MW00586004

because of her

JEWEL E. ANN

BECAUSE OF HER

JACK & JILL SERIES STANDALONE

JEWEL E. ANN

This book is a work of fiction. Any resemblances to actual persons, living or dead, events, or locales are purely coincidental.

Copyright © 2023 by Jewel E. Ann

Print Edition

ISBN: 978-1-955520-36-2

Cover Designer: © Emily Wittig

Formatting: Jenn Beach

PLAYLIST

"Cleanse" Boatkeeper
"Love Is The Answer" Natalie Taylor
"Kingdom Come" The Neighborly
"Have You Ever Seen The Rain" MR. RACER
"Deep Dark Sleep" Melanie MacLaren
"I'm Worried It Will Always Be You" Katie Gregson-
MacLeod
"Wings" Birdy
"Secret Garden" Molly Parden, Tony Anderson
"Blue Moon Revisited (Song for Elvis)" Cowboy Junkies
"Sweet Jane" Cowboy Junkies
"The Heart Asks Pleasure First" Michael Nyman
"Voyage dans la lune" Sad Piano Music Collective
"Outside, Alone" Peter Gregson
"Ironic" Davis Naish, AG
"Liebestraum (Love Dream)" Franz Liszt, Michael Krücker
"Claire de Lune" London Symphony Orchestra
"Nocturne Op. 9 No. 2" Frédéric Chopin, Olga Bordas

To my Jackson fans ... this is the end.

CHAPTER ONE

FRANCESCA

THERE's nothing notable about Boone, Kansas, other than the unkempt graveyard shrouded by cottonwoods where my brother, his wife, and their only child now rest. They moved from Chicago to give their son a better life.

Had they known how "better" would play out, they might have been more inclined to overlook the ninety-minute crawl to work or the occasional vandalism.

Now, their little family of three has a one hundred percent death rate. I'm not sure that's the definition of a better life, especially given that all three deaths were suicides.

A one-way street lines the tiny town square of crumbling brick buildings still home to a few local businesses that have stood the test of time. Murals line the alleys, a youthful touch to something old. I repeat my trip around the weathered square five times in the June sun before taking a brave breath and turning on my blinker to make a right down one of the more abandoned streets in the town.

My brother John and his wife, Lynn, chose this house

1

because they liked the oversized lot, minimal traffic, and abundant mature trees. Never mind the century-old homes with splintered siding, curling shingles, and crooked shutters. Our mom took one look and whispered, "It's horrific," while my brother, simultaneously, sighed contentedly and said, "It's perfect." He envisioned endless possibilities, and Mom saw nothing but a never-ending series of headaches in what our dad called "a thirty-year mortgage on a poor decision."

The irony? We grew up on a rundown farm in Iowa, where subsidies paid the rent.

Who could blame John for loving the place and the nostalgia that came with it. The house backs up to a cornfield, reminiscent of the days John and I hid from our parents. John mapped out a maze while I foraged for supplies in case we needed to hide out for days while our parents argued over money and who bore more responsibility for parenting.

John and I were inseparable, not just because we were twins. We complemented each other perfectly—my weaknesses were his strengths, and his were mine. We always said we were accidental twins, meant to be one person. Instead, we were two out-of-balance humans: either extremely good at something or extremely bad. John could barely spell his name but knew Pi to ... infinity. On the other hand, I poured over every book I could get my greedy little hands on and fell in love with Chopin long before I was old enough to need a bra. But if you asked me if two times two equaled four, I had to think about it for several seconds because eight seemed like a good option too.

The gravel crunches beneath my tires while I roll to a stop. I haven't been here since the funeral. I'd convinced myself it was nothing more than a nightmare. If I waited long enough, I'd wake up.

No such luck.

I knock on the warped wooden frame of the neighbor's screen door. (She has a key to their house.) It makes squeaky grunts while decaying boards creak with every tiny shift of my weight. I'm impatient to get this done so I can go home—anywhere that feels less real than Boone Fucking Kansas.

When Eloise doesn't answer, I glance at my watch. I'm an hour later than I planned. Stopping for lunch and procrastinating in the town square didn't help.

Dark, rich notes of hammering piano keys drift from her oversized two-car garage. It's a bonus garage behind the one-car attached to the house. I stroll along the cracked sidewalk under the maple trees to the access door, easing it ajar while poking my head through the opening. There's a black BMW sedan, weights, a hanging punching bag in the corner, and a man sitting at a grand piano with his back to me.

It takes several blinks to process this peculiar situation.

"Have you heard of knocking?" the man asks without missing a note, his body gently swaying to the rhythm and direction of his hands dancing across the keys.

It takes me a long moment to answer because ... *a man is playing a grand piano in a garage.* "Sorry. But I'm looking for Eloise Owen."

"She lives in the house," he replies in a clipped voice.

"Yes, but I knocked, and she didn't answer."

"Then she's not home, or she's dead," he says without emotion, which is odd since he's playing Alexander Scriabin's "Piano Sonata No. 9," quite possibly one of the most moving classical piano pieces ever written.

"Is that her car?"

"It is not." He glances over his shoulder, fingers coming to an abrupt halt. The man with short, grizzled hair and a clean-shaven face inspects me momentarily. He defies all stereotypes regarding aging men—a secret brotherhood of George Clooneys and Hugh Jackmans.

I step inside the garage and close the door to keep the heat out since a window air conditioner blasts cold air into the musty space.

The man swivels toward me on the bench, squaring his body in gray cargo pants and a tight black T-shirt. Tattoos cover his sinewy arms, and distrust lurks in his amber eyes. I'm not sure I've ever seen anyone with that eye color.

"She has a key to my brother's house." I jab my thumb in the direction of John's house.

"I'm not her keeper."

"No?" I slant my head to the side, feeling a little surge of attitude in response to his helpfulness. "Well, I didn't say you were. I heard the piano, and since she didn't answer her door, I thought maybe she was in her garage. I assume this is her garage?"

"I'm renting it." He folds his hands between his spread legs.

"I didn't know."

"Well, now you do." No detectable emotion accompanies his candid response.

"Yes." I chuckle and shake my head at his clipped responses. "I suppose I do. Would you, by any chance, have a cell phone number for her? I only have what I assume is a landline."

"I don't know if she has a cell phone." He crosses his arms.

Pressing my lips together, I nod several times. "I'll wait in my car."

4

"Your family was pretty fucked-up. Sorry for your loss," he says as I open the door.

Three suicides. I suppose that qualifies as "pretty fucked-up." What does one call a guy playing Scriabin on a grand piano in an old garage? He might qualify as fucked-up too. "Perhaps you're right," I say. "I'd call it unfortunate, like Alexander Scriabin's death."

He narrows his eyes.

"I certainly hope anyone who can play Scriabin like you would be well-read on the composer's history."

"Do you play?"

"I was a music theory professor."

"Was?" His lips twist.

"Long story. Sorry to have disturbed you." I turn.

"I can let you into the house."

"You have access to their house?" I squint. Why would Eloise give someone renting her garage a key to my brother's house?

"Sure." He retrieves a leather pouch from his car.

"Did you know Lynn and Steven?" I ask when he steps past me at the door.

"I was aware of the boy." His heavy steps carry him toward the house through the weed-infested grass littered with sticks snapping beneath his boots.

I'm not sure what that means.

"Can I ask why you're living in Eloise's garage?" I jog to catch up to him.

"Does it matter?"

"Just making conversation."

He stops at the front door and unzips the leather pouch.

"Wait. I thought you had a key," I say as he squats at the door and proceeds to pick the lock.

"I said I could let you into the house. You asked if I had

5

access. I said, 'Sure.'" He works multiple lock picks into the deadbolt keyhole.

It takes him less than a minute to unlock the door. When he turns the handle, letting it ease open on its whiny hinges, I feel a heavy wave of emotion roll over me. I don't believe in ghosts, but I swear I hear Steven's laughter and Lynn's soft hum that she made every time she nodded her head in agreement. I can see my brother on a ladder, hanging blinds. I can smell vanilla and brown sugar from Mom's chocolate chip cookie recipe that Lynn used to distract Steven from getting into all of the boxes before they unpacked.

This is harder than I imagined, and I haven't stepped foot into the house yet.

The zip of the leather pouch silences the whispers from the past. "Do you pick many locks?" I use him as a distraction to cross the threshold like it's no big deal like I wasn't paralyzed seconds earlier.

"I usually kick in a door if I need access and don't have a key." He smirks, focusing on the pouch for a few more seconds before lifting his gaze to mine. "I assumed you'd prefer the door remain in one piece for resale value."

Finding a tiny grin, I curl my hair behind my ear on one side. "One piece is best. Thanks."

He eyes my hair.

"I'm Frankie, by the way." I hold out my hand.

"Jack." He takes my hand, letting the handshake linger. Again, he eyes my hair.

"Sorry." He catches himself and releases my hand. "You remind me of someone, and the resemblance is distracting."

"Well, it's a false resemblance. I had long brown hair six months ago, and I chopped it off at my chin and bleached it blond." With a shrug, I touch the ends of my hair. "Midlife crisis, or so I've been told."

He returns a careful nod.

"Francesca, sorry I'm late."

I glance over Jack's shoulder at Eloise, gripping the handrail while making a slow ascent up the porch stairs.

"Oh my goodness," she says, out of breath. "Did I forget to lock the door? I could've sworn I locked it after tidying up yesterday. Since you're staying a few days, I wanted to dust and vacuum." Her gaze shifts to Jack. "What a pleasant surprise."

Is she ... blushing?

Eloise fans herself. "How did you manage to get him to come over here?"

"He picked—"

"I heard a car and saw her entering the house. Thought I should check it out," he says, offering Eloise a pleasant smile. He gives off a peculiar vibe that I can't figure out.

I reserve the right to hold his trustworthiness in question.

"Always looking out for me." She rests her hand on his arm and gives it a playful squeeze. She's flirting with him.

Again, he eyes me. Whoever I resemble must be someone he either loves or hates. The intensity is too strong for indifference.

"I'll leave you, ladies, alone."

"It was nice meeting you," I say as he steps onto the porch and begins to close the door.

He pauses, not looking back at me as he offers a slight nod. Then the door shuts.

"He's a *very* fine wine." Eloise smirks.

My brow lifts. Did she just say what I think she said?

Her wink confirms it. She's not wrong.

7

"You're the only one who's been here since ..." Her weathered face droops with sadness when she meets my gaze.

I wordlessly acknowledge her painful observation. My brother and his wife spoke highly of their eighty-something year-old neighbor, and she always treated them like family. I don't have to ask; she's still grieving. It's in her eyes, a reflection of my own.

"Since Lynn died," I finish her sentence.

She drops her chin. "Such a tragedy. I'm heartbroken."

"As am I," I murmur past the lingering pang of resentment from drawing the short straw. It's hard to say I'm too busy to go through their stuff when I no longer have a job.

"You'll want to turn down the thermostat. I had it at seventy-five since no one's been sleeping here."

It's a little warm, but it's better than outside. Less humid. However, the memories are more suffocating than any amount of heat and humidity. It's like they're still here. Everything is tidy. Lynn kept an immaculate home, even in death. A friend found her dead from a pill overdose atop a neatly made bed.

No dirty dishes in the sink.

Every piece of laundry was clean except the clothes on her dead body.

Even the empty pill bottle sitting next to a glass of water on the nightstand had its cap replaced. All the details were neatly checked off a list, including a note by the glass.

> Dear friends and family,
> Forgive me for any inconvenience or grief my death may cause you. I think it's best for everyone

if I'm not here to grieve John and Steven for eternity. Please take solace in knowing our family is reunited.

Love,

Lynn

My brother took his life three years earlier after losing his job and drinking himself into a severe depression—a gun to his head behind the garage. I hope that inclination doesn't run in the family. After leaving my position at the university, I inhaled a whole bag of chocolate chips. Suicide never entered my mind, nor did a drop of alcohol enter my body.

How Lynn managed to stay here is beyond me. She wanted to keep Steven at the same school. I get that, but this isn't the only house in Boone.

Then ...

My nephew hung himself in the backyard late on a Saturday night. The tree stands mere feet from where my brother put a gun to his head.

Lynn swallowed a bottle of pills the day after Steven hung himself. It's as if she knew it would be less burdensome for everyone to attend a double funeral rather than two separate funerals—always so *thoughtful*.

An unimaginable tragedy. A mother and son succumbing to years of grief.

But I never saw that.

Lynn had friends and family. She worked at a dance studio in Rhodale, one town to the north, and loved her job. Of course, she loved John and missed him dearly. But his death didn't cripple her. Last I knew, she was casually dating.

She killed herself because she lost her son.

The question that hasn't been answered is why Steven took his life. Because of a knee injury? Maybe I don't understand kids because I don't have any. Perhaps there's nothing logical to interpret from suicide.

"Lynn and Steven called you Frankie." Eloise touches her neck and clears her throat.

I nod.

"Your brother called you Francesca. Which do you prefer?"

"John called me Francesca because I hated it." I grin. "It wasn't funny when we were kids."

"It's a lovely name. Why don't you like it?" She can barely look me in the eyes, and her nerves are more distracting than the heat.

I blow out a slow breath. It's hard to look back. I hate looking back. "We were twins. And I was upset that he was a boy. I wanted to be the boy. To appease me, my parents said I could be 'Frankie.' But, as siblings do, John liked to get under my skin by calling me Francesca, and he did it with such exaggeration." I chuckle. "Fran-CHESS-ka!"

Eloise rubs her lips together, but it doesn't hide her smile. "He was full—" In the next breath, that hint of a smile vanishes.

"Full of life," I murmur, scanning the room for the umpteenth time. "The irony in someone so seemingly full of life just ... ending it."

"Do you still hate the name Francesca?"

God bless her. She's doing her best to keep things light.

"No. It's a family name. I abandoned my boy phase when Aiden Walker transferred to our school in the eighth grade. It was also the year my girly curves made their big debut." I smirk.

"Aiden Walker? Sounds like trouble." Eloise narrows her blue-gray eyes.

After twenty-five years, just the mention of his name makes me blush. "Oh, he was all kinds of trouble. My parents lost so much sleep over my obsession with him. My mom couldn't get me to wear a dress for anything. Not church. Not weddings. Not even my Great-Grandma Francesca's funeral."

Eloise's thinning eyebrows lift a fraction.

I slide my hands into the pockets of my shorts. "But Aiden made me want to curl my hair, color my lips deep red, and wear anything that showed off my newly developed breasts and sun-kissed legs."

"Oh, dear ..."

My head dips into a sharp nod, remaining bowed while my blush dissipates. "Oh dear, indeed. His winning smile, smooth voice, and subtle wink blinded me."

"Let me guess. He was the best athlete. Smart. And cared for his dying grandmother after school."

"No." I cough with a partial laugh while lifting my gaze from the scuffed linoleum floor. "He worked on cars with his dad, started smoking our junior year, got his ear pierced our senior year, and barely passed his classes to graduate."

"Ah, I see. My son is a diesel mechanic who can't spell to save his life. He hates reading, but he can fix anything with a motor."

"That was Aiden. And I liked him beyond reason." I laugh. "Really. There was no good reason to like him other than he looked at me like I was the prettiest thing he had ever seen. So, I left my boy phase and embraced whatever anyone wanted to call me. Francesca, Frankie, Fran, Fran-nie, or 'my girl.' That's what Aiden called me."

"Like the song."

I nod. "But my dad calls me 'Frannie Pants.' I'm not sure how that got started, but it stuck."

After a few moments of silence, Eloise blows out a long breath. "Well, dear, let me know if you need anything."

I offer a tiny smile. "You've done so much, and they adored you. My family won't ever be able to properly repay you for everything you have done, especially after my brother died."

She clears her throat and puts on a brave face. "It was my pleasure. And if you need boxes or help packing things, I'm happy to oblige."

"Thank you."

The door clicks shut behind her, but then she opens it again. Indecision spreads across her face while she presses her lips into a hard line.

"What is it?" I ask.

It takes several seconds before she looks directly at me. "A few days after the funeral, when everyone had left, I walked around the house." The discomfort in her expression deepens. "I needed to make sense of everything. And I thought if I ..." She shakes her head. "I don't know. I thought I'd hear them. Or see them. Or feel them. And I thought it might help me understand what happened."

My head bobs a few times. "I get that."

"I don't think Lynn was in the right frame of mind to figure it out. The moment they pronounced Steven dead, I think she died. Taking those pills was nothing more than a formality." Eloise eyes me with caution.

Again, I nod.

She closes the door and folds her hands in front of her,

head bowed. "I found something in Steven's room. I wasn't intentionally snooping. It was all very innocent. I walked around the house, opening closet doors and sliding open a drawer or two. I read over Lynn's whiteboard planner in the kitchen. There wasn't anything, in particular, I was looking for. But then I stumbled upon something in Steven's desk drawer."

I study the unease in her slumped posture and tightly folded fingers, knuckles turning white. "What did you find?"

Eloise's lips twist. It's a palpable hesitancy. "A letter."

"A suicide note?"

She shakes her head. "A letter from his girlfriend."

"Molly?"

"Yes."

Reaching for the fan, I pull the chain to move some air. "He seemed to adore her. I bet she's heartbroken. I can only imagine what it must feel like to lose your boyfriend so tragically. She had trouble keeping it together at the funeral."

"That might have been an act."

I glance over my shoulder while opening the blinds. "You think she was disingenuous with her grief?"

"You should come read the letter. Or I can go get it."

After one more glance around the lifeless room, I nod. "Lead the way."

Eloise shuffles her Crocs toward her house, occasionally stopping to bend down and pull a weed or two between the uneven bricks along the narrow path.

The drifting piano notes resume.

"Does Jack live in your garage or just use it for storage?"

"He lives there. I couldn't refuse his offer to rent it. He sleeps on a cot, although, now, he might sleep on the old sofa I gave him. There's a sink. He added a toilet. And I believe he uses the hose by the floor drain to bathe. I noticed he got a microwave. Jack's a rather ... interesting guy."

I hum. "I got that vibe too. But what do *you* mean by interesting?"

"He's secretive. For the most part, he keeps to himself. I know very little about him. Sometimes, he's gone for days at a time. And then there are long stretches where he plays that piano or goes for an hour-long jog. When he's here, he seems to do the same thing at the same time every day. I used to wonder if he was a serial killer because he's good-looking and eccentric." She grips the handrail to climb the rotting wood steps to her porch overflowing with potted flowers and two red-painted chairs. A string of windchimes hangs below the guttering, singing in the light breeze.

"Have you ruled out that possibility?"

"No." She chuckles, opening the screen door that droops on its hinges.

"But it's nice having him here like a bodyguard. I mean ... if he's not interested in killing me, maybe he'll protect me. And he's not bad company. Sometimes, he has dinner with me. And he's willing to help me out with certain chores."

My lungs greedily inhale the heavenly cool air laced with a vanilla scent when we enter her house.

Eloise pours two glasses of lemonade and slides one to me. "Let me grab that letter from the drawer of my secretary."

The AC is good, but this lemonade is better. Steven used to tell me how everything Eloise made was delicious. Her homemade pies. Jams. Chicken soup. And freshly squeezed lemonade. Steven said she was like a bonus grandma.

"I'm not showing you this to upset you. But if you're still

wondering why he did it, this might help shed some light on everything."

I stare at the folded sheet of paper before taking it. As I unfold it, the first thing that catches my attention is the doodles in the margins.

Broken hearts.

Skulls.

Headstones.

A figure hanging from a tree branch.

The letters R.I.P.

They are Steven's drawings. When he was younger, he doodled on everything, including walls and furniture. It infuriated my brother.

Dear Steven,

Do you believe in an afterlife? I do. I think when we die, we quickly come back as a new person —a do-over. Fearing death is weird. Don't you think? It's the fear of the unknown. But isn't every day an unknown? We should no more fear death than waking up each day, walking out of our house, and getting in a car.

I'm sorry about Colin. It was not planned. He was drunk, and I was angry at the world for doing this to you. I needed someone to take away my pain, but I couldn't ask you.

I know football was your life. If I lost my dad and then lost my ability to do the one thing I loved more than anything else, I don't think I would survive. I'd want a do-over. Lately, I've seen it in your mom's eyes. She's struggling to keep it together. I bet she misses your dad. It has to feel nearly impossible to wake up each morning. But she does it for you. And now she has to watch you go through rehab, knowing your dreams have been shattered.

Will there be enough money to pay the bills?

I wonder how often she must think of just checking out.

It has to be unbearable for her.

Just know that despite what happened with Colin, I love you. And I will always love you. But it's hard on me, too. It's hard to watch you suffer. Watching everyone at school look at you with so much pity is hard. It's never going to end. You will always be that kid who was supposed to be great, but one bad hit to your leg stole your future. In some ways, I bet it feels like it's stolen your whole life.

I can barely see the paper, and the ink blotches are from my tears because I love you so very much. I love you enough to understand if you don't want to do this any longer. If you don't want to be a burden on your mother. If you don't want to deal with all the pity from the people who say they are your friends. It's more than I would be able to handle. I guess what I'm trying to say is that it's okay. It's okay if you check out. It's okay to take the do-over.

Yours in this life and every life,

Molly xo

I read it once, frozen in place. Then I reach for one of the kitchen chairs before my knees buckle. And then I read it a second time. Slower. Letting each word echo, searching for an alternate meaning that isn't what it seems. *Did his girlfriend suggest he take his life?*

That's unimaginable.

Morbid.

Awful beyond any sense of my imagination.

Sure, couples argue. Sometimes, they say things in the heat of the moment, things they later regret.

But this was thought out. Well thought out.

It's vicious.

It's ... unforgivable.

"I know what you're feeling," Eloise says. "I felt it too. But I've had time to reread it. I've had time to interpret it in different ways. Maybe he was depressed. Perhaps he shared it with her. This letter may be nothing more than an immature girl trying to ..."

My gaze lifts to hers. "Trying to what?" I murmur in a weak tone.

She frowns, taking a seat next to me. "I don't know." Her knobby-knuckled fingers brush along the wood table like she's wiping invisible crumbs. "I don't understand their generation, but I also don't understand what having no hope inside you feels like. I suppose that makes me lucky."

I accept her apologetic smile with a tiny nod. "Did one girl have that kind of hold over Steven? Should one person's opinion or actions have the power to convince another human to end their life?"

"No." Eloise frowns, sliding her hand along the table to rest it on mine. "People can't break you unless you're weak. Steven wasn't weak."

He was weak. It's the only explanation.

And Molly knew it.

"I didn't mean to upset you. There's no changing the past. Since I took it from his room, I felt I had to return it to the family. That's all. It's best if you burn it and go through their things. Put the rest of this tragedy behind you."

The growing rage of thoughts in my head drowns out her words, but I manage a single nod.

CHAPTER TWO
FRANCESCA

I can't forget.

And I can't let it go.

It's not letting go of the past; it's justice in the present.

The plan was to spend a few days going through their belongings, sorting them into things to donate, items to sell, and anything sentimental the family might want to keep. By the fourth day, it's all done and time to arrange for a pickup of the items. Then I will drive home, leaving this house for the last time.

Again, that's the plan.

However, there's a wrinkle in this plan. That wrinkle is a piece of paper with four hundred and six words. Yes, I've counted them. I've read them. I've studied them. I've tried to read between the lines. I've attempted to put myself in Molly's shoes. I've imagined what Steven must have felt reading them for the first time, the second time, and a million times after that. Because surely he did. Right?

He must have read it repeatedly before concluding that she was right—his life was no longer worth living.

"Hey, Mom," I answer her call with as much enthusiasm as I can muster.

"Hi, Hun. How's it going? I told your dad I feel guilty for not helping you. But I still haven't fully recovered from my knee surgery, and I don't know how much help I would have been."

Pinching the bridge of my nose, I lean into the back of the sofa. "It's fine. I'm making progress. There are a few loose ends I want to tie up, so I think I might stay longer than originally planned. The house needs to go on the market. I'm not sure how long it will take to sell."

"Well, it's unrealistic for you to stay until it sells. That wouldn't be fair to you. But I hope you're getting out and going to eat and doing something. I can't imagine spending so much time in that house by yourself. And since you lost your job, I worry about you."

She's worried I'm going to take my life. I'm not John. Or maybe I am. I'm the half of "us" that doesn't feel like my life is disposable.

"Don't worry about me."

"Did you find your brother's baby book? I know it's silly, but I wanted to ask Lynn for it after he died, but it never felt like the right time."

"Yeah, I put it in a box with other stuff for you."

"Thank you, Francesca. Sincerely. I can't thank you enough for what you're doing. I know Lynn's family is incredibly grateful too. Lisa's still having a really tough time. I can't fathom how long it would have taken her to gather the emotional strength to go through their belongings. I think she'll go to her grave asking 'why?' But I don't think we'll ever know why."

The "why" is a "who." And the "who" is Molly Sanford.

And knowing that doesn't change a thing. Eloise knows it. And I know it, but I can't let it go.

"I'll call you when I'm ready to head home."

"Okay. Love you."

"Love you too." I end the call.

And then ... I take a little drive.

The Sanfords live halfway between Boone and Rhodale. Their property is impossible to miss because it's so out of place. A sprawling ranch—a mansion—surrounded by wheat fields transitioning from green to gold.

Armed with a small box of miscellaneous items I found in Steven's closet, which I assume belong to Molly, I park my car and swallow past the lump in my throat while ringing the doorbell. I need to look her in the eye and hopefully find eternal sadness and regret. Every day, I hope she thinks of Steven for the rest of her life. I hope she feels responsible for his death. Anything less is unacceptable.

A figure appears on one side of the glass-paneled, grand entry double door. A dark-haired woman with leathery skin and a kind smile. "Hello."

"Hi. I'm looking for Molly."

"Well, I'm Mrs. Sanford's assistant, Katheryn. Please come in." She steps aside. "Can I tell Molly who's here?"

"Uh ..." I draw in a slow breath. "I'm Steven Holter's aunt."

Katheryn's smile slides straight off her face. "I'm so sorry for your loss."

"Thank you. I've been going through their belongings and found this box of things I assume belong to Molly."

"I can give it to her." She reaches for the box.

I turn slightly and offer a stiff smile. "Actually, I'd like to meet her. Steven talked a lot about her. And I didn't get the

21

chance to have a formal introduction at the funeral. So if it's not too much trouble ..."

"Of course not. She's out back by the pool. Follow me."

"Thank you."

A girl with long blond hair in what barely qualifies as a bikini or clothing at all lifts onto her elbows from a padded lounge chair. She slides her sunglasses to the tip of her pierced-septum nose.

Katheryn doesn't stick around to introduce me. By the time I check over my shoulder, she's gone.

"Molly?"

"You are?"

I internally bristle at her rude excuse of a greeting. Did she not see me at the funeral or the burial? "Francesca. I'm Steven's aunt."

Her pouty lips gape while she reaches for a sheer coverup and swings her legs over the side of the lounger.

My nose wrinkles when I catch a whiff of her sunblock, a mix of harsh chemicals and an overbearing coconut scent. "I've been going through the family's belongings and came across this box of things in Steven's closet." For a brief moment, I stare into the box at the pink-handled hairbrush, gold hoop earrings, a small women's tee, a bottle of perfume, lip gloss, and a slew of hair bands. "I figured they must be yours." I return my gaze to hers.

She doesn't move other than fiddling with the silver ring on her middle finger.

"It's odd. They were already in this box like he was planning on returning them to you, or he was making it easier on whoever had to deal with his belongings after ..." I frown, letting her fill in the blank.

"I'm sorry for your loss," she whispers.

My loss? Yes. Steven was my family. But I remember

what it was like to be a teenager where everything was magnified. Every situation felt life-changing, and every emotion seemed to make a mark on my fragile heart.

Molly is numb. Her words carry no sincerity.

"He talked highly of you." I hand her the box and help myself to the lounger beside her. "I can't even imagine how someone your age deals with this kind of loss. I hope you've found counseling or someone to help you through this." I smile just short of sarcastic.

"Yeah," she whispers while inspecting the contents of the box. Anything to keep from looking at me. "They brought in extra counselors at school after he died."

"Did his death surprise you?"

She glances up at me, eyes narrowed. "W-what do you mean?"

"I mean, did you know he was suicidal?"

"Of course not!" Her fingers grip the side of the lounger, knuckles white.

"Hey," I hold up my hands. "I'm just asking. I'm trying to figure out what happened."

In an instant, her expression hardens. "He was upset about his injury. Football was his life. He loved it."

"Hello?"

I turn toward the woman's voice behind me, an older, blonder, caked-on makeup version of Molly.

"Hi." I stand, adjusting my shorts. "I'm Francesca, Steven's aunt. I was just returning some of Molly's belongings that I found in his closet."

"Oh." Her overly shiny Botox face makes a sad attempt at showing emotion, like reeling in a kite when there's too much wind. "I'm Corinne, Molly's mother. Our family is so sorry for your loss." She shifts her attention to Molly. "Moll, would you mind giving us a few minutes alone?"

She doesn't have to ask her twice. Molly shoves her feet into flip-flops and hugs the box while practically sprinting into the house without so much as a "nice to meet you" or "goodbye."

"Listen," Corinne twists her diamond earring, "Molly has yet to accept what happened. To my knowledge, she has not shed a tear except for the day of the funeral. We've tried to get her to talk to a therapist, but she's refused. I think the wound is too deep. And I fear she will let reality in and completely fall apart one day. So you'll have to excuse her if she seems unaffected. Everyone knew how much she loved Steven."

Did they? I could make a case for the opposite. However, I should leave. Steven is dead, and nothing I say or do will change that. But ... I can't. Life isn't fair. I get that, but what she did is unforgettable and unforgivable.

"Yes." I smile. It's hard to do without gritting my teeth. "I can't tell you how being with Molly helps me. It's surreal. Otherworldly. It's like I'm with a part of Steven again." I rest my hand over my heart. "I'm going to stay in town for a while. There's just so much stuff to go through. I'd love to stop by and see Molly again."

Corinne glances at her watch. "Uh ... yeah. I'm sure that would be fine. Molly's a busy young lady, but we'd happily accommodate you."

Only people with this much money would call spending time with a grieving person an "accommodation."

"Do you have other children?"

Her brow tightens for a second. "Just Molly. I'll walk you out."

I guess I'm leaving now.

"So you can imagine how devastated Steven's mom was after losing her only child."

24

"Of course. It would be hard to move on after a loss like that."

"Impossible." I turn toward her after she opens the door. "Is your husband around? I'd love to meet him, too."

"No. Archer works long hours. I barely see him. I'm afraid it's unlikely you will meet him." Corinne folds her long fingers with pointy nails in front of her and blinks unnaturally fast.

"Oh. A shame. Here's my number. Tell Molly to call me when she gets some free time."

Corinne takes my business card and reads it. "You're a professor?"

"Was. Long story. But that's my cell phone number."

"Thanks. I'll give it to Molly. It was nice meeting you," she says absentmindedly before catching herself. "Well, as nice as it could be under the circumstances."

Corinne's right. It's not every day that your only daughter convinces her boyfriend to take his life. It's certainly not the best circumstances.

CHAPTER THREE
JACKSON

JACKSON KNIGHT SQUINTS against the setting sun's glare while pulling into the gravel driveway. Along the side of the garage, there's a pile of split wood that wasn't there when he left earlier this morning. He told Eloise he'd split it for her; he just hadn't gotten around to it. And being June in the Midwest, it's unlikely she'll want to start a fire for at least three or four months at the earliest.

He inspects the perimeter and finds no one except the dead neighbor's relative sitting on the front porch steps, chugging a water bottle. His glance is enough to bring her to her feet. She makes her way to him.

"Shit," he mumbles, ducking his head and reaching for the door handle.

"Eloise said you wouldn't mind if I chopped that wood."

Frankie looks like his wife did when they met. But, unlike his wife, Frankie has a confidence akin to his twin sister. Her blue eyes hold his gaze. She walks with her chin high and shoulders back. But he's not in Boone, Kansas, to make new friends. Eloise is the necessary exception. So while Frankie's *eye-catching*, he needs to stay focused.

Her blond hair blows in her eyes as she approaches in frayed denim shorts, toned legs smudged with dirt, a gray tank top, and brown hiking boots. It's worth noting ... she's not wearing a bra. His sister shares Frankie's disregard for social decency.

"You don't say much." She wipes her arm across her sweaty forehead. "Eloise thinks you might be a serial killer." With a wry grin and a chortle, she shrugs a shoulder. "I guess that makes you the silent but deadly type."

The corner of Jackson's mouth curls at her astute observation. "That's fascinating."

"Murder is fascinating?"

"The world's obsession with death." Jackson nods toward the pile of split wood. "If you get another burst of energy, you can chop all those logs in half again so Eloise can lift them into her fireplace."

"Are you critiquing my wood-chopping skills?"

He eyes the pile of wood. "I'm saying Eloise can't lift heavy things."

"I'll split them again if it makes you happy."

Happy? Jackson searches his weary mind for that word. When was the last time he was happy? "Are you leaving soon?"

Frankie rests a hand on her hip. "Not as soon as expected. I'm trying to decide—"

"Okay. Then chop the wood again." Jackson slips into the garage and closes the door behind him.

After an hour of pounding the punching bag and lifting weights, he showers in the corner with cold water, opens a can of soup, and pulls up the surveillance cameras on his computer, rewinding the footage from the day. Then he checks his phone to track his target's current location.

Later that evening, he sits down at his piano and plays

something of his own. Just as he starts to tweak a rough part, there's a knock at the door. He assumes it's Eloise with cookies. She always bakes pizzelles because she's Italian, and it's her grandma's recipe with a secret ingredient. Well, she was born in France, but her ancestors are from Italy, and she has family there. Eloise jumps at any opportunity to take someone through her family tree.

When he opens the door, it's not Eloise.

"What do you know about toilets?" Frankie asks. She's showered with wet hair, tiny pink cotton shorts, and a white crop top.

Jackson concludes that she must be proud of her nipples since he's seen them twice in a matter of hours.

"I know it's a myth that Thomas Crapper invented it," he says.

Frankie inspects Jackson and his tattooed torso. When her eyes find his face, she blushes and clears her throat. "Mine won't stop running."

"Sounds like you need a plumber. Good luck with that." He starts to close the door.

She slaps her hand against the door to keep him from closing it.

"What were you playing?"

Jackson dramatically swings his arms like a crossing guard when she brushes past him. "Come on in," he mumbles.

Frankie scuffs her flip-flops along the concrete floor to his piano. The pads of her fingers feather across the keys without making a sound. "I taught my brother to play the piano. He wanted to learn just so he could impress Lynn." She grins, staring at the keys. "He surpassed me in no time. I was always first, but he was always better. When he ..." Her brow fills with lines. "When he took his life, I knew. I knew it the moment it happened. I called Lynn and told her to find him."

Blowing out a long breath, she shakes her head. "It was too late. The void inside of me was instant." Frankie peeks over her shoulder at Jackson with a sad smile. "We were twins."

He snags a T-shirt from the top of a camo duffle bag and pulls it over his head. Why is she dumping all of this on him? A stranger. But ... Jackson knows all about twins. He's felt that invisible bond in the most excruciating way.

When their parents died.

When they had to change their identities.

When he nearly lost her.

Even now, as he ties up the last loose end that keeps his family separated, he thinks about Jessica. She's always a whisper in his ear, giving him strength when he needs it and restraint when he's on the verge of losing all patience.

"What?" Frankie appraises him through narrowed eyes, sitting on his piano bench, hands gripping the edge.

Jackson lifts his gaze to her, blinking several times. "I didn't say anything."

"Your face says a lot."

"My face says I'm old and really fucking tired."

A smile tugs at Frankie's lips. "What are you? Fifty? That's not that old."

Jackson lifts an eyebrow for a second.

"You look sad. Not like you've had a bad day; more like you've had a bad life."

He's not a specimen for her to observe under a microscope. Retreating a few steps, he opens the door. "Sorry. I'm not an expert on fixing toilets."

Frankie inspects the room with a slow, sweeping gaze before she stands. "It's dark in here. Cold despite the heat.

29

Depressing. It might be affecting your *cheery* demeanor." She shuffles her feet toward him, stopping so close he can feel the warmth of her body and smell the sweet tones of her shampoo. "I don't think you're a serial killer." Wetting her lips, she cants her head to the side. "But if you are, hide my body when you kill me. I don't think my parents can live through another death."

She bleeds the same blood. Jackson internally bristles at the similarities between them. Of course, he will never tell her that. The sooner she squares away everything in that house and leaves for good, the better.

"Condolences for your losses," he says.

Her lips twist while she stares at his chest, her gaze a million miles away. "Thank you," she whispers. "And thanks for listening."

As if he had a choice.

CHAPTER FOUR
FRANCESCA

I CAN'T STOP REREADING the letter. My hatred for Molly and her pretentious family grows out of control. All I can think about is payback. Nothing can right this wrong. No amount of revenge will bring Steven and Lynn back. Still, I can't let her get away with this. If she doesn't learn a lesson, what's to say she won't compel another innocent soul to take their life?

Molly doesn't call, not that I expect her to. She leaves me no choice but to follow her to a coffee shop in Rhodale. Boone kids get bussed to Rhodale for school, whereas the wealthier families live in the heart of Rhodale with bike trails, fine dining, boutiques, and trendy cafés. Everyone drives a Tesla to save the earth yet swims in a heated pool and incessantly waters their pristine lawns.

I'm not opposed to upper-class life. I've lived it for years. It's the required holier-than-thou attitude that I struggled to accept.

Molly steps out of her black Model S and adjusts her short skirt and floral halter top before focusing on her phone as she walks to the hipster cafe, where a gentleman exits, holding the door open for her. She pays him no attention. Not a smile or a murmured "thanks."

I blend into the ten-dollar-latte crowd with a red gauze, strapless sundress and Birkenstocks.

Hair in a messy, low ponytail.

Round sunglasses.

As I approach the door, Molly steps up to a table by the window, bending over to kiss a guy who looks her age. I keep my sunglasses on and my back to her while I order an iced coffee and sit on the opposite side of the cafe.

She steals his drink and sips from the straw while her bare foot, not-so-discreetly, lifts to his chair, nestling between his spread legs.

Classy.

Corinne was right. Her daughter is a very busy young lady. While the kids from Boone are working summer jobs for ten bucks an hour, riding their squeaky-wheeled bikes around town, Molly Sanford's jerking off a kid at the coffee shop with her newly pedicured foot in exchange for a few sips of his syrupy coffee drink. I wonder who she will blow for a chicken sandwich at lunch?

She giggles.

The boy holds her foot, working it between his legs, lower lip trapped between his teeth, and a look on his face that sends a little bile up my throat. Molly's clearly still grieving, and this young man is taking advantage of her broken heart.

I'd like to say that the students I had in my classes were a little more controlled and possessed more social etiquette, but that would be a lie. The music majors were the horniest ones on campus. Music really does inspire.

While Molly grieves over coffee, I conduct a few internet searches on her parents. Corinne Sanford owns a custom jewelry store here in Rhodale. She's on the City Council and president of the school board.

Archer Sanford owns Sanford Real Estate and S&J, an engineering design firm.

When I glance up at Molly and her coffee mate, he pinches his eyes shut and grips the side of the table. Molly returns her foot to her white canvas sneaker.

"It's about time," I grumble, collecting my keys, phone, and coffee before moseying in their direction.

"Hey, I thought that was you." I plaster on a friendly smile to match my jovial tone.

All the color drains from Molly's face, but her friend's cheeks remain flushed from his orgasm or the embarrassing spoonful of cum in his pants.

Molly sits up straight. "Hi. W-what are you doing here?"

I hold up my drink. "Same thing as you. Did your mom give you my number?"

Molly shakes her head, gaze darting between her friend and me.

"Oh, that's disappointing. I wanted to spend more time with you. After we met, I realized you might be the one person who can help me find closure from Steven's death."

Now, her friend turns the color of the whipped topping on their half-empty drink. They share a look.

"I gotta go." He nearly knocks his chair over while standing, righting it at the last second with his fidgety hands.

"Colin," Molly snaps his name in a desperate plea.

"Colin?" I purse my lips.

"Y-yeah," he stutters, a light sheen of sweat beading along his forehead.

"Gosh," I tap my chin, "that name sounds familiar."

"Colin played football with Steven." Molly jumps in to save the day.

Only ... nothing can save her.

She is rotten to the core. And while I have no desire to take her life or even give her my blessing to take her own life, I don't think I can have closure without seeing her suffer to the point that she wished she were six feet under with Steven.

"So you and Steven were friends?"

Colin eyes Molly and clears his throat. "Yeah."

I nod thoughtfully. "That must be it. I saw your name somewhere. Steven loved doodling things. Pictures ... names ... dates ..." I shrug. "Well, it was nice meeting you, Colin. Take good care of this one." I stroke the length of Molly's ponytail, and goosebumps erupt along her skin while she holds her breath. "Steven adored her."

Molly's lips quiver. I'm unsure if she's on the verge of crying or passing out.

"Let's get together before I leave." I pluck Molly's phone from her hand, hold it to her face to unlock it, and add myself to her contacts ... as a *Favorite*. "Bye, kids." I keep my composure until I get to my car and pull onto the street, where angry tears spring from my burning eyes. "FUCK!!!!"

She tied the goddamn noose around his neck and kicked the ladder out from beneath his feet. And now she's jerking off his friend in public. It's not okay. It will never be okay.

When I return to the house, I head up the stairs to change my clothes to finish chopping the wood into manageable pieces for Eloise. Stepping into the bathroom, I notice the towel I had on the floor by the toilet is now hanging over the edge of the tub, and the floor is dry.

I flush the toilet and wait.

No leak.

After changing into my old shorts, a tee, and boots, I trudge toward the pile of wood by the garage just as Jack jogs up the drive, covered in sweat from his run. Who runs in long pants and a long-sleeved tee this time of year?

He eyes me for two seconds before opening the access door to the garage.

"Hey, did you fix my toilet?"

"Depends," he says with his back to me while he removes his shirt and uses it to wipe the sweat from his torso.

He's ripped. Shredded. Tattooed. And a bunch of other distracting things. I clear my throat. "On what?" I manage two words despite being sidetracked by his striptease.

"Is it leaking?"

"No."

"Then I fixed it."

Click.

The door closes behind him.

I shake my head. He's a hard one to crack.

———

"Dear, if you don't hydrate, I fear you'll pass out." Eloise holds up a glass of lemonade.

"Thanks," I grunt, striking the wood. "I'm about done."

She eases into a metal glider with chipping blue paint. "I'm not complaining, but I'm surprised you're still here. Do you still have many things to go through?"

I toss the last log onto the pile and prop the ax against

the garage. "No," I pant before gulping half of the lemonade. "It's Molly."

"The girlfriend?"

I nod.

"Oh, Frankie, I should have destroyed that letter. I knew nothing good would come from showing it to you. We can't get him back."

"I know. But I feel like there should be justice. What if I took it to the police?"

Eloise returns a slow headshake. "Molly's family is well-connected. Her mom had an accident years ago and didn't see a day of jail time. Three weeks of community service. And not the kind where you're picking up trash from the ditch. She watered the flowers at the parks every other morning."

"What accident?"

Eloise frowns, holding her hand over her heart. "She killed a man. She was drunk, but there was a 'mix-up' at the lab, and they didn't get accurate confirmation of her blood alcohol level. The only reason she saw community service was because there were witnesses. It never even went to trial. The Sanfords are untouchable."

"No one's untouchable." I scoff.

"If you go after them, they will ruin your life. Don't you think you've suffered enough? Nothing good will come of going after that girl. She'll get what's coming to her eventually. I believe we all pay our dues at some point."

"It's not right, Eloise. It's not just Steven. Molly Sanford is responsible for Lynn's death too. Justice matters." I'm knotted inside. And it's making me angry. "My dad's favorite line is 'life's not fair'. He's right. But that doesn't mean you let people literally get away with murder."

"Maybe you need a break. You've been staying in their

house, going through their things. Take some time before you make any decisions that can't be undone. Don't poke the bear unless you know you can survive."

I give her a nod to appease her and ease the concern along her face. When I speak, Jack plays the same piano piece he was playing the last time. I've never heard it.

"I don't know why he's living in my garage, but I'll miss hearing him play when he's gone," Eloise says, swaying to the dark notes.

"Have you asked him why he wants to live in your garage?"

She opens her eyes. "Yes and no. He generously paid me to rent it with 'no questions asked.' But I've nudged him for information."

"And what does he say?" I take several gulps of my lemonade. He has a grand piano in a garage. Sure, it's peculiar. But to me, it's also a sign of passion. A love for something so great he can't bear to be without it.

A soft chuckle bubbles from Eloise's chest. "Nothing. He just says he'd tell me, but then he'd have to kill me. Such a tease."

"A tease?" I narrow my eyes, shaking the ice at the bottom of the glass.

"Oh, he's kidding. Jack wouldn't harm a fly. I was kidding about him being a serial killer. I'm a good judge of character, and Jack is a kind soul."

"You think?"

"Yes. Honestly, I've wondered if he's dying. I read a book about a woman who found out she was terminally ill, so she left her family so they didn't have to suffer with her. Maybe he's dying."

My lips twist. "We're all dying."

"We are, but my husband said the best thing to do while you're waiting to die is to *live*. He had a good life."

"I like that motto," I reply sincerely, even though my thoughts have drifted to Jack and his comment about his age and tiredness. *Is* he dying?

"Can I get you more lemonade?" She pushes back in the glider for momentum to stand.

I shake my head, handing her my empty glass. "I'm good but thank you."

"No. Thank *you* for chopping all this wood. I hope it helped with your frustration and grief."

"It did."

"You should come to dinner tomorrow night. Jack is coming."

"That sounds nice. Thanks."

Eloise plods her way to the house in her Crocs. I consider taking a shower, but I opt for a good distraction that won't let me focus as much on revenge. I knock a little harder after three knocks on Jack's door and no answer.

The door swings open, and the shirtless man greets me with a hard sigh. He has a routine.

Workout.

Shower.

Get half dressed.

Play the piano.

"I didn't get to properly thank you for fixing my toilet," I smirk, "even if you did pick the lock to do it."

"*Properly* thank me?"

The cold air wafting from the garage feels fantastic, so I step inside. "Shut the door. No need to let out all the cold air."

"I didn't invite you in." He glowers while shutting the door.

I ignore his grumpiness. "Properly, formally, whatever. I meant I didn't get to thank you at all. So ..." I fold my hands in front of me. "Thanks."

"You're welcome." He rubs the back of his neck. "Is that all?"

"What were you playing?"

"Nothing in particular."

"Your nothing sounded good."

He draws a deep breath and releases it while lacing his hands behind his head. "Anything else?"

Sweet Jesus. That pose puts everything in its proper place. I can't help but stare at his tattoo-covered arms and torso. A few bold black words interspersed with intense colors: roses, hearts, branches, a dragon, numbers aligned in dates, and musical notes.

"I always wanted a tattoo. My brother had a few. But I was too indecisive." I smile, thinking about John's tattoos. "His were so random. His first one was PEMDAS because my dad said he needed to tattoo it onto his forearm. John took that as a challenge. He drew it in permanent marker and ended up excelling at math in high school. Of course, our dad told him this when we were fifteen, but it was the first thing my brother did when he was old enough to get a tattoo." I shake my head. "All for a laugh. He just wanted to make our dad laugh."

Jack releases his arms, letting them relax at his side. And it's tiny, but I detect the hint of a smile.

"I know we just met, but Eloise is fond of you, and so am I now that you've fixed my toilet, so I want you to know that you can talk to me."

He stares at me, unimpressed with my offer.

"I mean ..." I hug one arm to my chest. "If you have

something going on and no one to talk to, I'm a good listener. And I'm good at keeping secrets."

Jack blinks, offering me nothing but a blank expression. "I've killed more people than I can count."

I don't move. Not an inch. A blink. A breath.

This is the confession a killer makes before he kills his next victim. After all, if I'm dead, I can't tell anyone. He knows it. And now I do too. He's joking. Haha. *Right? RIGHT?!*

"I mean..." he bounces his head a few times, eyes rolled to the ceiling "...I'm not your brother, but I'm decent with math. It's not that I *can't* count that high. I'm just saying I stopped counting after like ... fifteen ... twenty."

I nod as if he's telling me about a teddy bear he lost as a child.

"Can you keep *that* secret?" Cocking his head to the side, he narrows his eyes at me.

"Y-yes." I swallow hard.

"If I were a killer, do you think I'd have time to watch a YouTube video to learn how to fix your leaky toilet?"

Every cell that makes up my body collectively exhales. "You're an asshole."

He grins, and it's the biggest grin I've seen from him. A stellar smile that fits such a sexy man.

"Can I ask why you're living in a garage?" I inspect his space with a scrutinizing eye.

"Do you think a guy living in a garage would want anyone to know why he's living in a garage?"

He's not a homeless man. Homeless men don't have grand pianos. Homeless men don't drive BMWs.

"Do you really shower with that hose over the drain?"

He nods.

"Is it only cold water?"

Another nod.

He's out of his mind. It must be this part of Kansas. Everyone's a little ... off.

"Shouldn't you be getting back to your job? Your husband? Kids? Golden retriever?" he asks.

"I screwed the dean's husband." My lips pucker like a duck's. "Maybe because I don't have my own husband."

His eyebrows slide up his forehead.

I shrug. "That's why I lost my job."

"I didn't need those details."

"I know. That's why I told you."

Jack eyes me like he's solving something. "My name."

"What?"

"The first tattoo I got was my name."

I laugh, but it comes out as a giggle. "Seriously? Where?"

He holds out his arms like he's seeing his tattoos for the first time. "It's been buried by other tattoos."

"You're supposed to get 'Mom' or your first love's name, not your name." I cover my mouth to hide my grin.

"It *was* for my mom." He rubs his jaw. "She always said, 'Don't ever forget who you are.'"

"You," I point a finger at him, "basically got PEMDAS as your first tattoo."

The ghost of a smile holds his lips despite the tortured soul deep in his eyes.

We stand in silence for a few seconds, just ... staring at each other. Does he see how tortured I feel too?

"I can't let go," I whisper.

Lines spread across his brow.

"They should still be alive. So I can't just ... let it go." With a painful laugh, I run my hands through my hair. "Eloise keeps reminding me that nothing I do will bring them back. And I know that. But ..." I shake my head and sigh. "I don't know how to move on."

"Letting go is hard." Jack's gaze drops to the floor.

"And holding on is an illusion." I open the door. "Thank you for fixing my toilet. Good men are a dying breed. So ... don't die."

CHAPTER FIVE
JACKSON

JACKSON KNIGHT HAS ONE GOAL—TO get back to his family.

He's close. So very close. But he can't let go of the possibility that he will rush things—miss something—and the consequences could be catastrophic.

"How are your kids?" he asks his sister, Jessica.

"They're good."

Jessica and her husband, Luke, sent their kids out of the country to an undisclosed location. Everyone's waiting for Jackson to finish this so they can have normal lives again.

Get married.

Complete college.

"It will be over soon." He stares at the ceiling from his cot in the garage, his phone on speaker beside him. "I hate this life."

"It's the only one you've got."

"Mmm ..." He sighs. "What if I'm wrong? What if he's not the last one?"

"We've been over this ad nauseam. He's it."

Again, Jackson hums. "When it was just us, taking

chances came easier. We have families now. Risking them isn't an option."

"Jackson ... *life* is a risk. Finish this and come home."

"How's Livy?" He shifts to his favorite subject.

She laughs. "You don't want to know."

Jackson throws an arm over his head. "He's knocked her up again, hasn't he? I should have killed him like I killed his father."

"Jackson ... she's alive because of him. And he is her *husband*."

He grumbles.

"How's Eloise?" Jessica asks. "Have you sweet-talked your way into her adult diapers?"

"Fuck you." He chuckles.

"She's your type."

"She's a phenomenal cook, but my type might be shifting." Jackson married a woman ten years his elder. He found older women to be more intellectually stimulating. He loved Ryn as no man had ever loved a woman.

However, his brother-in-law would argue that point. And that's fine because Jessica is, in many ways, the *greatest* love of Jackson's life.

His twin. And she deserves the world.

KILLING people has lost its luster over the years. Jackson no longer feels an ounce of adrenaline or fear for his life.

One last target. The final piece of the puzzle. Yet, the highest-hanging fruit.

His target is exorbitantly wealthy and well-protected. That's how Jackson knows it isn't over. Who needs that kind of security if there's no threat? And if his target thinks

Jackson is a threat, then he is an equal threat to Jackson and his family. It's hard to distinguish the prey from the predator—it depends on the day.

"What the actual fuck?" Jackson murmurs from his BMW parked outside The Lark, an overpriced steakhouse in Rhodale's Uptown Market. Frankie breezes past the outdoor seating area, wearing a strapless red dress and heels women wear when they want something from a man. He does a double take to make sure it's her.

It is.

His target does his own double take, holding out his hand to stop Frankie.

Such a predictable fucker.

He says something that makes her laugh, tossing her head back. While she's swept away in laughter, his target eyes her body like it will be his dessert this afternoon. He motions to the empty chair across from him. Frankie glances at her watch, and then she nods. He stands to hold her chair like a real fucking gentleman.

Over the next hour, they order what seems to be everything on the menu and get cozy. Too cozy. He inches his leg closer to hers under the table and jumps at any chance to reach across the table to touch her hand.

This is not the wrench Jackson needs in his plans.

When his target's security detail closes in to prepare for his departure, Frankie lets him put his hand on the small of her back and whisper in her ear. She laughs and nods. Then he hands her a card that she slides into her clutch. Frankie floats along on her merry way while the target gets into the back of an SUV.

CHAPTER SIX
FRANCESCA

To really know Molly Sanford, I need to know her family. As I slip out of my red dress and slide on a more casual romper and flip-flops for dinner at Eloise's, I can't stop thinking of my luck this afternoon.

Archer Sanford was a bit of a surprise today. I thought I might get a glance at him and his daily routine, but I never expected to be the bait he took so eagerly. All I did was walk past him at his table outside the restaurant. The next thing I knew, he was complimenting my dress.

"It's just a dress. But thank you."

"It's not just a dress. It's a goddamn statement."

I laughed at his gruff assessment and his unshakable confidence.

"And what statement is that?"

"You want to be noticed. Admired. Treated like the fucking queen you are."

Really, I never expected it to be that easy.

"What do you suggest?"

He grinned. *"Let's start with lunch."*

And just like that, I spent an hour with him and left

with his cell phone number. Corinne Sanford must be so proud of her husband for making sexual advances toward strangers in plain sight. But after watching Molly's behavior, I've decided there's a lot that's not right about Rhodale or the Sanfords.

"Come in!" Eloise calls when I knock on the door.

I step inside and kick off my flip-flops.

"We're on the deck," she says.

I set a pie on the counter and open the screen door to the deck where Eloise and Jack are lounging in chairs with her famous lemonade in a pitcher on the table between them. "Hi."

"Have a seat. Dinner's not quite done. Help yourself to lemonade," Eloise says.

Jack gives me an unreadable expression while I pour myself a lemonade.

"Hey. How was your day?" I ask him.

He sips his drink and returns a one-shoulder shrug. "Not as good as I'd hoped."

"Sorry to hear that." I sit across from them on the wooden rocker.

"What did *you* do today?" Eloise asks me.

"I went to Rhodale. I bought a pie for tonight. It's on the counter. Then I ran into Molly's dad."

"Frankie ..." My name floats from Eloise's lips on a big wave of disapproval—a familiar motherly kind of disapproval.

I shake my head. "It's fine. It was just by chance. He's an interesting man. I don't recall seeing him at Steven's funeral."

Jack scowls at me, so I don't give him any more attention.

"He wasn't at the funeral." Eloise sets her glass on the

table. "Neither was his wife. Just Molly and friends from school. Where did you see him?"

"He was eating lunch by himself on the patio at a restaurant when I walked by."

"And you introduced yourself?" Eloise asks.

"Um ..." I swirl the ice in my glass. "Not really. He complimented my dress, and that was about it."

Eloise scoffs. "A married man complimenting a stranger's dress. How uncouth. I've heard he flaunts his affairs."

"Mmm ..." I nod in agreement. She's not wrong. But I wanted him to notice me. However, I thought it would take more than casually walking past him. I planned to find a table on the patio and get his attention in other ways. He was just too easy.

I risk another glance at Jack and his corkscrewed lips and narrowed eyes.

"Well, I'm going to check on the roast." Eloise heads into the house.

"Everything okay?" I ask Jack.

"Molly was your nephew's girlfriend?"

"Yes."

"Did you know her?" Jack narrows his eyes.

I squirm under his visual interrogation. "No. Steven talked about her. I think he liked her a lot."

"Is she struggling with grief?"

Eloise must not have shared the letter with Jack—not that it's any of his business.

"I wouldn't say that."

"Can I ask where you live?"

It takes a few seconds for my thoughts to shift to this new line of questioning. After several blinks, I answer, "Hinsdale, Illinois."

"Is that where the dean's husband lives?"

I smirk, glancing past him to the hummingbird feeder. "No. He lives in Winnetka ... with the dean."

"So you're not a homewrecker? Do you make it a habit of dining with married men?"

I laugh. "No. The story's more complicated than that. Both stories. The dean forgave him, fired me, and I'm sure they'll live happily ever after. Something tells me Molly's parents don't stand a chance of happily ever after."

He nods slowly. "Don't you need to look for a new job? I'm surprised you're still here."

"Are you tired of me already?"

He almost suppresses his grin. *Almost.*

"Besides," I lean back and close my eyes, "one could ask you the same thing. Living out of a garage doesn't make sense when you drive a BMW and own a grand piano. I bet there's more to your story too."

"I've never made sense."

"Yeah, well, life doesn't make sense." I shake my head slowly, peeking an eye open.

Jack studies me over the rim of his glass before tipping it back.

"Dinner's ready." Eloise pokes her head out the door, and the herbaceous aroma wafts in my direction.

Jack waits and motions for me to go in first with a tiny nod and a quick once-over that gives me a chill—the good kind, not the serial killer one.

When we're seated, I look around the table. Eloise Owen has graciously made dinner for a man living in her garage and a relative of the dead family next door. Are they my new friends? Will we exchange phone numbers and keep in touch?

"Steven loved my roast and potatoes," Eloise says. "I used to make them for him when Lynn had to work late."

I take a bite of the roast and nod. "Mmm ... I can see why. It's delicious."

"Do you have someone filling in for you at school? Lynn said you're a professor, right?" Eloise asks.

Jack smirks over a mouthful of potatoes while he slowly chews.

Swallowing, I shake my head. "I'm between jobs."

"Oh? Why did you leave your last position?"

Jack eyes me, and with one look, I dare him to say a word like I used to dare my brother to rat me out at breakfast if I was out past curfew the previous night.

"There was a misunderstanding between the dean and me. And even if we worked things out, I feared it would affect my job at the university, so I left."

Jack focuses on his plate of food while his head makes a tiny shake.

"That's unfortunate." Eloise offers a sincere, sad smile.

Jack could learn a little compassion from her.

"It is, but it was for the best in the bigger picture. It would have been hard to take so much time off work to be here."

Eloise returns a thoughtful nod—too thoughtful. I'd prefer she not overthink my intentions or worry about me.

We eat. Silverware clink and tap. Occasionally, Eloise clears her throat, but words are not exchanged—the awkwardness of the silence multiplies.

Small talk to the rescue.

"So, Jack, what did you do before you became a garage dweller?" I tap my fork on my lips.

"Frankie." Eloise smiles while shaking her head. "Jack's a private person. And it's best if we respect that."

Is she saying that because she's respectful of his privacy? Or is she still thinking he might be a killer?

"Thank you, Eloise. Dinner was amazing as always." Jack slides back in his chair. "But I have some *work* to do." He avoids any sort of glance in my direction as if I'm not here. He exudes confidence in everything he does.

Shoulders back.

Chin held high.

A perfected poker face. Well, not all of the time. I think it slips with me. The tiny twitch of a grin. The subtle rubbing together of his lips. He's not immune to the hairline cracks in his composure where slivers of his human side shine through.

"That's all you're eating? There's plenty more," Eloise protests his early departure.

"I'll pop in for leftovers tomorrow," he says.

"Okay, dear. You are welcome to have dinner with me anytime."

"Don't worry," I say. "We'll get the dishes ... since that's what women do."

Halting, Jack sighs and grumbles, but I can't make out his words.

"No. I've got the dishes." Eloise blots her mouth with a napkin. "I don't need anyone's help."

"I wouldn't dream of letting you make dinner and not doing my part to help clean up." I rest my hand on her arm.

She nervously eyes Jack while he pivots.

"Sorry. You're right." With a tight smile, he retraces his steps, gathering his empty plate and glass. Then, he proceeds to fill the sink with hot, soapy water.

"Frankie, I can handle it," she says softly.

"You haven't finished your meal. Take your time. Jack

and I have everything. Besides, there's still pie." I carry my plate to the sink. "Do you prefer to wash or dry?"

With his head bowed to the growing suds, he scrubs the dishes while the sink fills with water. "What can I do to help expedite your trip home?"

Taking the clean dish from him, I dry it. "Why do you want to expedite my trip home? Because I suggested that you help do the dishes?"

"Yes. Eloise and I had a good thing going, and you're rocking the boat." He hands me another dish.

"Rocking the boat? What are you calling a good thing? She cooks and cleans, and you ... eat?"

"I mow the lawn, pull weeds ... I cleaned the chimney. And I chop wood. Oh, and sometimes I fix the neighbor's toilet."

"*I* chopped the wood." I search through her cabinets to find where the dishes belong.

"Stealing someone's job doesn't make it your job. Just like stealing someone's husband doesn't make them yours."

Someone's a bit chippy tonight.

"Touché. But, for the record, I didn't want him."

"You just wanted to have sex with him?"

I dry the next dish, peeking around the corner to see if Eloise is listening to us. "Did someone cheat on you?"

"No," he scoffs as if it's ridiculous.

"At least not that you know about, right?"

Jack eyes me with confusion. I wink, and one of his brows lifts a fraction—another tiny crack in his well-practiced composure.

"What are you two chatting about?" Eloise asks, carrying her dishes into the kitchen.

"Jack was just telling me about his family. He's been married five times. He has twelve kids and four grandchildren. The reason he's living in your garage is because his current wife made him choose between her and his piano. To be honest, he might have made the right choice. It's a beautiful Steinway & Sons. However, I haven't met his wife, so it's just my biased assumption as a music lover. No offense intended."

Eloise hands Jack her dishes, eyes big, mouth agape. "Is that ... true?"

"Part of it." He takes her dishes.

"Which part?" she asks, uncovering the pie I brought.

"My piano is beautiful."

Eloise eyes me, and I confirm with a smile that I made up almost everything.

"Well, I like Jack's mysterious nature." She gives his arm a gentle squeeze.

"Does anyone want pie?" I ask.

Jack hands me the last dish. "I'll pass. Thanks." A stiff smile accompanies his words.

"I'll have a piece." Eloise sets two small plates on the counter.

While I cut and serve the pie, Jack finishes the dishes. "Am I dismissed?" He dries his hands while examining me.

"You are. I'll save some pie for you." I give him a toothy grin.

"I'm good. Thanks again, Eloise."

"Of course, dear."

Eloise and I eat pie and discuss how the hummingbirds have recently found her feeders. I look forward to a time in my life when the highlight of my day is dinner with friends and hummingbirds. I look forward to the day I don't feel dead inside because my family needlessly died. Sadly, I don't think that day will ever come.

"Take the rest of the pie. It was delicious, but I'll never eat it all," she says when I stand to leave.

"You sure?"

"Oh yes."

"Well, thank you, Eloise. It's been a nice evening—a perfect distraction." I wrap up the rest of the pie.

"Frankie, I hope you find closure soon to return home in peace. I hope you've thought about what I've said. We can't change anything. Don't let your emotions steal another day of your life. Move on, dear."

I smile. "I know. Thank you for your concern. Good night."

"Good night."

CHAPTER SEVEN
FRANCESCA

It's a perfect day to shop for new jewelry, especially since Corinne Sanford is at the store. I've noticed she doesn't spend much time here. Living at the top of high society seems to be a job in and of itself—the poor dear.

When I open the chiming door, she and a bearded man glance up and step apart as if I caught them, but I didn't. At least, I don't think I did.

"Frances." She fakes a smile while the dark-haired gentleman in a suit disappears into the back of the store.

"Francesca." I return an equally fake smile. She knows my name.

As if she didn't hear me or it doesn't matter to her, she lifts her chin and clears her throat while adjusting the collar of her white button-down that's as starched as her smile. Overlapping gold necklaces hang from her pasty white neck that's streaked red like *someone* with a beard recently brushed up against her. I'd like to wrap my hands around it and scream at her for bringing such a monster into this world.

"What can I do for you?" she asks.

"I was in the area, so I thought I'd look for something for my mom. Her birthday is next month."

"Oh," her face softens. "I can help you with that. What's your price range?"

I'm jobless, and my mom's birthday was in January. We went to lunch, and I bought her a new suitcase for her trip to Ireland that she had to cancel because her grandson and daughter-in-law tragically died.

"A hundred?" I shrug.

Corinne's nose wrinkles.

"Five hundred?" I correct.

She nods. "I have a few things. Let me show you." She retrieves several displays from behind the glass counter.

"Did Molly mention I saw her at a coffee shop several days ago?" I ask.

"No. But I don't talk with her that often. She's busy, and so am I."

"Her new boyfriend seems nice."

Corinne pauses her motions, carefully setting the last display onto the counter while eyeing me. "She doesn't have a boyfriend. She's still grieving Steven."

My lips twist while I hum. "That's interesting. They seemed to be together."

"What do you mean by *together*?"

Inspecting the necklaces and bracelets on the displays, I shrug. "Molly was touching him in a way that I assume only a girlfriend would touch her boyfriend."

"Touching him how?"

I try on one of the bracelets. "Intimately."

"Holding hands?"

I shake my head.

Corinne spins the rings on her fingers like her daughter did when I visited her at their house. "Kissing?"

56

Another headshake. "It's not my place to share the details. And maybe I'm wrong." I hold up a necklace to my chest and glance in the mirror. "Perhaps times have changed. Maybe teenagers do more with or *for* their friends than we did years ago. If that's true, then Molly must be Colin's best friend."

"I don't know what you think you saw, but you must have mistaken it for something else. And I don't know who this Colin boy is. Believe me; I would know if my daughter had a boyfriend."

"You said it yourself. Molly is busy, and so are you. I'm sure she doesn't have time to give you the finer details of her life." I shift my gaze toward the door at the back of the store where the man in a suit escaped. "Just like I'm sure you don't have time to share the finer details of your life with your daughter..." I smile "...or your husband."

She's screwed, and it's all over her face. On the one hand, she wants to threaten me and kick my ass out of her store—out of this town. On the other hand, she knows I'm here because I lost my nephew, whom her daughter was dating. And you can't threaten a grieving person.

"Are any of these going to work for you?" she asks through gritted teeth.

"I fear not. But thanks for showing them to me. Nice seeing you again, Corinne."

I NEED to know who the guy was in the store with Corinne. There's a hundred percent probability that their relationship is as innocent as Colin's and Molly's. In the meantime, I text Archer Sanford. I don't plan on killing anyone, but

I'm not leaving until I've thoroughly fucked up their entire family.

Will it get Steven and Lynn back? Of course not.

Do I think it's what my brother would have wanted me to do? Absolutely.

That letter poisoned me, and it would have poisoned John too. And I can't just shake it off and leave town like it never existed.

> Me: It's Iris. The red dress?

> Archer: What a pleasant surprise. Can I take you to dinner?

> Me: I'd love that

> Archer: What's your address?

> Me: What's the address of the restaurant?

> Archer: Fair enough

He sends me the address.

> Archer: 7?

> Me: Perfect

> Archer: Wear that dress again

> Me: Boring

> Archer: Don't wear anything underneath it and I promise you won't be bored

The Sanfords are despicable. I need to figure out how far I'm willing to go to make them pay. Am I ready to sell my soul?

Molly humiliated Steven and then destroyed him. I'm going to humiliate her in every possible way.

I arrive at the restaurant ten minutes early. Then I slip into the ladies' room and slide off my panties. Yes, I'm wearing *the* red dress. After tucking them in my purse and checking my makeup, I return to the entrance just as Archer arrives with his bodyguards. Why all the protection? Is he running for president?

He removes his sunglasses, tucking them into his suit jacket while a triumphant smile bleeds across his face.

Here we are in another public space, and he unapologetically fucks me with his eyes. Sadly, I'm not immune to it. Archer's older than me, but it doesn't detract from his sex appeal. He's fit and tan with a head full of blond and gray hair. He has a sinful smile and a custom-tailored suit. His confidence alone would make the average woman do about anything for his attention.

I'm not the average woman, but I'm willing to play the part to regain some sense of control and right in the world again.

Before I can speak, he saunters past the dining room attendant. His bodyguard nods for me to follow Archer. We enter a private dining room, fit for a party of twelve, but there are only settings for two and champagne is already on ice. His bodyguards don't join us in the private room. I tamp down my nerves with Molly's words. That's all it takes because I have every single word of that letter memorized.

"Lady in red." He shakes his head while holding my chair as he did at lunch.

"Sounds cliché." I laugh while sitting.

"Iris," he whispers next to my ear, "you're anything but cliché."

I shiver because I don't trust him. I shiver because he's

undeniably sexy, and that's just a fact I can't avoid. And maybe it will make this easier, but I doubt it. I hate every single Sanford in this godforsaken town.

But *Iris* doesn't. She's enthralled with Archer, so much so that her panties are in her purse instead of where they belong. Sex is its own form of revenge, even though I've never wielded it like a weapon until now. Death changes people. After John died, I feared I would never be the same. After his son and wife died, I *knew* I'd never be the same.

"I didn't think I'd hear from you again," he says, sitting across from me.

"Oh? Why is that? Did you think you made a bad first impression?" I rest my napkin on my lap.

He smirks. "No. You seemed a little skittish the other day."

"Well," I reach for the stemmed glass of water and hope he doesn't see me tremor, "can you blame a girl? After all, you pulled me off the sidewalk and overwhelmed me with compliments, over-priced food, and champagne." I sip my water while holding up a finger. "All while wearing your wedding band and no explanation of a dead wife or recent separation." With unblinking scrutiny, I slowly return my glass to the table.

He twists his wrist, inspecting his ring. "Is this a hard limit for you?"

"It used to be, but I've unintentionally lowered my standards over the past year."

He laughs. "I'm not sure how I should take that."

A waiter slips through a side door and serves us hors d'oeuvres before pouring our champagne and exiting without so much as brief eye contact.

"I can't get you out of my head," Archer says.

60

I grin, lifting one of the hors d'oeuvres onto my plate. "So tell me about your family, Archer."

Again, he laughs. "My family?" While chewing, he wipes his mouth. "You're unlike any woman I have ever met."

"Because other women don't ask you about your family? I can't imagine why."

"And I can't imagine why you would."

I set my fork on the plate and rest my hands on my lap. "Attraction to me is more than physical. I need to 'get' you first."

"So you *are* attracted to me?" He eats up my words.

"I'm interested." I offer a wry grin.

"I'll tell you all you need to know about my family after you tell me what you're wearing beneath that red dress."

"Nothing. Wasn't that your request?"

"Are you lying?"

"Why would I lie?"

"Women lie to me all the time."

"That seems like a you-problem."

Archer eyes me for several seconds before standing. I focus on slow, even breaths with each step he takes toward me. He hovers behind me, tracing my bare shoulder with the tip of his finger. I'm not sure what his fascination is with this dress. It's off the rack. I bet Corinne has never worn anything off the rack.

His hand slides along my chest, and I can't help but make a slow, hard swallow when it dips beneath the bodice and cups my bare breast in a firm hold. My fingers twitch on my lap, wanting to grip something to stay in control.

His lips brush the hair at my ear, breath hot along my skin. "You have fucking perfect tits."

When he removes his hand, I start to relax, but in the

JEWEL E. ANN

next breath, his hands slide to my hips, and his lips skate down my neck. Greedy fingers gather the skirt of my dress, inching it up my legs. There's no way to stay calm. A stranger is touching me intimately. This isn't a game I've played before now. I don't know the rules. I'm not a cheater. That's on him. I hate his wife and daughter, so neither is on my conscience. Still, feeling physically attracted to someone who also makes my blood boil is emotionally stifling. If sin weren't pretty, it wouldn't be so tempting.

His fingers find skin, skimming my inner thigh until he meets my exposed flesh. Both hands grip my legs, and I can't keep my muscles from going rigid.

"Relax," he whispers, pushing my legs apart.

My mouth falls open to accommodate my labored breaths.

I can't do this ...

My mind screams while my tongue remains idle.

His middle finger slips between my spread legs while his tongue drags along my neck from my collarbone to my ear.

I gasp because I'm scared out of my fucking mind. I choke because I'm turned on. And I wonder if this is how Molly manipulated Steven. Did she seduce him only to torture him?

"I guess you're not a liar," he casually says while standing to his full height and straightening his suit jacket on his way back to his chair.

I force myself to eye him without a blink or a facial twitch while I slide my dress back down my legs. When I removed my panties, I had no illusion that he wouldn't want firsthand proof. However, no amount of mental cheerleading prepared me for this feeling. He is an awful man who married a horrible woman. And God should

62

have robbed them of their right to reproduce. But He didn't. And now I'm stuck grappling with the question of God's existence. Perhaps, for now, it's best if He doesn't exist. I have a feeling I'm not earning any points toward salvation.

"You were vague at lunch when I asked you to tell me about yourself. A dental assistant, originally from the West Coast, didn't give me much to go on."

"Wait. You were going to tell me about *your* family. I think I earned it."

"Tit for tat?" He lifts his eyebrows. "I can go all night if that's the case. What do you want to know first?"

"Do you have kids?"

"A daughter."

The waiter returns with cups of soup. When he leaves, I continue my line of questioning. "How many times have you been married?"

"Just once. First and last marriage."

He's committed. Not faithful but committed.

"How old is your daughter?"

He grins before sipping his soup. "You earned two questions. And I answered two questions."

"Does your wife know about your indiscretions? And do you know about hers?"

He grins. I take that as a yes.

"You said you were only in town for a few weeks, but you never said why you're here," he says.

"Mmm ... I suppose I didn't. I'm visiting family."

He nods, readily accepting my explanation. And why wouldn't he? There's no reason to be in Boone or Rhodale unless you live here or have someone to visit.

After the soup, the waiter delivers our salads.

"If the only way we talk is through an agreed-upon

physical exchange, then I'm not sure why we're here and not at a hotel," I say while stabbing lettuce with my fork.

He pauses his motions. "*Would* you go to a hotel with me? It's only our second date."

"We're not dating." I shake my head.

"No?"

"I don't date married men."

Archer chuckles, blotting his mouth while leaning back in his chair. "Then why are we sharing a meal twice in less than a week?"

I shrug. "I like free food. And I find it psychologically fascinating why people cheat. Maybe I should have been a psychologist instead of a dental assistant."

I'm not sure why Archer is into banking other than the apparent reason—money. Because I did a little research, and he has a master's degree in *psychology*.

A victorious grin slides up his face; he knows I've Googled him. "There is not one single answer. Happy people cheat. So do people who love their spouse. One can be perfectly satisfied with their marriage, even sexually satisfied, but they still cheat. So the typical troubled marriage or damaged person with a history of emotional baggage doesn't always define the reason for cheating."

"You've thought about this a lot."

He shrugs. "Perhaps."

"So why do you do it?"

"Because I can."

I laugh. "That implies there are married people who *can't* cheat."

"There are plenty of people who are incapable of cheating."

"The righteous ones?" I slant my head to the side.

"The miserable ones."

"So everyone in a faithful marriage is miserable?"

Archer's head bobs a few times. "Maybe half. Maybe more."

The waiter arrives with the main course—the catch of the day with eyes. I'm not eating it.

"You'd be miserable in a marriage, Iris."

"Why do you say that?"

"Because you wouldn't allow yourself this luxury."

Is cheating a luxury? I ponder that idea.

"How do you know?"

"Because you said you've never been married."

I roll my lips together for a beat and nod once before eating the red potatoes not near the fish's head. "So I'm afraid to get married because I don't trust myself to be in a monogamous relationship, or I know I wouldn't cheat and therefore feel trapped?"

"Your words, not mine." Archer smirks before taking a bite of his fish.

"Maybe I've just been career-oriented."

"Then you'd be the dentist, not the assistant."

I take personal offense on behalf of all dental assistants —even if I'm not one.

I have over a decade of college on my resumé. Would that impress him? I don't know. He seems to be more of a tits and pussy guy.

By the time dessert is served, Archer has his tie loosened and the top two buttons of his shirt undone. Also, he's had most of the bottle of champagne.

He drums his fingers on the table while I eye my chocolate tart. It's hard to eat with him staring at me.

"Do you not like dessert?" I ask.

"I like you."

"I'm not on the menu."

"You should be."

My laugh is a little nervous, a little forced.

"Dinner was lovely, and the conversation has been most interesting." I set my napkin on the table and slide my dessert plate away.

"Lovely and interesting ..." He wets his lower lip. "That's exactly how I'd describe you."

"Thank you," I say with a surprising amount of sincerity.

At first, I feigned interest in Archer Sanford and his blatant cheating. Now, I can say I'm genuinely intrigued. Sin is very intriguing. Too intriguing. Was Steven this intrigued with Molly? I can't imagine.

The waiter returns with coffee.

"Out!" Archer snaps.

I jump more than the waiter.

"I ... uh ... should go." Standing on shaky legs, I adjust my strapless dress.

Archer pushes his chair back. "Come here," he whispers as if he hadn't just lost his patience with a stranger.

Whatever my heart rate was when he touched me earlier, it's ten times that now as he unzips his pants.

"On your knees."

I think those three words will haunt me forever. Not because they're anything new. Not because no man has said that to me before now. No. They'll haunt me because I'm not Francesca. I'm Iris. And I deliberately put myself in this situation because I can't let Molly Sanford get away with murder. There's no room for ethics and morality when revenge is the only goal.

Sucking Archer's dick isn't the problem. It might even be part of the solution, just not tonight. Perhaps he's in this room with me because Corinne won't give him head. Or maybe she's willing to give him everything. Is that why some of the wealthiest people in the world are also the most dissatisfied with their lives? When you have everything, what's the point?

My parents fought about money and a messy house. They even fought about sex when they didn't know I was listening: Not enough time for sex. Too tired for sex because raising twins and running a farm was exhausting.

They didn't have everything; they had each other. Perhaps people who don't have everything know how important it is to hold on to what they do have. My parents had me and my brother. And they had each other. They still have each other. Even after losing a son, his wife, and a grandchild, my parents are stronger than ever.

"Archer, maybe the reason I've never been married is because I refuse to get on my knees for *anyone*."

He purses his lips, eyes narrowed in contemplation. "I will have you, Iris."

"That's the spirit." I saunter toward him, leaning forward to press a soft kiss to the corner of his mouth. "Never give up. Good night."

CHAPTER EIGHT
JACKSON

JACKSON WATCHES Frankie leave the restaurant. Once again, she's wearing that strapless red dress. And once again, she's spending time with Archer Sanford. After she climbs into her Lexus and heads toward home, Jackson stays until Archer exits the restaurant with his bodyguards.

He can't figure out why Frankie would give Archer the time of day, let alone lunch and dinner, in less than a week.

After exercising, a shower, and playing his piano, there's a predictable knock at his door.

"Leftover pie?" Frankie holds up the pie from the other night.

Jackson steps aside.

She's no longer in a red dress. For Jackson, she wears tiny shorts, flip-flops, and her usual tight top that shows her nipples.

"How was your day? Did you get a lot of work done?" She glances around the garage before plopping on the sofa facing his punching bag and weights.

"I always get a lot of work done." He grabs a titanium utensil with a spoon on one side and a fork on the other.

Frankie inspects it before eyeing him. "I'll take the spoon side."

He sits next to her and steals the pie plate. "If you didn't eat your share before you got here, that's too damn bad. We're not sharing anything."

She faces him, crisscrossing her legs on the cushion. "You seem a little agitated. Want to talk about it?"

"Nope." He shovels pie into his mouth. Of course, he's agitated. She's fucking around with his target, but he can't say a word to her about it. "How was *your* day?" he asks. "Surely you can't have much more to do around here."

"What are you talking about? I can't leave until you finish your piano piece. It's in my head, and I must know how it will end. Half a song is an unfinished story."

"Then you'll be here forever, which is a hell of a lot longer than I'll be here."

"Why do you say that?" she asks.

"Because I won't ever finish it."

Frankie steals the pie plate and his utensil, using the same end to take a bite of the pie and then another and another. "Why?" she mumbles.

He eyes her, again feeling the eerie familiarity of the women who have dominated his life, sometimes against his will. "Because the inspiration died."

Frankie taps the fork end of the utensil on her lips. "Then resurrect it."

"Her," he says, and it's barely a whisper.

"Did you say *her*?"

"Thanks for the pie." Jackson stands, staring at the ceiling and stretching his back with his hands on his hips. He's not here to talk about his life or eat pie with a woman.

And Frankie is the worst kind of woman. She's messing with his mind and pulling invisible strings. He has a job to do. And it would be much easier to do without daily visits from her perky little nipples. It would be easier if she'd stop stroking his piano keys before leaving her feminine scent in his space.

It's been ages since he's felt so uneasy about a woman. It's been forgettably long since he's needed to drink himself into a stupor or beat the shit out of something or someone to suppress the urge to fuck.

And if all that isn't enough, Jackson can't rid his mind of the predatory way Archer Sanford looked at her.

Did he touch her tonight?

Did she let him?

Does it matter?

That's the real question. Why should he care? Since Jackson's been tracking his target, he's seen him with numerous women. He's seen Archer parade them in and out of hotels. And he's never thought twice about the women other than they deserved to be fucked and forgotten. After all, it's no secret Archer's married. Fairy tales rarely start with infidelity.

When Archer dies (soon), and no one can find him (his lifeless body), there will be a long list of suspects with fake tits and lace panties on security footage of local restaurants and hotels—a crime of jealousy and passion.

Frankie doesn't move despite Jackson's gratitude for the pie wrapped in a not-so-subtle hint that he wants her to leave. She stares at him with sympathy. It used to bother him. Saying Ryn's name, even "her," was unbearable. But time has forced him into acceptance.

"Your wife died," Frankie says with reverence.

He nods.

"You started this song while she was alive, but now she's gone, and you can't finish it."

Another nod.

She stands and hands him the utensil. "Do I look like your wife?"

He narrows his eyes before whispering, "Yes."

"I'm sorry."

Jackson slowly shakes his head. "Don't be. She was beautiful."

Frankie finds a sad smile in return for Jackson's attempt to compliment her.

"Whatever you're doing ... don't. Just go home," he says.

"I can't because I need to make things right."

It makes no sense. Jackson can't figure out how messing around with a married man makes anything right.

"Your family died. Nothing will ever be right," he says.

"My brother wouldn't have wanted me to walk away."

"Then he wasn't a good brother."

Frankie winces. "You know nothing about my brother."

"I do. You just said he was the kind of guy who would want his sister to engage in a dangerous game for ... what? If it's not to save a life, it's not worth it."

Chewing on the inside of her cheek, she averts her gaze. "Get rid of the D minor chords. They're too melancholy. Stop lamenting. And maybe you're the one who needs to go home." Her gaze returns to his. She's unapologetically crass. And standoffish. She's goading him with words and tempting him with her physical presence—her physical existence.

If he touched her, what would she do? His next thought goes to his reaction—*his* level of control. If he touched her, could he stop? Would he want to?

"I *need* you to leave," he steps toward her, and she retreats, "before something bad happens."

Another step forward.

Another step backward.

She swallows hard when her back hits the door, staring at his chest. "If you try anything, I will hurt you. I've had self-defense classes. Please don't make me hurt you." She glances up at him.

Jackson hasn't had an erection this hard in a long time. He stares at the outline of her nipples while her chest heaves.

He'd fucking love it if she tried to hurt him. Throw a punch, a jab ... make him bleed. Make him *feel* again.

Frankie balls her hands at her sides and raises her chin slightly. Jackson can't help but grin.

"What are you smiling at? Think you can back me into a corner and intimidate me with your wolfish expression?"

He scrapes his teeth across his lower lip. "You're not in a corner, but I could find one and back you into it. I'd love to watch you squirm your way out of it."

"Three years." She swallows hard again. "I took classes for three years. I'll have you flat on your back in no time."

It's like she's trying to awaken his dick with her tongue; every word is a methodic stroke.

"As tempting as that sounds," he rests a hand on the door next to her head, "I have some work to do. Can I take a rain check?"

"Do you want me to be scared of you?" she whispers.

"If it makes you pack your bags and go home, then yes. I want you to be fucking terrified of me," he replies in a low, unwavering tone.

She lifts onto her toes as if hoping to press her lips to his. Will he let her? Absolutely not. Does he enjoy the torture of her proximity? Unfortunately.

"I'm not scared of anyone," she whispers.

Tying a woman up was never Jackson's MO. The need

for that level of control has always been his sister's weakness. And because of her, Jackson learned just how much the need for control can be a person's biggest weakness.

Frankie's entire body goes rigid when Jackson cups her jaw, gently forcing her head against the door until her unblinking eyes flare, and she swallows her next breath.

"You should be a little scared of everyone because humans are unpredictable."

Frankie grips his arm with both hands, digging her nails into his flesh. "Are you a little scared of me?"

Jackson lowers his face to hers, and she wets her lips. "I'm more than a little scared of you." His revelation brings something to life in her eyes, but she has no clue that his confession isn't a relinquishment of power or an acquiescence of her strength.

"Now get the fuck out of here." He releases her.

CHAPTER NINE

FRANCESCA

Molly Sanford's busy schedule would break the most dedicated Marine. I don't know how she does it.

Coffee.

Blowing Colin in his pickup before baseball practice.

And now ... a mani-pedi.

"Can I help you?" The young blonde at the counter smiles when I enter the nail salon.

"Do you have any openings for either a manicure or a pedicure?"

She nods. "Sure. We can do both right now."

"Perfect." I smile, feeling nearly as lucky and hard-working as Molly today.

After I pick my polish, the tech leads me toward the pedicure station. I point to the empty chair next to Molly. "Is that open? I know her."

"Of course."

Molly glances up from her phone screen, and her summer tan fades into a shade of fresh winter snow.

"Hey, Molly." I climb into the empty chair and set my key fob and phone on the tray between us.

"Hey," she mumbles.

"I'm glad I ran into you again. I came across something in Steven's room."

She stiffens.

I let it simmer for a few extra seconds before sighing. "He had a notebook. A journal. And he wrote so much about you in it."

Molly's nail technician glances at her because Molly's foot and the rest of her body shakes.

"He adored you."

Her head pivots to me.

I rest my hand on her arm. "He was so in love. I don't know how I'll ever be able to thank you for being there when he needed you the most. Your love and loyalty bled through his words." I frown, averting my gaze for a beat before shaking my head. "I just don't understand why it wasn't enough."

She's speechless.

"What do you miss most about him? What did you love the most? Did you two discuss plans for after graduation?"

"Um ..." She clears her throat. "I don't know. I mean ... I loved everything about him. He always complimented me. He bought me things. He took me to dinner. He washed my car. He was just a really nice guy."

Me. Me. Me.

I can't handle her level of cuntiness. A real word? No. But it needs to be a word as long as Molly shares space and oxygen in this life.

"How did you react when you heard about his death?"

She glues her gaze to her sparkly purple toenails. "I was ... devastated."

"Surprised?"

Her forehead wrinkles. "Of course."

75

"Me too. It was so unlike him. He loved his mom. He was her rock. Steven was everything his mom needed after his dad, my brother, died. Mature beyond his years. I think losing a parent forces you to grow up quickly. It's not fair, but it's life. You know?"

I lift one foot out of the water when the nail technician reaches for my leg. "You can't even imagine how his death will affect you for the rest of your life. Everyone's vulnerable and impressionable. That's just human nature. But at your age, your conscience is so malleable. Things you think are no big deal only magnify over time." Blowing a long breath, I pause to give Molly more time to stew.

"You're going to think of Steven's death forever. Not because you want to. No. You'll do it because time will make you question everything. You'll wonder if there was more you could have done to stop him. And that will feel like an inescapable prison of regret. And no matter how many therapists you see, how many times friends and family try to convince you that there was nothing you could have done, you will carry that burden. And I wish there was something I could say or do to prevent that from happening. But there's not. The only thing I can say to comfort you is that Steven loved you. I think he would have done anything for you.

"Sure, you were both young, but sometimes you just know. And I think he knew you were it for him. I think he was going to align his future with yours. I think you were his first true love. And maybe knowing you were his only true love will comfort you a little." I glance sideways and wait for her to look at me before I smile. "You should feel incredibly honored to have been *that* girl in Steven's life."

"Oh! Wait! Are you okay?" Molly's technician says in a panic, dropping the polish bottle in the soaking tub when

Molly and her half-polished toes flee toward the back of the salon.

She doesn't make it to the restroom before hurling all over the floor, her legs, and her pretty purple-polished toes.

Poor thing.

When my technician gives me a wide-eyed gaze, I offer an innocent half-smile and stare at my fingernails. "You know ... I think we should do a French manicure instead of the red you're using on my toes. What do you think?"

She's not thinking. Molly's caused too much commotion, not to mention the mess of upchucked coffee and what appears to be bits of scrambled eggs.

Gross. She must be so embarrassed. I bet she never returns to this salon. That's too bad.

I lean back, close my eyes, and think of my wildly successful start to the day. Next, I'll grab lunch. Maybe a massage. And I might even pick up something for dinner and invite Eloise to eat with me.

BY LATE AFTERNOON, my wild success screeches to a halt when I return to the house.

The fire engines.

The remains of my brother's house—a charred skeleton with a few areas still smoldering.

What happened? WHAT THE HELL HAPPENED?

I sprint toward the house, eyes burning with tears.

"Frankie!" Eloise reaches for my arm.

I whip around. "What happened? Who ... w-what?" I stab my hands through my hair as my voice cracks. The photos. The things I set aside for the rest of the family. It's ... gone.

"I just got home too. I was getting ready to call you."

I shake my head. I can't tear my gaze from the sight before me. It's just ... not possible. "What caused it?" I stutter a few words while dragging my feet closer to the house.

"Ma'am, I'm sorry. You'll have to stay back. Is this your house?"

"No." Then it hits me. "Sort of," I whisper.

The fire chief introduces himself and asks me a handful of questions. I answer on instinct. I can't focus enough to understand what's happening or what I'm saying. When he glances over my shoulder, I follow his gaze to the black BMW pulling into the garage.

My body reacts without thought, and I run toward the garage, limboing under the door before it shuts.

Jack steps out of his car.

All I see is red as I hurl my fist into his face. "What did you do?" I scream.

His head barely flinches from the impact of my punch, but I feel it up my arm to my shoulder.

"You can't make me leave by burning down my fucking house!" I grab his shirt and attempt to shake him.

He's unmovable. Face blank. Eyes blinking slowly.

"E-everything that was l-left of them w-was in there." I release him and bat away my hot, angry tears.

He *is* a murderer and a monster, and his lack of emotion or response only angers me more. I shove him with both hands and throw another punch. He catches my fist in the palm of his hand.

"Calm the fuck down. I didn't burn down your house. Maybe you left the stove on. Maybe—"

He's mocking me. I'm not stupid.

"I didn't leave the stove on! I didn't leave anything

plugged in. That is arson. And the only person who wants me to leave *that badly...*" I point toward the fire "... is YOU."

He scratches his scruffy jaw and twists his lips. "You sure about that?"

"What's that supposed to mean?"

Turning, he dismissively walks away from me, retrieving an apple from the brown paper bag on his sofa. "I don't know, Francesca. What *does* it mean?" he asks calmly before biting the apple. "A jilted lover? A wife who thinks you're fucking her husband?"

He's calling me a whore without saying the actual words. His indifference is infuriating. Is this a joke to him? A game?

I shuffle my feet several steps and snatch a crowbar hanging from a hook on the wall beside a handful of other tools. I'm done. Jack has lost it. His mysteriousness is no longer intriguing. He's playing me. And I am *done*.

"What the fuck—" Jack drops his apple and flies toward me, but not before the crowbar lands on the top of his piano, splintering the polished black wood. I feel like a Christian burning the Bible, a soldier burning the flag. But sometimes, that's the only way to make a statement.

Whoosh!

The air leaves my lungs.

I've never been flat on my back, pinned to the ground so quickly. Not by an impatient lover. Not by my self-defense instructor. Not even when I slipped on ice in the university parking lot and split open the back of my head.

In the next second, I'm on my stomach with my wrists shackled in his steely grip. "So it's okay that things that matter to me are destroyed, but your precious piano is untouchable? Let me go! Hel—"

His other hand covers my mouth before I can yell for help.

I squirm and try to scream behind his hand, but I can't do either. And the harder I try to free myself, the firmer his grip gets. And it's impossible to breathe.

"Calm the fuck down," he grits between clenched teeth. "You need to listen carefully. If someone burns down your house, it's time to get out of town."

My fight dies like my brother, his wife, their son, their belongings, and their house. It feels like their entire existence has been erased from history.

I don't fight. I don't try to scream. I wait while my mind spins. But the anger doesn't go away. It multiplies.

If Jack didn't set the house on fire, *she* did.

CHAPTER TEN

JACKSON

THERE'S ALWAYS A SNAG, but Jackson thought this time would be different.

Relocate.

Find the target.

Surveillance to confirm Archer Sanford is the last target.

Take him out.

Go home.

Fucking retire ...

Every target has a life—a shit fest—that would distract less seasoned assassins. An affair. A secret baby. A weird porn fetish. Drugs. You name it.

Archer Sanford has his fair share. A whore for a wife. A fucked-up daughter. A string of mistresses. A nephew running for public office in Massachusetts who has a wife and a male fuck buddy on the side.

Jackson couldn't care less. He's not into judging them; he's just here to eliminate *his* problem.

But now there's a limp woman on his floor with her problems scattered at his feet. He knows he should pick her up, deposit her on Eloise's porch, and wipe his hands from the situation.

"Go home." He releases her and runs his hands through his hair before lacing his fingers behind his head, tugging and pulling against the pent-up tension.

"She did it," Frankie whispers, climbing to her hands and knees.

Jackson doesn't care. It's not his problem.

"I'm going to fucking *kill* her," she seethes while standing and rubbing her wrists.

He feels it's unlikely that a professor of music theory possesses the emotional detachment to kill someone in cold blood. But Frankie has a look in her eyes that Jackson has seen in his sister's—who *has* taken a few lives over the years.

Jackson picks up the crowbar. "Fuck," he mumbles. "I don't want to know. I just ... don't want to know." He returns it to the hook on the wall, unable to look at his poor piano. "I Don't. Want. To. Know." Scrubbing his hands over his face, he turns and lets them flop to his sides with a deep sigh. He hates this feeling of knowing he's about to cave. "Who are you going to kill? And why? And just..." pinching his eyes shut, he shakes his head "...tell me everything. I'll take care of it. You just *go home*."

"Take care of it? You don't even know what *it* is. You just want to get rid of me." She balls her hands into tight fists. "And I don't understand what's bugging you about my presence. You have no issue eyeing me like a piece of meat. You invade my space. You bully me. You—"

"Bully you?" Jackson chuckles. "Oh, Francesca, you have no idea what bullying is if you think I'm bullying you."

"You put me in a chokehold and told me to go home. And..." she points to the floor, "...you pinned me to the ground!"

"You have *three* years of self-defense. You threatened to put me on my back. And you punched me. Then you took a fucking crowbar to my piano!" He risks a glance at his baby and winces. "It's called self-defense, Sweetheart."

"I'm not your sweetheart." Her pounding feet eat up the distance between them, and she jabs a finger into his chest.

Jackson has patience for days—years. He's had militant control over his emotions and timing with Archer Sanford. He's dealt with his sister trying to backseat drive his plans from the other side of the country. He misses his family so much that it's hard to breathe some days. But Francesca Holter has another thing coming if she thinks she's going to fuck up his plans while smacking him around one minute and playing the victim the next.

Hell no.

He cuffs her wrist, digging her finger out of his chest and walking her backward until the back of the sofa stops her retreat. Her hands fly to the side, gripping the worn leather to steady herself.

Eyes wide. Lips parted.

"I'll scream," she whispers.

Jackson's lips twitch while his fingertips skate up her bare arms. "I don't doubt that."

"W-what are you..." With each labored breath, her words stumble across her lips "...doing?"

His hands cup her neck. It's gentle and reverent.

Frankie's eyes drift shut.

The pad of his thumb traces her jaw to the corner of her mouth.

It hurts him to touch her.

It hurts him not to touch her.

And he needs her to go home and never look back, but he needs something else too—maybe even more.

When her eyes open, meeting his unblinking gaze affixed to her beautiful face, she turns her head a fraction so his thumb slides along her lower lip. He ducks his head, ignoring all whispers of reason. As he moves his thumb to replace it with his mouth, three hard knocks rap on the door.

Frankie jumps, gaze darting toward the sound.

Jackson distances himself, eyeing her while his heart pounds. What did he almost do?

Fucking stupid. A weak moment.

He turns to open the door. He wouldn't be surprised if his sister teleported herself here just to make him bleed for getting distracted.

It's not his sister.

"Have you seen Francesca?" Eloise asks. "The fire chief needs to speak with her again. I can't believe this happened. She must be devastated."

Before Jackson can answer, Frankie steps behind him. "I'm here," she says, wedging herself in front of him.

"Honey, I'm *so* sorry. The fire's out. They're investigating to determine the cause, but the chief wants to—"

"I'm coming," she says, walking toward the charred remains. Just as Jackson starts to close the door, Frankie glances over her shoulder. A look is exchanged, but he quickly shuts the door.

"Fuck." He sighs, staring at his splintered piano. Frankie may look like his wife, Ryn, but that's where it ends. He shrugs off his shirt and spends the next hour pounding his hanging bag and pushing through a grueling workout with his weights.

CHAPTER ELEVEN
FRANCESCA

THE LITTLE BITCH WILL PAY. I've never wished Molly Sanford physical harm—until now.

She's pure evil.

The fire department hasn't concluded their investigation, but I know it will come back as arson. I pissed her off at the nail salon, and she blamed me for her embarrassment, or she worried about the letter being in his room and decided to take care of it before I found it.

"Have you told your parents?" Eloise asks while showing me her guest bedroom.

"Not yet," I toss my purse onto the bed. It's all I have.

"You're welcome to stay as long as you need. But I think you need to return home and let this go."

"She burned it down." I narrow my eyes. How can Eloise not see that I can't walk away now?

"If she did, they'll trace it back to her." Eloise frowns.

I open my mouth and close it just as quickly. Does she hear herself? She told me the Sanfords were untouchable. Why would an arson charge stick?

"Do you have something to wear to bed?"

"I don't need anything. I'll go shopping tomorrow."

Disapproval remains etched on her forehead. She doesn't want me to go shopping tomorrow. She wants me to go home. She and Jack are on the same page.

"Good night, Francesca."

"Thanks for letting me stay with you."

With a sad smile, she nods and shuts the door behind her.

I collapse onto the bed and stare at the ceiling. Life hasn't been my biggest fan over the past few years. I'm a fan of optimism, but even the most loyal fans lose faith in their team when they've been let down repeatedly.

My phone vibrates.

> Archer: Still in town? I need to see you

I take a selfie of my face in this unflattering position and send it to him.

> Archer: Meet me at the B&B on 5th and Wilson

> Me: I'm not much of a breakfast person

> Archer: Cute. Be there in 30 min

> Me: Can't. It's past my curfew

> Archer: Wear that red dress

> Me: It died

> Archer: ? I'm tired. Not in the mood to play

> Me: Then go to sleep. We'll meet up when you're in the mood to play

> Archer: I like getting my way

I grunt. "Shocking. You're such a toddler. I might have been in the mood to meet you tonight had your fucking little offspring not burned down my brother's house."

> Me: Goodnight

I shut off my phone and toss it aside. Then I crawl to the top of the bed, rest my head on the pillow, and close my eyes for a few minutes.

A few minutes turn into the whole night.

I head to Target for a few essentials the following day before Eloise is out of bed. When I return, Jackson's mowing her lawn.

I park by the remains of my brother's house. There's a fire investigation team working the scene. Waiting in the car, I try to figure out what to do when they confirm it's arson. What I did to Molly at the nail salon was a four. This is a ten. It's like cutting out someone's tongue for spitting on you.

Stepping out of my car, I walk the perimeter.

"It was gasoline."

I turn toward Jack's voice.

He wipes the sweat from his brow with his arm.

"They said that?"

He shakes his head.

"Then how do you know?"

"Because I looked over things last night."

I cross my arms. "Did you Google 'searching for the cause of fires'?"

"Shouldn't you be on your way home by now?"

I frown before brushing past him. "I think Steven's girl-friend burned down the house."

"Why would she do that?" He follows me.

"Because she ..." Nope. I'm not telling him about the letter. I don't know him. "She's unwell."

"Then go to the police." He follows me.

"Why do you care?" I whip around just before reaching my car. "Huh?"

"For the same reason that I fixed your leaky toilet."

"Because I asked you for help?"

"Because you needed help." He slides his fingers into the back pockets of his jeans, drawing his sweaty shirt tight against his chest.

I let it distract me for five seconds before clearing my throat. "The only help I need is for you to stop telling me to go home. And if you could get Eloise to stop worrying about me, that would be great too. Can you do that, Jack? Can you help me in that way?"

He rubs his right eye like something's in it, then nods.

"When you stop playing that song you wrote for your wife, I'll take your 'life tips' with more than a grain of salt. But for now, I will not feel guilty for my emotions or my need to make the people who destroyed my family pay." I retrieve my bags from the car.

When I shut the door, Jack's twenty paces in front of me, heading back to the lawnmower.

I can't figure him out. I don't have *time* to figure him out. But it doesn't mean I don't want to know why he was going to kiss me. The bigger question is why I wanted (still want) him to kiss me. Why do I want to feel his hands on me again?

The intensity of his gaze.

The heat of his body.

The mindlessness of the bubble around us when we're alone.

I feel *seen* with Jack.

Perhaps it's music. Maybe it's grief. But it's something.

CHAPTER TWELVE
FRANCESCA

I LOVE BASEBALL.

John played shortstop, and our school won the state championship our senior year. There's nothing better than metal bleachers in the hot sun, concession stand popcorn, and fresh-cut grass.

"Oh, hey!" I adjust my new baseball cap before bounding up the bleachers toward Molly and her friends.

Her jaw drops, as does the phone in her hands.

"Shit!" One of her friends gasps, trapping the phone beneath her foot inches from falling underneath the bleachers. "That was close." She hands Molly the phone.

"Are you feeling better?" I make a shooing motion for her friend to move aside so I can sit next to Molly, my new BFF.

The girl with black streaks in her blond hair scowls, but she slides to the left.

"Popcorn?" I offer to Molly.

She returns a barely detectable headshake, swatting at a wasp.

"Do you think it was food poisoning? What did you eat before your appointment?"

Colin's cum?

"Nothing. It was nothing. I'm ..." She leans over and whispers something in her other friend's ear.

"I'm Frankie." I dust salt off my hand and offer it to the friend on the other side of Molly. "Steven's aunt."

Blood drains from the friend's face. Did she know about the letter? Did Molly tell her I'm in town? Did she help Molly burn down the house?

"Brea." The girl gives me a wimpy handshake.

"Steven loved baseball. Did he tell you I took him to his first Cubs game? Speaking of Steven, did you hear his house caught fire? Total loss. I'm not sure I can take much more devastation."

It takes less than a second to assess her guilt.

"What?" her friends ask in unison.

Molly swallows hard, eyebrows knitting together with a slight headshake. But she doesn't look at me. Her jaw is set, eyes glued to the game. She's a statue of guilt.

"They're pretty sure it's arson. I can't imagine who would do something so horrendous. It's like dancing on their graves. Don't you think?"

Her friends nod. They seem to have genuine sympathy... actual souls.

"Is that Colin?" I point to the pitcher.

Molly ignores me.

"Does he drive a truck? I was in town the other morning, and I swear I saw you get out of a truck."

"Were you in Colin's truck?" The girl who moved her ass over for me leans forward to interrogate Molly. "What were you doing in his truck?"

"Jesus, Sadie, just shut up," Molly bristles.

"There's your mom." Brea points to the bottom of the bleachers.

Perfect.

I stand. "Nice chatting with you and your lovely friends."

Corinne stiffens when she glances up at me just as I approach her.

"Hello again. Molly was just introducing me to her friends. Great afternoon for a game."

She glances around the bleachers and waves to a group of ladies a few rows behind us. "Yes. It is." She lowers her sunglasses with a smile as stiff as the rest of her body. "Are you leaving so soon?"

"I like to watch from behind home plate. Good to see you." I exit the bleachers and glance around the crowd. My gaze snags on the overdressed man in the concession line. I look back at Molly and Corinne, who are occupied with their friends, and then I meander toward the line.

Oddly, Archer's wife and daughter have no one protecting them from ... whatever threat lurks around him. But today, his bodyguards hang back a reasonable distance, almost blending in with the spectators.

"I'll take a black cherry snow cone," I say.

Archer turns ever so slowly like the smile that swells in tiny increments on his face. He slides his sunglasses to the top of his head. Then, his gaze circumnavigates the crowd, pinpointing his daughter and wife before returning his attention to me.

"Funny. I wanted something last night, but you weren't feeling so generous. Maybe I should make you buy your own snow cone."

"Next," the young man at the concession says.

I step in front of Archer. "Black cherry snow cone."

As I reach into my purse for money, Archer tosses cash onto the counter.

I smirk and take the snow cone. "I was going to pay." I mosey away from the baseball diamond.

"I like the idea of you owing me," Archer says, following me at a safe distance. He's willing to have lunch with me in public, but hanging out with me at the same venue as his wife and daughter appears to be the line he's drawn in the sand.

I laugh. "I don't think you'll get much for a three-dollar snow cone."

"I was going to get you popcorn too."

Again, I laugh, but this time, it's spontaneous. Archer has a funny side to him. Don't get me wrong; he's still an arrogant asshole of a man, husband, and father, but he's not the worst company.

"You like that? I can go back and get the popcorn."

"Thanks, but I already had popcorn." I worm my way toward the school parking lot, stopping at my car under the mature oak tree.

A good ten yards away, Archer's two bodyguards park themselves and scan the area while he takes advantage of the distance we've put between us and the spectators.

"I can't stop thinking about you," he whispers in my ear, pressing his chest to my back before I can open my car door. His erection supports his claim, and so does his hand coiling around me, sliding between my legs to cup my crotch.

I'm grateful for my choice of denim shorts instead of a dress. My brain has no conflicts of interest. I hate Archer's daughter and wife, so I hate him by default.

My body ... it's not numb to his touch, and that's fucking unfortunate. So when I close my eyes and concentrate on his hand between my legs, I think of Jack. When Archer's other hand slides up my shirt and under my bra to my breast, I think of Jack.

"I want to fuck you, Iris. I want to fuck every inch of you."

Splat.

My snow cone falls from my hand to the ground as Archer thrusts his erection against the curve of my ass.

"Why do you need bodyguards?" I grasp at anything to slow him down.

"Because I'm an important person." He bites my earlobe. "And certain people see me as a threat. Now, open the back door," he growls.

She burned down their house. She burned down their house.

Am I willing to go the distance? Am I willing to be the mistress to worm my way into their world only to destroy every part of it? Is this what John would have wanted?

I open the back door, and Archer spins me around so quickly it makes me dizzy—like his mouth covering mine and his hands gripping my ass to the point of pain—like the way he lifts my leg to press his erection as close as he can get it to his goal.

Grinding.

Grunting.

Fucking me with his tongue.

When he releases my mouth, I gasp for a breath. He nudges me to get in the back seat.

"Show me that pussy," he demands while unbuttoning his pants.

This is it? Right here in the school parking lot while his daughter and wife watch the baseball game a stone's throw from my car? Is this where I will give him something so I can take his *everything*?

I don't have much time to think this through. What do I get in return? If I give this to him, will he toss me aside? For a man like Archer Sanford, is it nothing more than the chase? Will he shift his attention to the next woman who catches his eye?

His dick bobs when he releases it from his briefs. Archer strokes it several times, eyes hooded.

My heart hammers so hard I can't catch my breath. Swallowing, I fumble with the button to my shorts, hands shaking while shifting my thoughts from my dead nephew and sister-in-law to the dean's husband. It was just sex. Just my body taking part in something sexual. It was something physical that distracted me from something devastatingly emotional. I didn't fall in love. I used him to escape. And I don't know what he got out of the deal. Maybe it was just sex.

If I don't think about Molly or Corinne, Archer is nothing more than a handsome man with a big dick. I bet he fucks like a stallion. I bet he'll make me come. So why am I on the verge of tears? I'm angry with myself for being this weak, for my shaking hands and constant need to over-analyze the situation.

Beep! Beep! Beep!

The penetrating sound of a nearby car alarm reverberates around us.

"Fuck!" Archer shoots an angry scowl toward his body-guards like it's their fault. He tucks his cock back into his briefs and zips his pants.

I sit up, running my fingers through my hair while attempting to slow my breathing. Relief washes over me. Saved by the bell.

No goodbye.

Barely a parting glance.

Archer hightails it back toward the ball fields.

It takes a few minutes for me to quit shaking. The car alarm shuts off, and I slide into the driver's seat and get the hell out of here.

CHAPTER THIRTEEN
JACKSON

JACKSON'S never been a baseball fan, and today is no exception. Francesca's messing with his head, forcing him to make rash decisions like setting off a car alarm to keep Archer Sanford from fucking her in the high school parking lot.

What the hell is wrong with her?

He knows all too well how grief can mess with one's judgment. He watched his sister dive headfirst into a messed-up relationship, disregarding the risk or the consequences. His wife (before she was his wife) let her ex-husband beat the living shit out of her because they had a daughter together, and she had no way to completely escape ... until Jackson came into her life.

"Beer?" Eloise holds up a bottle after Jack climbs the deck stairs. She grins. "I know you don't drink wine."

It's not his favorite green-bottled beer, but a solid step up from wine. He stopped drinking after his wife died, but given his current state of affairs, a beer might be just what he needs. "Thanks." He takes the beer and sits in the swivel chair next to her. Jackson's job is a lonely one by design. But he's too old to die alone, and being so far away from his family feels like a slow death. And ... he wants to see Eloise's new roommate.

"Did you have a wonderfully mysterious day?"

Jackson chuckles before taking a swig of his beer. It's familiar, almost forbidden. Eloise's respect for his privacy is most appreciated. "Mysterious? Yes. Wonderful? Not so much. How was your day?"

She traces the rim of her glass. "Let's see ... I cut back my tulips, opened a new bag of coffee, repaired the button on my favorite pants, and beat myself at Scrabble."

"Ahh ... living the dream." He grins, toasting her with his beer bottle.

She taps it with her glass and laughs. A few seconds later, her smile dies. "I'm worried about Francesca."

Jackson focuses on his beer bottle. "Oh?"

"I really wish she'd go home. It's not that I mind her staying with me. It's quite lovely, actually. It's been many years since I've had someone live with me. And my son doesn't visit often enough. But I think she must walk away from this tragedy—Lynn, Steven, the memories of her brother's suicide, and now the house. I worry that her grief over their deaths will cause her to do something rash. She's just so ... angry."

He nods several times.

"Maybe you could convince her."

Jackson grunts. "No. She won't listen to me. Sadly, she'll have to learn the hard way."

"It's the letter. I never should have shown her the letter."

Jackson shifts his attention to Eloise. "Letter?"

She frowns and glances behind us into the house. "A letter from Steven's girlfriend," she says calmly. "I stumbled upon it after the funeral. Molly, his girlfriend, all but told him to kill himself. It was just awful. She played on his emotions from his football injury. And she alluded to the fact that she cheated on him. There's no way to know if it's the reason he did it, but I showed it to Frankie." She shakes her head. "And I shouldn't have. Now, she thinks Molly is responsible for burning down the house, and she might be right. I suppose Molly would want to destroy the letter, but it's been months. Why wait to do it now?"

Jackson processes this new information and responds with a low, contemplative hum. All the pieces begin to fall into place.

What the hell is she up to? Revenge?

"I'm sure you don't know much about the Sanfords if you're not from around here. They live halfway between here and Rhodale. And they are wealthy and powerful. Nothing sticks to them. Nothing. I've tried explaining this to Francesca, but she won't listen. Maybe living close to Chicago, things are different. Perhaps there's more accountability. But not in Boone and Rhodale. The Sanfords and their wealthy friends are the beginning and the end. They control everything, including the law."

Jackson knows all about the beginning and the end. He knows what it feels like to be above the law and how getting tangled in that life destroys one's chance at having ... a life.

"Can I get you a sandwich? I have some leftover roast. I put ketchup on mine, but you might be more sophisticated. Mustard?"

Jackson grins. "I'm living in your garage. I'm not sure that makes me sophisticated."

"You have a grand piano in my garage." She eyes him with a smirk.

"Fair enough. How about a little ketchup and mustard?"

"You got it." Eloise disappears into the house, and his phone vibrates.

It's a notification from his surveillance cameras, the ones in the garage. He didn't lock the door. And Frankie has entered without permission. She strolls around the space, leaving her fingerprints everywhere as she feels the need to drag her hand along his car, sofa, punching bag, and piano keys. She inspects the wood that she tried to decimate. Then she sits on the bench, closes her eyes, and plays. His phone's volume is muted, so he can't hear the notes, but it's no less mesmerizing.

She plays like he plays—blindly, body swaying, a pained expression on her face.

Jackson stands just as Eloise returns.

"Did you change your mind?"

He takes the plate with the sandwich. "I forgot I have a call to make. Is it okay if I return the plate later?"

She gives him her flirty smile. "Of course."

"Thanks for the sandwich." He holds up his beer bottle on the way down the deck stairs. "And the beer."

"You're always welcome, Jack."

He takes his dinner to the garage and waits outside for a minute or so.

"Unfuckingbelievable," he mumbles.

Frankie's playing "Scarbo" from Ravel's *Gaspard de la Nuit*. One of the most challenging piano pieces ever written. Way out of Jack's league.

He doesn't subscribe to psycho bullshit about the universe bringing people together. No fate. No Karma. Just chance and dumb luck or lack thereof. Yet, there's something about Francesca that's made its way under his skin, latched on with razor claws, and won't let go.

Ravel isn't helping his situation.

Jackson opens the door.

Francesca doesn't miss a note.

He closes the door.

She freezes. The song dies on the pads of her idle fingers.

"You're trespassing."

"The door wasn't locked." She swings her legs around the bench to face him.

He shrugs. "The door doesn't have to be locked to trespass. A locked door might be more along the lines of breaking and entering. Both are illegal."

"So call the police."

He takes a swig of his beer. "I deal with things in-house."

Frankie wets her lips and nods several times. "So what are you going to do to me?"

Jackson doesn't need her attitude. Or her hands on his property. Or her tongue making a seductive swipe along her red lips.

"I'm not sure if entering uninvited is the greater offense or if playing the piano you tried to destroy requires the biggest balls."

Frankie stands. She's a small pint like his sister, yet, also like his sister, he doesn't trust her one bit.

"I had a shitty afternoon. I needed to release some stress. You weren't here, so I borrowed your piano. Neighbors borrow things from each other, right?" Frankie wraps her hand over his and brings the beer bottle to her lips, but she doesn't take a sip. She sniffs it, wrinkles her nose, and releases his hand.

"You need to learn boundaries," he murmurs.

Her gaze shifts from the bottle to his narrowed eyes. "Is this about the dean's husband again?" She plucks the sandwich from his plate and takes a bite.

Jackson's jaw grinds while he sets the plate and beer on the workbench he uses for a table. Then he turns and grabs her wrist as she brings the sandwich to her mouth for another bite. "Get your fucking hands off my dinner."

After pausing to swallow, she relinquishes the sandwich. "You're a terrible host."

"Then leave." He frowns at the ketchup and mustard dripping onto the floor since she squeezed the sandwich so hard.

"Is that really what you want?" Frankie strolls around the garage again, stopping at his punching bag.

"Why did you have a shitty day?" He deposits the messy sandwich onto the plate and wipes his hands on a rag before approaching her.

She draws in a slow breath as if she senses him behind her. "Because I'm human."

"And that's a bad thing?"

"Sometimes." She reaches behind her, taking his right hand and bringing it to her breast.

Jackson's dick twitches, and he tries to will it to show some self-control.

Her other hand reaches for his, guiding it between her legs. His chest pushes out with a deep breath he can barely control.

Jackson's dick has gone beyond a twitch; it's fully erect, and it's taking a lot of control not to move his pelvis into her.

Not squeeze her breast.

Not bend his fingers to feel the heat between her legs.

She let Archer touch her like this. She let him push her into her back seat.

She let him stroke his dick in front of her.

Jackson knows she would have let him go further; he just doesn't know why, like he doesn't understand why she needs him this way.

To erase Archer's touch?

To get off because some asshole set off a car alarm and interrupted them?

"What do you need?" he whispers next to her ear.

Her head lulls back, and her spine arches, pressing her breast into his hand. He loses the battle and squeezes it.

"I ... don't know," she moans, digging her fingernails into his other hand until he cups her harder between her legs.

"Why did you fuck the dean's husband?" His lips skate down her neck, but he doesn't kiss her.

"I d-didn't ..." She encourages him to squeeze her breast a little more.

His thumb brushes her nipple. No bra. Just a thin crop-top tee. He could easily slip his hand under her shirt, but there's a good chance his dick would break in half behind the zipper of his jeans with zero-way stretch.

"I fucked a guy..." she releases his hand over her breast and stabs her fingers through his hair as he nibbles the skin along her collarbone "...who happened to be married to the dean. Married men..." Frankie rocks her pelvis over his hand "...should wear their wedding bands." Her finger slides along the platinum band on his left ring finger between her legs. "Like you."

Jackson stills, and so does Frankie. Their labored breaths fill the bubble of space around them.

He's not married.

She knows it.

Jackson's hands fall to his sides as he inserts a few feet of space between them.

Frankie punches the bag once without glancing back at him. "Teach me to box."

"No."

She turns, eyes narrowed. "Why not?"

His thumb slides along his wedding band before he repeatedly pumps his fists. Any other man would ask her about this game they're playing, but Jackson doesn't because he knows it. He's distracting her from the guilt of her intentions, and she's doing the same for him.

The rules are simple: it means nothing; therefore, it changes nothing. That's why they don't talk about it. He knows if he fucked her right now, she would piece her clothes back in place, sleep at Eloise's house, and never speak of it again.

It's an awful life, one that Jackson's accepted. But he doesn't wish it upon anyone, definitely not a woman with a Ph.D. who can play Ravel and recently lost three family members and every last remembrance of their existence.

"You've had three years of self-defense. What can I possibly teach you?" He can barely ask it with a straight face.

"Self-control."

"Jesus ..." He shakes his head.

"What?" Frankie parks her fists on her hips.

"You remind me of someone."

She frowns, dropping her gaze. "Your wife."

"No."

She looks at him.

"Someone else. My wife was far more submissive." Jackson sits on his piano bench, folding his hands between his spread legs.

Frankie hesitates before acknowledging him with an easy nod. "Did you pluck her little cherry before she had the chance to get a backbone?"

Jackson shakes his head, ignoring just how wrong she is about Ryn.

"The cross tattoo ... were you the guy who valued a woman's virginity?"

He smirks because the story behind the cross tattooed on his arm is not that biblical.

"Many, *many* years ago ... a girl who happened to be a virgin—of legal age—said if I got a cross tattoo, she'd give me said virginity. In my defense, I didn't do it *because* she was a virgin. I did it because..."

Frankie giggles, shaking her head. "You just wanted to have sex with her. And why not? You knew a holy cross might also be useful for future expeditions."

Jackson's lips twist. "Mmm ... something like that."

"Does the cross still work for you to pop cherries?"

"Fuck ... stop." He rubs his hands down his face. "I'm too damn old for that."

"I'd let you pop mine."

His hands drop from his face to his lap while his grin simmers into a contemplative straight line.

"Well, years ago, I would have let you pop mine. The dean's husband popped it last year, so I no longer bear the forbidden fruit." She squares her body and punches the bag several times.

He doesn't buy that story, but Jackson likes it none-theless. "Pivot the ball of your back foot," he says.

With her hands fisted by her face, she glances back at him.

"Control it through your core, or you'll be off balance.

Let your lower body push your arm forward, and let your hips turn as your arm straightens toward the target."

She does it in slow motion. She does it all wrong, so he steps behind her, molding her body to his, one hand on her left hip and his other hand making a fist with hers.

"Pivot, push, strike."

"Pivot, push, strike," she repeats while their bodies move as one, repeating the motion until she gets it.

He steps back, and she puts more force behind it. "Ouch!" She shakes out her hand.

Jackson chuckles. "You need gloves, tape, and tougher skin. Is your goal to take up boxing or take out someone in self-defense?"

Frankie rubs her knuckles. "What do you think?"

Jackson reaches into his bag and pulls out boxing bandage elastic tape. "I think you need to leave your body intact and let me take care of it." He wraps her hands.

She glances up at him, but he keeps his focus on her hands. "Take care of what?"

"Eloise is concerned about you. She said your nephew's girlfriend wrote a disturbing letter."

"Disturbing? That's an understatement. Did she also tell you Molly burned down the house?"

He lifts his gaze to hers. "That's a bold accusation. Do you have proof?"

"Does it matter?"

"Save your hands. Save your dignity. Go home, and I'll make things right."

"My dignity? What's that supposed to mean?"

He nods toward the punching bag.

She faces it, punching it the way he showed her. "She cheated on him because she was so distraught over his football injury."

Smack. Smack. Smack.

"Then she told him it was okay to end things, to end his life." Frankie huffs and grunts with each jab. "Her mother is a cunt. Her father is ... well, he's a real piece of work. And I want the whole family to pay because they are all awful. And they think they can get away with murder."

Smack. Smack. Smack.

Frankie loses form and keeps punching the bag. Then she kicks the bag. "I hate them! I just HATE them!"

Jackson lets her fall apart. He waits for her to expend her last bit of energy. When she drops to her knees, hands balled at her face, body shaking, he hands her a bottle of water.

Frankie sniffles, lifting her red, tear-stained face.

"How are you making them pay?" he asks.

She takes several long gulps of water before rocking back onto her butt, knees bent. After wiping her face, she stares at the floor. "I'm going to ruin her reputation. I will make everyone see what a demonic whore she really is. And I will kick her mom off her pedestal, expose her indiscretions, and make her the laughingstock of Rhodale. Then I will run her out of business, off the city council and school board. Destroy her marriage and her whole fucking world."

Jackson squints, returning a hesitant nod. "And her dad?"

Frankie lifts her gaze. "I'm going to make him fall in love with the woman destroying his whole fucking life, but he's never going to see it coming."

He weighs his words, but he won't mince them. "You don't have what it takes to pull it off."

Frankie scrambles to her feet, chin up, jaw set. "You know nothing about me. I have absolutely nothing to lose."

"Your life."

She shakes her head. "My life? What life? I lost my brother and his wife. I lost the closest thing I had to a child of my own. I lost my job. And my parents won't live forever. You overestimate the value of my life."

Jackson holds back his instinct to wince at her words.

"Are you okay with a seventeen-year-old girl taking her own life because of you?"

She swallows, keeping her chin up, but she doesn't answer.

"Are you willing to fuck her father? Are you willing to be his whore? Do you really think he can love his whore?"

A tiny line of indecision trenches between her eyes, but her stubbornness prevails as it always did with his sister. "Yes," she says with a strained voice.

Jackson glances away from her at nothing in particular while pondering the questions only he can answer. Is he willing to let her destroy her life? Is he willing to let her potentially die? Is he willing to let Archer Sanford have her?

Jackson's not in Boone, Kansas for Francesca Holter. She should be nothing more than a sideshow in the Sanford circus. Jackson has a family, and they need him to stay focused.

"If they don't take your life, you'll wish you were dead by the time they're done with you. Are you good with that? Are your parents good with that? Maybe you should take a trip home and ask them how they feel about losing their last child. And fuck your brother if he honestly would have expected this from you. I would walk through fire to keep you safe if you were my sister. I would take a million bullets. I would let someone torture me. There's nothing I wouldn't do to keep my loved ones from suffering."

Frankie balls her hands at her sides. Lip stiff. Her eyes

set in a hard stare as if she could will herself to hide all emotion.

Jackson cups her face, and she exhales a tiny breath while leaning into it. "Go home," he whispers. "It's not worth your life too."

Her hands cover his. "Kiss me."

He slowly shakes his head. "I can't kiss you if you're going to let him fuck you."

She closes her eyes, squeezing his hands. After a beat, she turns her head, pressing her lips to his hand.

It's been a long time since Jackson Knight had this much trouble letting go of someone, but he does. He releases her face, and she makes her way to the door, peeling the tape from her hands and dropping it to the floor before it closes.

CHAPTER FOURTEEN
FRANCESCA

I'LL HAND it to Corinne; she's more discreet than her daughter. If you're going to meet your lover at a hotel, a Kentucky Derby-style hat with sizable black sunglasses is the way to go. Paying for a ride instead of taking her car is a nice touch too.

Arriving ten minutes apart.

Separate elevators.

Leaving thirty minutes apart.

A solid plan for an affair.

I watch from my car across the street. What's my plan? I don't know. But I have lots of pictures. None of them together, but it's a start.

> Archer: Miss me? What are you doing? Still in town?

"Spying on your wife, which is what you should be doing."

> Me: Touching myself

Archer: FU

I laugh.

Archer: I'm going out of town for a few days. Come with me

Me: I should go home soon

Archer: Terrible idea

Me: Where are you going?

Archer: Does it matter?

Me: Certainly

Archer: Somewhere I can fuck you without interruptions

"Kiss me."

"I can't kiss you if you're going to let him fuck you."

I feel Jack's hands on my face, my breast, between my legs, his lips on my neck ... I feel him everywhere, every second of the day. But it doesn't erase the pain and grief. It doesn't stop my need for revenge. I wish it did.

After stretching my neck and taking several deep breaths, I refocus.

Me: I fear you think I'm easy

Archer: We've had 3 dates. I've taken 3 cold showers. You're anything but easy

He's calling the baseball game a date.

Me: Where are you going?

> Archer: Name a place. That's where we're going

> Me: Bali

> Archer: Pack your bikini

> Me: I can't leave town. My grandma needs my help. How about dinner?

> Archer: Are you the main course?

> Me: I might let you touch my boob

> Archer: I might let you suck my cock

> Me: Lucky me (eye roll emoji)

He sends me an address with "7 pm." I reply with a thumbs up.

I tip my head against the headrest. Jack's messing with me even when he's not *with* me. What better way to get Archer to fall into my trap than a trip alone with him. He teed it up. All I had to do was say yes.

When I get back to Eloise's, the fire chief is out in front of the remains of my brother's house.

"Miss Holter." He gives me a polite smile. "It's safe to recover things from the main level. The investigation is complete."

"And?"

"Unknown cause. I'm sorry."

"What?" I shake my head. "It was arson."

"Inconclusive," he says.

"Who told you to say that?"

"The arson investigator." He walks toward his vehicle.

"That's bullshit."

"Sorry, Miss."

I bite my tongue and ball my hands to suppress my scream. At every turn, it feels like John, Lynn, and Steven are dying all over again. I navigate past the front door into the wreckage, fighting back tears. The boxes of items I set aside for the family are covered in soot and drenched from water.

I pull out John's baby book. The photos are wet but not burned. Sniffling, I hunch down and peel them from the curled water-stained pages.

"Inconclusive," Jack says behind me.

I nod without looking at him.

"Let me take care of it."

Standing, I shake my head, feeling on the verge of losing it. "What are you going to do? Kill them? *Are* you a serial killer? Why are you in Boone Fucking Kansas? Why are you living in a garage with a piano and a punching bag? Where do you go during the day? Who the fuck are you, Jack? Do you have a last name? A family? A life? Did you kill your wife? Is that why you can't finish your song? Was it an accident? Did she discover your secret? A storm cellar filled with human remains? Did you cheat on her? Did she take her own life because of it? It sucks when someone you love takes their life. Hundreds of thousands of people fight to beat cancer and other awful diseases every day. Do you know how disheartening it is to discover perfectly healthy people just ... dead because outside influences in life were just too much?"

My heart hammers out of control. "So *please* do tell me how you plan on 'taking care' of my situation."

"It's best if you don't know. Just walk away. Don't look back. Justice will be served, and you will be free of accountability."

"Why?" I whisper. "Are you dying?" My chest tightens from saying the words.

"Maybe." He slips his hands into the front pockets of his cargo pants.

"Go home, Jack. Don't die alone. I know you have a family somewhere who misses you."

His brow furrows. "Why do you say that?"

I toss the barely salvageable photos into the box and step in front of him, feathering the back of my hands along his cheeks and tracing the fine lines with my thumbs. "The eyes don't lie."

He slides his hand from my bicep to my hand on his face. "What do mine say?"

"You're not where you belong. Your eyes have so much longing and deep regret; it's soul-crushing."

Something in his face softens as he studies me, processing my words. With a tiny nod, he steps backward, turns, and heads toward the garage. Sometimes, there's no glory or joy in being right about things.

Feeling seen doesn't always feel comforting.

Being with the wrong person can feel more lonely than being completely alone. I fear I'm nothing more than a reminder of the people in his life whom he has lost or fears he may never see again.

Checking my watch, I pull in a long breath. I need to shower and meet Archer for dinner.

"Pizza?" I laugh when Archer and his bodyguards guide me to the back of the Italian restaurant—another private room.

"I don't have the patience for a seven-course meal

tonight." He loosens his tie when the door shuts, leaving us alone with a round table, a large pizza, and two glasses of wine. Archer reminds me of Robert Redford in *Indecent Proposal*, only he hasn't offered me a million dollars to sleep with him.

"You seem..." I pluck a mushroom from the pizza and pop it into my mouth, "...agitated."

Archer drinks his whole glass of wine. "My daughter accidentally burned down a house. Some place in Boone. The arson investigators have been up my ass."

There's knowing, and then there's *knowing*. My hand shakes, and I hug myself to mask my visceral reaction.

Why didn't I wear a wire? Would it have mattered? Could I make a case and get a fair trial around here?

"How does one *accidentally* burn down someone else's house?"

He eyes me, and I can tell he's formulating a lie. "Just kids being irresponsible with fireworks."

Does he know it was Steven's house? Does he know about the letter? This is so messed up.

"So what did you do?" I clear my throat and keep my distance despite Archer prowling toward me.

"Fixed it. That's all I do. Fix other people's shit." After his tie is undone and tossed onto the table, he unbuttons the top three buttons of his shirt. "Why are you so skittish?" He grins when my butt hits the edge of the table, and he's pressed to my body, hands roaming from my hips to my ass. "Jeans." He frowns. "Interesting choice. Let's get you out of them." He tugs the button while ducking to nip at my neck.

I grab his hand. "I'm having my period. Hence, the jeans."

He stills, slowly lifting his head. "I don't give a fuck." He slides down my zipper.

Again, I grab his hand. "Well, I do."

His gaze sweeps across my face several times, unsure if I'm trustworthy. Then his hand slides up my shirt, and I reach for his wrist, but he *tsks*, shaking his head. "You said I could touch your boob."

Slowly releasing the air in my lungs that I've held hostage since we entered the room, I rest my hands on the table's edge, maintaining eye contact with Archer as his hand covers my breast and he shoves my bra over it, squeezing my naked flesh.

He smirks for a second.

My lips part because it feels good, but at the same time, I feel nauseous in the pit of my stomach. I don't want his touch to feel good. I don't want to have a physical attraction to such an awful man. I close my eyes and imagine it's Jack.

Archer uses his other hand to guide one of my hands to his erection, forcing me to cup him and stroke him over his pants. "I'm going to fuck your beautiful mouth."

I can't breathe. He feels like the devil. The father of an evil spawn. Will he stop protecting her if I can crawl under his skin and infiltrate his vulnerable side? Can I weaken their untouchable empire? Their hold on everyone in this godforsaken town?

Archer shoves my shirt to my neck and sucks my nipple so hard I yelp.

He grins with his teeth digging into my flesh while he releases his cock from his briefs. Stroking himself, he eyes me while lapping his tongue over my breast.

This is *so* messed up. I don't feel like myself. The need for revenge has created this alter ego that takes over when I'm with Archer. A protective mask that I can shed when this is over. He's touching Iris. She's not me. She's immune to ethics and moral standards. She's disposable.

My fingernails scrape along the table. Again, I close my eyes and think of Jack. It's his mouth on my breast. It's him standing before me, stroking his cock.

Archer grabs my hand and shows me how he likes to be jerked off. When I draw my fist up his erection, he kisses me so hard I grunt into his mouth. His hand returns to my breast, squeezing it, pinching my nipple until I wince.

"Fucking don't stop." He breaks the kiss long enough to growl at me when my hand pauses.

I can no longer think of Jack. This is too wrong. The only thing that keeps me going is the words in Molly's letter to Steven. I kiss Archer back.

For revenge.

I pump his erection, eliciting approving moans from him. I think of how his daughter manipulated Steven in the most sadistic way. She walked him to the edge of a cliff and gave him a shove. She controlled him, and then she killed him.

And I'm going to control her family ... and then I'm going to destroy it.

Archer pistons his hips. He devours my breasts. His other hand grabs my crotch over my jeans.

This is gross and perverse.

It's wrong in every way.

Iris wants him. *She* likes the way he touches her—the pads of his fingers massaging all around her clit.

His mouth sucking *her* nipples.

Iris can do this. She'll do it even if I can't. She, not I, is okay with feeding Archer Sanford's prurient curiosity—his lascivious obsession.

She allows the sinful pleasure to penetrate her conscience, obliterating it when the heel of Archer's hand circles and grinds over her clit. *Iris* orgasms, fighting the tears from the instant onslaught of shame.

"Fuck ... fuck ... fuck!" Archer smacks the table beside me when he comes all over himself and on my hand.

His outburst shakes my confidence just long enough for him to shove his tongue down my throat and moan while guiding my hand to my breast, smearing his jizz all over it, marking me because he's an animal. Then he grabs his cock and rubs the head of it between my legs, dropping his chin to watch like it's the most mesmerizing thing he's seen—his cum soiling my jeans. "Goddamn ... I need to fuck you, Iris." He rests his forehead on mine, softly panting.

I close my eyes and hold deathly still. I don't want to see what he's doing. I don't want any of this to be real.

I don't want Steven to be dead ... but he is.

This is not as bad as death. It's remarkable how everything in my life has boiled down to the simplistic comparison to death.

"Let's eat," he whispers in my ear before tucking himself back into his pants and cleaning the wet spots on his shirt with a napkin.

I reach for my napkin, but he snatches it and shakes his head while smirking. "I want you to feel and smell me on you all night."

Any uncontrolled and unwanted physical attraction I (Iris) had toward him vanishes. I tuck in the front of my shirt and grab a slice of pizza with my clean hand; then I find a smile that's just sweet enough to feed his ego, even if I'm dead inside.

After Archer finishes the bottle of wine all by himself, I stomach a whole slice of pizza before he walks me to my car. He surveys our surroundings before kissing my cheek and sliding his hand up my shirt like he can fondle me at will. And maybe he can since I'm not stopping him ... *yet*.

"Good night."

I feel gross, but gross is better than dead (that fucking awful comparison), so I plaster on a smile instead of a verbal pleasantry. With as much self-control as I can muster, I pull out of the parking lot. As soon as I know he no longer sees my taillights, I push the accelerator to the floor. The road blurs behind my tears. It's hard to put things into perspective. I'm angry and heartbroken. Embarrassed. I'm grasping for something that I hope will feel like justice. But I don't know how long I can hold on. So I recite every word of Molly's letter, which feeds me. It strengthens my resolve again. I can do this.

By some miracle, I make it to Eloise's in one piece —physically.

Emotionally, I'm scattered along the road between Rhodale and Boone, Kansas.

"How was your night?" Eloise asks with her usual bedtime concoction mug of warm milk, honey, and turmeric cupped in both hands.

With my head bowed, I mess with my hair so she doesn't see my face while I beeline for the stairs.

"Did you have dinner alone? I would have joined you."

"I uh ... had dinner with a friend of Lynn's. Good night." I hide in a hot shower, giving my body a head-to-toe surgical scrub, including my tongue, which makes my stomach tighten and lurch on the edge of vomiting.

When the lights are off and Eloise is in her room, I stare at the ceiling from my bed, letting one more rogue tear escape. What have I done? And what will I do with this experience? Will I tell Molly when she's with her best buds? Will I tell Corinne she should keep an eye on the black mole Archer has next to his pubic hairline? It might be precancerous. Maybe I'll let them know together after I invite myself to lounge by their pool. Nothing goes better with a margarita than tales of how I jerked off their father-slash-husband in the back room of a restaurant, and he nearly came a second time watching me wipe his cum on my breasts.

What makes it so special is that Archer hasn't connected the dots yet. He doesn't know Francesca. He only knows Iris in the irresistible red dress, who doesn't mind screwing around with a married man.

Grief changes people on a cellular level. It rewires the brain. It's hard to remember how I saw the world before John and his family died. I don't recognize the reflection in the mirror. I'm not sure I ever will.

CHAPTER FIFTEEN
JACKSON

JACKSON STAYS FOCUSED while Frankie spends the evening with Archer Sanford. He thinks about anything but Archer's hands on her ... or worse. He isn't stupid. Frankie told him her game plan. And he knows Archer will take her any way and anywhere he can get her, even in the back room of a restaurant.

When Archer walks Frankie to her car and slides his hand up her shirt, Jackson's grip on his gun tightens. His finger caresses the trigger while he peers through the scope. He has a clear shot to take him out.

Frankie balls her hands at her side and lets Archer touch her. Jackson hates that. But he lets it go from his mind. He controls his impulses because that's what he's trained to do. And he knows how losing the people you love changes all the rules in life. The aching void festers into something toxic and out of control.

How can he tell Frankie that what she's doing is wrong when he's taken so many lives? Hurt so many people. Committed unforgivable acts. He's the fucking king of revenge.

The following morning, Jackson heads out for a jog in his long pants and long-sleeved shirt. (His tattoos make him too identifiable). A rhythmic creaking catches his attention. Frankie gently rocks in a wooden chair on Eloise's front porch. An oversized tee covers her knees, which are tucked into her chest. Her hands cradle a steaming mug of coffee. She radiates innocence. His sister always did too. Sometimes, innocence is nothing more than a sleeping monster.

Frankie has nothing to offer but a blank, lifeless expression when their gazes meet. Jackson will remove the hand that Archer Sanford shoved up Frankie's shirt. He'll remove any part of Archer's body that touched Frankie. And if that means he removes one finger at a time, so be it.

In the meantime, he beats his feet against the uneven terrain until exhaustion incinerates his thoughts. By the time he returns, the wooden rocker sits empty and idle. But the air fills with a familiar song. His song.

Jackson opens the door, and Frankie ignores him while she plays his song, the same lines repeatedly. It's not her song to play.

"Leave. I need a shower," he says, passing the piano and peeling off his shirt.

Frankie tests new notes and chords. They're good notes, maybe even the right ones, but Jackson doesn't want her finishing something that is, by design, not meant to be finished—the way his wife left their life together unfinished.

"Get the fuck out of here." He turns on the hose by the drain.

Frankie stops playing.

Jackson feels the weight of her stare, but he doesn't acknowledge it. His shorts and briefs join his sweat-soaked shirt on the concrete floor. The cold water numbs his aching muscles. It's been a long time since he showered with warm water. He rubs the soap bar along his skin and scrubs it into his hair until weak foam forms.

Frankie plays a movie score. It's romantic and vaguely familiar. She keeps playing while he dries off, but she's not looking at the keys. Her gaze remains glued to him while he wraps the towel around his waist and shakes out his hair before running both hands through it.

The melody slows until Frankie's hands pause, leaving the song unfinished.

"What's the movie?" he asks, twisting the top of a bottled water with his back to her. When she doesn't respond, he glances over his shoulder.

Frankie takes liberty with her gaze, making a detailed inspection of Jackson, lips parted, eyelids heavy. "*Amélie.* 2001 French film. Yann Tiersen. It's a waltz," she murmurs like an afterthought.

"I have to get dressed and..." he guzzles the whole water bottle "...work."

Frankie slowly nods, a million miles away. She stands, shuffling her feet toward him the way someone might approach a deadly animal injured on the side of the road.

He waits for her to make eye contact, but she keeps her gaze glued to his torso, confusion wrinkling the skin around her eyes. He wants to take her pain, but he knows nothing will ever be able to take away the pain she feels. That vast hole of nothingness takes on its own life with a pulse—each beat feels like a knife to the chest.

Jackson remains statuesque when her fingers touch his skin, tracing the intertwined lines of ink, one tattoo overlapping another. He can't hide the part of his body aroused by her touch, but she doesn't seem to notice. She's too busy skating the tip of her finger along his flesh like she's deciphering a treasure map from his chest to his abs

... back ... shoulders ... arms. She makes a slow circle around him.

Jackson waits, frozen, every muscle tense in anticipation of her descent. His tattoos stretch down his body, but she must remove his towel to follow them.

Frankie lifts his arm. He holds it up for her, cupping the back of his head. Her touch leaves goosebumps along his skin, and he expects her to notice, to acknowledge her effect on him, but she doesn't. Her touch fades, hands falling limp at her sides while she cocks her head, eyes squinted at his torso beneath his armpit.

Then her gaze lifts to his. "Jude," she says. "Your name is Jude." Her finger presses to his skin again, tracing the nearly indistinguishable lettering.

Jackson drops his arm. "No."

"No?" Frankie eyes him.

He tightens the towel around his waist and grabs clothes from the pile by his bag. "Jude died."

"When?"

"Many years ago." He tosses the towel aside and gets dressed.

"Who was he?"

Jackson buttons and zips his jeans. "We're not going to talk about this. Understood?"

"No. I don't understand."

"How was your date last night?" Jackson pauses his motions, arms threaded through his T-shirt. He berates himself for asking the question. It's irrelevant. He needs Francesca Holter to be irrelevant too.

"Did you..." she squints "...follow me?"

"No." It's not a lie. Jackson pulls his shirt over his head.

Frankie hugs herself as the room's mood, even temperature, changes. She averts her gaze and digs her nails

124

into her arms. His wife used to do that when he asked her about her abusive ex-husband.

Jackson peels Frankie's fingers away from her skin, and she inspects the indents in her arms as if unaware of how they got there.

"He said Molly burned down my family's house. Only ... he doesn't know I'm Steven's aunt. He doesn't know I could have been in the house."

Jackson slides his phone into his pocket with a hard sigh.

"Sorry. Am I boring you with tales of arson?"

"Frankie, you don't bore me, but your confession doesn't surprise me."

"Because I should know the Sanfords are awful humans? I should know they can literally get away with murder?"

"Something like that."

"How do *you* know that? Are you from this area? Are you hiding from your family when they're blocks away? Is that what you do all day? Spy on your family to see if they're okay without you?"

Her words don't phase him. Jackson's life has been built on secrets and lies. He envies anyone who has the luxury of demanding honesty and truth. "What..." he crosses his arms, "...can I do for you?"

"You can answer me."

"Fine. No, I'm not from this area, nor is my family. I'm not spying on my family. And they're okay without me for now."

Frankie's gaze drops to her feet, and she whispers, "Are you sick?"

"Mentally or physically?"

Her nose wrinkles. "Either."

125

"No."

"Why won't you tell me why you live in this garage?"

"I can't."

"Why?"

"I can't answer your whys. What else can I do for you?"

Frankie blinks and brushes past him, circling the garage's perimeter as if she hasn't done it multiple times before today. "Have you ever done something so morally gray that you know you'll never be the same? You know that selling your soul is not just a saying but a real possibility?"

"Yes," he says without hesitation.

Frankie eyes him, maybe to gauge his honesty. "Last night, I lost a piece of my soul. And I know I'll never get it back." She feathers her fingers over the hood of his car.

Jackson's mesmerized by this woman's touch ... even when she's not touching him. Her delicate fingers. Her innocence. Some people should never sell their souls—Frankie's one of them.

"You fucked Molly's dad."

She slowly shakes her head, focusing on a tiny chip in the paint. "I couldn't. Not yet."

"Why?" He eases his hands into his pockets so she doesn't see him pumping his fists.

Frankie's blue-eyed gaze finds his. "I haven't completely worked it out in my head." She shrugs. "I imagine Steven and Lynn went through the steps of working things out in their heads. When you know something is forever, that it can never be undone, there are steps that you take to reconcile it in your mind. A plus B equals C. You have to accept that it will always equal C. For the rest of time."

She leans her backside against the hood, hands on either side. "I haven't reconciled it in my head. At least, not when I'm with him. Alone, reading the letter from Molly, I feel confident—resolute. I feel brave and selfless. But when he touches me, everything blurs."

Jackson's jaw clenches.

"My confidence wavers. I fear he'll see right through me. Because as much as I tell myself it's just my body, I know it will be more because hatred is still a form of passion. It's just the other side of the same coin. To make it believable to him, I have to believe it, at least partly, myself. To make him want me, a part of myself must also want him."

"Francesca, don't ever let a man touch you unless you want it as much as your next breath. Selling your soul is worse than suicide. Dying is easy. Living is really fucking hard."

She shakes her head. "Why would you say that? Do you think it was easy for my brother, his wife, and their son to end their lives?"

"Yes."

Her face wrinkles with disgust as she pushes off the car and brushes past him toward the door. "You didn't know them."

"I'd rather die than ..."

She stops with her hand on the doorknob. "Than what?"

"Fill in the blank. How often have you heard someone say, 'I'd rather die than' ... lose a child? Battle cancer? Watch a lover die? Have someone torture you? A million other things that could happen to someone, and given the choice, they'd choose death. And sometimes your mind's not right. Something alters it, and we make permanent decisions that we wouldn't make if we were of sound mind. You didn't fuck Archer because you're of sound mind. You're alive despite the devastation of losing your brother and his family because you're of sound mind."

She bows her head as if his words are still making their way to her. Then she opens the door. "Being of sound mind is overrated."

CHAPTER SIXTEEN
FRANCESCA

I HATE BEING WRONG. It's an ego issue. A quintessential human trait that I've willingly accepted.

Revenge is a poison that never clears the body. It simmers into acceptance. That's the best possible outcome. Sadly, I haven't reached that outcome. Jackson's pep talk didn't help. It was sound advice, but I will forever be a defiant child: the girl who wanted to be a boy until the right boy came along to make me eternally thankful for being a girl. The student who wanted to be an overachiever more than a wife or mother. The aunt who regretted living the better part of her life alone with nothing more than a wall covered in framed accolades.

I don't know who I am now that my people who defined happiness are no longer alive.

Was it all a lie? An illusion? Were they not happy at all?

> Me: Can I borrow $1000?

> Archer: You can earn it

Me: A) I'm not an escort B) If I were, you would have had to pay 10K for the hand job

Archer: I've paid less

Me: Then stick with your bargains. Nice knowing you

I look up from my phone and smile at Eloise while she peels peaches for jam.

Archer: Where are you? I'll drop it off

I grin.

Me: My grandmother's peeling peaches for jam. I bet she knows who you are. She probably shops at your wife's store.

Archer: My wife's store? Someone's been doing her homework

Me: Yes. I was a straight-A student

Archer: In dental assisting school?

Fuck you, asshole.

I set my phone on the table, the screen side down. "Can I help you?"

"Yes. You could measure two-and-a-half cups of sugar into that glass bowl and cut that lemon for me."

"You got it." I stand, and my phone vibrates.

Archer: I'm sorry. You're amazing and smart. And sexy AF. I'll leave an envelope for you at the cafe where we met. Dinner next week?

130

Me: kissing emoji

"Have you decided what you're going to do?" Eloise mashes the peaches.

"Do?" I measure out the sugar.

"Are you going to the police with the letter from Molly? Are you going to let them know you think she started the fire? Or are you going home? Not that I want to see you go. But I hope you choose the easiest path to peace."

"I've had a few encounters with the Sanfords. Molly is awful, but I'm trying to decide if she's redeemable. I think that's what keeps me here. If I walk away, I have to feel at peace. I need to feel that she's learned a lesson."

Eloise frowns. "It could take quite some time for that to happen. I don't think you want to put your life on hold for that long."

"Maybe not. But since I'm between jobs, I have time if you're willing to put up with me." I seal the lid onto the container of sugar.

"Perhaps you'll find a job in Boone or Rhodale."

I hum. "There are no universities around here, but ... maybe I could teach high school music."

"You'd be overqualified, but I'm sure they'd be lucky to have you."

Staying ... I can't imagine that.

After the jam jars are filled, Eloise tends to her flowerbeds, and I take a trip to Rhodale and pick up the envelope with a thousand dollars. Then, as luck would have it, Molly's Tesla is parked at the school. The baseball team has practice. I turn on an audiobook and wait.

Forty minutes later, Colin leaves the field and nods toward his truck. Molly steps out of her car, straightening her denim miniskirt and one-shoulder tank top. Glancing around, she bolts to his truck and hops into the passenger seat. He tosses his bag in the bed, and the tires skid out of the gravel seconds later.

Keeping a safe distance, I follow his truck out of town to a wooded area by the river. When they turn off the main road, I keep driving and make a U-turn after I can no longer see his truck. I trek a good quarter mile down the gravel road before seeing Colin's truck.

Over the next hour, I camp behind a tree like a skilled hunter, only my weapon of choice is my camera and my prey is the two fuck-ups banging in the grass, smoking weed, and for the grand finale, Molly snorts a fine line of white powder off Colin's abs.

"Come on, baby." She reclines and taps the vile until powder falls right between her breasts.

"Can't. If I get caught, I could lose my scholarship."

"My dad won't let that happen."

Archer is everyone's hero.

"Your dad doesn't know about us." He traces the outline of white powder on her chest.

"Maybe he should."

Colin's hand stills. "Are you serious?"

Molly bites her lip and nods.

"What about Steven?"

"He's gone."

"But his aunt's still in town. Doesn't that freak you the fuck out? Like ... what the hell is she doing?" Colin asks.

"She's a psycho bitch. I should get a restraining order against her. She's stalking me."

Colin rolls to his side. "I wonder why? Maybe she's dealing with PTSD or something."

I don't think Colin's an accomplice of Molly's. An

asshole of a friend to Steven? Yes. But I'm not getting the vibe that he knows about the letter or that he's screwing an arsonist.

"I just wish she'd go home. It's bad enough that there's a freaking memorial for him at the school that I have to see every time I pull into the parking lot. But how am I supposed to move on when she's *everywhere*?"

My hand shakes as I hold the phone, taking video. The little bitch makes me livid. I can only see red when I'm around her.

When I have ample sex and drug footage, I return to my car and call it a day.

As I pull into the driveway, my mom calls me. I send it to voicemail. She's wondering why I'm not home. It's a valid question. I just don't have a good answer yet. Slinging my purse over my shoulder and clutching my phone in my hand like the world would end if I lost it, I fly up the front porch steps and inhale the mouthwatering smell of something on the grill. I think Eloise mentioned steaks.

"We're out back," she calls as soon as the creaking screen door snaps shut behind me.

We're.

Jack's here. My tummy does a little flip, but I don't know why. I'm not fourteen. I saw him naked the other day. And sure, I've replayed in slow motion a few hundred times the moment he dropped his towel to the floor, but it's only because he has so many tattoos.

And a nice cock.

And thick, defined thighs.

And an ass that makes me want to...

I shake my head, trying to erase those salacious thoughts.

"Hi." I smile at Eloise and try my best to give Jack nothing more than a two-second glance—an afterthought—before helping myself to a glass of lemonade.

After thinking about naked Jack, it takes several long gulps before I feel my body cool again.

"You seem cheery," Eloise says, eyeing me suspiciously.

Jack glances over his shoulder, giving me a once-over as well.

"I uh ... got a massage today."

"I've never had one. I don't know how I feel about a stranger touching my naked body."

Jack grins to himself at Eloise's comment.

"I used to get one every week. When I had a job." I sit next to Eloise.

"It would seem Francesca doesn't mind strangers touching her naked body." Jack flips the steaks.

"Oh, dear." Eloise hides her grin behind her cupped hand.

Jack keeps a straight face. I don't sense any humor in his not-so-casual observation.

"Human touch can be very therapeutic. And yes, sometimes it can be sensual." I wink at Eloise.

"And sometimes it can be inappropriate," Mr. Observant adds.

I frown at Jack, but he doesn't look at me.

"Those look pretty good, Jack. I like mine medium-rare." Eloise presses her hands to the chair and grunts while standing. "Let's eat inside. The bugs are out of control tonight."

We follow her into the house. She pulls a potato dish from the oven while Jack sets the plate of steaks on the table. I retrieve my vibrating phone from my pocket.

Archer: Iris! I'm a little drunk and a lot
horny. I need to see you

I bump into Jack, knocking my phone out of my hand. "Oh! Sorry. I've got it," I say, but not before he plucks it off the ground.

I try to take it from him, but his grip tightens for several seconds, just long enough to read the message from Archer. Jack loosens his grip, allowing me to slide it out of his hand while he eyes me.

I feel like an errant child, like he caught me, and now I'm in trouble. I also feel ashamed, even though I'm not meeting Archer tonight.

"I'm going to wash my hands. Be right back." I can't look at Jack as I slide my phone into my pocket and disappear up the stairs.

Me: I don't do drunk. Sorry

I hide my phone in a drawer and slip into the bathroom to splash cold water on my face. When I open my eyes, Jack's reflection is in the mirror, and he's closing the door behind him.

After patting my face dry with the towel, I turn toward him. "He's drunk. I told him—"

"I don't give a fuck what you told him." He reaches into his back pocket and pulls out an envelope—my envelope with the money from Archer.

"Where did you get that?" I reach for it, but he holds it just out of reach. "Did you go through my purse?"

"I picked it up off the floor at the bottom of the stairs. Did you stop at the ATM? This is a lot of grocery money.

Or did your massage therapist pay *you* for the service instead of vice versa? Is your massage therapist the same one who just texted you? What does a grand get these days? And who the fuck is Iris?"

"Not that it's any of your business, but if you want to call me a prostitute, just say it. Stop beating around the bush."

"Have you fucked him?" Jack asks through clenched teeth.

My heart thrashes out of control in my chest. I'm in over my head, but I refuse to admit it. Archer can't get enough of me, and the man I want touching me keeps me at arm's length. I have blurred intentions and knotted emotions. I didn't get a massage today, nor did I spread my legs for a grand. But I'd let Jack keep every dime if he'd just ... touch me.

Kiss me.

Acknowledge that I'm more than a thorn in his side.

He tosses the envelope onto the vanity. "I don't know how you do it. It's beneath you, and it won't change a damn thing." He turns to open the door.

"I asked for the money after the fact," I say.

Jack pauses.

"It wasn't sex. It was ..." This hurts. The shame. The loss. The confusion. "It wasn't sex," I whisper. "But he touched me, and I touched him. And I closed my eyes, and I imagined it was you. And it didn't make it better, but it made it bearable. And I hate that I can't let it go. And I'll hate myself if I *do* let it go ... let her get away with this."

"Don't fucking think of me when he's touching you." Jack turns, and his eyes burn with anger.

I bite my quivering lips together and nod, willing myself not to blink because tears will run down my cheeks.

His face wrinkles while he shakes his head. "Just don't ... let him touch you."

As I draw in a shaky breath, Jack steals it, kissing me hard. My palms frame his face, and I release a soft moan. He reciprocates, causing me to come undone with need. This need works the button and zipper to his jeans while he lifts me onto the vanity, wedging his pelvis between my spread legs. His hands shove my midi skirt up my thighs before shredding my favorite panties.

I feel safe in a stranger's arms.

I feel understood by someone I don't understand.

How is this possible?

My hand slips into his briefs, making long strokes up and down the length of his cock as his tongue teases mine before our mouths fuse in a deep kiss again. He works his jeans and briefs just past his rock-hard ass and grips my ankles, planting my feet on the edge of the vanity (one flip-flop on, one off), forcing my knees to draw back and my legs to spread as wide as possible.

"Oh ... god ..." I arch my back when he drives into me, pausing long enough to shove my crop top and bra away from my breasts so he can devour them while fucking me senseless—my head against the mirror, one hand tangled in his hair and the other pressed flat to the wall beside us.

I would *rather die than* ... have him stop. And I let him know as much by chanting, "Jesus ... god ... please don't ... stop. Don't ... ever ... stop."

He groans when I yank his hair, urging him to keep sucking and licking my breasts. My bare foot slips off the edge of the vanity, and I dig my heel into his taut ass like a jockey finding their grip in a stirrup. His muscles contract and release at a quickening pace.

I need the release, but that means it will be over.

"Don't stop ..." A drunken panic hijacks my words to the point that I barely recognize them as my own. It's not even a plea. I'm flat-out begging him not to stop.

How can something so senseless feel like the best decision I've made since John died? Why does absolutely nothing about this feel wrong?

Jack's hand smacks against the mirror next to my head as he moves faster and harder. I hug him, fingernails sinking into his back when I orgasm. My teeth claim his shoulder. I'm unsure if his low grunt is from his release or my assault on his flesh.

And then we're idle, completely still, save for the rise and fall of our chests and labored breaths marking time.

When he starts to pull away, I slide my arms around his neck and hug him, silently asking him just to give me a second.

A second to catch my breath.

A second to form a coherent thought.

A second to wipe a tear from my eye before he sees it.

He has no idea how much I've needed his touch. I needed it before I consciously knew it was *his* touch I needed. Finding something or someone you weren't looking for is quite possibly the greatest gift in life. This somehow simultaneously changes nothing *and* everything.

Jack ghosts his fingertips down my legs while his nose traces a line from my shoulder to my jaw.

"Is everything okay up there?" Eloise calls from downstairs.

We share soft chuckles. Jack eases out of me and pulls up his jeans. When my feet reach the floor, he's pieced back together and out the door.

"Everything's fine," he says, his voice fading while he descends the stairs.

It takes me a few minutes to freshen up. And it takes another minute or two to gather my composure while I stand at the top of the stairs. Jack shares his tips for the perfectly seasoned steak, and Eloise voices her frustrations over her late husband's refusal to use a grill because he believed charring meat created carcinogens.

I focus on each breath, willing my heart to slow its beat. But every time I think of Jack touching me, kissing me, moving inside me, I lose my breath. Heat fills my cheeks. And my knees begin to buckle.

Then I think about how long it's been since someone made me feel like this. And the answer is never.

"You've got this." I give myself a quick pep talk on the way down the stairs.

"It's warm up there. Isn't it?" Eloise smiles, taking a seat at the table.

"It's uh ..." I shrug, eyeing the food, the beverages, and Eloise's light blue plates. I look at everything except the other people in the room.

"Your face is red. It's a hot day, and heat rises," she says.

I risk a glance at her. "So hot."

She knows.

I know she knows.

We share a smirk.

Jack cuts his steak and chews it without regard for our subtle exchange.

"Smells delicious. You're a gifted grill master." I pick up my knife and fork, waiting for Jack to look at me.

His lips twitch while he slowly chews.

"I think Jack is probably gifted at many things." Eloise isn't going to let this slide. The elephant's not in the corner of the room; it's sitting on the table, but no one wants to acknowledge it directly.

He clears his throat, blotting his mouth with his napkin. "You're very kind."

"She's right." I stab a potato and bring it to my lips. "I think you've been holding out on us. A man of many hidden talents." I don't know if Jack is someone who blushes, but I'm going to give it my best effort. "You can fix toilets, play the piano, chop wood, mow the lawn, box, grill the perfect steak." I wet my lips and smile before biting into the potato. "Very talented with your hands," I mumble over the food in my mouth.

And there it is ... a pink hue spreads along his face. It might be the sexiest thing I've ever seen.

Eloise's doorbell rings. She sighs. "Who's selling what?"

When she heads to the front door, I set my fork on my plate and wipe my mouth. "Those were my favorite underwear."

Jack focuses on cutting his next bite of steak. "And now they're my favorite underwear."

"Why is that?"

He takes a swig of his beer and shrugs a shoulder. "Because you can't wear them again."

"You know that didn't make me your girlfriend. Right?"

He presses his fist to his mouth and clears his throat. "Girlfriend? I'm flattered that you think I'm that young."

"Age doesn't have anything to do with having a girlfriend. After my grandma died, my grandpa met a woman who was ten years younger than him." I laugh, shaking my head. "He was so proud of her. You'd have thought he won the lottery. He told everyone she was his girlfriend. Neighbors. Servers. Cashiers at the grocery store. And she embraced the label as a term of endearment. Whenever he'd say it, she'd pinch his cheek and kiss his lips."

Jack grins. "That's a great story."

I nod slowly, feeling the reality of time settle around my heart like a coat that no longer fits. "My brother was named after Grandpa John. He looked up to him like an idol. Grandpa John served in World War II as a pilot. He had a single-engine Cessna. And he'd take John and me up with him all the time. We'd fight over who got to be the copilot."

Jack sits back in his chair, resting his hands on the arms, giving me a soft smile and full attention.

"Of course, I rarely got to be the copilot because Grandpa was old-fashioned, and he thought a girl's place was at home, raising a family. He's one of the reasons I got my Ph.D. and never married. I wanted him to see a successful woman who didn't bake cookies and pop out babies." I frown. "But he died before I got my first job at a university."

"I'm sorry."

My gaze flits to Jack's. "Thank you," I whisper.

"I can't get over kids these days." Eloise rolls her eyes, easing into her chair. "I'm eighty-one. No twenty-something will tell me anything about Jesus Christ that I don't already know."

We laugh.

We converse.

We eat good food.

For the most perfect hour, I don't think of my brother, Lynn, and Steven. I don't think of the Sanfords or the dean's husband. For an hour, I exist only in this moment with these two beautiful humans.

"Thank you, once again, for a nice evening," Jack says to Eloise.

"You did the hard part. Thanks for manning the grill."

I hang back a few feet as they say their goodbyes on the front porch.

"Well," Eloise turns toward me, "I'll let you two kiss good night without me getting in your way."

I bite back my grin and give her a tiny nod.

Jack pinches the bridge of his nose and shakes his head. "Yeah, that's my cue to leave."

Eloise returns to the house while Jack treks toward the garage.

I glance over my shoulder to see if she's left us alone, and she has. But there is no "us." Jack's halfway to the garage, and I'm standing atop the porch stairs.

"Hey. That's all I get?" I holler at him.

Jack turns, giving me a head-to-toe assessment before the hint of a grin steals his lips. "You're not my girlfriend."

I lift my skirt and skip down the stairs in my bare feet, tiptoeing over the uneven bricks to the warm grass and eventually to him. "You're right. I'm not your girlfriend." I curl my fingers into his shirt and lift onto my toes. "But I'm the girl you kiss good night."

The pad of his middle finger presses to my forehead, and he uses it to trace a line down my nose. My eyes close. His finger skims my lips before his knuckles brush my cheek.

I lean into his touch.

His thumb hooks my bottom lip.

Just as I open my eyes, his mouth replaces his thumb.

Jack's touch is patient. Too patient.

And seductive. So seductive.

It takes a few seconds to realize he's peeling open my fingers. I grin, uncurling them and holding my hands up. "Sorry. I lost my balance."

Jack hums, giving me a shit-eating grin. "Be good." He turns and opens the garage door.

"What's that supposed to mean?"

"You know what it means."

Click.

The door closes.

CHAPTER SEVENTEEN
FRANCESCA

It's hard to separate teenagers from their phones. It might be easier to sever a leg from their body with dental floss. But I think I've got this. Brock, my new BFF and waiter, has agreed to get Molly Sanford's phone for me for a thousand dollars. I asked Archer for the money to see if I could manipulate him. I wasn't sure what I'd do with the money.

Until today.

"What's she drinking?" I ask from my booth on the opposite side of the restaurant during the lunch rush.

"Diet Coke." He plucks the wad of cash from my hand and pockets it. I think he knows her, but I don't think he's a fan.

"Get her a refill, spill it on her lap, then go to town cleaning up the mess, making sure to get her phone when no one's looking. But you have to do this when she's on her phone, so it's not locked when you take it. Got it? And don't let the screen lock before you get it to me."

"I think I can get her phone without spilling anything on her."

"I'm sure you can, but she's wearing white, so let's go

the distance with this." I dip my last few fries in ketchup and pop them in my mouth with a grin.

Brock eyes me for a second before he gets it. Sure, the main goal is Molly's phone, but for a grand, I'm going to fuck up her overpriced outfit and embarrass the shit out of her. Technically, her dad's paying for this lunchtime entertainment.

"Brock, if you can't do this, I understand. I mean ... you could get fired."

"Pfft. I have two other jobs. Who gives a shit?"

He makes his way to her table with a full glass of Diet Coke. I have to cover my grin with my hand when it goes down.

"Oh my god!" Molly explodes into a hissy fit, pushing back in her chair and standing. Her mouth opens in shock as Diet Coke soaks into her white clothes.

Her friends jump to attention, offering their napkins while Brock profusely apologizes and jogs to the kitchen to get rags to clean it up. He detours past my table, depositing the phone under my napkin.

I touch the screen, so it doesn't lock. I have a short amount of time to get the video onto her phone and a group text sent.

> Hey, just wanted to let everyone know Colin and I are a thing now.

After a few minutes, Brock walks past my table, snatches the phone, and returns it to the table, dropping it in Molly's handbag without anyone noticing.

Money well spent.

I exit the back of the restaurant and call Archer. Usually, I'd text, but a phone call feels more rewarding today.

145

"What?" he barks in an angry, clipped tone.

"Hello to you too."

"Iris, I don't have time to talk. I have to kill someone. Fuck! I just ... have to go."

"Sorry. Hope it all works out."

He mumbles a few expletives before a muffled "bye."

To be fair, I don't have kids. So I can only imagine how I might feel if my daughter announced her relationship status by sending out a group text with a video of her by the river getting nailed from every angle and a slow-motion segment of her snorting coke off her naked boyfriend's abs.

Is it fair to Colin? Perhaps not, but how fair was it to screw his friend's girlfriend? Colin is acceptable collateral damage.

I wait in my car parked across the street. When I see Molly exiting the restaurant, I roll down my windows. Her friends stop walking, gazes glued to their phones. Molly waddles like she has something up her ass, pulling her wet, stained shirt away from her body.

When she notices her friends are ten steps behind her, unmoving, heads bowed to their phones, she yells, "Let's go! I have to get out of these fucking clothes!"

They ignore her.

She huffs and retraces her steps back to them, glancing at their phones. It takes less than two seconds.

"Oh my god ..." Her fingers stab through her hair, clenching it while her head shakes in disbelief.

Nuclear meltdown.

She sobs, rifling through her purse for her phone. After she checks it, it gets hurled across the parking lot. Her friends huddle together as if they don't know what to say. They look terrified of her.

They should be.

She's a murderer. A whore. And she doesn't deserve the air she breathes.

I grin, slipping on my sunglasses and pulling away from the curb. I think that was worth a grand of Archer's money.

ELOISE SUBSCRIBES to the idea that life plays out as intended—a balance of good and evil. Today was a good day, maybe too good. And to balance things, my parents' Chevy Traverse is parked in the driveway of my brother's charred house when I return to Boone.

"Shit," I grumble, climbing out of my car and sliding my sunglasses onto my head.

They turn toward me when they hear my car door close. I may still be single because I choose to do everything by myself. My best friend died a week before I got my bachelor's degree. My family found out nearly six months later because I chose to deal with the grief alone. And I knew if I told them, I'd not only have my grief to deal with I'd have their pity and constant checking in on me. So yeah, Molly Sanford burned down my brother's house, and I haven't mentioned it to my parents. I guess word got out.

Mom's unblinking gaze affixes to me, mouth agape.

"What the hell happened?" Dad's not one to beat around the bush.

"It caught fire." I cross my arms and inspect the remains as though I'm seeing them for the first time.

"W-when?" Mom stutters.

"A few days ago."

"Why did we find out from the Helgusons?" Dad asks, eyes squinted.

"Who are the Helgusons?" The name's not familiar to me.

"They own the dance studio where Lynn worked," he says.

I nod several times. Makes sense.

"I'm responsible for the house, per John and Lynn's will. The insurance company will be out tomorrow. The cause of the fire was undetermined. I wasn't here when the fire started. I'm brokenhearted over losing the things I set aside for family, sans a few barely salvageable pictures. I haven't been able to bring myself to share more bad news. Sorry."

"Francesca, what is wrong with you? We are your parents. Why have you always insisted on keeping important things from us?" Mom gives the same speech I've heard many times before.

"Everything okay?"

I turn. Eloise to save the day. "Hi. Have you met my parents, Taylor and Erin?"

"We have. It's good to see you. I wish it were under better circumstances. You must have been devastated all over again when Francesca told you about the fire. I'm so sorry. Thankfully, she wasn't home."

My parents level me with matching scowls.

"Where are you staying?" I change the subject and regret it the second my parents eye the house where they would typically stay in Boone. "I'll get you a hotel in Rhodale."

"Nonsense. I have two spare bedrooms," Eloise says. "Francesca has been staying in one, but you're welcome to stay in the other."

"We don't want to intrude." Mom gives Eloise her

pouty face, the one Dad said made him drop to one knee to propose even though he hadn't yet bought a ring.

"It's no imposition."

"Eloise, thank you. It will only be for a night or two until we help Francesca settle everything with the insurance company."

I'm forty-one with over a decade of higher education to my name and plaques and accolades to fill an entire wall; I just returned from doing gangster-level revenge, and I recently had sex with a man who might be a killer. *Yet* ... I feel I will be grounded for the next two days. Phone taken away. And only allowed out of my room for meals and to use the bathroom.

Eloise leads my mom to the house while my dad retrieves their bags from the Traverse. A sweaty Jack returns from his usual late-day jog as I take one of the bags and follow my dad.

Lagging back, I offer a half smile to Jack. "Want to meet my parents?"

He opens the garage door. "Nope."

Click.

CHAPTER EIGHTEEN
JACKSON

JACKSON IGNORES his sister's incessant calling for as long as possible, and then he answers on the fifth attempt.

"I need an update," she says, minus a greeting.

"Nothing to update."

"Take him out and come home."

"I think Mitchell's alive."

"Mitchell?"

"The nerdy guy."

"You're the nerdy guy."

Jackson tosses his phone onto the sofa and peels off his sweaty shirt.

"The one with the eye patch."

"Donald Mitchell."

"Yes."

"You saw him?"

"Yes."

"Can you give me more than one-word replies? I haven't gotten laid in over a week. Luke's on his way home. And I'm wearing nothing but—"

"Shut the fuck up. I have never wanted to hear that shit. Why would you assume I've changed my mind?"

"Speaking of getting laid ... you need to prioritize that. It takes the edge off. Where did you see Mitchell?"

"I think he's Archer's pilot."

"Probably a pity job. Let him go. What must he be now? Eighty? If you wait long enough, his heart will give out mid-flight, and your mission will be over without you doing a damn thing. You're to take out the threat, not every person we ever knew."

He grabs his hand weights for shoulder presses.

"My parents are distracted. Hurry up and take off your clothes. I have fifteen minutes, twenty tops." Frankie barges into the garage, kicking her flip-flops off her feet while unbuttoning her shorts.

"Just ... damn! Who is that? Are you *getting laid?*" Jessica's disbelief bleeds from his phone.

Jackson drops the weights with a heavy *clank* and reaches for his phone while Frankie narrows her eyes.

Without another word, he ends the call.

"Who was that?" Frankie's eyes widen at him.

"It's personal." He resumes his lifting.

"Girlfriend?"

He ignores her with a tense face while pressing the weights over his head.

"Mother? Therapist?"

He holds the weights at his sides for squats.

"Doesn't matter," she says. "I've got a lot of energy ... nervous energy, frustrated energy, and an unexpected revenge high, which is a next-level energy. My parents showed up out of the blue. I feel like a teenager again, grounded for bad behavior. So now I have a rebellious sort of energy too."

"And why should this concern me?" he asks.

"Well ... *do* you want to get laid?"

He drops the weights again, blinking several times. "Play something." He nods to the piano.

She frowns. "Play something? Are you serious?"

He nods again.

Frankie pivots toward the piano. "Not what I had in mind," she mumbles.

"Take off your clothes before you play for me."

Frankie turns, resting her chin against her shoulder. "Is that your kink?"

"I'm too fucking old for kink. I simply know what I like."

She removes her top and shorts, depositing them on the floor by the piano bench. "And you like watching me play the piano naked?"

Jackson leans against the back of the sofa and crosses his arms. "We're about to find out."

Frankie gives him a thoughtful expression while removing her bra.

Jackson admires her body. On his long list of things he's too old to do, feeling guilty for this kind of pleasure is one of them.

She slides her underwear down her tan legs. Then, she sits at the piano, adjusting the bench to the correct distance from the pedals.

Perfect posture.

Fingers caressing the keys before pressing them.

Foreplay.

Jackson loved his wife to the ends of the earth. She consumed his heart ... his whole world. In many ways, she saved him. His need to protect her became the driving force for his existence. His perseverance.

He's experienced love, lust, hate, passion, revenge, and countless inconsequential, forgettable encounters. But never has he looked at a woman and felt so intimidated. Watching Frankie play the piano feels like an out-of-body experience. A transcendence to another life. It's the first time he's felt like a student unworthy of being in the presence of someone so gifted.

It takes him a few seconds to place the song. It's from *The Piano* soundtrack. A tiny grin pulls at his lips. Frankie's wit is subtle, humor so dry one might miss it or mistake it for something less brilliant.

Does she want him to stare at her leg? Touch her bare shoulder? Lie naked beside her in bed?

Her gifted fingers fly over the keys and stop without warning. The song has an abrupt ending—a chilling silence like a scene flashing to black instead of gradually fading.

"You're obviously Ada. Am I Alisdair or Baines?"

A slow smile builds on her face while she stares at the keys, and her hands lie idle on her thighs. "Depends. Are you going to cut off my finger or go down on me?"

"I'm well-practiced at both." He smirks. "Do you have a preference?"

Proving to be a worthy adversary, she slides her gaze to him and shrugs. "Not really. Do you?"

He takes a moment to consider her words, his surroundings, the circumstances that have brought them together, and the uncertainty ahead. By the time he opens his mouth to speak, Frankie's sliding into her underwear.

Bra.

Shorts.

Shirt.

Flip-flops.

She hits rewind on his fantasy.

"Time's up. Since you don't want to get laid or meet my parents, I must return to the house. If my dad catches me playing the piano naked in front of a guy *again*, I fear he'll ground me for life." She tucks her fingers into her back pockets and gives him a goofy grin, an amusing contrast to the naked virtuoso he witnessed just moments earlier.

"Again?" He narrows his eyes, rubbing his chin.

Frankie grins and pivots. "Again."

"Why do you have an unexpected revenge high?" He knows the answer, but he doesn't know it from her point of view. After watching her play his piano naked, Jackson has a burgeoning need to see the world from her perspective.

"I did something awful." Frankie opens the door. "And it felt good." She turns ninety degrees, head bowed. "I waited for the wave of guilt and regret. It never came," she murmurs.

"That's too bad."

Her gaze flits to his.

Jackson pushes off the back of the sofa. "Guilt and regret are vital to being a kind person. They're good for your conscience. Keeps everything in check. Sleep on it. And if you feel awful by morning, celebrate having a soul." He stops beside her.

She turns into him, resting her forehead on his bare chest, hands limp at her sides. "I know you think you're Alisdair, but I need you to be Baines."

He grins.

She lifts her head just enough to kiss his sternum, and then she's out the door. "Did you enjoy watching me play your piano naked?"

She turns at the bottom of the porch steps when he doesn't respond. Enjoy is not the right word. He enjoys a good steak and a cold bottle of Heineken. Francesca, naked at his piano, surpasses any word in the English language. At the opposite end of the emotional spectrum, he imagines it's how Molly Sanford felt this afternoon. Aghast times infinity.

He's officially made it his job to know Francesca Holter's every move.

CHAPTER NINETEEN
FRANCESCA

I PUT MYSELF IN TIMEOUT.

After dinner, Eloise serves homemade sangria to my parents on the deck. I hole up in my room for barely twenty minutes before my dad knocks twice and cracks open the door.

He's a farmer like his dad and granddad. My mom doesn't give him much credit for being observant. She feels like she raised us alone. Yet, there is very little that gets past my dad. He's reserved but far from oblivious. And he's never been one to beat around the bush. John and I used to joke that the cows were ratting us out because Dad managed to be in the field all day, yet he'd know that we'd done something nearly every day that warranted extra chores.

Mom would say, "You don't even know why you're punishing them."

He'd reply, "Look at them. I've never seen guiltier faces."

John shoveled manure while I milked the goats. Those were our usual punishments.

"They're gone, Frannie Pants." Dad closes the door behind him and sits on the edge of my bed, resting his hand on my leg.

I lean against the headboard and sigh. "I know."

"So why are you still here?"

I think I could tell my dad. He'd hate it, but accept it because he's a hundred times more rational than I am. He's also honest to a fault. There's no way he could keep this from my mom. And she runs on pure emotion.

Mom's not the type to seek revenge. She'd drown in a sea of helplessness and let it eat her alive.

"I don't have a job. Or a brother. I don't have Steven, the only child who felt a little ... like mine. My godson." Tracing the swirling pattern on the bedspread, I murmur, "I'm looking for closure. I'm waiting for it to make sense. And I know they're not coming back. I know it, but I don't *feel* it yet."

"So you're going to stay with a stranger for ... how long?"

"Eloise isn't a stranger. Steven adored her like another grandmother. And she's been nothing but kind to me. I think she's needed me as much as I've needed her. When Lynn and Steven died, Eloise felt like she lost part of her family."

Again, he squeezes my leg, and I give him a sad smile. "Come home with us. Your mom needs you. *I* need you." It's a rare moment to see vulnerability in my father's eyes.

I scoot closer to him, wrapping my arms around his neck. "I won't stay long. I just ... can't leave quite yet. It's difficult to explain, but I need you to trust me."

He hugs me tighter than he has in years, maybe ever. "I trust you," he whispers.

The following morning, we drive to Hertzville for breakfast at the cafe where Eloise used to work. It's an old joint with a slew of health code violations, stale donuts, and sludge for coffee. But the waitress is sweet and laughs at my dad's jokes, so it's worth the one-star food.

Until ...

Archer Sanford breezes through the front door with his bodyguards. This is the last place on Earth I would have imagined him visiting. Nobody with money or working tastebuds sets foot in here. I scoot down in the booth's corner behind my dad, ducking and slowly scratching my forehead to hide my face.

He heads to the back of the cafe and disappears into the kitchen. A few minutes later, he emerges like a king. Always dripping confidence.

I lift my coffee mug to my lips, scooting even farther down into the booth, eyeing Eloise to see if she notices him, but she's too busy dipping the last of her stale donut in her coffee. My dad gives me a funny look, forcing me to sit up straighter. And that tiny adjustment is all it takes for Archer to spot me.

I can't look away. He has a commanding gaze. With a subtle jerk of his head, he exits the cafe.

Archer: I don't like waiting

I peek at my phone and slide it back into my purse. "I need to use the ladies' room."

Dad scoots out of the booth to let me past him, still inspecting me with suspicion. I smile before heading toward the restroom, but I keep going to the exit at the back of the restaurant. Archer's SUV with blackout windows waits across the street. One of his bodyguards opens the back door for me. We're alone. There's no one in the driver's seat.

"Fuck ... what a surprise. I need this." He sighs, grabbing my hips and pulling me to straddle his lap before I can chirp a word.

I grip the door to steady myself, swallowing hard to mute my inclination to gasp from his sudden aggression. Archer buries his face in my neck and takes a deep breath while gripping my ass.

My hands look for a place to rest. I don't want to touch him, but our close quarters don't leave me much choice.

"Who are those people with you?" he asks muffledly.

I stiffen while he kisses my shoulder and pulls me closer to him—to his erection.

"Family. What were you doing in that cafe?"

"Business," he mumbles, nibbling at my neck.

"Y-you sounded distraught yesterday."

"Nothing you need to worry about." He grinds into me, sliding my shirt up my torso.

"I have to get back inside." I try to sound more matter-of-fact than desperate, but it's hard.

"Iris, I need inside too. Inside of you." He unbuttons my shorts.

"Archer," I push at his shoulders, "I can't do this right now."

His hand dips into the cup of my bra, and he groans.

The SUV suddenly shakes, the front of it slanting to the right with a pop.

Another pop and shake, and the other side sinks.

His bodyguards fly into the front seats. "Shots," one snaps while the other starts the engine. "Get down!"

Archer shoves me off his lap and hunches toward the floor.

I panic. I don't know what's happening outside, but I don't feel any safer inside with Archer, a man with a target on his back.

"Iris!" he barks when I stumble out the door and run off.

The SUV tries to pull away from the curb, but two more *pops* sound behind me.

I cover my mouth to muffle my scream. When I glance back, all four tires are flat.

Finding refuge behind the building, I rest against the crumbling brick, shaking and panting.

Someone's trying to kill him.

I wait ... and wait. There are no more shots. No commotion. No sirens.

After fixing my bra and buttoning my shorts, I close my eyes and run my fingers through my hair. When I return to the table, my parents and Eloise give me concerned looks.

My nose wrinkles. "Sorry. I'm uh ... not feeling well. Mind if we leave?" I shift my gaze to the front windows.

Another SUV pulls up next to Archer's. His bodyguards step out first, making no attempt to hide their drawn guns while scoping the area. Then they open one door, Archer dives into the back seat of the other SUV, and it quickly speeds off.

"Of course," Mom says. "You don't look well. It might be the coffee." She gives my dad a nervous smile.

No one notices the disabled SUV across the street when we exit the cafe and take a sharp right toward my parents' vehicle.

When we return to the house, Eloise rests her hand on my shoulder. "Let me know if you need anything."

"Thanks," I mutter, making a beeline for the bedroom.

I close and lock the door, resting my forehead and flat hands against it. Did I almost die this morning? My heart pounds, confirming that I was in danger, and no one knew it. Opening my eyes, I turn and jump out of my skin.

Jack's perched on the foot of my bed with his index finger at his lips.

I swallow my yelp, but my tears are a little harder to control.

There's not an ounce of concern on his face. No shock. No curiosity. No confusion.

My wobbly legs take me to him.

After all, there is something in his expression—firm jaw and eyes set into a slight squint. Anger. He looks angry.

"I'm going to remove his hands one finger at a time," he murmurs just above a whisper. He's eerily calm and pragmatic. "Then I will carve my knife into his face and remove his tongue and lips. And because I'm certain he's looked at you inappropriately, I'll shove the tip of my knife into his eyeballs just for good measure."

I wince, stumbling all over my emotions. He's lost it. Why is he saying this? Did he see me with Archer? Does he know I was in the line of fire less than thirty minutes ago? If he did, would he be this angry and calloused?

"I-I ... almost died this morning," I whisper, hugging myself to keep from shaking.

"You didn't."

My head jerks backward. "*You didn't*? Not ... what happened? Not ... are you okay?"

"I know what happened. And I know you're okay."

I open my mouth and snap it closed just as quickly.

Jack gives nothing away. His calculated words and calm voice make me dizzy.

"Did *you* try to kill him?"

His lips twist while he tilts his head to the side. "Did he try to fuck you?"

"Did *you* shoot his tires?" My tone has never sounded so incredulous.

He doesn't flinch. I think that's a yes. But I'm so bewildered, I can't see the lines, let alone read between them.

"Why would I do something like that, Frankie? After all, the poor guy had a crap day yesterday. His daughter sent a group text with a video attached. Do you want to know what was on the video?"

"How do you know that?" I breathe with barely enough oxygen to give the words life.

"You think you know the rules, but you're not even supposed to be in the game. Go home. Please."

"Game? What kind of game involves putting bullets in a man's tires?"

Jack brings his finger to his lips again when my voice escalates. "People in the protection business have to carry weapons."

"You're what? Protecting *me*?"

"I did today." Jack grips the back of my legs, tugging me to stand between his spread knees. "Let your parents take you home." He rests his forehead against my stomach and sighs. His shoulders relax.

"No," I whisper, combing my fingers through his thick hair.

Who is this man?

"Yes," he says, lifting my shirt and flicking his tongue into my navel while sliding my shorts and panties down my legs.

"Jack ..." My voice trembles.

"Was he going to fuck you?"

I shake my head when he meets my gaze.

He narrows his eyes. "Did he *want* to fuck you?" His middle two fingers slide between my legs.

I swallow hard before releasing a harsh breath. "Yes," I whisper.

Jack grits his teeth.

"Don't be mad." I feather my fingers along his stiff jaw to his lips. "Be Baines."

Confusion lines the corners of his eyes.

I guide his hand from between my legs and bring his fingers to his lips.

Realization softens his tense expression. "George Baines, huh?" He sucks on his wet fingers.

I nod.

Our gazes shift toward the door for a few seconds when we hear someone close the bathroom door.

Jack slides off the bed to his knees.

My pulse rattles my bones when he lifts my leg, opening me up to him. I bite my bottom lip and sink my fingers into his shoulders while he spears his tongue between my legs.

I squeeze my eyes shut and bite my lips together, trying hard not to make a sound.

It's torture.

When I can't keep my knee from buckling, he guides me to the bed and resumes his best George Baines. Ada was mute. I try to be Ada.

I fail. After thrashing my head side to side and twisting my body while his hands pin my hips to the bed, I grab the pillow and cover my face to absorb my deep moans.

Jack stands, wiping his mouth before peeling off his tee and unbuttoning his gray cargo pants.

I jackknife to sitting, yank the front of his briefs past his erection, and run my tongue along the length of his cock.

I'm confused by the day's events, stupefied by Jack's knowl-edge of Molly's video, and speechless. Ninety-nine percent of my conscience tells me Jack can't be trusted. But that remaining one percent is in control. That one percent wants to rid my body and mind of Archer Sanford. That one percent grips Jack's hard glutes and takes him deep into my mouth.

He cups my head in his hands.

Then that ninety-nine percent clears its throat and kicks me in the gut. It's ....*UGH!* It's really *my mom* who clears her throat.

Jack stills with his back to her, staring straight at the wall while tucking himself into his briefs and zipping his pants.

I snap my knees together. There's no hiding that I'm naked from the waist down.

"Francesca Adeline Holter ..."

I have no fucks to give at this point. We've been here before.

Jack's a soldier. He stands guard in front of me like my mom's not in the room. He even casually slides his hands into his pockets, but he doesn't look at her, not even a glance over his shoulder.

I lean to the side and give my mom a tight grin. "What's up, Mom?"

With her infamous O expression and slow-blinking eyes, she shakes her head. "Eloise wondered if a little ginger oatmeal might soothe your stomach. But it looks like you're getting your fill."

Rubbing my lips together, I nod several times. "I'm working on it. Tell her thanks."

She frowns at my dismissiveness and slams the door behind her.

Jack peers down at me and grins. "You didn't introduce me to your mom."

"I asked you yesterday if you wanted to meet my parents. You said no."

"I thought you locked the door."

"I did!" I snag my panties from the floor and charge toward the door. After I push the lock button, I turn the handle and open it. The lock's broken. Closing the door, I lean against it in defeat and step into my panties. "You should climb out the window."

He lifts an eyebrow, sauntering toward me.

"My dad owns a gun."

Amusement plays along Jack's lips. "I'll go out the front door when you're done."

"When I'm done, what?"

He eyes me while unzipping his pants. "I'll hold the door shut." With his pants open and his erection straining against his briefs, he presses his hands to the door over my head.

"I have a Ph.D. I don't get on my knees for anyone. I'll sit on the bed."

He ducks his head and kisses me. It's good. *Really* good. But a woman needs standards and limits. I undressed and played his piano yesterday. That's my limit.

"Adeline ..." he whispers. "A beautiful name for a beautiful woman."

Not fair.

Again, he kisses me. "A goddamn queen," he murmurs along my jaw to my ear.

I lower to my knees, but I don't look at him. "I'm *only* doing this because someone has to guard the door." My feminism is still intact. Sort of.

CHAPTER TWENTY
FRANCESCA

JACK FOLLOWS me down the stairs. I have no intention of introducing him to my parents.

1. He doesn't want me to.
2. He lives in a garage and might be a serial killer.
3. My dad won't be able to help himself. He'll feel obligated to ask Jack what his intentions are with "his daughter."

Do I want to know Jack's intentions? After today, I'm not sure. The reason I'm horny as fuck around him is *because* he lives in a garage and might be a serial killer. I don't know if I want to know the meaning behind his tattoos or how his wife died. How many kids he has. Or how far away from the cafe he was when he put four bullets in Archer's tires.

Was he on a rooftop like a sniper? I don't know. And even when I ask him questions, I only do it to feel sane. A normal, *sane* person would ask those questions.

Molly Sanford stole my sanity when she dipped her

feather in ink and sealed my nephew's fate.

"Jack, come meet Francesca's parents." Eloise derails the plan.

He shrugs at me and reroutes, carrying his confident self into the living room.

Maybe my mom kept her discovery to herself.

Nope.

Dad's in a wide stance beside the sofa, arms crossed and hands tucked into his armpits. It makes his chest look puffed out. It's the stance he's taken for years with men I've dated. Mom has a tight smile and laser eyes on me.

"Jack, this is Taylor and Erin." It's hard to read Eloise. Maybe she knows. Perhaps she doesn't. Either way, she's old-fashioned enough to insist on proper introductions.

"Hi." Jack offers a quick nod and a pleasant smile.

No "Nice to meet you."

No "I have the utmost respect for your daughter."

Nothing.

"Jack's renting my garage. He plays the piano," Eloise says.

My parents look constipated. It's killing them to act like their daughter wasn't sucking on his dick twenty minutes earlier. Eloise might be a savior. However, a real savior would have fixed the lock on the bedroom door or, at least mentioned, it was broken.

My mom presses her hand to her neck and clears her throat. "Francesca is a brilliant pianist. Or at least she was. It's been a while since I've heard her play. She might be in the middle of a midlife crisis."

"I played yesterday." I smile. "For Jack." I bat my eyes. "Naked."

Just before the collective gasp, I roll my eyes. "I'm kidding."

Jack? He's back in soldier mode like one of those guards at Buckingham Palace. They don't crack under any amount of pressure. Not a blink. Not a grin. Nothing.

My dad scowls, and my mom offers a little "tee-hee."

Eloise snorts. "Francesca, don't tease your parents like that." She rocks in her chair. "Jack's a perfect gentleman."

Mom's gaze shoots at him, but he keeps a soft, neutral expression.

"How old are ya, Jack?" Dad asks.

Jack scratches his jaw. "I've lost track."

"What do you do?" Mom asks.

"Depends on the day. Some days I do a lot, other days not so much."

I bite back my grin when my parents share a funny look.

"Thanks for the introduction," Jack says. "I'd better get back to work."

"Bye, Jack." Eloise continues to either play the part or reside in a bubble.

When the screen door clicks behind Jack, Mom glares at me. "Francesca, what is going on with you? I think you need help. And I think this started before Lynn and Steven died. You've been spiraling out of control since John died. Or is this a midlife crisis? Either way, you need to see someone before you ruin your life."

"I need to water my flowers." Eloise slowly stands, giving me a sympathetic smile before abandoning me.

"Frannie Pants, we're worried about you. We love you more than anyone. Don't push us away. We'll do whatever it takes to get you the help you need." Dad sits beside Mom and reaches for her hand in solidarity.

It's them against me.

They used to do this whenever John and I got in trouble together. They knew they had to stick together if they didn't want to be railroaded because John and I were always a unified force.

"I'm between jobs. I'm financially independent. I'm taking care of things after my brother's wife and son killed themselves. I was fortunate enough not to die when the house started on fire. But I'm somehow having a midlife crisis or irrationally grieving and 'acting out' because I'm getting laid?"

"Francesca, you were ..." Mom clenches her jaw. She can't even say it. "*Doing that* while your father and I were in the same house. A house that's not your house. And you were ... *doing that* with some random guy who lives in a garage and has no manners whatsoever."

"For the record, he went down on me first, so you can't say he has 'no manners whatsoever.' And yes, I was *giving him head* in a bedroom with the door closed while other people were in the house. It's no different than being in a hotel room. The fact that you barged in on us is not my fault. It's yours. Think of all the times John or I happened to open your *unlocked* bedroom door without knocking, only to discover that you like to do it doggie style or that Dad wears socks during sex. So before you point fingers and accuse someone of uncouth behavior or suggest that their actions are somehow a 'crisis,' maybe you should focus on yourselves. Or maybe you should start giving me some goddamn credit for all the hard work I've put into my life, the amount of success I've achieved, and how I've managed to do it without drinking myself to death and putting a bullet in my head."

Tears fill my mom's eyes, and Dad hugs her while looking at me. It's not anger; it's pity.

I scrub my hands over my face. "You have no idea," I mumble, "what I have done for this family."

CHAPTER TWENTY-ONE
JACKSON

"Who did you find to touch your pee-pee?" Jessica asks Jackson the second she answers her phone.

"I'm compromised." He sighs, holding the phone to his ear with one hand while stabbing his fingers through his hair with his other.

"Leave," she says in a sharp tone.

"I can't."

"You know the protocol. Get out *now*."

"Protocol? What protocol? There is no protocol. I'm the cleanup crew without an employer. No backup. No extraction team. Nothing. Either I get it done or die trying."

"Or you walk away and let the chips fall where they may."

Jackson shakes his head, pacing the garage. "I can't let the chips fall where they may. I want to see my daughter and—"

"Then go see her. Be with her."

"Then I'll never see you again."

"Fin de journée" (*End of Day*), Jessica whispers.

"No. The Days ended. They died. Ryn died. *I'm* ending this."

"Why are you compromised?"

"I put four bullets in his tires."

"Did someone see you?"

"No. But he's going to be guarded like the damn president now."

She sighs. "Then why did you put four bullets in his tires?"

Jackson continues to pace the garage, feeling jittery because he's losing focus. And he's losing focus because Frankie did, in fact, touch his pee-pee.

"The girl. You're compromised because of a girl."

Jackson bristles. "She's a woman."

"We're all just girls at heart when it comes to love. Who's the *woman*?"

He stops his pacing and stares at the ceiling. "The aunt of the boy next door who took his life."

"Oh, the double suicide?"

"Correct. She was supposed to go through their things, sell the house, and go home. But she ..."

"Met you. And you charmed her. Wait ... no. That's not possible. You ... drugged her? No. That's not your MO. Seriously, I need to know. Is she a witch? That's the only explanation. I don't care if she's a Victoria's Secret model or an heir to some throne. You have a type, and she tragically died."

She did. Ryn was his type. But she died. And so did the man he was with her.

"She has a Ph.D.," Jackson says.

"So? She's smart. That's not enough."

"In music theory."

Jessica withholds her comeback for a few extra seconds. "I'm listening ..."

"I've never seen anyone play the piano like she does."

"Well ... damn," Jessica whispers.

He doesn't add the fact that she's stubborn as hell, just like his sister.

"Anyway," he massages his temples, "she's seeking revenge on the Sanfords because she thinks their daughter is responsible for her nephew committing suicide."

"Is she?"

"I don't know. Maybe. How the hell am I supposed to know? And why should I give a shit?"

"Because you can't think of her as collateral damage if something goes wrong while taking out Archer."

"She's going to get herself taken out, and it won't have anything to do with me."

"And you're not going to feel inclined to protect her. Correct?"

It's an unfair question for his sister to ask on a day that Frankie got on her knees for him.

"Just be on alert. Be smart," he says.

She laughs. "Have you met my husband?"

"He's a good man."

"You've never thought that."

Jackson nods to himself. As with all the women in his life, no man will ever be good enough for them. "Tell him hi."

"You mean tell him to keep his dick out of your sister."

"I think you tie him to your bed on the daily. I'm not blaming him for your issues."

"Fuck you."

"Love you too, Jess." He grins, ending the call.

THE FOLLOWING DAY, Jackson waits on a park bench across from Archer's office. He's intentionally reading a book close to an older woman and her dog. And occasionally, he glances at her and smiles, giving her little dog a scratch, which seems to please the lady. To anyone watching them, they'd assume he knows the lady.

When Archer emerges from the building, he's flanked by security. Just as Jackson suspected, the tire incident made his job harder. When the motorcade pulls away from the curb, Jackson jogs to his car and follows Archer.

He stops for lunch at the same restaurant where Jackson first saw Frankie having lunch with him. Only this time, he's meeting his wife for lunch. He's not as affectionate toward her. No brushing his leg against hers, no resting his hand on hers. They couldn't be more distant, and their hand gestures show they're having a dispute. Before they finish their appetizer, Corinne Sanford throws her napkin at him, stands, and slings her handbag over her shoulder.

Archer leans back and glances around with a slight headshake. They're probably arguing over Molly. Do they send her to a convent or hire her out for money since she's proven she'll spread her legs for anyone?

Jackson's surveillance of their house has shown Molly at home since the video text. She's locked in her ivory tower. Before leaving the restaurant, Jackson takes pictures of the new additions to Archer's security team.

When he returns home, the only car in the driveway is Frankie's. He hears a rhythmic knocking from the distance, closer to the house that burned down. He makes his way around the rubble.

Frankie's going to town with an ax on the thick trunk of the oak tree, sweat dripping down her face and saturating her gray tank top.

"Chainsaw would be easier."

She stands with a huff and drops the ax.

"Where are the folks?"

She swipes her arm across her brow. "They disowned me and headed home."

He nods slowly. "And now you're mad at the tree?"

"My brother blew his brains out a few feet from this tree. Then Steven hung himself from it. The house is gone. The memories are buried in soot. But this fucking tree remains unscathed."

"What's next on your revenge list? The wife? The husband? The dog?"

Her nose wrinkles. "Do they have a dog?"

Jackson shakes his head.

"The wife has a boyfriend. I think I should catch him cheating on her. It would devastate her more than her husband cheating on her. And clearly, I'm going to burn down their house at some point."

"Cheating *and* arson. You'll have quite the resume when you're done with them. I'm concerned that your idea of getting him to cheat on her is seducing him yourself."

She shrugs. "Is that a problem?"

He refuses to back down from the challenging gleam in her eyes.

"Maybe I should fuck Corinne just for good measure. Let's blow up the entire family in a sex ring."

"Sex ring? Doesn't that imply the involvement of children?"

"Molly's seventeen."

Frankie's head jerks back as she winces. "Are you

174

implying you're going to have sex with Molly? What is wrong with you?"

"What?" He slides his hands into his back pockets. "Is that too far? Is there a line you won't cross to get revenge?"

"It's not me. I'm taken aback that you'd do such an awful thing."

He nods several times. "Is it awful because she's seventeen or that I'm the one willing to fuck her?"

"Both."

"Interesting. I have no issue with you spreading your legs for Archer or Corinne's lover. It makes my day. Nothing weird about it at all. In fact, I don't know why you didn't try to seduce Molly's boyfriend. You're a MILF. You could pull that off."

"I'm not a mother. And that's different."

Jackson ambles back toward the garage. "Keep telling yourself that."

CHAPTER TWENTY-TWO

FRANCESCA

> Archer: I'm sorry

AFTER GIVING up on the tree, I glance at his message on my way back to the house. My hands are blistered to the point of feeling debilitated.

> Me: I don't think there are enough "I'm sorrys" for nearly getting me killed

> Archer: You weren't the target

> Me: I don't want to be collateral damage. I'm out

> Archer: Can I see you?

> Me: I'm out

> Archer: You're not that weak

"Fuck you," I murmur.

> Me: I'm not that stupid

Archer: I'll do anything to see you again

Me: I have a boyfriend

Archer: Maybe you should set him up with my wife

I ease my achy, sweaty body into the wooden rocker on the porch and stare at his text.

Me: I'll run it by him

Archer: Tell me about him

Me: He's private

Archer: Good in bed?

Me: Not sure. We don't use a bed

Archer: See me tonight

There's nothing more dangerous than a man with something to prove, especially one who feels threatened by another man.

Archer: PLEASE

Me: Raincheck

Archer: I'm not that patient

Me: I'm not that submissive

Archer: You will be

"How do you feel about carnivals?" The door creaks when Eloise opens it.

I tuck my phone into my pocket. "I've never been asked

that before. How should I feel about them?"

"A friend of mine asked me to assist her. It's from six to eleven tonight in Rhodale. I could use a ride there. She'll bring me home, so you won't have to stay the whole time."

"What does your friend do at the carnival?"

"Palmistry." A conspiratorial grin steals Eloise's lips. "She's very accurate."

"Maybe I could use a palm reading."

"I was thinking the same thing."

"Did you ask Jack?"

"Yes, but he said he doesn't go out at night."

I narrow my eyes. "Is that so? Past his bedtime?"

She laughs. "Perhaps. It's just another mysterious thing about him."

"Maybe nighttime is when he chops up the bodies."

She glances at the garage and hums. "I've thought about that. He never stays past sunset when I invite him to dinner."

"Exactly."

"I feel bad for you, Francesca."

I narrow my eyes.

"I like Jack, but I fear he's using you for ..." Her nose crinkles.

"Sex?"

She nods.

"What if I'm using him for sex?"

Her eyes widen as if the idea is unbelievable. "Are you?"

I think of our sexual encounters, which only once led to actual sex. I don't count oral, just like I didn't count it in high school with Aiden Walker.

"I don't know." I chuckle.

As if he knew we were talking about him, Jack jogs up the drive. He's definitely a creature of habit.

"Speak of the devil," Eloise says.

"The devil indeed. Why do you suppose he runs in pants and a long-sleeved shirt?"

"To sweat more, I suppose."

I stand. "I'm going to see if he'll make an exception and come to the carnival with me."

"Good luck," she says as I descend the stairs.

"You need a shower," Jack says, eyeing me just before opening the door.

"So do you." I follow him into the garage. "Want to shower together?"

"I don't have hot water." He removes his shirt, tosses it on the floor, then grabs the tape and wraps his hands.

"I don't mind." I lose my shirt and my shorts. "You should come to the carnival with me tonight. I'm taking Eloise. I'll win you a stuffed animal or buy you cotton candy."

Jack eyes me while securing the tape. I toss my bra aside along with my panties.

He punches the bag.

I turn on the hose and gasp when the cold water hits my skin.

"Told you it's cold." He continues to punch the bag.

It's fucking freezing, but I stifle any further reactions. After a quick rinse-off, I set the hose by the drain and grab his soap bar. It doesn't suds well without hot water, but it's good enough. I rub it over my body, giving my breasts extra focus.

Jack sneaks several quick peeks. When I rinse off, I make sure to get everything clean, aiming the nozzle between my legs while my other hand slides between them.

"Fuck," he mumbles, punching harder.

The cold water has goosebumps blooming along my skin and my nipples harden more than ever. I feel sensitive and *responsive* everywhere.

"Do you have an extra towel?"

"Nope." His leg swings to the side of the bag, landing with a harsh smack.

"I'll just walk around until I air dry." I wring out my hair and peruse the perimeter of the garage.

Jack grumbles something else that sounds like a string of expletives, but I can't say for sure. Then he rips off the tape, strips, and rinses off with soap and the hose. I suspect he's doing it *just* for the cold water.

When my backside feels dry, I sit on the piano bench and play another song from *The Piano*. And then another ...

Jack uses the lone towel to dry off before wrapping it around his waist.

My fingers pause, and I slowly lift a leg over the piano bench to straddle it, wholly exposed to him. "Baines is the endgame. I like him, but Alisdair loved her too. It took him a while, but I think he loved her. I know it's an unpopular opinion. He was her husband. And he made the biggest sacrifice by giving her up. He could have removed all her fingers and forced himself on her, but he never went that far despite the temptation and complete blow to his ego that his wife was cheating on him."

"He tried to rape her when she was on her way to Baines's place. He cut off her finger." Jack's face sours while he runs a hand through his wet hair.

"Passion is the least rational feeling. We say 'making love,' but love is a broad term. I think the church likes to use the word to make sex seem like more than just two people getting off. But it's passion, a carnal urge. It doesn't make sense. And both Baines and Alisdair treated Ada like a sexual object. The only difference is that Baines used her piano as a bargaining chip, and Alisdair used his role as her husband. But Ada didn't care about marriage and promises. She cared about her piano. Baines had the bigger bargaining chip. Who's to say that had Alisdair used the piano to his advantage, Ada might not have fallen in love with him over time? He was a handsome man. Nice body. Inviting smile. And Ada was a very sexual being."

Jack's gaze finds a permanent home between my spread legs. He wets his lips and nods. "Fair point."

"I have to get ready for the carnival."

Jack shakes his head and murmurs, "Not yet."

His patience pushes me to my limit. So, I go for the jugular. "Archer messaged me. He's desperate to see me. I wonder if he'll be at the carnival." I stand, naked ass swaying toward my discarded clothes by the drain.

"I'm not doing this. If you parade around here naked, don't say his name. It's like you want him dead. Is that what you want, Francesca?"

I turn with my dirty clothes gathered in my arms. "If I say his name, you'll kill him?"

"I'm going to kill him. You mentioning his name will only expedite it."

I laugh—the nervous kind. This is a game, but unlike any game I've ever played. And the mysterious side that drew me to him has taken a wrong turn. I can't read him. Is he telling me the truth disguised as a joke? Or is he joking just to test me? To see if I trust him like I've tested Archer.

I play the game even though I've not been given the rules. "I mentioned his name because he's transparent with what he wants."

"What does he want?"

I smile. "Me."

"What do *you* want?"

"Revenge."

"Bullshit."

I bristle at his sharp response.

"If you really wanted revenge, you'd show that letter to everyone in this town and Rhodale. You'd plaster it all over social media. It would go viral, and you know it. But you're afraid that might cause her to end her life. Is her life worth more than your nephew's? If the answer is no, then what are you waiting for? Do you really think fucking her dad and exposing her mom will fill the void left by losing your brother's family?"

"What do you know about revenge?"

"Everything." Jack sucks all the oxygen from the room with his one-word reply.

I step into my dirty shorts and pull on my shirt. "I'm taking Eloise to the carnival."

He grabs my arm when I pass him. "He's playing with you."

"Maybe I'm playing with him."

"If he wants you, he'll have you."

I jerk my arm from his grip. "He'll get nothing more than I willingly give him."

He releases my arm. "I need you to do me a favor."

I stop at the door.

"Don't blame me."

"For what?" I ask.

"For being right."

CHAPTER TWENTY-THREE
FRANCESCA

"It's Betty's Between the Lines." Eloise points to her friend's stand with a palm sign.

"Got it. I will look for some junk food and check in with you before I leave." I scuff my flip-flops toward the food trucks and stands—the distant screams from the roller coaster echo. I stop for ride tickets on my way to the food trucks. The bells ring amongst the thudding of balls and pinging targets. Uplifting laughter and squealing children buzz past me with their parents, trying to catch them. Popcorn, grease, mini donuts, and cotton candy saturate the thick summer air.

Occasionally, a welcome breeze catches the skirt of my light blue sundress, offering several seconds of reprieve from the suffocating humidity.

"I'd like a pretzel with cheese and a bottle of water, please." I pull a folded twenty out of my purse.

"Make it two pretzels."

I stiffen when a hand presses to the bare skin on my lower back.

Archer tosses a fifty on the counter before I get my

twenty laid down. "No raincheck needed after all. It's fate. And you look stunning in this shade of blue. And here I thought red was your best color."

Pinning a believable smile to my face, I turn.

He eyes me while trapping his lower lip between his teeth. "*Fate* is a beautiful thing. Don't you think?"

"Where's your wife?" I take my pretzel and water. The white paper crinkles in my shaky hand while my other hand grips the icy cold water.

"Where's your boyfriend? Did you already introduce him to my wife? Maybe he can join her and my accountant at their favorite hotel."

"Your wife's screwing your accountant? That doesn't sound good." I escape his possessive hand while he gets his pretzel and change.

"On the contrary." He catches up to me with his not-so-discreet bodyguards. "My accountant can remind her just how much she stands to lose if she fucks around on me and asks for a divorce."

I swallow a bite of the salty pretzel, finding it hard to push it past the lump in my throat because Jack's words keep repeating. They're robbing me of my confidence. He's making me feel weak. And the last thing I can afford to feel around Archer Sanford is weak.

"And what happens if *you* ask for a divorce after fucking around?"

"I told you I won't ever ask for a divorce. She's my wife and the mother of my child."

I constantly have to remind myself that Archer has a degree in psychology. Somewhere in the corners of his complicated mind, he's constructed his idea of family.

Wife.

Child.

Mistress. *Mistresses?*

And each role holds importance and balance in his world.

"How do you eat this shit?" He tosses his pretzel into the trash.

"It's a carnival. It's part of the experience, like the Ferris wheel and the House of Mirrors. Trekking through dirt mixed with peanut shells and tumbling wrappers. Music so loud you feel like you're in a fog. Chugging machinery. Air brakes whooshing. Sticky metal handles and cracked padding shoved into your gut to keep you from flying out of a ride. And yes ... stale pretzels with fake cheese sauce. It's all quite nostalgic." I grin, taking another bite of my pretzel.

"Not to sound like a broken record, but you're a dental assistant. I'm not surprised that a carnival triggers nostalgia for you."

"Annnd ... I'm done." I shove my pretzel *and* cheese into his white collared shirt.

He holds up his hands. "What the fuck?"

"On behalf of all dental assistants, I hope all your teeth rot out of your mouth and you choke on your dentures." My flip flops pound toward the rides, and I hand over a ticket for the Ferris wheel. I'm not really mad. He's an asshole; that's nothing new. I want to see if he grovels. I need to know what kind of hold I have on him.

"Sir, your ticket!"

Archer jumps into the seat with me, causing it to rock backward as it moves to let the next people onto the ride.

I angle my body away from him and cross my arms.

"Look, Iris. I'm sorry. I'm an asshole. I won't even try to deny it. And all I meant was that you've lived a sheltered life. I want to show you the world. Private jets. Weekends at spas in Bali. The Amalfi Coast. I'm honored to be the one who gets to be with you when you experience those things for the first time."

"If you really wanted revenge, you'd show that letter to everyone in this town and Rhodale."

Jack's words continue to haunt me.

"And getting shot at. Don't forget that. Nothing screams romance like gunshots while a guy tries to get into your pants. Do you feel honored to be the first guy to endanger my life?"

"Are we having our first fight?" He slides his hand to my leg.

I dig my nails into his skin.

"Is it wrong that the more you fight me, the harder my dick gets?" His grip creeps higher on my leg and tightens as we reach the top of the Ferris wheel, where it stops to let on more riders.

The humidity vanishes. All I feel is ice creeping up my spine. This is Jack's fault. He's in my head. I was focused. I didn't have to think. I just acted. I felt in control, even if I willingly gave Archer the feeling he was in control.

But now I'm suffocated by self-doubt, which is making me weak. And Jack's voice keeps getting louder.

"If he wants you, he'll have you."

"Not like this." I grit my teeth to steady my voice. "Not here."

My leg burns from his brutal grip. My nails sink deeper into his hand. "You're hurting me."

"Then just relax." His other hand grips my throat, and he kisses me.

A silent scream has never been so deafening. This is for revenge.

For John.

For Lynn.

For Steven.

Archer's hand forces its way to my panties, and he rips at the crotch, stabbing his finger into my flesh, trying to gain entrance. He wants me to fight him. He gets off on it.

So I don't. My mind slides into a dark place outside my body because it's just that ... a body. A shell. The empty part that will remain on this earth long after my soul moves on.

I kiss Archer back. I release his hand. I relax my legs.

It's just a body.

Jack's wrong. Archer can't reach me. He can physically invade me. He can use me for his sick pleasure. But he will never invade my mind like Molly invaded Steven's. He will never have my love or my respect.

I do the opposite of fighting him. My leg swings over his lap, so I'm wedged between him and the bar. He pulls back with a glimmer of panic as the car rocks.

"Fuck me right now," I whisper before grabbing the back of the seat and kissing him as brutally as he kissed me. "Right here," I say next to his ear before biting it. *Hard.*

"Fuck," he growls, wincing at my attempt to pierce his ear.

"Yes," I hiss, grinding against his erection. I'm angry and determined to beat him at his own game.

Archer's willing to parade his affairs around town for the world to see, like he's daring anyone to say one word to the king. But is he willing to do more than have dinner with women who are not his wife? Is he willing to have sex with me on a Ferris wheel at a carnival filled with kids who go to school with Molly? Parents who attend the same school events? Clients of his?

The ride moves another few spots and halts again.

Archer's hand grips the side of the car.

"Make me scream ..." I lift onto my knees, which makes the car swing more.

"Iris!" His body stiffens, and panic spreads across his face.

I unbutton his jeans and ease down the zipper. When I slide my hand into his briefs, he's limp. My gaze waits for his, but his wide eyes are too busy darting in all directions as his hands claw at anything to secure himself while we rock beneath my movements. "I thought you would be my favorite ride at the carnival."

Archer's eyes flit to meet mine. "What the fuck is wrong with you?" he asks breathlessly.

"If I had a dick, I'd say adrenaline gets me hard."

His jaw clenches. "Sit down."

I remove my hand from his flaccid cock and plop down beside him, making the car swing just as it starts to move again.

"Stop the ride!" Archer barks as we descend closer to the bottom. He fumbles with his jeans to get them zipped and buttoned. "Stop the goddamn ride!"

It stops at our car.

Archer grabs my wrist and drags me off the ride like an errant child getting pulled out of a store after throwing a fit.

His men surround us, funneling toward an exit but taking a quick right before reaching the security guard at the ticket gate.

"I have to take my grandma home," I say less confidently.

Archer ignores me, his grip on my wrist feeling just as unforgiving as his grip was on my leg. We pass a tent, a row of portable toilets, and a gravel area filled with RVs before cutting toward an alley with two SUVs.

While my heart pounds, my mind plays the reasoning

game again. It's just my body. He can do whatever he wants. My mind will let go. I'll let it float away from my body.

Relax.

Relax.

Rel—

I gasp when the men around us drop to the ground like dominos in a series of thumps and cracking sounds.

"Run!" Archer jerks my arm in the direction we came as the last man standing behind him puts himself between Archer and the lifeless men on the ground.

I stumble to my hands and knees at the sudden change in direction.

"Iris!" Archer tries to turn back, but his last security guard shoves him to keep going.

I don't run. I can't. My body shakes, but I can't move. I can only wait on my skinned-up hands and knees for something.

A bullet in my back?

Each breath pulses out of my nose as tears fill my eyes. When the first tear hits the dirt, I inch my gaze behind me.

There are three men—blood pooling around their heads.

I choke on a sob as the thud of heavy boots in the dirt treads toward me. Pinching my eyes shut, I pray.

"Let's go." It's Jack's voice.

I slowly open my eyes, but I'm still paralyzed, my ears ringing and my heart pounding. He's the color of night. Black-painted face. Black beanie. Black shirt, pants, and boots.

"Who ..." I flip over, scooting away from him. My feet skid on the gravel while my hands keep propelling me backward. "Who a-are you?" I shake my head repeatedly, trying to distance myself from him and the dead men.

He holds out his hand. "We have to go."

I continue to shake my head while trying and failing to get my footing to stand on shaky legs. "Don't touch me!" My gaze flits to the dead men on the ground. "You ... you *killed* them!"

He shoves a gun into the back of his pants. That's when I notice he has a bigger gun hanging from a strap over his shoulder. "Look at me."

I can't. There's too much blood pooling around their heads.

"Look. At. Me." He squats in front of me and grabs my face. "I'm not going to hurt you. But we have to get out of here right now."

"Who are you?" My unblinking gaze meets his. This isn't happening. I'm a music professor. My idea of revenge involves public embarrassment and exposing affairs. This is not the same thing.

"Tonight, I am your savior. Let's go." He pulls me to my feet, but the second I look at the dead men again, I stumble, and nausea twists my stomach into tight knots.

When I can't tear my gaze away from the bullet holes in the men's heads and their dead eyes pointed at the night sky, Jack scoops me into his arms. He treks out of the alley and tucks me in the back seat of his car. Seconds later, he floors it before I can sit up straight or catch my breath.

I don't move for miles. I remain on my side, staring through blurry tears at the back of his seat. Jack doesn't say a word.

"Don't blame me."

"For what?"

"For being right."

My hands cover my face, and I shake uncontrollably. Eventually, I realize we've been on the road too long. We're not going to Boone. I try to sit up, but my body won't cooperate. If I move, then this is real. And right now, I need it to be a nightmare from which I can awaken.

I want my life back.

My family.

Maybe even the job I lost.

When the car stops, Jack opens the back door. "Get out."

I don't move. "You were right," I whisper.

"Yeah, well, I didn't want to be right." He plucks me from the car and carries me to a room at a rundown motel.

It reeks, and it's stuffy like there's no air conditioning. Jack sets me on the edge of the bed. Then he closes the door and the blinds before tossing the room key (an actual metal key) on the nightstand.

Slowly, he hunches in front of me. "Are you okay?"

I shake my head. "W-what just h-happened?"

"I saved you from yourself."

My hands shake, so I ball them into fists, but they still tremble. "Why are we here?" I whisper.

"I don't know if we can go back to Eloise's. I'm on Archer's radar now. And you can't go back either. You can't go home. Not until I finish this."

I sniffle, wiping my eyes. "Finish what? I don't understand. You ... y-you killed those men."

"Did he hurt you?"

Hurt me? He *killed* three men. Three men who probably have families. That's three families without fathers and husbands. Steven lost his father and look how that turned out.

I touch my leg on instinct, and Jack doesn't miss it. He

191

lifts my dress. I have a red mark that will be a bruise by morning. Jack eyes me, and I swallow my emotions, refusing to look directly at him. I didn't kill anyone. Why do I feel such shame?

"I'm fine," I whisper.

His jaw muscles tick, working his teeth overtime while he pushes my dress further up my legs. I grip his hand to stop him. This only hardens his expression more. He pushes past my grip until my dress is at my waist and the partially torn crotch of my panties is in plain sight.

"Did he stick his fingers inside of you?" Jack's voice is tight, a rubber band stretched to its limit.

I shake my head. How do I tell him I don't actually know? I let myself escape to a different place. Then, I gathered the confidence to take back control.

"Did he fuck you with his fingers?" His words cut through the air, and it startles me.

"No," I say before choking on a sob, shaking my head over and over. "I-I'm fine. I was in control. Y-you messed with my head." I push his hand away from my leg and wipe my nose with the back of my arm. "It's flesh and bones. It's not me. It's not who I am. It's a vehicle." I hold my ground despite what feels like a building collapsing in my chest, sharp-edged boulders landing in the pit of my stomach.

"It's *your* body," he says after a hard swallow.

When he looks at me again, I tip my chin up. I want to remind him that he's right. It's my body. Not Archer's and not *his*. But I can't because I think he killed three men tonight to save me. To save my body. *I* did this. Three families will grieve the unnecessary deaths of their loved ones because of me.

"I saved you from yourself." Jack's words echo.

He drops his head in my lap, reverently kissing my bare legs. "You want a shower?" he whispers.

I don't want his kindness. It makes me feel weak. And I can't feel weak when I have to be stronger than ever. Right now, admitting how badly I messed up takes the most strength.

"I have to go back. Eloise will know something's wrong."

"No. You're not going anywhere."

"Jack—"

"If you leave, I can't protect you." His hands grip my waist to keep me from standing.

"I don't need your protection."

"He was going to rape you."

I shake my head over and over.

Pained lines crease his forehead. "I know you think it's just flesh and bones, just a vehicle. But this flesh and bones is how you experience the world. It gives you perception. The mind needs a body, and the body needs a mind. As long as you're alive, you can't separate the two. If he takes something you don't willingly give to him, it won't just break your body; it will destroy a part of you that will never mend."

I blink back a new round of tears. "I'm willing to give it to him if it makes things in my world a little less wrong."

Jack frames my face with his hands, desperation filling his eyes. "They're gone, Frankie. Nothing can make that less wrong. And maybe you're willing to give him your flesh and bones, but I'm not."

I touch my fingers to his black-painted face. "You killed three men." More tears escape when I blink. "It's ..." My lower lip quivers. "It's my fault."

His Adam's apple bobs. "It's Archer's fault." He stands,

leads me to the bathroom, turns on the shower, and lifts my dress over my head. I cover my breasts, but I don't know why. Archer didn't take anything I hadn't willingly given him before today. But that's just it ... Ada hated her husband because he tried to take what she wasn't willing to give. And she didn't fall in love with Baines until he surrendered, giving her freedom.

Control changes everything.

When I lost control tonight, everything changed. And when I took it back, it changed again.

"Do you need some privacy?" Jack sets my dress by the sink.

"No," I whisper, letting my hands slide from my breasts to my sides.

Jack's gaze flickers past me to the shower for a second. "If you need time to—"

"I don't."

If he treats me like I'm broken, then I am.

In silent acquiescence, Jack removes his clothes. I ease my ripped panties down my legs. He takes them from me, tossing them in the trash.

I step into the shower first. The water's not steaming hot, but it's better than his hose in the garage. Jack joins me, and I take the washcloth from his hand and start cleaning the paint from his face.

"You don't have to do this."

"I want to," I murmur, taking my time to wipe every inch, every tiny crease, clean. I need to believe that somewhere in his heart, or at least in a remote corner of his conscience, he's struggling emotionally because he had to kill three people today—because of me.

He shampoos my hair and then his. I slowly spread the soap over my body, stopping before my hands reach the top of my legs. Jack blinks, drops of water clinging to his eyelashes.

With our gazes locked, I take his hand and guide it between my legs.

"Frankie," he rasps, but he doesn't remove his hand or move his fingers. They stay idle, gently pressed where Archer's had been on the Ferris wheel.

"I'm okay." I'm not asking for sex or for this to go any further. Maybe I'm not doing this for him as much as I'm doing it for myself. *I'm okay*.

Jack skates his fingertips over my flesh, taking his time. His hand slides to my hip, breast, and neck before cupping my cheek. "You're okay." He presses his lips to my forehead.

I'm not broken.

Cracked? Yes.

Bruised? Yes.

Knotted? Yes.

Some days, barely breathing? Unfortunately.

But my heart beats. And even when it feels like a curse, I remind myself it's a gift, not just a choice.

HOURS LATER, as Jack sleeps beside me, the sheet low on his waist, both hands resting on his chest, I wonder how I got here. I've never felt this lost, this uncertain. The blinking neon motel sign lights up his skin every time it flashes through the threadbare curtains. My fingers trace his tattoos, the veins down his arms, calloused fingers, and abs.

And ... lower.

He stirs, head easing to the side, tired eyes peeling open. I stare at him for a few seconds. "Are you broken?" I whisper because the life in his eyes seems to fade a little more every day.

He blinks slowly.

My hand slides along his growing erection.

"Down there?" he murmurs, lifting a single brow. "It would appear the answer is no."

A tiny smile steals my lips as best as it can. My heart is too heavy to embrace his humor fully.

"What is ... this? Us?" I release him and skate my hand up his chest. "Who am I to you?" I slide a leg over him, straddling his torso while kissing along his neck.

His fingers tangle in my wet hair while he sits up, so we can look into each other's eyes. My nipples brush his chest when I lift onto my knees and lower onto him, letting him fill me physically ... emotionally ... and all my tiny fractured places.

Jack's teeth scrape along his lower lip, masking his grin while he hums. He deposits a series of slow kisses all over my face. "You're the girl I kiss good night." His hands grip my hips, moving me over him while we kiss.

Under different circumstances, that would make me the luckiest girl in the world.

CHAPTER TWENTY-FOUR
JACKSON

"You killed three men." Frankie's groggy voice seeps into the bathroom while Jackson shaves.

He pauses briefly before rinsing the razor, hoping she accepts that he did it for her and stops mentioning it.

"Because of me." She slides her legs over the edge of the bed and combs her messy hair with her fingers.

Jackson continues shaving. "Good morning."

She grunts. "Good?"

"Above average."

"You *killed* three men yesterday."

So much for that minor detail slipping her mind.

"It's complicated." He wipes the residual soap from his face with a towel.

"Finishing that song for your wife is *complicated*. Killing three men is criminal." Frankie appears in the doorway with a sheet wrapped around her.

Jackson nods slowly. "I'll pick up clothes for you today."

"I have clothes."

"Not here."

She rubs her eyes. "I'm going to need more than the word *complicated*."

"Messy."

Her hands drop to her sides, and she frowns.

"Dangerous." He twists his lips. "But mostly ... really fucking complicated."

"I'm leaving." She pivots. "Where's my dress?"

"In the trash."

"You threw away my dress?" Frankie turns again, pushing him aside to inspect the trash in the bathroom. "It's not in the trash." She searches the rest of the motel room.

"The dumpster behind the motel's office."

Frankie's attention snaps to him, lips parted. "Why would you throw away my dress ... the only thing I have to wear?"

Jackson's list of reasons for disposing of the dress is long and *complicated*. "If we're on the same page, I'll pick you up some other clothes today."

Confusion wrinkles her face while she blinks several times. "On the same page? Sorry, you'll have to explain what's on the page before I can confirm or deny if I'm *on it* with you. And you have to use more than a few words to describe the page. I'll need to know why you killed those men. Who are you? And what are your intentions for Archer Sanford and me?"

Jack retrieves a toothbrush from his small toiletry bag and squeezes a dab of toothpaste onto it.

"Where did you get that toothbrush? The razor?" She shakes her head and stutters, "The w-whole bag?"

"Wal-Mart," he mumbles over his foam-filled mouth.

Frankie's gaze circumnavigates the room. Jackson's wearing black combat boots, but a pair of running shoes is by the bed. And he's wearing different jeans than he wore yesterday. She opens the TV console drawers.

"Why do you have clothes here?"

He spits and wipes his mouth. "Plan B."

"Jack, I need you to elaborate." Frankie tightens the sheet around her body. "You killed three men," she whispers.

"Are you going to run?" He crosses his arms, leaning into the bathroom door threshold.

She glances down at her sheet-clad body as if that's all the explanation he needs.

"If you fear for your life, that won't stop you," he says.

"I ..." She shakes her head. "I don't know if I should fear for my life. You won't tell me anything." Her voice escalates. "I just know that you *killed three men*!"

He flinches.

Tears fill her eyes as she shakes her head. "I just want to go home."

He retrieves his phone from the nightstand. "I wanted you to go home weeks ago."

"Fine. You were right." She bats away her tears. "Is that what you want to hear? I should have gone home when you told me to go home. I'm sorry. Just ... let me go home."

"He'll kill you, but not before he kills your parents and anyone he thinks is close to you."

"Why?"

"To protect his family. To seek revenge for what you've done to his daughter. But mostly, he'll do it to get to me."

Frankie swallows hard. "He doesn't know I had anything to do with his daughter."

He shrugs a shoulder. "Let's hope not."

"W-why would he want to get to you? Because you killed his men?"

"Because I'm the man who's going to kill him."

She continues to shake her head. Jackson could never have anticipated Frankie the way he wasn't ready for Ryn. But Frankie's here, and he can't pretend she doesn't matter.

"So *I* can go home," he adds to justify what he's done and still has to do.

A deep sadness fills her eyes. "Where's home?"

Jackson's blank expression gives nothing away. It's as if he doesn't know the answer. "I'm not going to hurt you." He grazes his knuckles across her cheek.

She closes her eyes.

"Please be here when I return so only the bad people die."

Frankie winces, but she doesn't open her eyes. He leaves her with a kiss on the crown of her head and a click of the door behind him.

CHAPTER TWENTY-FIVE
FRANCESCA

IF YOU WANT to know someone, ask what music they like. Music is a fingerprint on one's soul. Eighty-eight keys are infinitely more revealing than twenty-six letters.

I don't know much about Jack that can be put into words. But I've heard him play the piano, so I know what touches his soul.

That fingerprint keeps me in this motel room despite three dead men. Wearing his tee from the console drawer, I inspect every item of clothing in the room, every essential in his toiletry bag, and every nook and cranny that might hold a clue.

He didn't rent this room last night. He's had this space. A safe house?

I look for my purse and phone, but neither is in the room. Maybe they're in his car. Did I have my purse when Archer pulled me off the Ferris wheel?

Eloise.

Oh god ...

She'll be worried about me, especially if she discovers Jack is missing too.

I startle when Jack opens the door. He doesn't say anything. Bags in one hand and a gun in the other, he checks the room, behind the curtains and the bathroom. Then he holsters his gun.

He has a gun and a holster.

I have pepper spray.

"Where's my purse?"

"Back of my car."

"And my phone?"

He shrugs, setting the bags on the bed. "I disposed of it."

"Why?"

"Because he has your number." Jack slides a black backpack off his shoulder and retrieves his laptop. "Which means he can track you."

"Eloise will be worried sick. And she'll call my parents." I pull the clothes out of the sack.

"I took care of it." He sits on the bed and opens his laptop.

"What do you mean?"

"I've talked with her and said you were with me for a few days."

"You went to her house?"

He shakes his head. "Stopped by the senior center where she walks when it's hot."

I hold up the thong underwear he bought me. "I don't wear these."

"Fine." He shrugs, focusing on his computer.

"I like a bikini cut." I inspect the rest of the clothes. There's a small shirt, an oversized shirt, two extra small white tank tops, size two shorts, size six jeans, and a frumpy, medium prairie dress in stunning shades of mustard yellow and shit brown. "No bras?"

Jack smirks. "Is that a trick question? I know your nipples have an aversion to bras."

I frown before shrugging off his shirt. Jack eyes me while I don the dress.

"Ada wore more of a corseted dress. Sexy and forbidden. This is just …" I look down at the tent dress "…anti-sexy. A sister-wife vibe."

There's so much exhaustion in his eyes. He tries to smile but fails at infusing any believability into it.

"Tell me about her," I say softly.

A tiny worry line creases along the bridge of his nose. "Which her?"

I pull up the dress skirt and kneel on the opposite side of the bed, fiddling with the tag on the sleeve. I'd make another sister-wife reference if he weren't so tortured already. "Just…" I risk a glance at him "…tell me about the women in your life."

Jack closes his laptop, sets it aside, and rests his hands on the edge of the bed with his head bowed. "I shouldn't trust you or anyone at this point."

"But you do because I'm here. I'm in a dingy motel room with you and don't know your last name. I don't know why you kill people. I have every reason to leave. To run. Yet … I'm here because you haunt me with everything you've never said. If I trust you, a stranger, with my life, don't you think you can trust me with yours?"

After a few breaths, Jack's head bobs in a barely detectable nod. "I have a twin sister."

My heart skips on a silent gasp just as chills course along my skin in all directions. It's not possible that this man's path has crossed mine.

"We've been to hell and back too many times to count.

She's the only person I trust completely. I trust her with my life."

There's no more blinking back the tears. I let them fall. What if John would have trusted me with *his* life? Would I have failed him? Did I fail him by not being there for Steven? Somewhere along the way, should I have been the one to convince Steven that no girl's—no person's—opinion matters more than his right to feel worthy of love? Of *life*?

"My wife..." Jack continues, "...took everything bad inside of me and made it good. There wasn't anything I wouldn't do for her—except let her go. Even when I knew it was the only way to truly love her," he shakes his bowed head, "I just really wanted to have a chance at that kind of love. That kind of life."

When he doesn't continue, I struggle to find the right words. How did she die? Am I allowed to ask him that? Just when I find the courage to do just that, he continues.

"We have a daughter."

I swallow hard because I think I've known he has a family. The eyes never lie.

"I raised her alone. She has her mother's heart, passion, and ability to forgive the unforgivable." He lifts his head and stares out the crack in the curtains. "But she's me too." The hint of a smile touches his lips. "She's fierce and unrelenting. She's stubborn. Too smart for her own good." The muscles in his jaw flex. "And I failed her. I didn't protect her mom. I let my guard down. I showed vulnerability when the enemy showed patience." He rubs his temples. "So I have to be patient too. And it's unfathomably hard because I miss my life."

I don't know if I have the emotional capacity to formulate a response. He's told me so much, yet ... nothing at all. I *feel* him. But without clarity, I cannot understand him. Two feet are between us, yet I don't know how to bridge the divide. Jack's words carry an intimacy that feels almost sacred. He holds his life and memories in a guarded, impenetrable space. I think it's so guarded because he feels the fragility of those memories.

I understand.

My memories of John, Lynn, and Steven feel defenseless and I am the soldier tasked to keep them alive in some small way. Humans are a culmination of the love we share. If I let the memories die, I think I will die too.

"I was standing in line," I say, clearing the emotion from my throat, "at a CVS." I laugh through a few residual tears. "And the person in front of me was making small talk with the young man at the cash register. She said, 'Can you believe it's already the last day of November?' November thirtieth. My birthday. *John's* birthday. I don't acknowledge that day. And I've asked my parents never to acknowledge that day again. The mind instinctively tries to protect us. It's easy to let it block memories. Self-preservation is a good thing.

"But then, some overly chatty woman at a fucking CVS had to kick through the patched hole in my heart. And I just ... started crying." I run my hands through my hair and blow out a shaky breath. "It was a hemorrhaging pain that wouldn't stop. And a kind man behind me rested his hand on my shoulder—such a simple gesture. I didn't look back. I just grabbed his hand for dear life, so afraid that he would let go and I would feel the full weight of reality. The avalanche of grief, the suffocating, unbearable loneliness that I was half dead."

I bite my trembling lip for several seconds. "The guilt of being alive," I whisper.

Jack turns his head, eyeing me over his shoulder.

"He bought the notecards and Sharpies that I dropped on the floor and added a tissue box. Then he walked me to my car, but I was still shaking with grief. So he drove me home. He wasn't the most handsome man in the world. And he hadn't said more than a few words to me. But he had kind eyes and an even kinder touch. I kissed him. And I didn't want to know his name. I didn't care if he said a word to me. Several hours later, I woke up alone in my bed. Yet ... I didn't feel alone. I felt like my brother had a hand in ensuring I found the right people in my life when I needed them most."

"The dean's husband?" Jack asks.

I smile, wiping my cheeks. "Yes."

He narrows his eyes. "Do you think your brother is the reason our paths crossed?"

I shrug.

Jack's contemplative gaze drifts to the side.

"But I find myself in new territory," I say. "I want more."

His gaze returns to me with the obvious question on his face.

"But I'm afraid to ask your real name. I'm afraid to ask how your wife died. I'm afraid to ask why you're planning on killing Archer Sanford. Because I've never been invested in someone who doesn't have a familial obligation to love me back. I've always felt like needing someone means I am not enough. I am *less*."

I crawl toward him, trudging my way through this painful divide. "But when I'm with you," I press my palms to his cheeks, "I feel like I'm more. Wholly alive. And everything I told myself I didn't want a few weeks ago..." I touch his lips, "Well, it's all I want now."

The pads of my fingers trace his lips, and his eyes drift

shut, a silent surrender. "Jude Day," he whispers before opening his eyes. "My wife was killed by the people who trained me. And Archer needs to die so I can see my daughter again."

"Jude Day," I whisper, staring at his mouth while my fingers feather along his jaw.

"He had to die so that Jackson Knight could live."

I nod slowly. Jude Day became Jackson Knight. My Jack.

"How old is Jude Day?" My eyes flit to his.

"Thirty."

I nod again. "And Jackson?"

He turns his head and bites my thumb. "Older."

I smile before kissing his cheek. "And Jack?"

He lifts my dress over my head and tosses it onto the floor. "How old is Francesca Holter?"

"Forty-one."

He flatters me with his slow inspection of my naked body before an appreciative smile bends his mouth.

"Jack, how old are you?"

My words hang unacknowledged in the air while he removes his shirt.

His boots.

Pants.

And briefs.

With a ginormous level of confidence, he stands at the side of the bed. "How old do you think I am?"

I don't know. That's just it; he's a walking contradiction. From the neck down, he could pass for thirty-something. A-hot-as-fuck thirty-something. But the tiny lines along his face and the peppering of gray in his hair put him in his late forties ... early fifties?

"Cat got your tongue? No guess?"

My lazy, unabashed gaze leaves his erection, canvases his cut, tattooed torso, and settles on his handsome (and, yes, mature) face. "Fifty?"

"Fifty," he repeats. But it's not a confirmation. He's done this to me before.

I need to know. I need the truth. I want *more*.

Walking on my knees to the edge of the bed, I slide my hands along his chest to his shoulders. "Tell me."

He wets his lips, threading his fingers into my hair. "It's just a number," he whispers before kissing me.

I welcome every touch. His hand feathers down my backside, dipping between my legs. Jack plays *me* one note at a time. My fingers sink into his back, urging him on top of me.

He touches my lips before kissing them. His thumb drifts down my neck, and his lips follow. A taste follows every touch. Our bodies move in tune. A perfect rhythm. We're "Liberstraum."

"3 Nocturnes Opus Number 9."

"Claire de Lune."

We're a symphony of labored breaths and soft moans. Colliding flesh. A creaking bed.

He rolls us, so I'm hovering above him. I kiss the corner of his mouth and whisper, "Don't stop."

Jack grins, wrapping his arms around my body, holding me to him as close as possible. "I won't."

CHAPTER TWENTY-SIX
FRANCESCA

"You're watching him?" I ask, groggy, while lifting my head from Jack's abdomen.

He's holding his laptop high on his chest, angled to the side not to wake or move me. "I am."

I scoot toward his head to bury my face in his neck. "I *feel* music when you're inside of me."

He chuckles. "Chopsticks?"

I giggle, but my laughter dies when I turn my head and focus on the screenful of live video feeds.

Archer's office.

His house.

Private jet.

A feed that looks like a body cam.

The inside of an SUV.

I stiffen. "Did you see me? The day you shot his tires outside of the cafe, did you see me? Did you see Archer …"

"Trying to fuck you? Yes."

A hard knot forms in my stomach and another swells in my throat. I roll to the side and sit on the edge of the bed with my back to him. "I wasn't thinking about you," I whisper. "When I decided to get revenge, I wasn't—"

"I'm aware." Sometimes, Jack can be so blunt, so detached. He's mastered what I've tried and failed to do with the Sanfords.

His practiced indifference does little to lessen the shame I feel. Was I going to let Archer have sex with me? My shaky hand covers my mouth because I know the answer. "Did you set off the car alarm at the school?"

"Yes." Jack's continued forthrightness sends a shiver along my spine.

All I've wanted is for Molly Sanford to feel a fraction of the pain, embarrassment, and regret I feel right now. "I wanted revenge more than ... anything," I murmur.

"I get that. But you wanted it on your own terms. You were willing to fuck him, but were you willing to let him fuck you? Rape you?"

I cringe.

"Because I wasn't willing to let either scenario happen."

"Because we kissed?" I turn my head, resting my chin on my shoulder.

I can't kiss you if you're going to fuck him.

"Because you touched my piano."

Sliding the ugly brown dress over my head and down my body, I stand. I don't need further explanation. Jack has an intimate relationship with his piano. It's a window to his soul. Eighty-eight keys and an infinity of emotion. He plays those keys to remember his wife. He plays them to find closure. But he won't let the song end because that kind of love never dies.

And he let me touch his piano; he let me into his world from the first note.

"When are you ending Archer's life?"

"Soon."

I pad to the bathroom, stopping just inside the door. "Then what?"

"Then it's over."

THEN IT'S OVER.

Those three words will haunt me—maybe forever.

I don't ask a single follow-up question. I shower, and Jackson orders food. We eat on the bed with his computer and the live feeds in front of us, including the surveillance cameras around Eloise's garage. If they were pointed a little farther to the south, he would have footage of Molly Fucking Sanford burning down my brother's house.

I start to say something about that, but it doesn't matter now. So I step over every invisible line between us. They no longer matter. And I ask about what does matter.

"Where's your daughter?"

"In an undisclosed location." He takes a bite of his sandwich and then types a few lines into a notes app.

"How old is she?"

"Younger than you."

I shake my head before sipping my drink. "That's a relief. Forty is younger than me. Is she forty?"

"Nope." He stays focused on the cameras.

"Is she Livy or Ryn?"

Confusion clouds his eyes when he looks at me.

I shrug a shoulder. "I've thoroughly inspected your body. I could sketch your tattoos. All of them."

He casts his gaze on the mattress between us. "Livy."

"Livy," I echo him, stabbing my fork into my salad. "Ryn was your wife. And Gunner?"

A reluctant smile steals his lips before his eyes alight with something I know is a great memory. "Ryn's German Shepherd. He wasn't a fan of mine for a long time. Eventually, she convinced me to make a 'permanent' commitment to him. And in return, he would be loyal to me forever."

"And?"

Jack chuckles. "Hell no. He hated me 'til the day he died."

I giggle. "I almost had a dog." I shovel wilted lettuce into my mouth.

"Sounds like a close call."

"It was. Right after I got my master's degree, my roommate decided to move to Greece. She had a golden retriever. Goldilocks. 'Goldie.' And she couldn't take her to Greece, so she begged me to keep her."

"What happened?" He takes another bite of his sandwich.

"After Natalie left for Greece, Goldie ran away."

"You lost her dog?"

"No." I scrunch my nose. "She ran away. Broke through the screen door. She had on one of those 'have-your-people-call-my-people' tags with my phone number and Natalie's. But no one called."

"Did you post flyers?"

"I had her photo printed on milk cartons."

Jack rolls his eyes.

"Par for the course. Everyone leaves me." I sigh. "When I decided to get my doctorate instead of finding a mate and popping out babies, the universe knew I was giving conventionalism the middle finger. And it's not for a lack of trying. I've put forth a capital E for effort. I have never broken up with a guy. I've always been the one getting dumped. Then my brother left me. Lynn ... Steven."

Jack drops the rest of his sandwich in the sack. "Jesus, Frankie. That's a depressing story."

"You're saying that to deflect from the train wreck that is your life. I have never killed anyone. I haven't lost a spouse or a lover. I've never had to change my name or identity. And I've never lived out of a garage."

"It's like you haven't lived at all."

I smirk. "Touché."

After a few seconds, silence seeps into the room. As much as we try to use humor to escape from the reality that we are staying at a one-star motel because Jack killed three men to save me from Archer, the truth oozes to the surface like a wound that won't stop bleeding.

"You said you've killed more people than you can count. You said it casually when you knew I wouldn't believe you."

He clicks on one of the live cameras and zooms in on Archer and the man with him. Then he glances at me.

"I believe you," I whisper.

Jack gives it some thought. "It was my job. I protected people by removing threats."

"Threats to whom?"

"Families of agents."

I nod slowly. "You were CIA? FBI?"

"I was nothing. We didn't officially exist. We started out protecting DEA agents' families. The government reacts— retaliates. The satisfaction from revenge is short-lived. It changes nothing."

"Yeah," I whisper.

"But imagine intercepting that letter from Molly. Imagine removing her from your nephew's life. Imagine him still living. That's what I did. I saved lives by taking lives. Eliminating the threat before anyone died."

"Why is Archer a threat to your family?"

He leans back, resting his head on the wall. "I left the organization, but not without making enemies. I didn't realize how many enemies until my wife died in a car accident. I always suspected it wasn't an accident, but everyone thought I was crazy. Turns out, I wasn't crazy. It wasn't an accident. The organization dissolved after I left. But unbeknownst to me, alliances were made. My wife died because of me. And my daughter was a target too. So, she's taken on a new identity in a new location. The world thinks she's dead. She has a headstone in a cemetery. But I can't see her unless I end this, for her safety. So that's what I've been doing for the past year. Removing the threats, one at a time. And I believe Archer is the last one. If he's gone, the remaining few will scatter because they won't have the incentive or means to come after me or my family. Archer funded the people who killed my wife and came after my daughter."

This isn't real. I'm holed up in a motel with an assassin. Weeks earlier, I drove to Boone to go through my brother's family's belongings. Sell the house. And return home to find a new job. "What do you need from me?" I set my half-eaten salad aside and rub the back of my neck.

Jack eyes me with confusion. "I need you to do what I say so you don't die."

I laugh. This just ... isn't real. Die? I'm a music theory professor. Death, to me, means cancer, a heart attack, or a stroke. Unexpected death means a car accident. Lottery-statistical death means a drive-by shooting while walking through the rougher areas of Chicago at night or being at a mall when a shooter decides to take innocent lives. Being an actual target doesn't even occupy space in my head, no matter how hard I try to comprehend his words.

"What does 'not dying' involve?" I ask.

"Staying put."

"In this room?"

He nods.

"For how long?"

"As long as it takes."

I stand, shaking my head. "That's not an acceptable answer. Are we talking days, weeks?"

"As long as it takes." Jack's patience exceeds mine by miles.

"My family will look for me."

"Not if you let them know you're taking time to process. Taking a trip. A drive across the country to put yourself back together."

I cross my arms. "How do I tell them this? A messenger pigeon?"

"It would take too long to train a homing pigeon. I'm thinking of a burner phone," he deadpans.

"You're not funny."

"No?" Jack twists his lips. "I've been told my humor is subtle yet refreshing."

I make a weak effort to smile, but I can't. "Nobody looks for you? You just take him out, and nobody investigates? You're not a wanted criminal?"

"I've been a wanted criminal for most of my life. A nameless, faceless criminal who leaves no trace."

"So what happens when it's over? You go home? Where is home?"

He shakes his head. "I can't give you that."

"Why not?" I feel a pang of disappointment.

"Deniability."

"Deniability? For what ... if I'm captured and tortured for information about you and your family?"

Jack doesn't respond. That's my answer.

"You've lived an awful life," I murmur.

His gaze drifts from me to the window, and he gently nods. "But I wouldn't trade it for anyone else's life." He jerks his head to the bed and glances at his phone. "I have to go."

"Where?"

"Can't say." He hands me another phone. "Call your parents. Don't give anything away. Lie."

I stare at it for a few seconds before taking it.

"Lie like your life and theirs depends on it."

"Because it does?" I glance up at him.

"I'm the best at what I do."

He kills people. Is that something to brag about?

"Me too," I say with a shrug.

It takes him a minute, but when he gets it, he hums in agreement. "You're brilliant. A virtuoso." He drags his middle finger down my nose, the pads of his other fingers closing my eyes. That finger lingers on my lower lip while he ducks his head. "Exceptional in every way," he whispers before kissing me.

Our noses rub together after the soft kiss.

"I ..." The words catch in my throat because they scare me.

He scares me. Losing him terrifies me. So maybe I save myself—my heart—if I don't say it.

Jack narrows his eyes, waiting for me to finish.

I smile, keeping my gaze on his chest while I rest my hands on it. "I will wait here like you asked me to do."

He doesn't seem to buy it or press me on it. With a slight nod, he turns, slides on his holster, grabs his computer, and leaves me with an aching heart and an unspoken declaration of love.

CHAPTER TWENTY-SEVEN
JACKSON

"It's time to disappear for a few weeks," Jackson says to his sister the second she answers the phone.

"Are you still paranoid or has something changed?" Jessica sounds condescending.

"I took out three of his bodyguards."

"Why?"

"Doesn't matter. Just disappear for a while."

"Because of her?"

"Her? Are you referencing yourself? Livy? Surely, not just Francesca."

"So much for an easy target."

"Archer's never been an easy target," he snaps.

"Because your paranoia has made it so difficult." Jessica sighs.

"Paranoia? Like how everyone called me paranoid after my wife died in an accident that wasn't an accident? Had I followed my gut on it, I would have been more protective with Livy."

"More protective? I think the only way you could have been more protective would have been to lock her in a safe."

"Exactly."

"Jackson ... stop."

He blows a long breath, passing several bikers while noticing he's driving twenty over the speed limit. The bikers flip him the bird in his rearview mirror. "Frankie got in over her head with Archer, so I had to step in."

"And you took out three of his men, but not him? How? Why?"

"I had to extract her before I could get access to him. The point is, if taking out his tires didn't already alert him that he's dealing with one of his own, three clean shots taking out his men left no room for speculation."

"We'll disappear, but not for long. *End this.*"

Jackson rubs his temples while his other hand remains white-knuckled on the steering wheel. "I'm tired ... so fucking tired."

"Yeah," she whispers. "Just come home alive."

"I don't ..." He bites his lips together.

"You don't what?"

"I don't care about that. Not like I used to. If I can give Livy the opportunity for a normal life again, that's all that matters."

"She won't want it if you're not in it."

Jackson knows she's right. He also knows Jessica, of all people, has been in his position. Worse. Jessica has endured so much worse.

"Love you," he says in defeat.

"Alive, Jude," she calls him by his given name when she needs him to know she's serious. "Understood?"

He lets up on the gas while passing the stone-embellished sign at Rhodale's city limits. "I've always understood. It's all about luck."

"Jude—"

"Disappear, Jess." He ends the call.

Archer's at his office. Jackson gives a little more breathing room today instead of taking his usual parking spot across the street. Archer knows he's a target. His new security detail outside of the building has doubled in size and no longer carries concealed weapons. They have automatic rifles gripped in their hands—presidential-level detail with earpieces and bulletproof vests.

"I'm fucked," Jackson mumbles.

Maybe Livy lives on an island for the rest of her life. He'd have a better chance of threading a carrot into a cockroach's vagina than getting a clean shot of Archer.

Hours later, a group of six men in suits exit the building. Archer's in the center of the cluster, an impossible target. He gets into the middle of the three SUVs, and they pull away from the curb in a motorcade.

Jackson follows them to Archer's house. The middle SUV pulls into a garage, closing the door behind it. Shades block every window in the place. He doesn't anticipate Archer hanging out on his deck barbecuing anytime soon, so he heads back to the motel.

When he opens the door, Frankie doesn't move. She's asleep with Wheel of Fortune on the TV. He kicks off his boots and slides into bed with her, spooning her backside and nuzzling his face in her hair while his arm snakes around her waist.

"Is he dead?"

"No."

"Why not?"

Jackson exhales. "He's untouchable at the moment."

"What does that mean?" Frankie rolls to face him. She's the epitome of an island in the storm.

"I think I'd have better luck taking out the president."

JEWEL E. ANN

Frankie frowns. "Because of me."

He closes his eyes since she's all about the eyes, reading into them too often. "Because he just is."

"I can get close to him."

Jackson opens his eyes.

Frankie chews on her bottom lip with palpable nervousness and indecision. "He doesn't know about us. He abandoned me last night. I bet he's been blowing up my phone, wherever it is."

"Yes, that's a great idea. I'll give you the gun, and you can kill him. Then you can go to prison. Nice knowing you."

Her gaze drops to his chest. "I'm in this too. I want to help. I have nothing to lose."

"Your life."

"What life?"

"A long one with possibilities you can't even imagine yet."

She rests her hand over his heart. "It's my fault he's untouchable. You just don't want to say it." Her eyes shift to meet his gaze. "So I'm saying it. And you can't deny it. I won't kill him. But I can expose him. I can get you access to him. I can find out where he's going to be. I can lure him wherever you want."

"You're not bait."

She fists his shirt and tugs it with frustration. "But I could be."

He inspects her, looking deep into her eyes like she does to him. Not because he's giving it serious consideration; he's trying to figure out how someone so brilliant can let their mind go into such a dark place.

"I know his weakness."

220

Jackson doesn't ask because it doesn't matter. He's not letting her see Archer Sanford ever again.

"It's me," she whispers. "He knows I know his game. And he hates that I play it better than him. It makes him desperate and reckless."

"It makes him dangerous and unpredictable."

"So—"

"No," Jackson snaps.

"Then give me a gun."

Jackson sits up, resting his elbows on his bent knees and his head in his hands. "We're done talking about this."

"I don't think we are."

His wife wasn't like this. Ryn got upset with Jackson, but she also knew when he needed space, when he needed her to stop talking and stop pushing. Frankie doesn't back down.

"I'm the only card you have to play."

"It's not a game." He digs his fingers into his scalp, fighting a headache.

She crawls in front of him, constantly invading his space. "I am not living in this disgusting motel room for the rest of my life. Maybe you have the patience of a saint, but I don't. So if you don't have a plan, we go with mine."

"There is no *we!*" He lifts his head and grabs her wrists. "So just give me some goddamn space to figure this out."

After the initial shock wears off, she jerks her arms from his grip. "Have at it." She climbs off the bed, slips on her sandals, and leaves the motel with a hard door slam in her wake.

"Shit," he grumbles, shoving his feet into his boots and chasing her. "Frankie."

"Go think, Jack." Frankie stomps toward the road as if she has somewhere to go and the means to get there.

He blows out a long breath filled with mumbled expletives.

"I can hear you." She keeps marching.

"Then you know I'm not in the mood to chase your ass down the road."

"Go back to the motel. Fight *your* war. Don't let me and my stupid ideas get in the way."

"I just needed space because you were all up in my face."

"I'm trying to give you all the space in the world, but you're following me. Jack!" she screams when he grabs her arm, turns her around, and tosses her over his shoulder to haul her back to the motel room.

"I knew … I just knew, from the day we met, that you were going to be a royal pain in my ass," he says.

"I'm not in your face!" She pounds her fists into his back. "And I'm not up your ass."

Thud. Thud. Thud.

Her unrelenting blows don't phase him. He kicks the motel room door shut behind them and tosses her onto the bed. Frankie's eyes narrow, and steam billows from her flared nostrils.

Jack rests a hand on his hip and sighs. "I don't know what to do with you."

"Let me go."

He shakes his head. "Can't."

"Because you think Archer is going to hurt me?"

Again, he shakes his head.

"Because you think I'm going to blow your cover?" She crosses her arms, flipping him attitude with every word.

Another headshake.

"Then what? What is your problem?"

"You. You're my problem."

She scowls. "It's not your job to protect me. You're not my savior. You said it yourself; there is no *we*."

"I lied," he whispers.

Frankie's sheer stubbornness sends the start of another word out of her mouth, but she swallows it back just as quickly.

"I can't let you go because I don't *want* to let you go. Sometimes, I am Baines. And sometimes I am Alisdair. And your stubbornness is most certainly Ada. I can't stop thinking about you. And I can't let you go. My feelings are far from pure, and they're undoubtedly irrational. So that makes it my job to protect you ... to save you. So here *we* are in a place I swore I would never be again." He holds his hands to his sides in surrender for a few seconds before letting them drop. A white flag.

Frankie's jaw works overtime. Jack can feel the intensity of her warring thoughts and flared ego. She is Jessica. She is *him*.

He waits.

She deflates an inch at a time, a slow surrender. "We're in a tiny motel room with one bed. You might not want me up in your business, but I don't have a choice because you won't let me leave."

"You're right."

Frustration continues to line her face even though her body is relaxed. She's still ready for the fight that he's not giving her. "I'm hungry," she says gruffly.

"I'll order dinner," he replies with the utmost patience.

That patience seems to irritate her. "And I need to exercise. I have to burn off this energy, or I'll lose my mind."

"Okay."

Frankie takes a quick breath as if she anticipated a rebuttal, but she releases it with more control. And her words lose their fight, but they're no less sincere. "And my parents' anniversary is in two weeks. I *will* be home for it. They made me promise I would end my 'time away' by then." She pulls back her shoulders to show authority, to show Jackson she's not asking for permission to leave in two weeks. It's happening no matter what.

Jackson suspects his sister's patience has an even shorter timeframe, so he returns several tiny nods even though he has no clue how to get to Archer Sanford in the next two weeks.

He steps closer to the bed.

"I think I owe it to my dignity not to let you use your body to persuade me to change my mind."

He eyes her. "How would I use my body to persuade you?"

Frankie's blue eyes inspect the length of his body as though she's searching for the answer to this question. "I get ..."

"Get what?" He slides his hands into his back pockets.

"Distracted."

"My body distracts you?"

"The way you've chosen to mark yourself distracts me. You have many forms of self-expression, some rather subtle and nuanced. I find every one of them enrapturing."

Jackson regards her with no discernible expression because he finds everything about Frankie equally nuanced. Intriguing. And unexpectedly disarming.

"You make an eloquent appeal. However, I just want to know if I take off my clothes, will you take off yours?"

The corner of her mouth quirks, and Jackson feels victorious. She's strong, maybe even militant at times, but he's her weakness. Everyone has at least one. He has several, and they're all women.

"For an old man, you sure have a lot of sexual stamina."

He shrugs a shoulder. "Making up for lost time before I die."

"Lost time?" Frankie stands and slides her hands in the pockets of the prairie dress, holding it out to the side until it looks like a tent. "And this does it for you?"

"I think we've established what *does it for me*."

Frankie grins. The real deal. She doesn't attempt to restrain it as she points a finger at herself. "Me? I do it for you?" She's teeming with confidence, even in the prairie dress.

Jackson's wife struggled with confidence because an awful man beat her down. Jackson built her up, piece by piece. In the process, she made him human again. A lover. A friend. A husband. A father.

Two very different women. The man who married Ryn would not have known what to do with Francesca Holter. She wouldn't have complemented him the way Ryn did. She would have challenged him in all the wrong ways. Jackson would have seen Francesca Holter as competition. He would have seen her as an equal in some ways—an over-achiever with a chip on her shoulder and a complete inability to stay in a relationship. Their similarities would have been a toxic combination.

Not now.

"Your expressions," she whispers. "They break my heart."

Jackson shakes his head, trying to brush off whatever look she thinks is heartbreaking.

Frankie turns her back to him and slides the curtains another inch, letting the setting sun slash through the opening. "Let's go out to eat."

"If I thought it was a good idea for us to go out to eat, do you think we'd be sleeping in this motel room?"

"I don't know. For every single thing I *know about you, there are a hundred things* I don't know about you. I know you're okay with sleeping in a garage and a shitty motel. I hope it's out of necessity, but maybe you have an aversion to luxury. Maybe you don't have a romantic bone in your body." She chuckles. "Maybe you're sexy and romantic on the surface by sheer accident."

"Accident?"

Frankie presses her hand to the window like she's in a prison, longing for her freedom. "You have a sexy body, but I don't think you have that body to be sexy. Watching and listening to you play your piano is like tantric sex. Well, it's what I imagine tantric sex feels like."

"What is tantric sex?" Jackson cringes the second he asks the question.

How does she bait him into these conversations?

"A fellow professor and her husband went to a retreat. I don't think it was called a retreat, but that's what I had in my head when she explained it. From what I gathered, it's very powerful lovemaking. The fusion of desire, sexual energy, and passion aligns with your heart and spirit. It's healing and transcendent. An orgasmic state that feels psychedelic."

Jackson presses his lips together to keep from showing any discernible reaction.

She smirks. "But I've never been married. I've never been in a committed relationship, so it was laughable to me. Then..." she twists her lips for a second "...I watched you play your piano with your shirt off. And you asked me to play the same piano without wearing any clothes. And I realized we share something intimate through music."

Jackson opens the door. He's not into this conversation.

"Will you settle for the drive-thru and eating in the car?"

Frankie rolls her eyes. "Stop sweeping me off my feet."

Tacos and a shared side of nachos in the front seat of his BMW.

Their first official date.

"It's a little tacky that you drove us back here to eat in the motel parking lot. The least you could have done was drive us somewhere secluded with a view. I might've felt more inclined to do something like give you head or let you see my nipples."

Jackson snorts with his fist at his mouth while he swallows before choking on his food.

Frankie crumples her empty wrapper and stuffs it into the sack while slipping off her shoes and placing her bare feet on the dash, her dress sliding to the top of her thighs. Jackson hasn't felt this mesmerized by a woman since Ryn crawled around on the floor, cleaning the bathroom while unintentionally shaking her backside. She was hired to clean the house. And he was in the middle of a renewed vow of celibacy.

The timing couldn't have been worse, much like now.

Life and the powers that be don't seem to give two fucks about timing.

"I saw your nipples the first day we met. They're always excited to see me. But I'm intrigued by your other offer." He wads up his wrapper and adds it to the sack. "Let's go find a view I like." He backs the car out of the parking spot.

"I need to like the view too."

As he pulls onto the main road, Jackson chuckles. "You'll be staring at my balls."

CHAPTER TWENTY-EIGHT
FRANCESCA

Jack finds a secluded lookout over a lake. A few boat lights are in the distance, with the last shade of sunlight fading to darkness. He puts his car in *Park* and unbuckles. Then he presses a button, and his seat slides back.

I scratch my cheek, hiding my grin. When I risk a glance at Jack, he lifts his eyebrows.

"Well, here we are with a nice view in a secluded spot." He unbuttons his jeans. "It's *the least* I could do. Your words. So I believe *the least* you can do is follow through with your intentions."

I press the button to release my seat belt. "I thought someone your age would turn me down, citing something to the effect of 'front-seat blowjobs are unbecoming of a lady. And you, my darling Francesca, are too much of a lady. I can't let you commit such a salacious act. Let's find a song befitting the moment and dance under the full moon. Holding you in my arms fulfills my heart's desire more than oral sex ever could.'"

Jack slowly blinks at me with no perceivable reaction to my words. "You lost me at *someone your age*."

Making duck lips, I tap my chin. "Of which I don't know. So I don't know how I lost you there."

"You're right." He drags down the zipper of his jeans. "You lost me at the part where front-seat blowjobs are unbecoming of a lady."

I frown. It's a little fake, but I'm not sucking his dick with a smile, even if I'm happy to do it.

Standards matter.

I lean over the console and slide my fingers into the waist of his briefs to free him.

Before I expose him, he drags in a sharp breath and slowly releases it, stopping my hands from going further. "What song?"

I tip my head back and gaze up at him, resting my hands on his thighs. "Huh?"

Jack stares out the windshield. "If we dance under the full moon, which is only a three-quarter moon, what song is befitting of the moment?"

I sit up, grinning out of control while Jack tries to act like he's making a huge sacrifice.

He's not.

He's being incredibly romantic.

I snatch his phone and bring up his music app while hopping out of the car. He takes his time. When I find the right song, I set the phone on the hood and slide my hands around his neck.

Jack looks over my head at the lake but can't hide his tiny grin. As Patty Griffin starts to sing "Heavenly Day," I softly sing the words.

No clouds.

No trouble.

The smile on Jack's face.

Yeah, it's enough for me.

With his hands around my waist and our bodies swaying to the music, I rest my ear against his heart.

Archer Sanford doesn't scare me.

The thought of dying doesn't scare me.

The only thing that scares me is falling in love for the first time since Aiden Walker over twenty-five years ago.

I lift onto my toes, resting my lips next to his ear. "I'm not wearing a bra."

"I know."

"I'm not wearing *anything* under this dress."

"I know."

"Then what are you waiting for?" I ask.

"For the song to end."

I grin, kissing his earlobe.

While the song reaches its last few lines, Jack gathers my dress in his hands, dragging it up my legs until his fingers brush my naked ass. His lips whisper along my cheek.

With the last drawn-out "Heavenly Day," he lifts it over my head.

I close my eyes, feeling the warm breeze wash over my skin while his hands frame my face. "My brother and Lynn danced to that song at their wedding. I caught the bouquet." Opening my eyes, I chuckle. "Guess I proved the meaning behind that tradition is not accurate."

"You're not the marrying type?" He tilts his head.

"Apparently not."

"And not the girlfriend type?"

I *love* where he's going with this line of questioning. My heart has never been one to swoon for anything but a brilliantly composed piece of music. Until now …

"Just the girl I kiss good night."

Yes!

Jack's maturity bleeds through in his patience. It didn't in the bathroom at Eloise's house, but tonight, he's perfectly content taking his time. His phone plays another song. Cowboy Junkies' "Blue Moon." His kiss is soft and slow while his hands skate along my arms to my backside. We begin to sway again.

The dirt and grass under my feet are a cool contrast to the warmth of his hands and lips and the playful tease of his tongue against mine. Every moment with Jack feels like a contrast of senses. I steal this perfect moment and pretend my life hasn't been a tragic dumpster fire for the past six months.

"Jude, Jackson, Jack ..." I unbutton his jeans and drag down the zipper while kissing his neck. "You might be the greatest experience of my life." I glance up at him while sliding down the front of his briefs. "Does that make me pathetic?"

He blinks slowly, a heavy, drunk blink, while my hand wraps around his erection.

"Or does it mean you're extraordinary?"

He wets his lips while the corners of his mouth quirk into a sly grin. "Maybe both."

I bite my lip to hide my grin. The playful side of Jack has helped mend me in a way I can't properly articulate with words. I just *feel* it.

His smile fades, and his middle finger draws that familiar invisible line down my nose before stopping at my lips. "But you have it backward. I am the pathetic one. *You* are by far the most extraordinary one."

I wrap my lips around him and follow through with my original offer.

He stops me when he's close to release. We kiss, letting the intensity ebb and flow.

"Jack ..." I start to say those words. Those three words. Everything inside of me feels ready to burst with unspoken emotions.

He kisses my neck and chest, turning us so I'm backed into his car door. In one smooth move, he lifts me and fills me.

"Jack ..." I try again.

He pumps into me, offering a labored, "Hmm?"

I love you.

"Just ..." My mind blurs. The moment engulfs me. All coherent thoughts dissolve. "Don't stop."

He doesn't. Then he does, but only to slow the moment, to fully enjoy the give and take—the thrill of riding that edge of pleasure. And the fear of knowing when it's over, we can no longer pretend the world is on pause. The awful, grievous reality will seep back into our existence.

My fingers sink into his back, and he grips my legs tighter.

"I love you," I whisper. Barely a whisper. It's more like a loud thought. An exhale with my orgasm that sounds like those three words.

Complete mental hysteria.

Jack thrusts into me harder. And I hope his erratic movements and tiny groans block out my *loud thoughts*.

When he stills, glutes rock hard, lips consuming mine, I say a prayer. God hasn't been the best at answering them. Or maybe he has answered them, and I haven't been the best at accepting his answer.

Please say Jack didn't hear me. Or please strip my words from his memory. PLEASE!

"Frankie," he whispers, out of breath. Keeping me pinned to the car, his hands find my face again. "Frankie ...

Frankie ... Frankie ..." He showers my face with kisses and gently rubs his face against mine.

It's affectionate, intimate, and a little heartbreaking because I feel him clinging to this moment as much as I am.

My hands cover his when his forehead comes to rest against mine. "I'm afraid one day soon you won't kiss me good night."

He lifts his head, a sad expression stealing his handsome face while he nods gently. "Me too."

I don't cry, but I want to. I *need* to. My body needs to release these emotions to regain some semblance of control, but not now. Not in front of him.

On the way back to the motel, Jack reaches for my hand without taking his eyes off the road. When he squeezes it, my heart constricts.

I don't say anything when we get to the motel room. Instead, I head straight for the shower, locking the bathroom door behind me. And I hope the water and loud fan drown out my gentle sobs.

CHAPTER TWENTY-NINE
JACKSON

Love is a fickle emotion, especially choosing to love someone who is not family. It's the kind of love that feels like a real choice.

Jackson didn't miss Frankie's words.

I love you.

He remembers falling in love with Ryn against all better judgment. And when she died—when he spent days at her grave, sleeping on her grave—he swore he'd never let his heart fall like that again. He had his sister and his daughter. They were all his heart could take. Ryn's death didn't just break his heart; it killed a part of it. A spot that would never come alive for anyone else.

Whatever he feels for Frankie can't be love. Even if it's familiar, like the emotions he felt when he met his wife, it can't be. At best, it's an imposter kind of love.

A really good imposter.

It's awakened his hunger for normalcy again. It's awakened his desire for the kind of intimacy that takes over like a storm raging out of control.

He turns the handle to the bathroom, but it's locked. As he opens his mouth to say something, two hard knocks are at the motel room door. Jack retrieves his gun and peeks out the window from the curtain, but he can only see someone's shoulder and part of their leg—dressed in all black.

Opening the door slowly, he aims the barrel of his gun through the crack first.

"Nice place ya got here," the irritatingly familiar voice says.

Jackson opens the door but keeps his gun pointed at the man. "What the fuck are you doing here? And where is my daughter?"

Slade Wylder, the asshole who stole his daughter, crosses his arms.

"It would appear I'm here to dig your old ass out of this mess. And *my wife* is in good hands."

Jessica. The only person trustworthy enough to watch Jackson's daughter is his sister.

"You can put down your gun."

Jackson shakes his head. "Nah. I'm good."

Slade scratches his scruffy jaw. "She's pregnant." He grins with pride.

Fucker.

"Yeah. I heard you stuck your dick in my daughter again. I might need to remove it to feel better about the world again."

"Speaking of dicks. I heard someone has willingly chosen to fondle your gray balls. Where is she? I can't wait to meet her. How's your memory? Do you remember to take your pill so you can have a nice four-hour erection?" He brushes past Jackson, ignoring the gun pointed at his head. "Does she know you're a grandpa?" Slade turns his head, eyes narrowed while hearing the shower and fan. "She's here? You've taken her hostage?"

Jackson shuts the door and holsters his gun.

Slade picks up the prairie dress Frankie discarded on the bed before entering the bathroom. His mouth bends into a smirk, and Jackson wants to wipe it from his face with a firm fist.

"Sexy," Slade says, tossing the dress back onto the bed.

"Go home."

"Can't." Slade inspects the rest of the room before sitting on the end of the bed, hands folded between his spread legs. "Jess said to let her know when they can leave."

They.

Jess and Livy expect this to end so she and Slade can resume a normal life, out of hiding, with real jobs. Kids in school. Barbecues with neighbors.

Jackson wants that too. It's what he's always wanted. It's the reason he's gone so long without seeing his family. But now that he's at the end, finishing the job feels impossible. And the last thing he needs is Livy's husband losing his life. She would never forgive him.

"I've got it handled."

"You're staying in a motel that probably has bedbugs and cockroaches. You look tired. The kind of tired that someone looks before they're lowered into the grave." He blows out a long breath. "I promised Livy I'd handle this."

"Well," Jackson surveys the parking lot before closing the blinds, "looks like you lied to her. She won't be happy about that. But if you want a nice room at The Four Seasons and wait for me to finish this, I'll let you take the credit. I love my daughter so much I'm willing to let her think you're her hero."

"I saved your life ... and hers."

Jackson shakes his head. "You took a bullet because you were clumsy."

Slade eyes him, and the truth is exchanged, but neither will make the other admit it.

"You left me to die," Slade says.

Jackson nods several times while leaning against the door and crossing his arms. "But you just *had* to hold on for the paramedics." He rolls his eyes.

"Who would put his dick in your daughter if I died?"

Jackson fists his hands and steps toward his son-in-law just as the bathroom door opens.

A wide-eyed Frankie wrapped in a towel stares at Slade.

Wearing a punchable smirk, Slade's gaze slides to Jackson. "Are you going to introduce me to your piano teacher?"

"No." Jackson opens the door. "Go home."

"Jack?" Frankie says his name slowly.

"Jehovah's Witness. He was just leaving. I told him we were both going to hell. Unsavable savages." Jackson knows Slade won't say anything revealing to Frankie because he doesn't know what she knows or what's safe to share.

"I'm Francesca." She holds her towel with one hand and combs her hair with her other. "How do you know Jack?"

Slade eyes Jackson.

"Why did you tell a Jehovah's Witness that I'm your piano teacher? I mean ... I could teach you a lot, but that's beside the point."

Jackson narrows his eyes at Frankie.

Slade sniggers.

"You can't tell me who you are, can you?" She gives Slade a curious expression, lips corkscrewed.

Again, Slade looks to Jackson for a response but gets nothing.

She shrugs. "Well, you're nice to look at, so—"

"Christ, Frankie, just go back in the bathroom and put some fucking clothes on." Jackson drops his head and rubs the back of his neck.

She flashes Slade a grand smile while snagging one of Jackson's T-shirts from the drawer. Then she slips it over her head and lets the towel drop to the floor after the tee swallows her petite body.

"Are you staying?" she asks Slade. "Jack and I spoon, so one side of the bed is free."

"Francesca!" Jackson grumbles. "Slade is my daughter's ..." He can barely say the word without choking on it.

"I'm her husband," Slade says, clearly feeling confident it's okay to share that information.

Frankie's jaw drops. "Livy is one lucky girl."

"A word." Jackson grabs Frankie's hand and pulls her outside, shutting Slade in the motel room alone.

She crosses her arms. "What a lovely surprise. Is he here to help? He looks helpful. Quite capable. And why didn't you mention that Livy has a husband? I don't see his name tattooed on you anywhere. But seriously, did you tell him I'm your piano teacher? I'm flattered. Really."

Jackson waits patiently, unenthused by her spiel. "Are you done?"

She presses her lips together and nods. "For now, but I reserve the right to follow-up questions."

"No more questions. I'm not answering the ones you asked. I just need you to listen and do exactly as I say. Can you do that?"

He knows the answer is no, but he hopes she'll attempt it anyway.

Frankie shrugs a shoulder.

Jackson frowns. "That guy in there? I don't like him. So

you don't like him. He's supposed to be protecting my daughter, but he's fucking that up by thinking I need his help more than she needs his protection. He's not staying with us. Don't engage with him. Don't look at him. I will probably kill him if he doesn't do as I say."

Her brows shoot up her forehead.

He opens the door and drags her back into the motel room. "Time to go," he says matter-of-factly to Slade, keeping the door open.

"Livy wanted me to show you photos of Wylder. Do you want to see them?" He holds up his phone.

Fuck.

"Who's Wylder?" Frankie asks because she can't follow simple instructions.

"Jackson's grandson," Slade says.

Jackson gives Slade a look. His daughter doesn't know how to play fairly. She knew Jackson would be upset about Slade's arrival, so she used one of Jackson's greatest weaknesses to soften his reaction.

"Jack," Frankie whispers before pressing a hand to her mouth.

He swears her eyes are welling with tears.

"You're a grandpa? H-how old *are* you?"

"Fif—" Slade starts to speak.

"I will *end* you. Got it?" Jackson warns Slade.

"I want to see Wylder. How old is he? Do you have a picture of Livy too?" Frankie bleeds estrogen all over the motel room floor.

Jackson misses the woman who danced naked with him and sucked his cock with great enthusiasm. This Frankie looks ready to bawl her eyes out and run to the local craft store to buy yarn to knit his grandson a stuffed bear.

"He's eighteen months." Slade shows her his phone. A phone Jackson can't call, just like he can't contact Livy because the world believes she and Slade are dead. That's what's kept them safe and alive.

"Oh, my goodness. Look at that blond hair." Again, she gasps.

"That's Livy." Slade beams when he shows her a picture of Jackson's daughter.

He can't take it any longer. Jackson steps behind Frankie to look at the photos. He's not going to cry, but it hurts like hell. Livy looks radiant. And happy. She's the most beautiful woman in the world. And Wylder, with his shaggy hair that's nearly white, is a spitting image of Livy. *Of Ryn ...*

"We just told Wylder about the baby," Slade says.

Double fuck.

Frankie spins around, too overwhelmed with emotion to speak.

Jackson tries not to look at her, but she's demanding his full attention, so he glances down at her with a bored expression. Neutral. Unaffected. He's done nothing wrong. "Apparently, he's knocked up my daughter *again*. See why I'm going to have to kill him?"

"Well, as tempting as a threesome with the old man sounds, I'm going to grab food and get some sleep," Slade says, pocketing his phone.

Frankie turns. "Where are you staying?"

Slade chuckles. "There's no way I'd share that information."

She rolls her eyes. "He's joking about killing you."

Slade heads toward the door. "He's not."

When the door shuts behind him, Frankie returns her attention to Jackson. "You have a family. *Grandchildren.*"

Her flat hands rest on his chest. "It's time to go home. Let me help you end this."

Tension pulls at his brow. "I'm going to shower."

"Jack ..."

He shuts the bathroom door.

CHAPTER THIRTY
FRANCESCA

"WE'RE NOT TALKING ABOUT IT," Jackson says when he slides into bed after his shower. He rests his hands on his chest and stares at the ceiling while I shut off the television.

"Not talking about what? Your family? Your age? My willingness to help you kill Archer. The mind-blowing sex we had by the lake earlier? Why you act like you despise your son-in-law?"

"Yes. All of it." He rolls toward me and pulls me into his arms, scissoring his legs with mine. "Except for the sex. We can talk about that."

"I was pretty good tonight." I kiss his chest. "Well above average. You were okay. You could have washed your car before pinning my naked body to it. And I feel like you could have said thank you for the blowjob. But now that I know you're a grandpa, I feel a little bad. You could have fractured a hip, thrown out your back, or gotten a hernia from holding the weight of my body for so long."

"I'm a young grandfather."

"I know you're 'fif.' 'Fif' what? That's what I need to

figure out. I'll do some more investigating. But in the meantime—"

"Do you love me, Francesca?"

Whoosh ...

Those five words punch the air out of my lungs. Tears sting my eyes. He heard me. Even if I meant it, I want to take back those words. This isn't the time or the place to fall in love. It was a stolen moment like this is a stolen moment.

I could die.

He could die.

Or he could get caught and spend the rest of his life in prison.

Nothing good can come from loving him. Not for him. And not for me.

"It's a simple yes or no," he says.

There's nothing simple about it. About us. I've known him for barely a month. And in that time, I haven't *known* him at all.

I roll away from him and sit on the edge of the bed, my fingers clenching the mattress while my heart races, and panic sets in until I feel nauseous. "I'm not this person," I murmur.

"What person?"

"Vengeful. Unhinged. Dancing naked. Unemployed. A resident of Boone. A whore willing to have sex with an awful man." I shake my head. "So asking me about my emotions when nothing about this feels real, it isn't fair. If I say yes, it might be a lie. If I say no ... that might be a lie too. Because I'm not *me*, and you're not *you*."

"I am me."

I rest my chin on my shoulder, eyeing him for several seconds. "Liar. I know you feel that's true because you've spent so much of your life *not* being who you are that you've allowed yourself to believe you've become a different person. But I ..." The words are there, but I can't arrange them in a way that makes sense. "I don't think anyone is meant to live the life you've lived. I bet your wife had to feel like *everything* to you. A glimmer. The sun, oxygen, love, hope, redemption, and peace. I bet your soul was starving for joy. A sliver of happiness that's the essence of the human experience."

Slowly lying back on the bed, I stare at the ceiling. "I've seen tiny glimpses of that joy in you. Very tiny." I roll toward him, tucking my hands between my cheek and the pillow. "When you play the piano. When Eloise shamelessly flirts with you."

The hint of a smile pulls at his lips.

"When Slade showed you the pictures of Wylder and Livy."

He rests his hand on my hip. "Do you love me?"

A tear slips out, and gravity carries it to the pillow. "Is it okay if I do?"

His hand skims up my body from my hip to my face, and he doesn't say a word, but he smiles. And a train of more tears follows that first one.

I WAKE up a few minutes after five in the morning to no Jackson. He's not in the bathroom, and his car's gone. I turn on the TV and wait for him to return. By nine, I'm going stir-crazy. So I visit the main office.

"How can I help you?" A young woman with a baby in a wrap carrier asks me.

"Good morning. I lost my phone, and I need to order a

ride. Would you be willing to order me one if I paid you?" I have the burner phone, but I can't use it to get a ride.

She inspects me for a few seconds. She nods once she determines I'm not nearly as sketchy as this motel.

"Thanks." I dig cash out of my purse and set it on the counter. "I need a ride to S&J Engineering in Rhodale."

Before I met Slade and saw pictures of his family, respecting Jack's wishes and plans was easier. He has everything I didn't think I wanted. And he needs to get back to that life. I have nothing and virtually no one waiting for me. It's too late to save my family, but it's not too late for Jack's.

If there was any question if Archer would be at work, there's not now. When I step out of the car, I'm greeted at the entrance to the engineering firm by four armed guards.

"By appointment only," one of the guards says, stepping before me when I reach for the door.

"Tell Mr. Sanford Iris is here to see him."

The guard scowls for a few seconds before making a call while stepping away from me. When he turns around, he opens the door for me without further explanation. The second I enter the door, another guard gestures for me to follow him.

After a pat down, a scan with a metal-detecting wand, and a purse search, he nods toward the elevator. It's a two-story building, so getting to the second floor doesn't take long. The doors open to a relatively empty space with large windows, exposed air vents, and a brunette with a friendly smile sitting behind a glass desk.

"Mr. Sanford's office is in the corner." She nods toward the glass-walled office with blinds that prevent me from seeing inside.

"Thanks."

The guard at the door opens it for me. I return a stiff smile and step inside the office.

Archer's sitting on the edge of his desk, ankles crossed, hands gripping the side. Sharp as always in a suit. "Where the hell have you been? Why haven't you answered my calls or my texts?" He stabs his hands through his hair before pushing off the desk.

My breath hitches in a silent gasp when he hugs me.

"Fuck, I thought you were dead," he whispers.

His forehead wrinkles when he releases me, holding my shoulders at arm's length. "Tell me."

I clear my throat, shaking off his reaction to seeing me unexpectedly. "I lost my phone that night. And I didn't know if it was safe to come here." I infuse a believable amount of panic in my voice. "I thought about calling the police but didn't know what to say. After the incident at the cafe in Hertzville, I was afraid you were ..." I shake my head a half-dozen times.

After several slow blinks, he nods. "It's okay. I've made a lot of enemies over the years. Success can do that. I'm afraid it also comes with a risk. I'm *so* sorry." Again, he hugs me.

I push him away. "Three men died! What is going on?" I feign outrage.

Archer holds up his hands in surrender. "I don't know what you want me to say that I haven't already said."

I sigh and deflate. "There's nothing you can say. I just wanted to make sure you're okay. I'll be going home soon."

"You ... care." A slow smirk grows along Archer's face. "You came here because you care about me."

I couldn't care less.

"Doesn't matter. I can't do this. It was fun until it

wasn't. And I'm going home. So ..." I cross my arms and offer him a resigned smile. "I hope you stay safe."

Pressing his lips together, he slips his hands into his front pockets and drops his chin. "On the Ferris wheel, you were different. I wasn't expecting that." He lifts his head.

I shrug. "I like control. You tried to take it from me. And I wasn't okay with that."

He grunts a laugh. "Control, huh? Well, you're talking to the King of Control."

"Then you know we're not compatible."

"Or we're exactly what the other one needs. If no one challenges you to submit control, you'll never know you had it."

"Sounds like the ramblings of a psychology major."

Archer lights up. He loves that I've researched him. "Perhaps."

"You've made my visit ... interesting."

He cocks his head to the side. "So this is goodbye?"

"This is goodbye."

"Have dinner with me one more time."

I shake my head. "I think my luck is running out. I choose life over death by gunfire."

A guilty grin steals his lips. "My wife and daughter are out of town. Come to my house for dinner. I promise you'll be safe there."

"I shouldn't." I take a few steps toward the door.

"You're right. You probably shouldn't. But I can tell you want to."

He's so sure of himself.

"I have plans tonight," he says. "Come tomorrow. I'm sure you know where I live since you seem to know every-thing else about me."

"Archer ..." I play hard to get.

He steps around his desk and sits in his fancy chair. "I'll let you pick the meal. I'll give you all the control." He leans back, fingers laced and resting on his chest.

I don't say anything. Not even a nod or headshake acknowledging his invitation. When I exit, he lets me go without another plea. Either he doesn't really care if I come to dinner, or he's sure I won't be able to stay away. I'm banking on the latter.

CHAPTER THIRTY-ONE
JACKSON

"Where have you been?" Slade asks when Jackson opens the door to the motel room.

Jackson frowns. "She shouldn't have let you in."

"She didn't. I let myself in. She's not here."

His gaze slides to the dark bathroom and the open door. "Where the hell is she?" Jackson checks the bathroom even though he knows she's not there. "Did she leave a note?"

"She did not. Where have you been?"

"Doesn't fucking matter. Where is she?" He again opens the motel room door, surveying the surroundings, and steps outside. "Goddammit." He stomps toward his car.

"She's at her brother's house. Well, the neighbor's house," Slade says, standing in the doorway when Jackson stops and turns. "But she was in Rhodale visiting Sanford before that."

Jackson doesn't ask how he knows that. Slade's doing what Jackson would have been doing in his shoes—keeping an eye on the target and the unknown. Frankie is a big unknown to Slade, even if Jackson's dick is well-acquainted with her.

"She's going to get herself killed," Jackson grumbles.

"You're going to get her killed by not ending this."

Jackson steps into Slade's personal space. He still remembers how slamming his fist into Slade's smug face felt. "What do you think I'm doing?"

"I think you're getting laid while you shit your pants on this one. You're thinking like a father who's trying to protect his daughter. There's a reason surgeons don't operate on their family."

"You don't have a clue." Jackson heads toward the car.

"Sanford should be dead. You're afraid you missed something. You're afraid he's not the last one. You're afraid Livy's going to die like her mom. If you were protecting anyone but her, you would have more confidence. You're scared. Why the fuck do you think *I'm* here?"

Jackson opens the car door. "I don't know why you're here. So go take care of my daughter before I deem you as expendable ... more than I already do."

His anger builds the closer he gets to Eloise's place. There hasn't been any activity on his cameras around the garage, but it's only been forty-eight hours. Even if Archer doesn't suspect Jackson, he will need to stalk Frankie. And she's doing all she can to lead them to Eloise's house, the truth, and the garage filled with Jackson's belongings.

He waits down the street, using binoculars to look for anything unusual. Then he slides on a baseball cap and walks to her house instead of pulling into her driveway. As he reaches the front porch stairs, he hears laughter coming from the back of the house, so he walks around to the deck.

"Jack," Eloise greets him first because Frankie's sitting in a chair with her back to him.

"Eloise," he greets her with a stiff smile.

"Francesca was just telling me about your romantic getaway."

He climbs the stairs, and Frankie swallows hard, eyes wide, hands gripping the arms of the chair. "Was she?"

"Yes. She said you took her dancing."

He hums. "Well, she begged me."

"I did not beg you." Frankie finally acknowledges him.

"You were on your knees. If that's not begging, I don't know what is."

Frankie's face turns deep crimson. "I had to bend down to tie his shoe. He's getting up there in age."

"Oh mercy ... tell me about it." Eloise flicks her wrist. "I only wear slip-ons."

Jackson eyes Frankie, but she remains statuesque with a triumphant grin pinned to her face. "Someone has some attitude today."

"Me?" Frankie's jaw unhinges.

"Oh dear, trouble in paradise already? Maybe you two should have taken a longer getaway."

"Agreed," Jackson says. "In fact, I wasn't aware our getaway was over until I returned to the hotel, and you weren't there."

"The *hotel,* huh?" Frankie lifts her eyebrows. "Sorry. I'm pretty sure a hotel comes with amenities. Did I miss the pool and fitness center at our lovely little inn?"

"Do you two need a minute?"

Jackson says, "Yes," as Frankie says, "No."

With a nervous laugh, Eloise rocks herself to stand and opens the screen door. "I need to change some laundry anyway."

Jackson grabs Frankie's arm and drags her to the garage.

"I think I've been manhandled enough." She tries to pull away from his grip.

He releases her when they're in the garage, and the door is closed. "If you want to get yourself killed, then just say it. But I won't put my family in danger trying to save your ass every goddamn day."

"For your information," Frankie crosses her arms, "I've been the one risking everything for you and your family. When I woke up to an empty bed with no note and no way to contact you, I decided to go see Archer."

He clenches his teeth, hands fisted.

She turns and takes a few steps away. "I went to his office. It's under heavy security, but I got right up to see him because he trusts me. And *I'm* the key to ending this for you and your family. I can get to him anywhere, anytime. In fact, he wants me to have dinner with him at his house tomorrow night because—"

"Because his wife and daughter are in Paris for the next two weeks, and he thinks he can fuck you at his house without anyone putting a bullet in his head first."

Frankie deflates. "How did you know Corinne and Molly are in Paris?"

"Because it's what I do!"

She startles from the boom of his voice.

Jackson takes a deep breath and pushes it out his nose. He's too close to this woman but can't pretend she doesn't matter. It wasn't until he met Frankie that he realized how empty he'd become inside since leaving on this lonely journey to make things right in his world again.

"When Livy was six or seven, she wanted to help Ryn do everything in the kitchen. Chop vegetables. Dump pasta in boiling water. Frost cupcakes. So Ryn would let her help, but it took twice as long, and something usually got messed up. But mainly, Ryn had to watch Livy's every move to ensure she didn't hurt herself. Then we'd make a huge deal about it, so Livy felt like she was helping."

Frankie's face sours. "Wait ... are you comparing me to a six-year-old trying to help in the kitchen?"

"I'm saying your 'helpfulness' is far from helpful, even if your heart's in the right place. I'm saying I can do my job safer and more effectively without you."

"You just don't want him touching me."

Jackson clenches his teeth, holding his tongue for a few extra seconds before responding. "Do *you* want him touching you?"

She flinches. "Of course not."

"I realize you don't know what it's like to be married or even in a relationship, but it usually involves an aversion to letting other men touch you. And we don't have to label what's happening between us, but if we're being real ... I am neither Baines nor Alisdair. I will not stand by and watch someone touch you *or* torture you. And I won't get my revenge with a sex video or fucking a married woman. I sold my soul to the devil a long time ago. So, I'm the guy who will take someone's life without blinking, flinching, or even giving it a second thought. I won't beg you to listen to me or do as I say. But I will gag you, restrain you, and put you someplace out of my way until I am done with Archer Sanford so that I can see my daughter again, and your parents don't have to lose their last child."

Frankie's lips part, but no words are spoken.

Jackson knows she's thinking about last night, what they did, what he said, what she said. But he can't be blinded by intimacy or any illusion of love. If he lets that happen, his family will die. And Slade Wylder will be waiting with a big, fat I-told-you-so.

"You'll never get to him without me," she whispers.

"Watch me."

Frankie turns in a slow circle, taking in the garage like she's seeing it for the first time ... or maybe the last time. Then she sits at the piano. "How did you know I was here?"

"Slade."

She nods, fingers caressing the keys without pressing them. "You have him following me now?"

"No. He's following you because he doesn't trust you."

She starts to play a slow song. A sad one. "Why doesn't he trust me?"

"Because Archer's still alive."

She pauses her fingers. "And that's my fault?"

"No, it's mine. But Slade doesn't see it that way."

Frankie continues to play. "Why?"

"Because I took out eight people in one year, and I've been here to take out the last one for eleven months. Eleven months of looking for any sign that he's not the last one."

"I haven't been here eleven months."

Jackson walks around the piano while she plays. She's the living, breathing definition of grace, making everything look effortless—a oneness with the piano. "One shot. I used eight bullets to kill eight men. I've used seven bullets here, and Archer is still alive. Precision is the reason I'm not a wanted man. It's what makes me a ghost. Everything is quick, neat, and traceless."

Her eyes narrow at him, but her fingers keep playing. "I'm distracting you."

"You're complicating things."

Frankie stops playing. They stare at each other. He lets her see everything in his eyes and hopes she can see his soul because then she'll know. She'll know how he feels about her. And she'll know whatever they've become ... it ends now. And that's just the fucking awful unfairness of life. He has to make a choice, and from her glassy, red eyes, she knows it without him saying a word.

"It's time for me to go home," she whispers.

Jackson swallows hard before he returns a slight nod. He didn't have this with Ryn, this last goodbye. And while it seemed unfair at the time, he now realizes the idea of closure is an illusion. Once someone has planted themselves in your heart, it's forever.

There is no closure to infinity.

"Has anyone ever told you that your love for your family is the most beautiful thing in the world?"

Her words unearth his past. They peel back a layer to the life he buried, and he can hear Ryn as if she were standing before him.

"*I want the guy that kissed his sister on the head and whispered, 'You've got this.'*" *A laugh of incredulity bubbled up her chest. She shook her head with a painful grin. "That sounds so ridiculous, doesn't it? That touch ... the one that made me love you? It wasn't even me you touched. I fell in love with you because of how you love your sister."*

He sits next to Frankie and plays the song he can't finish.

She closes her eyes and lays her head on his shoulder.

When he stops, his hand rests on hers, lifting it to the keys. "Finish it," he whispers.

"Jack," she says in a thick voice as though she knows he's asking her to help him let go.

"Finish it, then go home."

She slowly lifts her head, letting an unacknowledged tear trickle down her cheek while her fingers cling to his last notes, taking something incredibly sad, and bringing it back to something filled with optimism. Every note comes easily; all she's needed is his permission to finish the song.

When she finishes, there's a finality to what he started. There's a new finality to the life that inspired it. Her foot on the pedal and her fingers on the keys become weightless together.

It's perfect.

"When Ryn died, I slept on her grave for days." He stares at the keys. "I abandoned Livy. I was a mess. Just me ... and a bag filled with bottles of alcohol. Eventually, my sister and her husband carried me to their car and took me home. They forced me to shower and put myself back together for Livy's sake." He grunts a laugh. "Jess said, 'Time's up. Now you move forward again.' I never knew how badly I needed someone to give me permission to move on until her words put everything in perspective again. And I thought this song needed to go on forever without an ending until ... now. Love is so fucking crippling. It's a minefield—a bunch of ... potholes waiting to make you stumble. And when the source of that love dies, you're left in the dark—lost and confused—until someone takes your hand and shows you the way out. Until you find a new light."

He rests his hand on hers.

She sniffles, abruptly standing and wiping her eyes with her back to him.

"Tomorrow, at this time, it will all be over. One way or another," he says.

The hardest part of taking someone's life is making it out alive. If Jackson takes that out of the equation, Livy can be free by this time tomorrow. Jessica can resume her life. And Frankie can find peace again, knowing Molly Sanford lost someone she loved.

Nothing will be right.

Revenge won't fill the holes.

256

But a new chapter can begin because the previous one has ended.

And he will do it all ... because of her.

"It's beautiful," Jackson says. "The ending to the song. I don't think it was meant for me to finish it."

Frankie hugs herself, but Jackson doesn't miss her shaking, trying to hold in her emotions despite the tears that cannot be contained.

"Tell your parents I'm sorry for my inappropriate behavior. As a father, I knew better. I should have acted better."

Her laughter escapes as a sob while she shakes her head. "*You* tell them. If you have something to say to my parents, you'd better tell them yourself."

Jackson winces at her angry tone. Sometimes, doing the right thing can take time to feel right. He lived with his sister's wrath for doing the right thing when she couldn't see it right in front of her.

Jackson wraps his arms around Frankie's shoulders, so she doesn't have to turn and look at him if she doesn't want to. Frankie leans her head back against his chest.

"Why did you let me love you?" she whispers through a mess of tears and broken syllables.

He kisses the crown of her head. "That's my line."

"Jack ..." She covers her face and sobs.

He turns her in his arms and lets her feel every emotion she needs to feel. When her tears end and her grip on his shirt loosens, he holds her face and wipes it dry. "Time to go home."

Frankie closes her red eyes for several seconds and acquiesces with a barely detectable nod. She lifts onto her toes and presses her lips to his. Just as quickly, she turns and hastens to the door.

Jackson takes several long strides and grabs Frankie's arm, turning her back into him, kissing her the way he wished he would have kissed Ryn goodbye the morning she died. Frankie locks her arms around his neck and opens her mouth to accommodate his demands, his need to take everything he can in case it's the last time in this life that he feels pleasure, desire ... *love*.

She pushes him away, covers her mouth with her hand while a new round of tears well in her eyes, and runs out the door.

CHAPTER THIRTY-TWO
FRANCESCA

THROUGH TEAR-BLURRED vision and snot running from my nose, I pull out of the driveway.

No goodbye to Eloise.

No retrieving the few belongings I bought after the fire.

No looking back.

Passing the cemetery, I slam on the brakes. There is one goodbye I need to make. I wipe my eyes and nose before stepping out of my car. The path to their graves is a short one. Lynn appreciated John being buried close to the road so she could say "hi" to him whenever she headed out of town.

The wind picks up, ushering in cooler air with the promise of distant storms. Crossing my ankles, I lower to my butt and curl my hair behind my ears. I still don't know what to say to Lynn and Steven, so I sit with John.

I trace his name in the granite.

"I'm trying to pinpoint when this started," I say. "When you decided your existence was inconsequential despite having a wife and son. A sister. Parents." I pick at the grass. "Did it make it easier for Steven to feel the same way about his life?" I rip out a handful of grass and let it scatter in the breeze. "Did I blame Molly for something you did?" I laugh. Clarity is never punctual. Had I never seen that letter, or had I been able to walk away sooner, my heart never would have had the chance to fall in love.

Maybe that was never the plan if there is such a thing as a plan. Have I spent forty-one years waiting for my path to cross with Jack's?

"It's all gone," I whisper. "Your house. Your things. Your family." Rocking forward, I kneel and rest my hands on his headstone. "I'm going to take the best of us and go ... *live*."

"That's touching."

A voice has never shaken me to the point of my teeth chattering ... until now. The temperature plummets. And my heart thumps and lumps with a suffocating panic.

I stand on weak legs and face Archer. Fifteen feet of isolation with him from his bodyguards. The question is ... are they here to protect him or to corner me?

Sliding off his sunglasses, Archer blows and wipes them with his sleeve. "Your nephew dated my daughter. Did I miss that in one of our conversations?" He squints while sliding his glasses back onto his smug face. "I mean ... I might have. You were rather distracting."

"What do you want?" I say as steadily as my nerves will allow.

"I want to know why you said your name is Iris. I want to know why you said you're a dental assistant instead of a professor of music theory."

I clear my throat. "You seemed interested in me the day I walked by your table. And after your daughter wrote Steven a letter giving him permission—encouraging him—to take his own life, I became very interested in your family.

What kind of parents raise a young woman to do something so unimaginable?"

"What are you talking about? Molly did no such thing."

I scoff. "You can't possibly be this confident in your defense of her when she snorted cocaine off the chest of her boyfriend after letting him fuck her ten different ways. Can you?"

Archer's expression hardens like his white-knuckled fists. "You took that video."

"I took the video. And I used your money to ensure it made it to everyone in her contacts." I step closer to him. "And for five full seconds, I felt like I had avenged Steven's death." I glance over my shoulder at his headstone. "But he's still dead, and Molly's in Paris."

Archer looks behind him at his security detail. "Let's go, Francesca."

"Who told you my name?"

"Who told you Molly's in Paris?"

We have a stare-off, and I cross my arms, standing my ground. "I'm not going anywhere with you."

He laughs. I've never heard a more sinister sound. "You don't have a choice. Tell me ... have you been fucking Jude Day while stroking my dick on the side?"

Hearing him say "Jude Day" zaps the air from my lungs. Had he punched me in the face, I wouldn't feel more speechless.

"My beautiful girl, are you okay? You've lost every ounce of color in your face." He steps forward, reaching for my cheek.

I whip my head back.

With a smile more ominous than the distant clouds, Archer tucks his hands into his pockets. "Looks like we're about to find out how you adapt to losing control." He shrugs a shoulder. "You might be surprised how much you like it." His mouth twists. "In fact, I think someone as fucked-up as you— someone who gets off on revenge— might find this thrilling."

This?

Archer jerks his head toward me, and two of his men close in on us. I retreat until I bump into John's headstone and nearly trip. Then I sprint toward my car but only get a few feet.

"No!" I shriek when both men grab my arms. My next breath catches in my throat, suffocating me behind the calloused hand, silencing my screams. They drag me to the SUV.

As I try to kick and wriggle out of their hold, I catch a glimpse of Archer's face getting into the other SUV. He's grinning.

CHAPTER THIRTY-THREE

JACKSON

JACKSON RETURNS to the motel to get Slade. Since he's here against Jackson's wishes, he will use him to get to Archer. Then he will make him get the hell out of Kansas before Jackson breaks Archer's neck. But he won't do that before he makes him pay for touching Frankie.

"Gotta hand it to you." Slade shakes his head, having made himself at home on the bed, ankles crossed, boots on, TV muted. "You've learned to prioritize rather well."

"What's that supposed to mean?" Jackson takes a piss in the toilet.

"Risking it all for Livy, consequences be damned."

Jackson zips his jeans. "I've always risked everything for her."

"Is this the first time you've risked another innocent life for her?"

Jackson sighs, leaning his shoulder against the wall, arms crossed. "You're far from innocent."

"I'm talking about Frankie."

Jackson shakes his head. "I sent her home. Archer dies tonight."

Slade rolls his lips together, head shaking. "I GPS-chipped her vehicle. She stopped at the cemetery but was nowhere to be found when I drove by. Any guess as to where she is now? I have a guess."

Jackson doesn't respond right away. All he sees is red, but he's unsure if it's because Frankie lied to him about going home or at Archer for consuming so much of Jackson's life and touching the woman he ... *loves*.

He lifts the mattress, forcing Slade to move. Inside the hollowed box springs is an arsenal.

"What's the plan?" Slade asks, selecting two semi-automatic guns and several grenades.

"Put that shit down. I plan to end Sanford, and you're going home to care for my daughter."

Slade chuckles, stealing more weaponry. "I'm not allowed to let you go on a suicide mission."

"What makes you think I'm dying?"

"You have no plan. You're outnumbered. And you have to extract a hostage before you can take Sanford out. Oh ... and you're just old."

"Fuck you." Jackson fastens his tactical vest. "I don't have a vest for you, so you can't go."

Slade heads toward the door. "Do you think I came without my own gear?" He opens the door.

"Then why are you stealing my shit?" Jackson hikes several guns onto his shoulder, along with a range bag of extra ammunition.

"Because I'll need to be more heavily armed than you once you get caught."

He follows him out the door. "What makes you think I'm getting caught?"

Slade shakes his head while trekking to his vehicle. "Again ... you have no plan. You're outnumbered. And you have to extract a hostage before you can take Sanford out. And you're just old."

"I will find Livy a nice Christian guy who worships her, second only to God. He'll have a boring job that pays well and a healthy fear of her father. She'll grieve you for a while, but she's done that before, so she'll know the routine." Jackson slams his trunk.

Slade eyes him over the roof of his car with the driver's door open. "I can't let you die. I really, really *want* to, but I can't. So stop a half mile from Sanford's place and have a plan or be ready to follow mine."

Jackson frowns and mumbles, "We'll never follow yours, dipshit."

WHEN HE PARKS his car off the road by a cornfield, Jackson stares at his phone, bringing up Jessica's contact.

> Jackson: I love you. Tell Livy I love her too

Before he finishes typing the text, he deletes it. As much as he wants to say goodbye, he can't give her a chance to panic and text Slade.

Tap. Tap. Tap.

Jackson glances out his heavily tinted window at Slade waiting for him. He leans back and closes his eyes, blowing out a long breath. Maybe his last long breath.

"Is she a voluntary hostage?" Slade asks when Jackson opens the door.

"What are you talking about?" Jackson pops the trunk.

"Did Frankie go willingly to his house, or do you think

she was taken?" Slade slips on his sunglasses. "And how the hell are you not tracking him?"

"I am, but I was with her right before she went to the cemetery. I didn't check his location because I ..."

He was grieving her and preparing to leave this earth for the women in his life to have the chance to live. He dropped the ball when he should have had his eye on Archer and ensured Francesca got out of town safely.

"Doesn't fucking matter. He has her and knows I'm here, which means he knows I'm responsible for recent events."

"Well," Slade starts trekking through the field to get closer to Archer's property, "this isn't ideal."

Jackson follows him, not saying a word.

"You have to pretend she's nobody," Slade says. Jackson doesn't respond, so Slade stops and turns. "Where's your head?"

"Fuck you—"

"No!" Slade shoves Jackson.

Jackson grabs Slade's vest.

"You can play the disgruntled father who hates his daughter's husband another time. You can make a list of regrets about that woman." Slade points toward Archer's house. "But I need to know your head is in this. I need to know you're detached from everything but your weapon and target. Or you need to get back in your car and wait for me to finish this."

Jackson keeps a tight grip on Slade, jaw clenched. But he knows Slade was trained by the same group who trained him. He knows he's saying what Jackson would say if the tables were turned. Slade's not Livy's husband. He's nobody's son. He's a soldier with his weapon and a target. And he's that way because his goal is to get home alive.

"If this is your suicide mission, let me spare you the work. I'll snap your neck right now. Today's not my day to die, you grumpy old fuck. So get your head straight, or say your last prayer." Slade shoves Jackson, so he's forced to let go.

Jackson brushes past Slade. "I am the lamb."

"We don't need—"

Jackson whips around. "My fucking head is *in this*. There has never been a day that my head wasn't *in this*. That's why this grumpy old fuck is still here. But we both know there is skill, finesse, and luck. There's always luck. So *I am the lamb*. Understood?"

Slade knows because he was the sacrificial lamb who saved Livy's life. He nods once.

Jackson's shoulders relax. He's resolute in his mission and resigned to the possible outcome. And as much as he hates the circumstances that brought Slade into his life, there isn't anyone else he'd want to have his back. Slade is a young Jude Day.

CHAPTER THIRTY-FOUR
FRANCESCA

I'm unsure how long it's been—maybe an hour or two. The door to the library opens, and the chandelier lights illuminate. After spending so long in the dark, shades drawn, I wince at their brightness, while gagged, wrists and ankles tied.

"Sorry. It's extra dark in here since I have to keep all the shades in the house closed," Archer says, ungagging me.

I cough a few times.

"I'll get you some water."

"I don't need water." I scowl at him.

He loosens his tie and unbuttons his shirt before shrugging off his jacket. "You've put me in an impossible situation." He tosses his coat and tie over the back of a floral upholstered chair, one of several in this two-story library filled with floor-to-ceiling shelves. "Molly's my daughter, and while parents don't condone everything their children do, I'm hardwired to love and protect her."

I continue glaring at him unblinkingly.

Strolling the room's perimeter like he's looking for a particular book, he sighs. "I realize you don't have children, so you don't know what that's like. But for what it's worth, I apologize on behalf of my daughter if she wasn't there for your nephew in his time of need." He pulls a book off the shelf and thumbs through it.

"There for him?" I try to readjust, pain slicing through my shoulder from being shoved onto the floor by his guys. With a grunt, I sit up against the side of a chair. "She told him to kill himself. She gave him all the reasons why he should do it. *Your evil spawn* led him to the cliff's edge and kicked the back of his knees! And his name is Steven. Fucking say his name! Remember his name. I will never let Molly forget it."

Archer lifts an eyebrow while returning the book to the shelf. "You'll never see my daughter again, so I think she'll have the rest of her life to forget."

His words settle into my gut like a knife, twisting and digging deeper. *He's going to kill me.*

"Tell me." Archer sits in the chair across from my spot on the floor, folding his hands between his spread legs. "Were you going to voluntarily have sex with me to insert your claws into my family?"

Voluntarily?

"Were you going to wait until my daughter despised you before telling her I was fucking her worst enemy?" He laughs. "It's brilliant, really. I probably would have done the same thing if I were in your shoes. After all, some things are worse than death."

"Then let me go."

"Can't." He drums his fingers together. "You're the bait."

"For Jack?"

"Jack?" Wrinkles line Archer's forehead. "Jackson." He nods slowly. "That's right. He changed his name and never

269

changed it back. We trained together. Did he tell you that? Well, we didn't train for the same job. He trained to kill people; I trained to determine if he was of sound mind to do it ... to keep doing it." He grins. "Have I lost you? Did he tell you he was an assassin?"

I don't respond.

Archer's gaze drifts around the room with a slow sigh. "He was good at it. Too good. The epitome of a natural-born killer. Had they not harnessed his 'potential,' he might have been a serial killer hunting innocent people. I did multiple psychological assessments on him, and the guy's not right—zero attachment. But ..." He meets my gaze again and shrugs. "The final decision wasn't mine. So they gave him an arsenal, and he used it like Rambo."

He's wrong. Jack's attached to his family. I think he's even attached to me. And he's not a natural-born killer. The eyes don't lie.

"What's that look?"

I shake my head.

"You don't believe me?"

I continue to shake my head.

"I'll be right back." Before he reaches the door, he turns and smirks. "Don't go anywhere."

I struggle again to free my hands, but there's no way out. They're zip-tied along with my ankles. I can't physically save myself, so I must convince him to let me go. This isn't my battle. I don't have to be the bait. Jack's coming for him without knowing I'm here.

"Oh, good. You're still here." Archer closes the door. "I found these in my safe. I'm not sure why I kept them. A sixth sense told me I'd need them for a rainy day. And I think storms are headed our way. How appropriate." He pulls photos from a letter-sized envelope. "I lost count. And god only knows what his number is now, but Jude's kill number was higher than anyone else's." He shows me one picture at a time, holding each one in my face before tossing it on the floor next to me.

Dead people. Mostly men, but a few women. Some of them have bullets in their heads, like Archer's bodyguards at the carnival. Others have their throats slashed. Some are missing body parts—including several who are decapitated. There must be over a hundred photos.

I flinch and turn my head at one that's nothing more than a torso—missing all four limbs and the head.

"Ah yes ... this one was personal to Jude. I don't remember why, but he killed him slowly."

Jack's words replay in my head. *"I'm going to remove his hands one finger at a time. Then, I will carve my knife into his face and remove his tongue and lips. And because I'm certain he's looked at you inappropriately, I'll shove the tip of my knife into his eyeballs just for good measure."* Jack's words relentlessly echo.

Killing Archer will be personal because of me because I couldn't walk away and deal with my grief like a normal person. I couldn't take Eloise's advice.

John used to say "no regrets" about everything. Not me. I've spent my life regretting so many decisions. And I have to wonder if John said those words to himself before he put a bullet in his brain. If there's life after death, is he somewhere seeing the bigger picture and feeling regret?

If I could do it all over again, I would have torn up the letter from Molly and gone home. That would have meant I would not have fallen in love with Jack. And that would have been a missed opportunity for my heart, but this whole scenario would be different. Archer would still die, but not like the grotesque pictures on the floor. Slade would have stayed with Livy. And Jack would be reunited with his family by now.

My thoughts return to Archer when he stops on a photo of a woman with a bullet hole where her eye used to be.

A woman.

She must have been bad too. A killer. *Right?*

"She was a red herring," Archer says.

I lift my gaze from the photo to him. My insides feel like acid, such an overwhelming feeling of nausea and something akin to grief that I have to fight the urge to buckle over and choke on the bile working its way up my throat.

This isn't the Jack I know. It's not real.

"She was sent to distract Jude so her boyfriend could kill him. It was the closest he'd ever come to getting caught, having his identity compromised. She tried to seduce him, and she tried to poison him when that failed. He caught her and..." Archer cringes "...he ended her before taking out her boyfriend an hour later. On his post-evaluation, mandatory after every hit, I asked him how it felt to kill a woman for the first time. He said when he decides to kill someone, they're no longer human; therefore, they're no longer male or female."

Detachment.

Those same hands that touched me intimately, that same finger that he traced down my nose to my lips, and those knuckles that ghosted along my cheek belong to the same man who killed and mutilated those people. Again, I have to look away.

"I don't blame you for not wanting to see them—for not wanting to see *him*. But I fear you think I'm the bad guy, and I'm not. I broke ties with the organization and started a new life. I don't know why he's coming after me. He's unhinged. I heard his wife died years ago. I bet he just ... snapped."

"You funded the man who killed his wife. You invested in a different group. You didn't break ties with *everyone*."

A muscle by his right eye twitches. "He must love putting his dick inside of you. There's no way he casually shared that information with someone he deemed as nothing more than a quick fuck. Perhaps I'll confess all of my secrets, too, when I'm balls-deep in your pussy."

No matter how hard I clench my teeth, I can't hide my disgust and swallow the burning bile back down my throat past its growing lump. "Twenty seconds ago, you feared I thought you were 'the bad guy.' And now you're confessing your intentions of raping me. Which is it? Are you another innocent victim," I nod to the pile of pictures on the floor, "or are you a bad person who needs to be eliminated?"

A slow smile takes over Archer's face. "Depends on the day."

"Today?"

"I don't know, *Francesca*. Why don't you tell me?" He glances at his watch. "The night's still young. Will you willingly finish what you started with me on the Ferris wheel? Or are you nothing but a cock tease just asking for it? And when I take what you were, in fact, offering, are you going to scream rape? I mean ... I'm sure you'll scream. And either way, I'll come harder than I ever have because you, Professor, made me wait so long. And my patience is gone. In fact," his smile swells, "we have a piano in the other room. Molly was supposed to play it, but she never practiced. Want to know who played it the most?"

A new wave of fear hits me, not because I fear him raping me. I fear what he's about to say.

"Steven." He slowly shakes his head. "Your nephew, a

goddamn maestro. Molly used to playfully push him off the bench because she said he was making her look bad in front of her parents."

Angry tears burn my eyes.

"Would you like me to fuck you on the white polished wood? Would you feel closer to Steven?"

"Screw you," I grit through my teeth.

"We will. Soon. But first, I need to know we're not under attack. You see, Jude Day is a slippery motherfucker. So, my men are patrolling the perimeter of my property. And they'll end him if he's out there. Which I imagine he is because I'd be looking for you too."

I shake my head.

"No?"

"He thinks I went home," I whisper.

"Perhaps he thought that. But I'm sure he's tracking you."

I shake my head again. "What makes you think your men can kill him?"

Given the pile of carnage on the floor, he knows it's a valid question.

Archer's gaze drops to the photos. "He's good, but he's not immortal. And he's outnumbered. But I suppose..." the corner of his mouth twitches "...he could have his sister with him." With a belly laugh, he throws his head back. "Wouldn't that be something? Has he told you about his twin sister? Fucking Jessica Day."

With a long whistle, he shakes his head. "Now *she's* the ultimate headcase. Jude will kill someone without much thought. That's why he's still able to pose as a normal human. But Jessica likes to manipulate her victims. She'll toy with them because she doesn't live for the kill like Jude; she likes to watch people suffer like she did. She enjoys bringing people an inch from their last breath and keeping them barely alive until they're gasping for a way to end their own life just to escape the misery."

None of this feels real. There's no way this is Jack's life, his family. His twin.

Archer glances around the room as if it's made of glass windows, encompassing his property. "Can you imagine two people their age taking on my fully armed twenty-some-thing men? They're not true immortals. I bet their joints ache like mine do some days. I bet they drink more whiskey and tequila than Gatorade and Red Bull. You just don't get to your late fifties and not feel like you're deteriorating by the end of a long day."

Late fifties?

"Maybe you're too old to live this life," I say, resigned to whatever happens to me.

"This life? The good life?" He narrows his eyes.

"Control is exhausting. Revenge is exhausting. Looking over your shoulder. Needing armed men around you at all times. Maintaining the illusion that you have a good life. A solid marriage. The perfect child. Wearing a tie you seem to hate because you're always adjusting it like it's strangling you. Maybe you're the one who needs to submit to control, not to remind you of what it feels like to have it, but rather to remember what it feels like to be human—to be vulnerable."

Archer bobs his head. "Conceivably. However, this world is not a utopia. You conspired with the enemy to kill me. So *human* I can no longer be."

"I didn't conspire to kill you or anyone. I was at the cemetery telling my family goodbye before going home." My voice escalates.

"And before that, you were with Jude Day. You can't

untangle yourself from this web you've willingly helped weave. So here we are, waiting to see who dies first. Will Jude let it be you? Or will he die to save you?"

"Is there a scenario where I live?"

He stands, adjusting his belt. "If six guards and myself die before you, then yes. But you seem pretty smart, so do the math. Now, I'm going to shower before we make our way to the piano because I'm considerate. Care to join me?"

"Yes," I say, feigning every bit of confidence.

His eyebrows lift a fraction. "I wish I could trust you."

"I doubt it. I think you get off on the fact that you know you can't trust me. So why don't you untie me, and let's play."

Archer chortles. "Did he teach you something? Can you snap my neck? Break my nose? Is that you're idea of playing? It was Jessica's. I think we'll have more fun if you're restrained. You had your chance. It's not my fault you were too weak to follow through." He exits the library, leaving the photos on the floor.

I stare at the parts of them that are exposed in the scattered pile.

Jude will kill someone without much thought.

Turning away from the photos, I lean my head against the side of the chair and close my eyes before they fill with a new round of tears. I just want to go home.

CHAPTER THIRTY-FIVE
JACKSON

"There are six guards and eighteen cameras," Slade says, trekking back toward Jackson.

"We need to disable the cameras," Jackson mumbles, lifting his gaze from the scope of his rifle and massaging his neck.

"I'm listening." Slade rests a hand on his hip.

Jackson feels every ounce of his scrutiny. He hears all of Slade's unspoken words. They don't have a team—no one to cut the electricity. An assassin's greatest tool, besides patience, is the element of surprise. There is no time for patience, and with a hostage, the element of surprise is lost.

Archer's well-prepared for his attackers. He's waiting patiently because he can. If Jackson focuses on saving Frankie's life, he can make a plan that might not get executed in the next few hours. He has no time if he goes one step further and attempts to keep her safe from other things Archer might do to her. In fact, he might be too late.

He hears her words.

"It's flesh and bones. It's not me. It's not who I am. It's a vehicle."

Frankie is strong, but she's not Jessica. And even his sister would say only death can separate the mind from the flesh and bones. Maybe she can survive whatever Archer might do to her by having a laser focus on the only thing that could feel like a silver lining—that she's still alive. The question is, will that feel like a gift or a curse?

"Pretend it's too late for her," Slade says. "It's the only way we can do this. You need to let all thoughts of her go."

"You're not thinking of Livy?"

Slade glances at Jackson while pulling his binoculars out of his vest. "No."

He doesn't expect Slade's answer to be that quick and resolute. At this moment, he realizes Slade is the better assassin. He's old enough to have a sharp mind and a steady hand from experience. Jackson remembers the confidence that came with those honed skills. But despite losing so much, he still has infinitely more than he's ever had. That *more* makes clearing his mind nearly impossible.

Jackson feels the gradual dulling of his edge, the growing whisper of doubt, and the tiny cracks in his confidence from carrying the world—*his* world—on his shoulders for so long. He no longer feels an unwavering certainty of the outcome. However, his unshakable determination keeps him moving because the one thing he knows with conviction is that he will do this or die trying.

"Livy and Wylder will get me killed. Thinking about them is like—"

"Removing the part of your vest that covers your heart," Jackson interrupts to finish the phrase he heard a million times during his training. They don't think about the people they love. There's no room for vulnerability, and love is the most vulnerable emotion.

"I'll take the back three. You take the front three," Slade

says, grabbing his night vision goggles as the last of the day's light vanishes. "Three shots, no more than a few seconds apart. Anything longer, any hesitation, and we're—"

"We're going to burn it down," Jackson says, eyeing the vast array of landscaping lights illuminating the property.

"What?"

"There are too many cameras. Someone's live monitoring the feed. Maybe in the house, maybe at a remote location. Since we can't cut the power, we will set it on fire. The 9-1-1 response time is approximately twenty minutes this far out in the country. So from the time the alarms sound, we have fifteen minutes to make the kills and remove ... any hostages."

And he knows Frankie would want the house to burn.

"Smoke out?"

"Yes," Jackson says, plodding back toward the vehicles for fuel.

"It will obscure our view," Slade calls, following him.

"And it will obscure their view as well. But first, it will draw them away from the house so we can take them out without cameras catching us." When he reaches his car, he retrieves a drone.

"Ariel view?"

He shakes his head. "I'm going to drop fireballs on the roof."

"Where did you get that?"

"I made it after seeing them used for prescribed fires. There are fifty balls in here."

"Won't they roll off the roof?"

"They ignite on impact. There won't be anything to roll."

"Smart."

Jackson smirks, feeling oddly gratified by Slade's

279

compliment. "Aren't you going to ask me how I know where to drop them?"

"No. If you don't have the layout of his house memorized, then I will lose what little respect I have for you."

Jackson shuts the trunk. "At least one of us has respect for the other."

"Livy didn't get pregnant right away. I had to stick my dick in her a half dozen times a day for a solid two weeks every month before—"

Jackson pulls out his handgun and presses it to Slade's forehead. "If you ever use the word 'dick' in the same breath as my daughter's name, I'm going to cross another thing off my bucket list."

"You're such a morbid fuck."

Jackson drops his hand and pounds his boots back into the field toward the house. He's never known where the line's been with Slade. Jackson killed his father because Slade's father did some unforgivable things to Jackson's family. They've never discussed it. And he can't imagine the day will ever come when there's a need to mention it. Still, it's hard to point a gun at Slade without recalling the day he put a bullet in his father's head. And occasionally, like a few seconds ago, Jackson can't help but wonder if Slade looks at him and thinks of him as the man who killed his father more than the man partially responsible for bringing Livy into this world—into Slade's world.

"When we get into the house, I take Sanford, and you take any hostages," Jackson says.

Francesca. They both know there's only one hostage, and her name is Francesca.

"Don't dick around. Once I get her out, I won't return for you."

"I wouldn't have it any other way," Jackson says, deploying the drone toward the house.

"Don't die, old man," Slade says, continuing toward the house, fully armed.

"Well," Jackson mumbles while the drone approaches the roof, "we're all going to die, eventually." When the first fireball illuminates, Jackson grabs his gun in one hand and his knife in his other hand while taking long strides toward the house.

CHAPTER THIRTY-SIX
FRANCESCA

WHEN THE DOOR CLICKS OPEN, I don't turn toward it. I don't even open my eyes.

It's just a body.

When a large hand grips my arm, pulling me to my feet, I squeeze my eyes shut tighter.

It's just a body.

I let my thoughts slip away, back to the previous night with Jack. His hands on my skin. His mouth fused to mine.

Music.

Dancing.

And love.

"Do you love me, Francesca?"

My ass hits the piano, a jumble of keys making a discordant cacophony. Everything beautiful about music prepares to die.

Don't open your eyes.

"Fight me. Make my dick hard," Archer says, cutting the ties around my ankles and my wrists.

I have no fight left inside of me. The gravity of this moment disappears, and I float.

It's just a body.

Words leave me.

Time ceases to exist.

The brevity of life illuminates behind my closed eyes. I hear John telling me to hurry up while we sprint through the fields after Dad promised to mark our asses because we left the gate open and two of the cows got out. I can barely keep up because I'm giggling so much after John handed Dad a black marker to do the marking. My brother was full of *life.*

"Open your eyes," Archer demands while yanking my jeans and panties down my legs.

I see the happy tears in Lynn's eyes when she shows me her engagement ring. She promises to take good care of my "other half." Lynn had the life I never dared to pursue. She had a husband who adored her. A son who was her best friend. A job. Friends. *Happiness.*

The cool wood presses to my back. This time, my heels land on the keys, making a harsh, unforgiving sound as the strings' vibration spreads beneath me.

"Open. Your. Eyes!" Archer's unkind hand grips my jaw while his hips nudge my legs apart.

I open my eyes, pointing my empty gaze at the ceiling.

It's just a body.

Archer can take every ounce of my flesh, chasing something he will never catch because I left the best of me with Jack. And he will protect it until his last breath.

I feel the embrace of Steven's arms after John died. He made me feel genuinely needed for the first time in my life. I never wanted him to let go. And I never wanted to let him down. But I did. I let all of them down.

"You might enjoy it," Archer says while his unconscionable fingers probe between my spread legs as my eyes drift shut again.

It's just a body …

The first tear slides down my cheek, taking my pain with it. I just … let go.

"Why did you let me love you?"

"That's my line."

Jack loves me.

"Get up!"

I blink open my eyes, but everything's blurry, and words are muffled because I've allowed myself to leave my body, if only for a moment.

"GET THE FUCK UP!" Archer repeats.

A sharp pain radiates from my wrist to my shoulder when he yanks my arm. I stumble to the ground on my hands and knees, naked from the waist down. When I lift my head, Slade's figure comes into view. It's all just a bad dream. Everything's in slow motion. *This* is not real.

Archer starts to pull his pants up his legs. Jogging pants. When did he change out of his suit? I blink slowly. Wait … I … I think he showered so he could be clean when he forced himself onto me.

Smoke.

I smell smoke.

And as everything speeds up into real-time, I hear alarms blaring.

Then I see him.

It's just my body …

I'm sorry.

Please forgive me.

I love you.

CHAPTER THIRTY-SEVEN
JACKSON

THREE SHOTS. Three seconds.

Jackson spots the three armed men retreating from the house's perimeter as flames engulf half the roof. He drops to his knees and lifts his rifle, eye on the scope.

Blink.

Blink.

Inhale.

Exhale.

Pause ...

No breath.

He lines up the crosshairs. Not even a minuscule movement.

One.

Crosshairs.

Two.

Crosshairs.

Three.

Then he runs toward the door, through the entry, left, right, another right, gun in one hand, other hand reaching for his knife.

"Stop," he says to Slade when he sees him stalking toward Archer, gun pointed at his head.

Archer pulls up his pants, and Jackson's gaze shifts to the floor behind him. Francesca is next to a white piano on her hands and knees, missing clothes below her waist. Jackson tightens his grip on his knife and holsters his gun. Archer won't die from a bullet. He won't die quickly. And he won't die with dignity.

Francesca blinks, and tears spill onto her cheeks.

"We have ten minutes tops," Slade says, aiming his gun at Archer's head.

"Where the fuck did you come from?" Archer asks Slade because Slade and Livy have been "dead" for nearly two years.

Slade doesn't say anything because one of the rules is that once a target's captured, there's nothing left to say. Words waste time. Words can fuck with the mind. There's a reason they tell people who are looking death in the eye to confess personal information. It humanizes them. And humans, by nature, aren't meant to kill their own.

Jackson ignores everyone but Frankie. He pockets his knife, kneels before her, and helps her to her feet. It's as if time stands still. He should be numb inside. That's all he's ever known when taking out a target. But tonight, he feels everything. As she stands on shaky legs, he dresses her.

"Jackson," Slade says.

But he ignores him because he can only hear Chopin. And he can only see Frankie sitting at his piano with her fingers effortlessly flying over the keys, making something impossibly hard look utterly effortless. She has a mesmerizing, timeless grace.

After her underwear is in place, he patiently threads her

feet through the legs of her jeans and pulls them up her shaky legs ...

Zipper.

Button.

Then he climbs to his feet and takes her tear-stained face in his hands while she softly sobs.

He smiles before pressing a kiss to her wet lips. "Good night," he whispers like they're in a room alone. No fire. No one he needs to kill. Just a man kissing *the girl* good night. After he releases her face, Jackson faces Archer, who seems dumbfounded by his actions.

With a slight nod at Slade, Jackson curls his hand around his knife again, holding it at his side, his back to Frankie. Slade steps behind Jackson and takes Frankie's hand to lead her out of the burning house.

Something explodes in an adjacent room, sending smoke billowing toward them.

Archer jumps back and coughs on the black cloud of smoke.

Frankie coughs as she and Slade exit the room. "Jack!" she screams.

Jackson doesn't move. His lungs eat the smoke, no longer feeling the need for survival. Time isn't of the essence when you're willing to make the ultimate sacrifice.

"I did nothing," Archer coughs, stepping backward when Jackson moves closer. "I ... I transferred money." He coughs some more. "I'm the fucking bank! You know that's all." He stumbles several more feet until he hits the wall, knocking a painting off its hook onto the floor.

"My wife."

Archer shakes his head. "I didn't ask for a name. It's a fucking business, and you know it. You k-know the *game*." He coughs again and again, barely catching a breath.

Jackson shakes his head. "My life is not a game!"

"FUUUCK!" Archer buckles at the waist when Jackson buries his knife between Archer's legs.

Blood instantly soaks Archer's pants.

This isn't how Jackson wanted it. He wanted Archer to suffer more. But there's too much smoke. Flames will descend upon them any moment.

Jackson removes his knife, no longer able to keep his lungs from sending him into his own coughing fit. "Did you stick your fingers inside of her too?"

Archer falls to the ground, curled onto his side. "AHHH!" His lungs release what is close to his last breath when Jackson presses Archer's hand to the floor and cuts off his fingers one at a time.

Archer's cries die. No more coughing. His eyes barely blink. And there's nothing but a weak wheezing sound pressing through his lips.

Another explosion sends flames through the wall, knocking Jackson on his back, feet from Archer. He lifts his throbbing head, barely able to see the outline of Archer through the thick smoke. The blazing heat makes standing impossible, so Jackson army crawls toward Archer. When his hand bumps the knife, he takes it and lunges forward, making his own excruciating cry from the pain as the blade lands somewhere in Archer's limp body.

Jackson can't breathe. It's suffocating, like nothing he has ever experienced. He's been close to death, but never like this. When he tries to pull the knife out, his hand goes limp. Everything goes limp.

Everything fades to black—except for the music.

It's the song he wrote for Ryn. She's twirling in a circle, holding Livy—blond hair and ribbons flowing in the breeze. He has a perfect life.

"Daddy!" Livy squeals when he hugs them both, nuzzling his face into Livy's neck before kissing his wife's red lips.

Then ... nothing. It's as if someone unplugged the television during his favorite scene of his favorite movie.

"Get the fuck up ..." Angry words echo a million miles away, but they fade as quickly as they bring him out of silence.

In the next flash, he's dancing with Frankie to "Heavenly Day."

"I'm not wearing anything under this dress."

She's breathtakingly ... well, everything about her is breathtaking. She's a second chance when he never thought he deserved his first one.

"The lamb? No. Do you really think I'll be allowed to return home after letting you sacrifice your old ass to torture someone when you could have put a bullet in his head and walked out with me? No. And here's the thing ... I don't want you to ever fucking forget that I came back for you, unlike some asshole who leaves people for dead after they save your only child."

Thunk!

Jackson's lying on something.

"Jack!" Frankie's voice cracks in panic.

"Take his car," Slade says.

"Where?"

"As far from here as possible."

"Then what?" Her voice shakes.

"Then nothing."

Just play another song, Frankie. I'll dance with you all night—with or without your sister-wife dress.

CHAPTER THIRTY-EIGHT
FRANCESCA

I TAKE his car back to Eloise's. It's as far as I can safely drive. And even the ten miles to Boone feels like a stretch for using the word "safely." Halfway there, the sky opens and unleashes buckets of rain and blinding streaks of lightning.

Pulling into the garage, I focus on the rhythmic windshield wipers for long minutes before pressing the button to close the door behind me. Killing the ignition, I stare out the windshield at nothingness in a numbing quietude. This morning, I was with Archer, feeling in control.

Lemonade with Eloise.

An emotional goodbye with Jack.

The cemetery.

It doesn't feel like the span of twelve hours. It feels like weeks, months ... years.

I don't know what to do or where to go. Is Jack still alive? If he is, where was Slade taking him?

My maniacal laugh cuts through the silence. I don't recognize it as my own. "The world thinks he's dead." Tears accompany my hysterical laughter. Jackson Knight's not his real name. And Jude Day died.

No real name.

No number.

No address.

I'm in love with a ghost.

Stumbling in the dark, I go from the car to the sofa and collapse, drawing my knees to my chest.

———

THE GARBAGE TRUCK wakes me with screeching brakes and the clang of the lift. I slowly sit up and rub my eyes. For some reason, I glance around the garage, hoping to see Jack.

The idle piano keys and boxing bag tell the ending of this story. I won't see him again. Maybe he's dead, and if that's the case, I'm glad I don't know. If I figure out how to drag myself off this sofa, say goodbye to Eloise, and drive home, imagining he's alive will make it easier—imagining he's reunited with his daughter, waiting for her to give him another grandchild.

It's a long walk to the cemetery, but I need my car. And by some miracle, it's here. The door unlocked—key fob in the console where I left it. I can see why John thought this was a safer place to raise a family.

When I pull into the driveway, Eloise is on the porch in her wooden rocker, her usual spot, so much for sneaking around the back of the house to get showered and out of these smoky clothes before she sees me.

"Francesca. Oh my goodness! Are you—"

"I need a shower." I hold out a flat hand. "Can I just do that before we talk?"

The concern along her face deepens, but she returns a hesitant nod.

"Thank you," I whisper, heading into the house.

I peel off my clothes and drop them in the trash can that's too small to accommodate the bulk. When the hot water hits my head, I slick back my hair and close my eyes. The first wave of emotion hits me, and I squat in the tub, hugging my knees to my chest. After a while, the water begins to run cold; I grab the soap bar and scrub every inch of my body. But no matter how hard I scrub, I still feel Archer's flesh pressed against mine.

I can still smell his pungent cologne and the liquor on his breath.

My hands move frantically, but I still hear his voice. So I drop the bar of soap and cover my ears.

Breathe in.

Breathe out.

I am not a victim.

When I first became interested in piano and classical music, my parents scrounged the money for a piano teacher. Bertha Cabral lived a few miles down the road, an elderly lady who appeared sweet on the outside. But when it was just the two of us in her piano room, she used a tiny twig (an actual stick from a tree) to literally whip me into shape.

"Shoulders back." She'd snap the twig at the middle of my back so I'd arch it.

"No lazy wrists." She'd flick the underside of my forearms.

Bertha was as practiced with that twig as I was with the piano. She never left a welt or a mark that remained visible long enough to show my parents.

And if I started to cry, she'd say, *"You are too weak to ever be great, Francesca. The great ones channel their emotions into the notes but are ironclad on the outside. You will never be great if you can't stop being this weak girl who sits at the piano just to drivel for an hour."*

I mentally whip myself with that tiny twig and suck it up. No driveling.

"Good morning," I say, carrying a cup of coffee onto the porch to join Eloise. I even manage a believable smile as if she didn't see me at my worst thirty minutes earlier.

She eyes me with caution while I sit in the other rocker. "Long night?" Her gaze shifts to my wet hair before sweeping along my face.

I nod, sipping my coffee. "Long night."

"Where's Jack?"

Taking a minute, I swallow and gaze at the garage. It's just. Not. Real. "He went for a jog."

Eloise nods slowly, but I don't detect an ounce of trust in her wordless response.

"Dear, are things not going so well between you two? Is there something you want to discuss? I hope you know you can trust me with anything."

With a deep breath, I harness the courage to keep going and let go of the people I have loved with my whole heart— the ones I have lost forever. And I whisper the only truth I know right now because I don't trust myself. I don't know which parts of the previous twenty-four hours are real. "I'm going home."

Eloise's brow furrows. "You are?"

I nod.

After a long moment, she smiles. "I think that's the right decision." She's being incredibly kind. I saw my reflection in the bathroom mirror. I looked like death warmed over. I had soot on my face and clothes.

"I suppose you heard."

My gaze lifts to hers. "Heard what?"

"There was a fire at the Sanford's last night."

I grip the coffee mug tighter.

Eloise eyes me, and I feel translucent, but I don't blink. Instead, I let her see deep into my eyes that fill with the tears I refuse to set free.

She sips her coffee, breezily averting her gaze to the road. "I saw it on the news this morning. They're not disclosing names, but there were casualties."

"Tragic," I murmur.

"I do hope Jackson returns soon."

She hopes he's alive. I see it in *her* eyes. All the things she's not saying. She's giving me the deep breadth of space to share what I can—if I can—and only when I can.

"I'm going to pack my things." I stand and reach for the door. "Jack ... gave me his piano since it's damaged. So if he forgets to tell you, and you see a moving truck show up, don't be alarmed. I'm going to make arrangements as soon as I get home."

Eloise quickly blots the corners of her eyes and offers me a brave smile. "He must have really cared for you."

Cared ...

Past tense.

"I think so," I say without looking back at her.

CHAPTER THIRTY-NINE
JACKSON

"Welcome back," Jessica says to Jackson. The warmth of her hand spreads along his arm when she gently squeezes it.

He has no recollection of time, but it feels like he's been asleep forever.

"If you try to die again, I will kill you."

"If—" His voice breaks into a partial word at best.

Jessica lifts her head. "Shh. You have laryngeal burns from smoke inhalation. And ..." Her eyes fill with tears, but she glances away and wipes them while pulling in a shaky breath. "Your heart has stopped twice."

Her words lack clarity. Why would his heart stop twice? And who felt the need to bring him back to life *twice*?

"Livy's here." She smiles. "Well, she took Wylder outside to play."

Jackson's gaze scans the room. He's in a big plastic bubble with machines all around him, portable lights, and a slew of electrical cords.

"Slade called in a favor. So did I. So did Luke." She shakes her head like she's mad at him for making them use up all of their favors. "It took a week to get you stable enough to transport you from a makeshift hospital in Kansas to a makeshift hospital here in San Francisco. Your doctors are old—pulled out of retirement and, quite honestly, struggling with dementia. But you're alive, so let's not leave anyone a bad review."

He tips his chin into a tiny nod. His throat feels raw and irritated, like he needs to clear it, but his body thwarts the slightest attempt to do anything but lie still and breathe.

"Good boy." Jessica winks. "Be right back. Livy's going to bawl her eyes out. Just be prepared."

Livy ...

It's been over two years since Jackson's seen his daughter. And he's never met Wylder in person. Livy's not the only one who might bawl her eyes out. She's here, which means whatever he did ended things—Day, Knight, and everything in between.

God, I hope it's over.

Livy pulls back the plastic curtain, tears already soaking her cheeks. Jackson knows he has no chance of keeping it together. Behind her, Slade's holding Wylder, who hides his face like he's shy.

"Daddy," Livy chokes as she hugs him.

He inhales her floral scent as her blond hair brushes his face. "Livy," he whispers, falling into silent, uncontrolled sobs.

She doesn't let go, and he's OK with that. His hands rest on her back. Jessica and her husband, Luke, file into the space too.

When Livy loosens her grip on him, she wipes her eyes and sniffles. "Meet your grandson." She takes Wylder from Slade and sits him next to her on the edge of Jackson's bed.

He smiles, wiping his eyes before resting his hand on Wylder's head.

"Wylder, this is your grandpa."

Grandpa.

Jackson's still unsure about that title, but he's deeply in love with the blond-haired boy who giggles when his nose is bopped. "He's ... perfect," Jackson whispers.

"The doctor said your throat should be fine in a few weeks. So, as long as your heart stops trying to quit, the prognosis is good. Do you remember much from going in and out of consciousness?" Livy asks.

He rolls his head from side to side, still mesmerized by the little boy on his bed. When Jackson's gaze shifts to Slade, something unspoken passes between them.

This boy will never hurt a soul. He will live a beautiful life. We will give him everything no one else in this room has had the privilege of experiencing—peace.

"Someone's awake." The doctor enters the bubble.

"Let's give him some space," Luke says.

Everyone exits except Jessica, his other half. The doctor pokes, prods, taps, inspects, shines a bright light in Jackson's eyes, and asks him a few questions.

"If you stay stable for twenty-four hours, your family can get you out of here, and my brother can move his airplanes back inside." He winks at Jackson before slipping out of the bubble.

Jessica grins. "Dr. Swen's brother owns a small aviation company, and his wife sells medical equipment. You can thank Luke for this private hospital. Then, you can thank me for the unofficial medical care in Kansas. And finally, you can thank Slade for the helicopter that got you to the doctors I lined up right after the fire."

That's why Jackson was supposed to die. An ambulance couldn't be called because there was no clean-up team, and "unofficial" medical care was not only exorbitant, but it was also nearly impossible. So, his family had to drain a lot of their savings to do the impossible.

"You should have let me die," he says with a raspy whisper.

Jessica returns a crestfallen expression. "You're probably right. I've thought that about myself more than once. It's weird to think of the ways we've ended lives in a matter of seconds. Yet, we've gone to the ends of the earth to save lives too. What makes one life more precious than another?"

Nothing. It's all just a game. An awful game.

"Le début," she says, squeezing his hand.

"The beginning," he says, turning his hand so their fingers interlace.

CHAPTER FORTY
JACKSON

WYLDER TODDLES along the hardwood floor while Livy chases him. It's a big open space where Jackson's piano used to be.

"You should get a new one," Jessica says, glancing up from her computer while Luke paces the deck on the phone with a patient.

Jackson stands from his recliner and scoops Wylder when he skitters by him. Wylder squeals as Jackson blows on his belly. He knows it's the most beautiful sound in the world, far exceeding anything that can be played with black and white ivory keys. Livy's grin reaches her ears, and her eyes fill with emotion as they have since Jackson's been home for the past three weeks.

"I have all I need right here," he says with a voice that's almost back to normal.

"What happened to your piano? Isn't it in Kansas?" Livy asks, picking up Wylder's toys before someone steps on them.

"It's gone," Slade answers her, closing the front door behind him.

She lights up, padding her way to him. Everything about him softens with her. His hands rest on her hips while she lifts onto her toes and kisses him, arching her back to accommodate her pregnant belly.

Jackson sets Wylder onto his chubby bare feet, who dashes toward his mom like a wind-up car, eventually hugging her leg.

"How do you know?" Livy lifts Wylder onto her hip, but Slade steals him from her. He doesn't like her carrying two children. It makes Jackson despise him a little less.

"I sent someone to clear out the garage. The car was there, but the piano was gone," Slade says.

Jackson heads to the kitchen, looking for something to throw on the grill for dinner.

"I bet she took it," Jessica says, hopping onto a barstool.

"Who?" Livy wedges herself between Jackson and the fridge. "We're having tofu kabobs."

"*We?*" Jackson eyes her when she turns toward him, holding a covered bowl of marinated tofu.

"Jessica promised it would taste like chicken." Livy shrugs, squeezing past him to the counter. "Who took your piano?"

Jackson shuts the fridge door and leans against it, arms crossed, gaze glued to Jessica. She knows the look has nothing to do with tofu's ability to taste like chicken.

"Your dad met someone," Jessica says slowly, testing the water.

Jackson's gaze slides to Slade.

"I told her to take your car and get as far away as possible." Slade lifts Wylder onto his shoulders.

Jackson knows what he told her, so he nods slowly.

"Hello? Who is *she*? You met someone?" Livy asks with wide eyes. "Why does everyone keep me in the dark?"

300

"Because you're in the business of growing humans, which requires no stress," Jessica says, rubbing Livy's back.

Livy rolls her eyes. "I'm not that fragile."

"Her name is Francesca ... Frankie." Jackson feels a mix of emotions just saying her name. "She's a professor of music theory."

Livy's lips part for a breath before pulling into a huge grin.

Jackson's smile is more subdued. Things ended too bittersweet. "She got tangled in my business." He opts not to revisit Frankie's pursuit of revenge. "She lost her brother and his family. She was in Boone dealing with their things. They were Eloise's neighbors."

"And?" Livy's wide eyes circumnavigate the room, looking for anyone to elaborate.

Jessica and Slade know it's not their story to share, so they keep their expectant gazes on Jackson.

"She was in the fire. Slade saved her. And that's when he told her to take my car and get as far away as possible."

"Did you ..." Livy's enthusiasm wanes. "I mean ... was there something between the two of you? Or just a love of music?"

Jack stares at the floor for a few seconds, wondering if he should tell his daughter the truth. How will she feel about her father moving on from her mother?

"Dad?" Livy says softly.

He lifts his gaze. It doesn't help that Livy's the spitting image of Ryn. Telling her feels like telling Ryn. And who tells their wife, the mother of their only child, that someone else has made her way into his heart?

And does it matter now?

"Mom's gone. She's never coming back. If you found

someone, she would want you to take another chance on happiness ... on love."

Jackson returns a thoughtful nod. There are too many people in the room for it to be so silent. "She was what I needed. And I think I was what she needed. But that wasn't her life. It wasn't my life. *This* is my life."

Livy and Jessica share matching frowns.

"Luke, do something." Jessica jerks her head in Jackson's direction.

Luke narrows his eyes at Jessica.

"He's not thinking straight," she says through clenched teeth as if Jackson can't hear her.

With a sigh, Luke eyes Jackson. "Would you like to talk about this with me in private?"

Jackson answers with a look. It's the are-you-fucking-kidding-me look.

Luke shrugs at Jessica. "There you have it."

"Steaks for the men, fake chicken for the ladies?" Jackson pulls steaks wrapped in white butcher paper from the fridge.

CHAPTER FORTY-ONE
FRANCESCA

Dear Molly,

Do you believe in an afterlife? I don't. I think when we die, that's it. We don't come back as a new person—no do-overs. Fearing death is weird. Don't you think? It's the fear of the unknown. But isn't every day an unknown? We should no more fear death than waking up each day, walking out of our house, and getting into a car.

I heard about that video by the river. I'm sure it wasn't planned. I bet someone just happened to see you get into Colin's truck, and their curiosity got the best of them. I bet it was someone you crossed. How unfortunate.

I know it must have been embarrassing for you. If someone did that to me, and I lost my dad, I don't think I would survive. I'd want a do-over.

I bet your mom's struggling to keep it together.

After watching her teenage daughter snort cocaine off a naked guy's stomach and then losing her husband so tragically, I bet she's struggling to keep it together. I bet she misses your dad. It has to feel nearly impossible to wake up each morning. But she does it for you. And now she has to watch you deal with the ramifications of being a sexually promiscuous drug addict who convinced her ex-boyfriend to kill himself.

Will she find time for her extra-marital affairs while finding a new home?

I wonder how often she must think of just checking out.

It has to be unbearable for her.

Just know that despite what happened with the leaked video, I forgive you for writing that letter to Steven. It was hard at first to move on from Steven's death, knowing that you were responsible. It was hard to watch you not suffer the way I was suffering. But I take great solace in knowing that it will never end. You will always be that selfish girl who cares for no one but yourself. And in some ways, I bet the consequences of your selfishness feel like they've stolen your whole life.

I can barely see the paper, and the ink blotches are from my tears because I fucking forgive you. I forgive you so much that I don't ever want you to feel like you're not worthy of the air you breathe. I never want you to feel like your life is

*not worth living. I want you to own your mistake
and move on.*

    It's not okay to check out.
    It's not okay to take the do-over.
    There is no do-over.
    There is only DO BETTER.
    Sincerely, Francesca

A MONTH AGO, I hugged Molly after her father's funeral
and handed her this letter (laced with her own words to
Steven) before I walked away. Not one single word was
exchanged. I needed to see the pain in her eyes. I needed to
see a glimpse of real emotion.

It's true. I don't want her to die. I think a little evil
resides in all of us. Molly's had horrible role models. And
the truth is... my brother was a terrible role model for
Steven. He not only lost his job, but he also took up
drinking like a retired banker takes up golfing. Lynn said he
was drunk nearly every day before noon, about the time it
takes to play eighteen holes. Then for his grand finale, he
took his life most spectacularly... leaving his brains stuck to
the backside of his goddamn garage for his wife *and son* to
see. Who does that?

I had the chance to do better, to be better. But I wasn't.
And I will live with the consequences of my actions for the
rest of my life. But I'm okay with that because life *is*
precious. Everyone has something to give and to gain.

Every mistake is an opportunity—a chance to be
humbled, to learn, to grow, to make amends, to *do better*.

Unlike how she wrapped her horrific message to Steven

in poisonous Saccharin, I didn't sugarcoat anything for Molly. Truth? She will think of Steven every day for the rest of her life. And she'll think of me. We will forever be reminders that bad decisions come with accountability. The memories of us will be her new god—the north of her new moral compass.

"I have a new job."

My therapist smiles curtly. "You've mentioned that several times, but you haven't said how you feel about your new job?"

I gaze at my glass of water on the oval wood coffee table between us. I should have asked for ice. I hate the taste of her water. She needs a glass pitcher instead of a metal one. "Privileged." My gaze shifts to hers, assessing her assessment of me. "I'm a terrible patient. Just say it."

Dr. West shakes her head. The last time I saw her, I'd lost my job. And I needed someone to tell me I wasn't an awful person.

She's good at listening but not reassuring. I never did get her to say the words I wanted to hear. Now, I want to talk about the fire, but I don't know how to bring it up, and we're on our third session this month.

"How would you describe your mood?"

"Melancholy."

"Why do you suppose you feel melancholy?"

"Because I ..."

Dr. West doesn't hurry me. She's patient. Maybe too patient. Sometimes, I want her to drag more out of me and do it faster than she does with such benign, open-ended questions.

Drawing a slow breath, I let it and everything else out simultaneously. "I went to Boone to go through their belongings. I met a man. Fell in love ... I think. And another man sexually assaulted me. But I didn't fight back. In many ways, I let him. So, I'm not sure where that falls on the spectrum of assault. It's messy. I've been trying to 'check in' with myself to see if I'm suppressing a catastrophic breakdown. And I don't ... well, I don't know how I feel. Maybe there's nothing to feel. I dealt with everything in the moment, and I'm good. Or perhaps I'm headed for a massive breakdown with no warning, like when I lost it at the CVS and had sex with the dean's husband. Thoughts?"

She nods slowly. "I'm so sorry you experienced that. Are you ready to walk me through it?"

I don't want to tell her about my revenge plans or the suicide note. I want her to tell me it's okay to put it behind me and move on. Maybe we can run through it instead of walking through it—no need to dwell.

"I've known a handful of married women who had sex with their husbands when they didn't want to ... so ... without consent." I stare out the window at New York in the fall; trees adorn it in shades of gold and orange. "Is that a gray area of applied consent or 'the right' to have sex with your spouse? I can't imagine why marriage would change bodily autonomy. I, however, was a willing participant for weeks, but it never went that far for different reasons. Then, the night I was not a willing participant at all ... that's when it happened. He was angry because he felt betrayed since I found a new guy."

When Dr. West doesn't respond, I shift my attention back to her, running my hands nervously over my gray wool pants. Omitting ninety percent of the story will likely yield a ten percent success rate with this therapy, but I must try.

"Did you report it?"

I glance at my watch. "Time's up."

"We have five minutes."

I stand. "I have class. Thank you. I'll schedule another appointment, but I don't know when. But you think I'm good, right?"

Her lips part, but nothing comes out.

"Good enough?" A nervous laugh escapes as I slide my bag onto my shoulder.

"Francesca ..."

"Have a good weekend." I skitter out the door, tossing the receptionist a faint grin before speedwalking out of the building. When the cool air hits my skin, I stop and just ... breathe.

"You might enjoy it."

"He's dead," I whisper to myself.

THERE'S something gratifying about teaching grad students. By this point, they're dedicated and have a greater appreciation for the professors who are not merely teachers ... we're mentors. I served my time with undergrad students. Molding ripe, young minds comes with its own level of fulfillment, but it also comes with the tedious patience of weeding through the ones who are lost and not ready to be found.

Some days, I still feel lost, but more and more, I feel like I'm ready to be found. The days I get lost in the past, the man with the piano, I couldn't care less about the rest of the world. But that's not living.

If he were alive, he'd come for me. Right?

If I truly loved him, I'd make finding him my full-time job, even if it led me to his grave. Right?

If. If. If ...

It's been months. No more ifs.

"Professor Holter? Did you get a chance to glance at my outline for the conference research paper?" A young man pokes his head into my office. "Sorry." He cringes. "Your assistant wasn't at her desk. If you're busy—"

"It's fine. I haven't looked at it. I'm sure it's on my to-do list. I have a long to-do list." I lift my eyebrows and give him a tight grin while leaning back in my desk chair after being hunched over my computer for hours.

"Sorry. My mom's starting chemo in a week, and I wanted to get it written before I cannot concentrate."

My fake grin fades. "What's your name?"

"Jack Ebertt."

Jack … Well done, John.

Of course, my brother knows I'm struggling. Even in death, we share an unbreakable bond. He knows I need a sign that everything's going to be okay.

I twist my lips while sitting straight again. "Jack..." I search for his outline "...I just so happen to like the name Jack. So let's go look over your outline." Closing my laptop, I slide it into my bag.

"Go?"

"Lunch. I'm starving." I stroll toward the door.

"You're ... I mean ... we ... we're going to lunch? Together?"

I nod toward the exit. "If you want me to give you feedback on your outline before your mom starts chemo, then yes." I brush past him.

He follows me. "I didn't expect you to be so ..."

I glance over my shoulder just before the stairs. "So what?"

"Kind." He gives me a sheepish grin. "Most of my instructors are not so ..."

"Kind?" I laugh, taking the stairs. "Well, most of my

students don't go out of their way to get ahead so they don't fall behind when they know a family member will need them. You could have used it as an excuse not to complete the paper, but you didn't. And, like I said, I'm a fan of the name Jack. So thank your mom for that when you see her." I push through the door to the campus. "Thank your mom for everything."

This feels good. *Living* feels good.

Dr. West doesn't need to tell me I'm good. It's a decision I'm making on my own. I can be a victim or a survivor. I choose the latter.

CHAPTER FORTY-TWO
JACKSON

"Idaho," Jackson says, staring off from his deck into the trees of his wooded lot in Hyde Park.

"Yes," Livy hands him a cup of coffee and leans on the railing beside him. She took a job at a law firm in Boise, and Jackson made an offer on the house across the street from hers and Slade's. "I think we're going to love it here."

He hums in agreement.

"As long as you and Slade can manage not to kill each other."

Jackson grunts. "He needs a job."

"*I* have a job. An excellent job. Do you have a problem with Slade being a stay-at-home dad?"

"He's going to get restless."

Livy nudges his arm. "You mean, you're going to get restless watching him stay home instead of doing his manly duties of supporting me while I stay home and raise the kids as mom did."

"You're putting words in my mouth." He turns so he's facing the opposite direction as her.

She smirks before sipping her tea.

JEWEL E. ANN

"I'm going to miss our mornings together when you start your job."

"Me too, Dad." Livy smiles. "We spent too much time apart. And I didn't know if I'd ever see you again. So this is magical."

Jackson nods.

She pushes off the railing. "What are you going to do? You need a hobby."

"Playing with Wylder is my hobby."

"I love that, and so does he. But you have virtually no furniture in your house. No piano. No workout room. You don't have a job. No golfing buddies."

"I don't golf."

Livy sits in his deck chair. "You have one chair on your deck. You need another chair. You need someone to sit beside you and help solve the world's problems."

He frowns.

She returns a wrinkled-nosed grin. "Okay. You don't need to solve the world's problems. You've done enough of that. But you could use a friend. A companion. Maybe a dog."

Jackson chuckles, bringing his coffee to his lips. "Dogs don't like me."

"Not true. Jericho likes you."

"He doesn't. Your husband made sure of it."

"Well," Livy shrugs because she knows it's true, "maybe not a dog. Maybe you should join a club. Or teach self-defense classes again. You were good at that."

"Sweetheart, I appreciate your concern, but I can plan my days just fine."

She tucks her chin like she did when she was young.

"You're too old to pout."

"I'm not pouting," she says in a pouty tone before sighing. "Where is she?"

"She?"

"The woman you met in Boone?"

He shrugs. A lie. Jackson knows she took a position at a university in New York. He knows she bought an older three-bedroom home. He knows she joined a yoga and Pilates studio. And he's pretty sure she has his piano.

"You haven't thought about looking her up?"

"Why would I do that? She probably lives on the other side of the country. And I live in Boise with my family."

"Well," Livy stands and wraps her hand around his wrist while kissing his cheek, "Slade and I will be here raising our family, doing everything you've already done, so feel free to come and go as you please. We're not going anywhere."

"Where do I have to go?" He eyes her over the rim of his coffee mug.

She shrugs, heading into his house. "I'm sure a smart guy like you is only a quick internet search away from that answer."

CHAPTER FORTY-THREE
FRANCESCA

Back to the basics.

Today, I've chosen a lecture on advanced aural skills. It's a ninety-minute lecture, and I call for class participation to keep everyone focused. Since I offered extra credit for attendance, the auditorium is packed for the first time this semester.

"In conclusion, honing your skills for critical listening, notating four-part chromatic harmony and melodies, as well as advanced rhythm, meter, and instrumentation, will be invaluable assets for many of you in your future careers. Thank you for attending today's lecture. Can we get a round of applause for the willing and not-so-willing volunteers?" I smile and clap.

Laughter follows with a big applause before chatter erupts while the students gather their belongings to exit the auditorium.

As I collect my things, sliding them into my messenger bag, several students line up to ask questions. While addressing the last student, my gaze flits to the lone person sitting in the lecture hall.

"Thank you, Professor Holter. Great lecture," the young woman says, slinging her bag over her shoulder before climbing the stairs to the exit.

"Thanks." The delayed sentiment falls from my parted lips, eyes unblinking, after she's ten steps away from me.

When the door clicks shut behind her, I search for my voice, but it's nowhere to be found.

"You're a sight to behold," he says.

I laugh, but it sounds like a sob as I blink back tears. If I can hold it together, today will be the perfect day. Maybe the best day of my whole life. "You stole my line."

"Professor Holter, I could listen to you all day. Extraordinary as always."

It's a nearly impossible feat to keep from crying. He's alive.

And he's here.

"Thought you were dead." I set my mic and battery pack on the table with shaky hands.

"Me too."

I climb up the middle aisle of stairs and slide into his row, legs getting shakier with each step. Jack doesn't move. He waits patiently in his chair like a good student.

"I'm glad you're not." I sit beside him, hugging my bag and staring at the lectern.

"Me too," he whispers.

"What brings you to New York?"

"Fall foliage."

I grin without taking my eyes off the lectern. When I focus on it, my emotions stay in check. "It's stunning," I murmur.

"Stunning indeed."

A silence seeps between us for a long moment.

"Dark hair," he says.

I touch my hair. "It's my natural color. I decided blondes don't have more fun." I cringe. "Sorry. I know your wife had blond hair, as does your daughter and grandson. I just meant it wasn't for me."

"I feel like I'm seeing you for the first time. And ... I'm speechless," he says.

That thing in my chest that's supposed to keep me alive feels like it's on the verge of exploding. My watch vibrates with an alert. "I have meetings the rest of the afternoon. Are you, by chance, staying around for a day or two?" I stand, sliding the crossbody strap over my head.

"By chance, I believe I *will* be here for a day or two." He rests his hands on the arms of the chair and stands. Just his proximity could burn me to the ground, not to mention his grin.

These arms of mine want to wrap around him, but I won't be able to let go. And I do have meetings.

"Where are you staying?"

"Cheap motel."

My lips roll together to hide my grin as I nod. "Sounds like you. If you'd like a step up from a cheap motel, I'd be happy to offer you a room at my house."

"Is that so?" He slides his hands into his pockets. He's not in black. I'm not sure I've seen him wearing blue jeans. I definitely haven't seen him in a white undershirt and a blue checkered button-down. White sneakers. A little gray in his five o'clock shadow. He looks like *life*.

"Yes." I clear my throat. "Either way, if you don't have dinner plans, I'll be home by six." I turn and make my way to the exit. "Feel free to wait for me there. Help yourself to anything in the fridge."

"I'll need an address ... and a key," he says, right behind me.

I turn when I get to the door. "No, you won't." I smirk.

"My days of nefarious activities are over."

Pushing through the door, I laugh. "You found me here."

"That's basic internet information."

"Well, maybe I'll see you later. Maybe I won't."

I'm *dying*.

My heart's clawing at my ribcage, and my tummy's doing acrobatics. Playing cool has never felt this excruciating. As I stroll toward the opposite end of the building, I cave for a second and glance over my shoulder.

Jack's leaned against the wall, fingers tucked into his front pockets. A face-splitting grin. And he's just watching me.

ZERO CONCENTRATION. Less than zero.

I smile and nod during my meetings. When asked questions, I fumble my words only to have to request the question be repeated. Two fender benders on the way home force me to reroute, taking twice as long to get there. When I pull into my garage at six-thirty, I'm bummed that there's no car in my driveway.

Maybe he took a cab.

"Breathe," I whisper against my racing pulse before opening the house door.

Beautiful notes fill the space around me when I step inside. I don't recognize the song. Lowering my bag to the floor and slipping off my ankle boots, I pad my way to the great room with my favorite centerpiece and person perched on its bench.

Jack eyes me without missing a note. "You fixed Black Beauty."

My fingers slide along the lid. "Black Beauty?"

He nods.

"You named your piano?"

"Of course."

I know the song. He's playing "The Story" by Brandi Carlisle, but he's added some parts.

"Did you not have a piano?" He glances at his hands for a second.

"I did. A nameless piano."

"What happened to it?"

"It's at the university on loan. I didn't have room for two." I sit next to him, facing the opposite direction. When my arm brushes him, my breath catches in silence.

"Why take Black Beauty?"

I lean into him. "You know why," I whisper.

He stops playing, leaving his hands resting on the keys. "I got her after Jessica and I were relocated to Omaha. Beauty made the trip from Omaha to San Francisco. San Francisco to Kansas. And Kansas to New York."

I glance up at him. "Where will she go next?"

Jack's brows tighten for a second. "I'm not sure."

It hurts to see him as much as it breathes life back into my soul to know he's alive. So much has happened.

"Don't cry," he whispers.

I shake my head a half dozen times even though I can't speak actual words. If I don't blink, I'll be fine. No tears.

Then ...

That amber-eyed gaze sweeps along my face as his knuckles brush my cheek.

Don't cry.

His middle finger touches my forehead, drawing that

invisible line down my nose while the pads of his other fingers ghost over my eyes, forcing them to blink—forcing me to set the tears free.

I'm a goner. My lips quiver beneath his touch.

"I'm sorry I let it happen," his voice cracks.

Again, I shake my head but can't speak past the emotion clogging my throat. There's so much I want to say, but I physically can't.

I stand, wiping my eyes and taking a few steps from the piano. "Y-you did nothing wrong." Sniffling, I swallow over and over to find space for the words to come out. "Let's ... let's grab dinner." Drawing a superhuman breath, I turn and smile while wiping my eyes again. "I'm starving."

"Frankie ..." Worry lines trench along his forehead.

"Do you like pizza? I haven't had pizza in a while."

Sliding the bench back, he stands but won't match my smile. Not even close. "Francesca ..." He steps toward me.

Again, I swallow past the emotion and hug myself, so he doesn't feel the need to do it. I am a survivor. Not a victim.

As much as I've missed him and prayed he wasn't dead, what kept me from searching for him was this right here— standing on the edge of *this* moment. The expectant look on his face like I have something to explain or confess. Because the last time he saw me, I was half-naked on my hands and knees. I can barely look him in the eye, let alone speak of what happened that night.

"Can we not look back? I'm not. I'm just ... living."

"I ... I need to reconcile all of this in my head." He slowly shakes his head as if he doesn't understand why *I* don't understand.

"Have you reunited with your daughter?"

When he doesn't answer, I'm forced to lift my gaze to him. He doesn't answer me intentionally because he wants me to look him in the eye. Does he think I'll see all the things he wants to say? Because I do. I see the unspoken words and emotions that are too strong for words. That's why we don't need to discuss it.

"Yes. Livy is back where she belongs. And I've held Wylder." The hint of a smile pulls at his mouth.

I hate that he's suppressing his joy. I *need* to see his happiness. It validates all of my emotions. What happened wasn't for nothing. It was for something so much bigger than anything in my life. Family is precious. So *very* precious. And Jackson has his back, and I have no regrets.

I smile, hoping he feels my sincere happiness for him. More smiles. More about his family. "I bet he's happiness personified."

Jack's emotional struggle is palpable and heartbreaking, but he shows me a little more, and he's never looked this beautiful. "He's so innocent. It's ..." He shakes his head.

"Just as it should be." I think of Steven at Wylder's age. A little towhead too.

I'm not fooling myself; I know Jack can't let this go, but he blows out a long breath and offers a grin that feels like a truce. "Pizza sounds perfect."

CHAPTER FORTY-FOUR
JACKSON

JACKSON SPENT years keeping other people safe, often strangers to him. Yet, for all the lives he helped save by taking a life that wasn't worth saving, nothing makes up for losing Ryn. And nothing will erase the guilt he feels over Frankie.

She drives to the restaurant, talking non-stop about her students and all the work that went into her lecture today. Jackson smiles on cue and nods in timely intervals.

"Tell me to shut up." She chuckles after they're seated in a booth. "I've been yammering on about my life. Tell me about Livy and Wylder. Are you still Jack, or have you returned to Jude Day?"

Is she giving him the mere surface of her existence, or is she that strong? Is she a Jessica Day? An expert at shedding her skin and moving on. Are they really going to make small talk?

He sips his water, glancing around the restaurant. "Still Jackson Knight."

"Why not go back to Jude?"

He shrugs.

With a sad smile, Frankie shakes her head. "Sorry. It's not fair of me to ask you to go back in time if I'm not willing to do it."

He wishes she would.

"I met my wife as Jackson Knight. He's the one who fell in love with her."

Before Frankie can respond, they place their order with the waiter. By the time they're alone again, Frankie's eyeing him intently. "I can't believe you're a grandpa."

"No?" He leans back, crossing his arms. "Why is that?"

Her cheeks flush. "You have the uh..." her lips press together for a beat "...the stamina of someone much younger than fifty-*something*."

"Thanks. You don't fuck like an old lady either."

Frankie snorts, covering her mouth.

Jackson's trying hard to stay in the moment and follow her lead, but he can't shake the reality of what happened. He'll never forget.

"I'd like to think I'm feeding your ego, not bruising it." She runs a hand through her straight dark hair that barely brushes her shoulders.

"Same." He smirks.

She melts into a relaxed posture and an equally soft expression. "I'd say I've forgotten how much I've missed you, but that would be a lie. I've missed you every day in the most unforgettable way."

"Same."

She blushes again and clears her throat. "Can we talk about the present?"

"Of course." He slides his glass and silverware out of the way when the waiter delivers their salads.

Frankie retrieves her fork from the rolled-up napkin. "Where are you living?"

"Boise, Idaho." He stabs his fork into the lettuce. "Livy took a job at a law firm there, so I followed them. Bought a house right across the street."

She nods while wiping her mouth. "Livy's an attorney. That's great."

"It is."

"Are you the nanny?"

He chuckles. "Much to my chagrin, Slade's the nanny. I'm just the adult in the room."

"Have you two buried the hatchet?"

"No. That hatchet can't be buried." He takes several gulps of his water while glancing around the restaurant. "A truce is as good as it gets. As long as he treats my daughter with the love and respect she deserves and swears to lay down his life for hers from now until eternity, I will tolerate him for the greater good."

She taps her fork against her lip. "So you think he's perfect for Livy. That's all you had to say."

"I said no such thing." Jackson rolls his eyes, but it doesn't stop him from grinning.

"You didn't have to."

Over the next hour, Jackson suspends his guilt over Frankie long enough to tell her everything Wylder does that's irresistible, smart, and advanced—basically, all the ways he sees himself in his grandson. Then, on the way home, Frankie confesses everything she's done to make things right with her parents after the incident at Eloise's house.

He can't help but wonder if ignoring the past bestows failure upon the future or if it's the only way to ensure its success.

"Did you decide to stay at the Holter Hotel? Or did you get a room at a one-star motel with a high probability of bedbugs, unlaundered towels, and zero amenities?" Frankie steps out of the car and heads into the house.

Jackson closes the door behind them. "I'm not sure I can afford this five-star hotel unless you're offering the 'friends and family' discount."

She giggles while dropping her purse onto a credenza. "I might be able to extend the 'friends and family' discount if you make coffee in the morning."

"Deal."

The awkward moments of silence have multiplied as the night's progressed. Now, there's an extra-long pause—a deafening silence between two idle bodies standing five feet apart.

It's refreshing to see Frankie in her world. This older house is filled with antiques and painted wood trim. Creams, grays, and blues fill each room with splashes of pink and gold. Chandeliers and patterned upholstered furniture. It's a classic beauty, just like Francesca Holter. But it doesn't matter where they are or what they're doing because it won't erase what happened. There's not enough beauty in the world to cover that kind of ugly.

"Well," Frankie looks away first, "there are two bedrooms upstairs. You can—"

"I love you," Jackson interrupts with a declaration that seems to knock her off kilter. "I didn't come here to find my piano or see the fall foliage. I came here because I love you. And I miss you. And I *need* to know what happened the night of the fire. I can't stop thinking about it." He feels weak in his confession, but the women in his life have always been his greatest weakness and his greatest strength.

Frankie is no exception.

CHAPTER FORTY-FIVE
FRANCESCA

I'M NOT IN DENIAL. I'm actively not acknowledging what happened that night. There's a difference. Denial implies I think it's untrue or not real. I know what happened is true and bone-chillingly real.

"I'm sorry," I whisper, forcing my gaze to his, compelling myself to *actively acknowledge* his pain. "I'm sorry you can't stop thinking about it. But I *need* you to let it go. If I keep ripping off the bandage, it will never heal." With a hard swallow, I search for the truest thing I know I can share without ripping open that wound and bleeding out. "I blame PTSD and alcohol for my brother blowing his brains out. I blame Molly for Steven losing his way. And I blame an awful reality on Lynn giving up. Every time I let myself relive that day, I'm one step closer to leaving this life."

Jack winces. "Frankie ..." My name breaks in half as it falls from his lips.

"I know you're hurting, and that makes me hurt too. But if I'm okay, can't you be okay?"

His Adam's apple bobs, jaw clenched, eyes reddening.

He's constricting my heart, squeezing it so hard it feels like he's trying to rip it apart one chamber at a time. "Ryn gave me everything. And I gave her everything. And that's how we—"

"I'm not your wife," I say in a voice I don't recognize. Am I angry? Jealous? Hurt?

None of the above. I'm just being honest.

He bows his head, rubbing the tension from his neck. The waves of frustration are palpable and suffocating. "I cut off his fingers—"

"Stop." I manically shake my head.

"One at a time ..."

"Don't." The bandage tugs.

Pulling.

Taking flesh with it.

"I shoved my knife into his groin, and he—"

"Stop!" I cover my ears and continue to shake my head. A sob rips from my chest.

I see Archer above me—evil born of frustration and the misguided perception that a woman's affection can be taken.

It can't. It can only be given.

"I need this ..." Jack lifts his gaze, face scrunched. "Because you were on your ..." He chokes on his words, eyes bleeding with pain.

"P-please don't ..." I cover my mouth, releasing tears as unrelenting as this man.

"You were on your knees ... naked. It's not a wound that can heal. It's a fucking disease. And it's only going to spread if you ignore it. You won't die today, but over time... it will kill you."

"No ..." My head won't stop shaking. He doesn't know what he's talking about. He's just being cruel. "W-why are y-you doing this?" I lean forward with a wave of nausea because I smell the pungent soap that clung to Archer after his shower. I feel his fingers between my legs.

"Fight me. Make my dick hard. You might enjoy it."

Jack takes two long strides to hold my face in his hands, forcing me to look at him while I sob. "Frankie, tell me what he took from you." His whole body vibrates, as if he's one blink from falling apart with me. "It's the only way I can give it back to you," he whispers, kissing my tear-stained lips and every inch of my face. "Give me your pain."

I can't go there. Resting my hands on his chest, I push him away, stumbling back several steps. "No." I sniffle, wiping my eyes while drawing in a shaky breath. "I don't need this. I-I don't need y-you to give me anything. *You* feel guilty." I shake my head and wipe my nose. "Don't. You, of all people, know that life is really fucking hard, and nothing worth saving comes without sacrifice. I ..." Jabbing my finger into my chest, I swallow hard. "I decided to go down that dangerous road. I willingly sold my soul ... offered it as a sacrifice for the greater good. And here I am, alive and moving forward. I have a job—a life. And I now know that you're alive and reunited with your family. Can't you just let me be happy for you? Happy for me?"

The hint of an eye twitch is the only thing that remotely cracks his sullen expression. "I'm not built that way," he says.

"He's dead," I whisper.

"Doesn't matter."

"You killed him. What more do you need?"

"The truth."

"I'm not your wife. I don't need you to piece me back together."

"My wife's dead." He swallows hard, barely holding it together.

I wince. "The *truth* is … nothing I can say will change what happened. There's no revenge to seek. There are no broken pieces of me waiting to be mended. If it's *you* who needs this, then maybe you should talk to someone."

"I'm trying to fucking talk to you!" He raises his voice.

I stiffen. "Maybe a therapist—"

"My sister's husband is a shrink. I don't need a goddamn therapist. I need you."

More tears fill my eyes. "It's too … cruel," I whisper.

"Frankie, I'm not …" He runs his hands through his hair, shaking his head while his eyes gloss over with emotion. "I'm not being cruel. I need—"

"I'm not doing this." I turn and head toward my bedroom. "You're asking for too much."

"Goddammit!" His feet pound the squeaky hardwood behind me.

"Don't!" I whip around after reaching my bedroom, holding a flat hand out and losing the battle with another round of tears. "Don't cross that threshold. I'm taking my space. I'm being very clear with my words, and if you think you can bully your way in here and force me to tell you anything, then you are no better than him."

Jack flinches like I smacked his face.

I swat at my tears. "You …" My voice cracks. I hate this so much. "If you really love me, you will never ask me to relive that day."

He rests one hand on his hip and angles his torso away from me while his other hand rubs his eyes, and he clears his throat with a clenched jaw.

"Jack," I whisper.

After a pregnant pause, he looks at me.

I stop trying to hold back my tears. Every blink sends another one down my face. "It's embarrassing," I can barely whisper the words. They escape on shaky breaths, and my chest feels like it's splintering out of control. "And d-degrading." Covering my mouth, I hold my breath to stifle a sob. "Hu—miliating." I shake with more sobs. "And I … I fucking *h-hate* that you saw me on m-my hands and knees with no …" I can't finish.

If I tell him, I won't be able to look him in the eye ever again. And if that makes me weak, so be it. I'm nobody's hero. Years of schooling, mentoring, and living have not changed me when it comes to love. I'm just a girl who loves a boy. I'm just a girl who wants the boy to see the best of me.

If I truly loved him, I would give him everything.

If he truly loved me, he would never ask for everything.

We are at an impasse.

Staring at the ceiling, I wipe my eyes and will away any new tears. "I don't want that kind of love." I look at him and want to erase that indissoluble, forlorn expression on his handsome face. "I need to see where you end, and I begin. If loving you means surrendering *everything* that makes me who I am, I will always fall short."

Jack drops his gaze. After a few seconds, he turns and heads toward the stairs.

When he's no longer in sight, I close my door and sit on the velvet bench at the end of my bed, hands resting on the edge while I release the rest of my emotions one tear at a time. It feels like I'm choosing myself over him. Am I not being empathetic enough? Am I incapable of that kind of love?

I rub the heel of my hand over my heart, trying to ease the deep ache. Then I sniffle and bury my face in both hands while I cry harder.

After a shower and a cold washcloth for my swollen eyes an hour later, I slide on my nightie and pad my bare feet to the piano. My fingers caress the idle keys several times before I play "Outside, Alone" by Peter Gregson.

Closing my eyes, I sway gently. Music has, in many ways, always been my first love. Perhaps it will be my last. If my greatest love affair is with these notes and the images they inspire, the peace they bestow, I will die having experienced an emotional dimension unlike any other.

Music reaches further than words. It stretches past the heart and settles into the soul, where it belongs. Music bestows hope. It unearths memories. It sparks joy. It's without judgment. And it never dies.

When I play the last note, I feel Jack at my back. I keep my fingers resting on the keys and open my eyes.

"I should leave," he says.

I stare at my fingers, slowly letting them slide from the keys to my lap. "I know," I whisper.

He feathers his fingers down the sides of my neck to my shoulders, sliding the thin straps of my nightie down my arms. "But I can't."

Closing my eyes, I whisper, "I know."

I understand it's difficult for him to leave, but I also know he can't stay without knowing everything.

"Tell me to stop," he whispers at my ear before dragging his lips down the same path as his fingers along my shoulder.

It's gentle.

It's kind.

"I can't." I know where he's taking this. And I'm scared out of my mind, but I don't stop him.

He kisses my shoulder while his hands cup my exposed breasts. I grab his wrists, and he pauses.

I can't do this ...

Yesterday, I didn't feel broken. I felt strong. Confident.

Now, I know that wasn't real. It wasn't reality.

Jack releases my breasts, and I release his wrists. Then he places my hands over my breasts where his had been.

"You're so beautiful, my love."

I laugh, but it releases as a sob.

A shaky. Frightened. Sob.

I can't do this ...

He guides my hand along my stomach. "Benevolent." His lips skate along my neck while he slides my hand into the front of my panties.

My heart tramples itself as one beat tries to rush past the next, skipping it altogether.

"You're simply exquisite." He presses my finger over my clit and slides it farther between my legs.

Each breath rushes out with a sharp *whoosh*.

Jack's giving me back control over my body.

"I end things, Frankie." His lips brush my jaw.

I close my eyes, inching my legs apart.

"I don't know how to let them go." He squeezes the hand over my breast, and my back arches into *our* touch. "But I'll let it go if it's the only way to hold on to you."

Pulling our hands from my panties, I turn toward him. When I kiss him, he cradles my face in his hands, threading his fingers into my hair. I stand, nudging the bench to the side while my nightie drifts down my legs.

Jack kisses me deeper; my nipples brush his bare chest.

I reach behind me and close the fallboard. He ends the kiss, eyeing the piano behind me for a second.

"Not here." His concerned gaze meets mine.

I can't tell him about that night with Archer, but I can show him. And maybe it will create a new memory to replace the old one. Perhaps I'll be able to play happy songs again.

Removing my panties, I gaze at him and whisper, "Here."

"Francesca ..." he shakes his head.

Pushing onto my toes, I grab his biceps and brush my lips along his. "I'm giving you all I can. And it's so much more than my flesh and bones." I slowly kiss him. "It's more than I've ever given anyone."

Again, he grabs my face, kissing me hard. Is he angry? Hurt? Conflicted?

It doesn't matter because he lifts me onto the piano and guides me to lie back with one hand between my breasts while his other guides each foot onto the fallboard. The cool wood presses to my skin seconds before his mouth dips between my spread legs.

I moan, closing my eyes even though I'm afraid of what I'll see when they're shut.

Will I see Archer?

Will I hear his words?

Will I smell smoke?

Will I feel humiliated?

"Jack ..." I draw out his name. All my senses spin in my head. But when they come to life, when they are no longer blurry, it's him. Only him.

When I look down at him, his eyes are drunk but focused on me. He hums, and they drift shut for a beat while his tongue penetrates me and the pad of his thumb teases my clit.

My fingers scrape along the smooth wood while the waves of pleasure build into something bigger, something so intense I can't hear anything over my breaths and the pounding of my heart.

I want to moan and cry ... I want to scream his name, but I can't because my heart is wholly lodged in my throat. My hips jerk while one hand finds his hair, and my other squeezes my breast, pinching my nipple right when I orgasm. Everything blurs, and I feel like I'm floating.

My eyes blink open while he's removing his briefs. It's as if he's going through the motions, but those motions don't hide his indecision. It's like a dagger's carving lines on his face that will never heal. His gaze affixes between my spread legs while he rubs the head of his erection against me. It's warm and wet.

When our gazes meet again, my heart falls to pieces. He's so goddamn tortured.

I sit up. He doesn't stop me. I wonder if he's hoping I stop this from going further.

My middle finger touches his forehead. "Jack ..."

His brow tenses beneath my touch.

I drag my finger down his nose to his lips like he's done to me so many times. "You were born of innocence. It's time to return." I smile, brushing the pads of my thumbs across his lips. "Make love to me. No one's ever done that."

He takes a moment. I'll happily give him forever if that's how long it takes him to *let go*.

He pushes into me and stills. Our foreheads meet while he wraps me in his protective arms. "Fuck ..."

I grin. There's the man I love.

He pulls partway out and, just as slowly, thrusts back into me. We find a rhythm. We find each other.

We find now, lose yesterday, and hold on for tomorrow.

CHAPTER FORTY-SIX
JACKSON

NEW YORK IS on the opposite side of the country from Idaho—for anyone who needs a geography lesson.

Jackson doesn't.

He's all too aware of the distance between the women he loves. After three days with Frankie, of which she spends most of her time at the university, he gets a text from Livy while on his morning jog.

> Livy: I'm in labor. It's early. Not too early.
> The midwife says everything is fine. Don't
> rush home. Love u

Jackson sprints the rest of the way back to Frankie's house. It's a little before six in the morning, and she's already out of the shower, drying her hair for work.

When she sees his reflection in the bathroom mirror, she grins. He winks and peels off his sweaty clothes. His ego gobbles up every tiny glance she aims in his direction—the way she wets her lips while her gaze moves down his naked body.

"I fucking love you," he says just to get her attention before he steps into the shower.

Heat blooms in shades of pink along her cheeks. She knows he caught her staring.

He needs to book a flight home. He needs to say good-bye. Then, he needs to figure out what will happen when he leaves. When this baby arrives, Jackson won't want to leave anytime soon. He's already agreed to help with Wylder.

But he's in love with a brilliant music professor who lives in New York.

After his shower, he books the next flight to Boise and packs his bag.

Frankie's sipping coffee in the kitchen while sliding her thumb along her phone screen. Her smile fades when she glances up at him and sees his bag.

He drops it by the door. "Livy's in labor."

Frankie's smile returns. "Do you need me to book you a flight?"

"Just did."

"Do you need a ride to the airport? I can call in—"

"I have a rental car parked on the street." Jackson takes her coffee and sips it before setting it on the counter.

Frankie looks so brave, but he sees the slight wobble of confidence in her eyes. She knows they haven't discussed the logistics of their geographical challenge. He pulls her into him and kisses the top of her head.

"Had I known you were leaving so soon, I wouldn't have let you go for that jog." She slides her hands into his back pockets and kisses his sternum. "What time is your flight? I can go in late. It's just a boring meeting."

He chuckles. "Had I known you only had a boring meeting, I would have pulled you into the shower with me. My flight's in less than two hours. I have to go."

"Go be a grandpa. I'll send you a cardigan." She wriggles out of his arms and grabs her coffee, hiding her sad smile behind the mug.

"Come for Thanksgiving." He glances at his watch, not wanting to miss his flight.

"I'm not sure how my parents will feel about me missing Thanksgiving after ..." She trails off, finishing her thought with a somber expression instead of actual words.

"I understand." Jackson, once again, steals her coffee and sets it back on the counter. "We'll figure something out. Maybe next month, I can bring Wylder out here and give Livy and Slade time alone with the baby."

Frankie lights up, wrapping her arms around his neck. "I would love that so much."

"Yeah?"

"Yeah." She kisses him.

His hands lower to her ass. All he wants to do is pull her skirt up her slender legs and lift her onto the counter. He's unsure which feels more unbearable: missing his flight or leaving without a proper goodbye that involves being inside her.

Listening to her moan into his mouth.

Feeling her tremble from his touch.

With Frankie, he doesn't feel like a fifty-*something* grandpa. He feels like a twenty-something who can't get enough of the girl he loves. When he's not fucking her, he's thinking about it, actively plotting the quickest way to get her naked.

Francesca Holter is his fountain of youth.

"I can be quick," she murmurs over his lips while stroking him on the outside of his jeans.

Fuck me ...

"I have it on good authority that you don't get on your knees for just anyone." He bites her lip and grins. If he keeps it playful, his hard-on might deflate before he has to go through airport security.

She slowly pulls her lip from his hold. "And we know you're not *just anyone*." Her little temptress fingers unbutton his jeans and pull down his zipper.

It's not a good idea. He'll miss his flight. Livy's in labor.

But ... his dick doesn't understand why he needs to make this flight. All his dick knows is Frankie's on a mission to wrap her warm, wet mouth around it. And his dick is a huge fan of Francesca Holter's mouth.

"Frankie ..." He says with a pained voice.

She wrinkles her nose. "Sorry. You're right." She glances at her watch. "We're adults with responsibilities. You've been an awful influence on me these past few days."

"Get on your knees," he says, shoving the front of his jeans and briefs down just enough to release his erection.

Frankie lifts a brow. "Are you—"

"On your fucking knees," he says in a firm tone, but he can't help but smirk because he's biting his tongue to keep from saying "please." A man needs to have standards. He's saving actual begging for a last resort.

Frankie blinks several times before matching his smirk and lifting her skirt to kneel before him. She wraps her hand around the base and circles the head with her tongue.

Eu-fucking-phoria.

He blinks heavily, lips parted, when she takes him in her mouth. Then, his phone vibrates in his pocket.

"Goddammit," he grumbles, instantly feeling guilty, thinking it could be Livy. Sliding it out of his pocket, he answers it, even though it's not Livy.

"What?" he snaps.

Frankie's lips pull into something resembling a grin, but she doesn't stop what she's doing, and he's confident he's never idolized anyone ... until now.

"Livy's in labor. And I'm just now finding out you're in New York?" Jessica asks in a scolding tone.

"Not a good time." He bites his lip.

Fuck that feels good.

"Are you getting on the plane?" Jessica quizzes.

"I'm getting off."

Frankie stops, eyes wide in disbelief.

Jackson slowly shakes his head at her and pushes into her mouth a little deeper.

"You're already in Boise?"

"No."

"Then where are you getting—oh god. Are you having sex?"

"I have a flight to catch. I'll call you later." He slides his phone onto the counter, which makes Frankie release him and stand.

She straightens her skirt, tucks in her blouse, and sips her coffee like she didn't just have his dick in her mouth.

"I hate my sister," he grumbles, zipping and buttoning his fly.

Frankie dumps the last of her coffee in the sink and wraps her arms around his waist. "Go witness a miracle." She walks forward, forcing him to retreat slowly—a dance to the door.

"I'll call you." He kisses her one last time, wishing he could take her with him.

Frankie wipes a little lipstick from his lips. "You better. And you better send me lots of pictures."

Jackson can't contain his grin. *Miraculously,* so much of

his life has turned into a miracle. Despite the death. The grief. The agony of living more than one life. Somehow, he's found his place of peace, and it's a goddamn miracle.

He doesn't look back when he heads out the door, but he calls to her, "I fucking love you."

THERE's a pang of disappointment when Jackson arrives at the birth center to his sleeping daughter with a babyless belly and the guy who knocked her up asleep in a recliner with a tiny baby pressed to his bare chest.

Slade peeks open one eye when Jackson approaches him. But Grandpa Jackson gets shot down with a tiny head-shake. Slade's not giving up his baby just yet.

"Fucker," Jackson mumbles.

Slade closes his eyes and smirks.

"Daddy," Livy's groggy voice draws Jackson to her bed.

"Hey, baby." He kisses her forehead. "I missed it." He frowns, sitting next to her.

She eases her body to a sitting position, rolling her eyes. "You didn't miss anything. I wasn't going to let you watch."

"Where's Wylder?"

"Jess and Luke have him."

Jackson nods, trying to hide yet another punch of disappointment. They made it before he did.

"Where's Frankie?" Livy's gaze jumps over Jackson's shoulder to the door.

"New York."

"She didn't take you back?" Livy pulls out the pouty face she's perfected since she was old enough to figure out that her dad's a sucker for it.

"I'm not a lost puppy."

"You are."

"Are you going to tell me who's under that blanket?" He jerks his head toward the baby.

Livy grins. "Your granddaughter, Ryn Adeline James." The second she says it, tears fill her eyes—the happy kind. And in the next blink, they slide down her flushed face.

Jackson's chest constricts while he works his words past the congestion in his throat. "She would be so proud of you." He wipes her tears just before kissing her forehead. "Adeline?" He narrows his eyes.

"It's Slade's mom's middle name."

Jackson nods. It's Frankie's middle name. This might be the most perfectly named baby ever. "Now tell that oaf of a husband of yours to give me my granddaughter."

Livy giggles through her tears. "Baby, let my dad hold her."

Slade lifts his hand from Ryn's back and gives Jackson the middle finger.

"Baby, I need something to eat."

Slade sighs, slowly sitting up in the chair.

Jackson wastes no time reaching for the tiny baby. Slade stands with her, turning and giving Jackson the stink eye.

After a stare-off, Slade nods to the chair. "Sit down, old man. I don't want you dropping my daughter."

"Listen, fucker—"

"Language!" Livy scolds.

The men hold their tongues while the baby exchange is made. Jackson cradles her in his arms so he can inspect her precious face. "Ryn," he whispers with tears stinging his eyes. His wife would have been so in love with her grandbabies. She would have been the best grandma. Always so kind and overflowing with love. Always the nurturer.

Always the peacemaker in the room. Truly the glue that held everyone else together.

In the next breath, he thinks of Frankie.

CHAPTER FORTY-SEVEN
FRANCESCA

"Jack, she's precious," I gush, calling him after a long day at school. He sent me several dozen pictures. He's a proud grandpa, indeed.

"I can't stop staring at her," he confesses.

I laugh. "I don't blame you. How's Livy?"

"She's amazing. They're heading home in an hour. We had to wait two days to leave the hospital when she was born. Times have changed."

"What's Wylder think of his little sister?" I open my bakery bread and grab a plate for a sandwich.

"He's already the protective brother. He wants to hug her to death, and he keeps chanting, 'my baby.'"

"Oh ..." I press my lips together and shake my head.

"You're not crying, are you?"

"No." I sniffle.

He chuckles.

"I'm *so* happy for you and your family."

"Thank you. I was taken aback when they told me her name. It's ..."

"Perfect. Ryn is the perfect name. I'd be incredibly

honored to have my imaginary grandchildren named after me." I laugh.

"As fate would have it, Ryn's middle name is Slade's mom's middle name."

"Yeah, you didn't tell me her middle name, how much she weighs, or any of the good details. And why are you calling it fate?" I smash avocado onto my sourdough bread.

"Her middle name is Adeline."

I pause my spreading and stare at my phone on the counter. "That's ..."

"In your words ... *perfect*."

"I fucking love you," I whisper.

"I fucking *miss* you already."

"Don't waste your time missing me when you have grandbabies." I can't help but sniffle again. "You have *grandbabies*."

"Are you sure you're not crying? We should FaceTime."

"I'm a mess." I wipe my eyes with my arm and continue constructing the perfect sandwich. "Go be with your family. I don't want to keep you. And text me your address so I can send a gift."

"You should hand-deliver it. Anything less is a little tacky."

"I'm choosing to ignore your ridiculousness. Just let me know when you're bringing Wylder to New York. I'll plan something fun for us."

"I'll get to work on that."

I cut my sandwich and bite back my grin as if I need to hide my excitement from someone. "I want daily pictures. Video too. And don't forget to text me your address."

"Got it. Just uh ..." He mumbles something to someone in the background, but I can't make out what he's saying. "I gotta go. I'll call you later."

Just as I start to say, "I love you," he says, "Bye," and ends the call.

While I eat my sandwich, I look online for the perfect gift, but then I decide to buy something in person and send it with a handwritten note. That feels more personal, like what one should do if they enjoy giving the baby's grandpa blowjobs.

OVER THE NEXT FOUR WEEKS, I either talk with Jack on the phone every day or FaceTime. I like the FaceTiming best, especially if I happen to catch him in a recliner with either Wylder jumping on him or Ryn sleeping all nestled in his neck. By now, I've virtually met Livy, Jessica, Luke, and two of their three kids.

Some days being a responsible adult sucks. I want to toss clothes in a bag and book a flight to Boise. And just when I think having a job is overrated, Jack texts me a picture of his plane ticket.

Jack: I'm stealing Wylder and flying to NY. He likes mangoes, grapes, and hummus. Stock up. Can't wait to see you

Me: DYING with excitement!!!

I reread the text a half-dozen times on the way to my car, nearly getting backed over by another vehicle because I'm not focused on anything but Jack and Wylder. They'll be here this weekend.

With an unstoppable grin and a bounce in my step, I fish my key fob from my bag and unlock my car. Then ... I can't breathe.

CHAPTER FORTY-EIGHT
JACKSON

JACKSON PICKS up dinner for Livy and Slade and helps pack Wylder's bag for their weekend trip. Then, he steals Ryn for some cuddle time.

"Dad, you can't take your eyes off Wylder for one second, or he will be gone," Livy says while transferring the take-out to a plate.

"Good idea. I'm glad you said something," Jackson kisses Ryn's tiny head and rolls his eyes.

"Sorry. I have to say it. I know you know, but I would never forgive myself if anything happened and I didn't say it."

"How about I guard him with my life like I did for you?"

She sits at the kitchen table and gives him a tiny grin. "That's a great idea."

Slade doesn't say a word; he just smirks with amusement.

My phone vibrates in my pocket as I ease into the rocking chair. I retrieve it and read the message from Frankie.

Frankie: Something came up. I'm sorry. It won't work for you and Wylder to visit this weekend. Please apologize to him for me

Jackson reads her text a second time before calling her. It goes to voicemail.

He tries again and again, but it goes to voicemail. "Hey, call me. What's going on? Is everything all right?" He ends the call and sets his phone on the arm of the chair, hoping she calls right back.

"What's up?" Livy asks with a concerned look on her face.

Jackson slowly shakes his head. "I'm not sure. Frankie texted that something came up and the trip won't work this weekend."

"Is everything okay?" Livy wipes her mouth.

He rubs Ryn's back. "I don't know. I tried calling her, but she didn't answer."

"Maybe it's something with her family. She might be on the phone with one of them and is unable to take your call."

"Maybe," he murmurs, staring at his phone.

Over the next thirty minutes, he tries her a dozen more times with no answer. And five texts go unanswered as well.

"I'm heading home," he announces, handing Ryn to Livy when she sits on the sofa.

"Still no answer?"

"No answer." He tucks his phone back into his pocket.

"So, are you still going?" Livy rests Ryn on her shoulder over a burp rag.

He shrugs and shakes his head. "No. I ... I don't know. I assume the answer is no, but I can't know that until I talk with her. *If* she answers my call."

"I'm taking wild child upstairs for a bath," Slade announces, slinging a giggling Wylder over his shoulder.

Livy gives him a smile and a quick nod.

"Love you," Jackson says, bending down to kiss Livy on the cheek.

"Love you too. And I'm sure everything's fine. After all, you didn't give her much notice. In her excitement, she probably forgot about some other obligation."

He nods slowly, making a sad attempt at a reassuring smile. Something feels off. "Probably."

As he crosses the street to his house, he gets a text.

> Frankie: Sorry. I've been out and unable to answer my phone or return your texts. Again, I'm sorry. We'll plan it after the holidays <3

He narrows his eyes at her reply. How did they go from this weekend to after the holidays? It's mid-October. Before he even reaches his door, he calls her.

After three rings, she answers. "Hey." Her voice sounds gravelly.

"Am I waking you?" He glances at his watch. It's nine her time.

"No. I, uh ... had a day. A long day. Lots of talking. It took a toll on my voice."

"Frankie, what's wrong?"

"Nothing."

He closes his door and turns on the lights. "Why can't Wylder and I visit this weekend?"

She clears her throat. "I forgot I have a speaking engagement."

Livy was right. But he's still uneasy about something. She seems off.

"How long is the engagement? All weekend?"

Again, she clears her throat. "It's at an institution in Philadelphia."

Jackson sits at his desk, putting her on speaker while he opens his laptop. "Oh yeah? What institute?"

"What?"

"What institute are you speaking at?"

"Um ... Curtis. What does it matter? I won't be here, and that's why this weekend is not good."

She's not lying about the Curtis Institute of Music in Philadelphia.

"What is your topic?"

"Jack ... I don't mean to be rude, but it is late here. And I have to be up early. Can we talk about this another time?"

"Sure." He looks for anything involving Curtis and Francesca Holter. There's nothing.

"Good night," she whispers.

"Frankie?"

She doesn't answer, but he knows she's still on the call.

He laces his fingers behind his neck and closes his eyes briefly. "I fucking love you."

"Yeah, you too." She ends the call.

CHAPTER FORTY-NINE
FRANCESCA

TODAY, I get out of bed.

I shower.

I might even eat.

There are a slew of messages from my parents and Jack. I missed my dad's birthday, and they know it's not like me. Jack wants to know how the speaking engagement at Curtis went.

So many questions.

Staring at my phone, sitting next to my plate of untouched oatmeal and a cup of lukewarm coffee, I contemplate booking a trip far away from here. But that would require leaving my house. And I can't bring myself to open the blinds, let alone unlock a door.

I've never felt so weak in my life. Not when my brother and his family died. Not when Archer pinned me to his piano. Not when Jack begged me to tell him about that night.

There was this wall of false confidence that I'd constructed to keep everything in check. If I said I was fine, then I was fine. Mind over matter. The past died. And Jack was my future. That's *all* that mattered.

I didn't believe in ghosts. I reconciled everything that had happened into manageable compartments in my mind. Then I closed the doors to the compartments that held the horrific memories. Problem solved.

Until everything blew up in less than sixty seconds.

I reach for my spoon, but my hand shakes too much to grip it, so I fold my hands in my lap, squeezing them tightly until I no longer feel them shaking. Every time I close my eyes, I see Archer hovering above me. In the next breath, I see the scattered photos of Jack's victims on the library floor.

Sleep evades me at every turn. I'm painfully tired, almost nauseous from it, but I can't sleep. The second I begin to doze off, I wake with a gasp, my heart racing, my lungs starving for my next breath. Anxiety and panic attacks have me held hostage in my own home.

Is this how John felt? Utterly broken? Useless? Helpless? Hopeless?

I don't want to die, but I've lost my way and no longer know how to live. The shame is crippling. I don't know what to do or who to call. My parents know nothing, less than nothing. My friend list is empty at the moment. And Jack's too emotionally invested. This would crush him.

Dr. West would be a possibility if I could leave the house, but I can't. The last time Jack tried contacting me, it took forever to steady my voice to make my words sound believable. He doesn't know I had barricaded myself in the closet to feel brave enough to speak. To lie.

That's what my life has become: one big lie.

I shuffle my feet past the piano, but I can't touch it. I can't look at it, so I cover it with several blankets. Then I go back to bed.

CHAPTER FIFTY
JACKSON

JACKSON CALLED to confirm Frankie's speaking engagement at Curtis, but there was no speaking engagement. And she's gone silent on him again. No returning his texts. No answering her phone.

His plane lands just after noon on Monday, and he takes a cab to the university. When he gets to her office, a young brunette greets him with a wide smile.

"Can I help you?" she asks.

"I'm here to see Francesca Holter." He cranes his neck to see into her office, but the blinds are closed.

"I'm sorry. Professor Holter won't be back until next semester."

Jackson's face scrunches. "Are you sure?"

She nods.

"Why?"

"She's taken a leave of absence for personal reasons. That's all I know."

Jackson stares at her name on the door. "Thanks," he murmurs.

When he arrives at her house, all of the blinds are

closed, and he doesn't detect any lights are on. He's pretty sure she's not here. Perhaps something happened to one of her parents. But why would she keep that from him?

He knocks on her front door and rings the doorbell. No answer. Making his way down her driveway, he gets a feeling that he can't explain. Taking another step away from her house feels all wrong.

Everything about this feels wrong.

Retracing his steps, he rings the doorbell several more times and bangs on the door. Then, he makes his way to the back of the house. Again, all the blinds are closed, and there's no detectable light. The French door is old. He remembers the wind howling through its cracks from his visit because it's warped. With one kick, the door springs open.

The house is dark and silent. He flips on a light. A whole bowl of oatmeal is on the table, but it's dry like it's been sitting there for a while. His piano is covered in blankets. And everything feels terribly wrong.

Jackson creeps down the hallway toward her bedroom, peeking into the hallway bathroom first. Her bedroom door is closed, and the handle's locked. He makes a fist to knock but stops because ... it's all fucking wrong. He doesn't want to give someone who shouldn't be here any sort of warning. So he kicks open her bedroom door.

It, too, is dark. Her bed is unmade. But there's no sign of her. He checks her bathroom.

Nothing.

There's no lock on her closet door, but it's closed. Jackson slowly turns the handle and opens it. He flips on the light.

Nothing.

As he goes to turn off the light, he sees something move

out of the corner of his eye. There's a foot beneath a pile of clothes under a section of hanging dresses. His gaze slowly moves over the pile of clothes and stops on the tip of a knife pointed outward, shaking.

His heart plunges into the pit of his stomach when he sees eyes. Her eyes. "Jesus," he whispers, taking a step closer.

"D-don't," Frankie's trembling voice cuts through the silence, and the knife she has gripped in both hands shakes even more.

"Frankie—"

"Don't!" Her voice breaks into painful syllables, wild eyes unblinking.

He stops, holding up his hands. "I won't come any farther," he says slowly. "I'll stay right here. Okay?"

She doesn't answer.

Jackson wants to kill something or someone because the woman he loves is *broken*. It hurts so badly to look at her; he can hardly take it.

Who the fuck did this?

His mind jumps to Archer. Is this his worst fear coming to life? Was Archer not the last one?

Jackson squats slowly, then eases onto his butt, hugging his knees to his chest, eyes on Frankie's puffy eyes and pale face. He feels inadequate. If there's no one to kill, he's at a loss for the right thing to say or do. This is Jessica's and Luke's area of expertise. They would know what to say and what to do.

All Jackson can do is wait.

"I'm not going anywhere," he says softly. "And I'm never going to let anything happen to you again. You're safe. I love you, Frankie."

Tears fill her eyes, but it doesn't stop her from shaking. It doesn't loosen her grip on the knife.

So he waits.

And waits.

Nearly an hour later, they're having the same silent standoff. And he can't help but wonder how long she's been holed up in her house. And he doesn't want to imagine what fucking awful thing led her to this situation.

"I'm tired," Frankie whispers, and when she blinks, a single tear breaks free, making its way to her quivering lips. "But I can't sleep."

"What do you need, my love?"

"Sleep." Her voice sounds raw and weak.

"Do you want me to carry you to your bed?"

She slowly shakes her head.

"Do you want me to take that knife and guard the door while you sleep here?"

Frankie seems to think about it for a few seconds, then, ever so slowly, she nods.

Jackson inches forward so as not to make sudden movements and holds out his hand. Frankie stares at his hand for a moment. Then, her shaky hands release the knife. It falls to the floor. Jackson carefully retrieves it, keeping his gaze locked on hers the whole time. Scooting backward, he closes the door to the closet and leans against it.

"Can I shut off the light for you?"

Again, she pauses before relinquishing a tiny nod.

"Sleep peacefully. You're safe now. I love you." He turns off the light.

CHAPTER FIFTY-ONE
FRANCESCA

I DON'T KNOW how long I sleep, but I feel a little less scared when I peel open my eyes in the dark closet. Recalling why I'm in the closet takes me a few seconds. After all, I'd made progress.

I left the bedroom and fixed a bowl of oatmeal. Maybe I didn't eat it, but leaving the bedroom intending to eat was progress. After I returned to the bedroom, I climbed into my bed. Again, I drifted in and out of a restless state of light sleep, interrupted by awful visions that startled me.

Heart pounding.

Fear surged through my body.

Wait ...

Then there was a loud noise, like someone breaking into my house. I grabbed the knife under my pillow and hid in the closet. Was it just my mind playing tricks on me?

"Frankie?"

I jump, fumbling in the dark for my knife. Again, my heart pounds. Again, fear surges through my body. My labored breaths become deafening. A light illuminates. A phone screen that allows me to see the floor. A hand slowly slides my knife toward me. The closet light turns on, burning my eyes. With squinted eyes, I scramble for the knife. Clutching it in my hand, I scoot back as far into the corner as possible while my eyes adjust to the light, and Jack comes into view.

His back's against the door, knees bent, hands at his sides.

"Hi," I whisper.

He waits a few seconds before whispering "hi" in return.

Why is he here? I told him not to come. What am I supposed to say?

"Did you break in?" I find a weak voice.

"Yes."

I clear my throat. "Why?"

"Because you didn't answer your door."

"Why are you here?"

"Because I was concerned."

"Why?"

"Because you said you had a speaking engagement at Curtis, but when I called, they knew nothing about it."

I don't respond because I don't know what to say.

"Frankie, why are you in the closet with a knife?"

"Because I heard someone breaking into my house."

His brow tenses when he returns a slow nod. "You were really tired. You've been asleep for six hours. It's almost nine p.m. Why were you so tired?" Jack's gaze slides down my body.

I realize he's eyeing the knife I have tightly clenched in my hands, pointed toward him. "Is Wylder here?"

"No."

Thank God.

"Frankie, have you taken any medication recently?"

"No."

Again, he gives me a slow nod with a wrinkled brow. "Would you like to get out of this closet?"

"Sure." I wiggle out of the pile of clothes and stand on shaky legs.

Jack climbs to his feet. "Would you like me to return the knife to the kitchen?"

We stare at said knife in my hand. After a beat, I slowly extend my arm, keeping a good distance between us. He just as slowly takes the knife. Then, he opens the closet door and waits for me to exit.

But I can't because that would put me too close to him. And I can't be close to him because he might touch me. I can't be touched.

We have a silent stare-off, and then he heads toward the kitchen, flipping lights on as he goes.

"Your oatmeal is cold. Can I make you something else to eat?"

My bare feet pad along the hardwood floor behind him, keeping a safe distance. "Okay."

He slips the knife into the wooden block and turns toward me, his gaze making a slow inspection of my body.

I must look awful.

"How's the baby?"

Jack doesn't look surprised by my question. He has no discernible expression at all. "Ryn's good. How are you?"

"I'm uh ..." The open door snags my attention. I try to close it, but it won't stay closed. Inside, my mind is screaming, "CLOSE. CLOSE. WHY WON'T IT CLOSE?" I try to hide my panic, but I can't stop slamming the door, praying that it latches so I can lock it. So I feel safe.

"Easy. I'll get it fixed." Jack rests his hand on my arm, and I jump away from him, hugging myself. He frowns. It's disbelief or outright shock. Dropping his chin, he stares at his feet for a few seconds before closing the door as far as it will go with the splintered frame.

When he looks at me again, I feel the whole weight of his unspoken words.

My nails dig into my arms. "Something … happened."

With absolute patience, he waits. No pushing. Not even a nod or word of encouragement. The complete control he's showing with his idle tongue and respect for the space I need is unlike anything I ever imagined love could be.

"I was leaving the university. I'd just gotten off the phone with you. And a man …" I draw in a shaky breath. "He covered my nose and mouth and shoved me against my car. I couldn't breathe. I couldn't move. When I closed my eyes, all I could see was Archer. And all of my self-defense skills died." I wipe a tear and swallow. "I felt so helpless," I whisper. "So weak."

Jack takes a controlled breath and lets it out slowly but doesn't move or say a word.

"All I remember is crying. I don't know what he was saying to me because all I heard was Archer's voice, his words. Then, he shoved me to the ground and ran off with my purse." I wipe more tears. "I had to crawl under my car to retrieve the key fob and phone I'd dropped when he grabbed me. And ever since then, I've heard Archer's voice. And I've imagined the man who robbed me seeing my address on my driver's license and coming to find me." I shake my head like I can shake this unsettling feeling, but I don't think it will ever disappear. "And I see … you."

He squints.

"I see all the photos Archer showed me of your victims."

With a wince, he rubs his neck.

"That man in the parking lot triggered something awful,

and now all I see ... all I feel... all I hear are the absolute worst things. And I'm scared *all* the time. And I think ... oh God, is this how my brother felt? Is this how Lynn and Steven felt? Trapped in their heads? Haunted by events that plagued their lives?" I release my fingernails from my skin and thread them into my hair, digging at my scalp instead. "Will anyone be able to touch me again? Am I..." my face scrunches, trying to hold it together "...b-broken?"

Jack averts his gaze in deep thought. "Do you want to die?"

"No."

"Then you're not broken."

My lips part to protest. How can he know that? "Tell me what you're thinking."

Amber eyes find mine. "I think you're not broken."

I shake my head. "Not that. Tell me what you're really thinking. I won't let you touch me. You found me in a closet with a knife. You have to be angry at me for not being more careful. Or do you still feel guilty about Archer? Or are you wondering how you got mixed up with me in the first place? Or are you—"

"No," he cuts me off. "I made what happened with Archer about me. I couldn't see that your needs mattered more than mine. I'm sorry you've had to experience so many awful moments in your life. I'm sorry you had to see photos of my victims. And if I could take it all away from you, I would. But I can't. So I don't want you thinking about me and my feelings. I just ..." There's so much desperation in his face. "I just want to know how I can help you."

Rubbing the heels of my hands over my swollen eyes, I release a slow breath. "Food."

"I'll make you something."

We eat dinner in complete silence, but I feel safe. I can breathe.

He takes my empty plate, and I instinctively slide my chair away from the table to avoid him getting too close.

He frowns.

I do, too. "Sorry," I murmur.

"Don't apologize. I won't touch you until you ask me to touch you."

His kindness makes my heart ache. What if that day never comes?

After the dishes are done, he returns to the table. I haven't moved. I feel so fucking lost.

"You should try to sleep."

I nod.

"Where would you like me to sleep?"

My gaze flits to the broken door.

Jack heads straight to the living room and drags the sofa to the door. "This is where I'll sleep."

I don't deserve him. But I *need* someone to make me feel safe until that door gets repaired, so I relinquish a nod. "Thank you," I murmur. I walk toward my bedroom and say, "Good night."

Just before I reach my room, Jack says my name.

I stop.

"I fucking love you."

A flood of emotion surges through me. I can't even speak; it's too strong. I can only nod and hide in my bedroom for the night.

CHAPTER FIFTY-TWO
JACKSON

Jackson fixes the door. He hires a security company to cover the house with alarms and cameras inside and out. Every night, he sleeps on the sofa to monitor the house while Frankie stays holed up in her bedroom with the door locked.

He makes her meals.

Orders grocery delivery.

Laundry.

House cleaning.

And not once does he ask why Black Beauty is covered in blankets.

In fact, they don't talk much at all.

Frankie slowly makes progress by showering every day. Yesterday, she even curled her hair. While Jackson rakes the leaves in her yard, she does yoga and sits in a meditative pose for a good twenty minutes.

"I have no clue what I'm doing," he confesses to Jessica on the phone while arranging pumpkins and gourds around Frankie's front porch to get in the Halloween spirit. He's noticed a lot of kids in the neighborhood.

"Sounds like you're doing everything you can and then some. Luke agrees. What else can you do if she won't see a therapist?"

"I don't know if she'll see one. I'm afraid to ask." He sits on the top step and gazes out at the treelined street.

"Has she left the house yet?"

"No."

"Have you suggested it?"

"No."

Jessica laughs. "Well, you can offer to take her for a drive without it seeming as invasive as suggesting therapy."

"Maybe."

"Have you talked with Livy?"

"Yeah," he says, stretching his legs and crossing his ankles. "She's adamant that my place is here. And I agree. But I feel torn into two pieces at the moment."

"You're feeling that way because you went so long without seeing your family, and now that you have them back, you don't ever want to leave."

"Mmm," he agrees with a low hum.

"Has she talked with her parents?"

"Yes. But she's acting like she's working and staying busy like nothing happened."

"Well, I understand that. But at the risk of sounding like Luke, I have to say she needs to tell her parents what happened. Maybe not the part about Archer, but she can tell them she was robbed in the parking lot, and they would understand that it shook her."

"I'll suggest it. Maybe. I don't know. I'm so afraid of losing her."

"Keep doing what you're doing. She'll come back to you. Your love is enough. Trust that."

"Thanks, Jess."

"Love you."

"You too. Bye."

Jackson removes his shoes and steps into the house. Frankie's in the kitchen. It smells like pumpkin spice.

"Whatever you're doing, don't stop," he says, leaning against the counter without getting into her space.

She focuses on the batter she's stirring in the stainless steel bowl and doesn't try to hide her grin. "Muffins."

"Perfect." He washes his hands. "Have you thought about telling your parents about the robbery? Just that part. It might feel like a weight off your conscience. I'm sure lying to them is exhausting. And they would understand that something like that would leave you unsettled and fearful."

"If I tell my parents, they'll come here."

"Is that a bad thing?"

She drops muffin liners into the pan and shoots him a quick look. "I'm going to say yes because they'll see I'm not okay. And they'll feel like my reaction to having my purse stolen is extreme. Then, they'll worry about me. And they've dealt with too much grief to have my problems thrust upon them."

Jackson hangs the towel over the dishwasher handle. "When parents have kids, they take on *all* of their problems. And there is no expiration date. Ryn had a daughter when we met. She was a real piece of work. They had a rocky relationship for years. And when Ryn died, Maddie flew in from Baltimore for the funeral and left the next day. I haven't seen her in so long. But ... I have someone who keeps an eye on her whereabouts and gives me updates. I'll have someone check on her for the rest of my life because Ryn would have wanted it. Maybe you're not giving your parents enough credit. I think they'll be relieved that you're okay."

"*Am* I okay?" Frankie slides the muffin pans into the oven.

"You're baking. That's a good sign."

She closes the oven and leans against the counter, gripping the edge. A sad attempt at a smile plays along her lips for all of two seconds before it falls from her face. "I so badly want you to touch me, but when you get close, I tense up. I *fear* your touch. It's an awful feeling. I don't want you to represent Archer Sanford. I don't want to see you and, in the next breath, see a pile of pictures of dead bodies. I don't want to think of you and remember it was your voice I heard seconds before a man grabbed me, took my purse, and shoved me aside like trash. You represent everything I *love* about my life right now. But you also represent everything that made me lose my faith in humanity."

Jackson's gaze drops to the floor between them.

"That's not *okay*. I feel like I ran twenty-six miles of a marathon, and just as I saw the finish line, I tripped. Broke my nose. An arm. A leg. And lost half of my teeth. And everyone cheering me on looked at me like ... how? How does one come so far only to fall and completely unravel with just two-tenths of a mile ahead?"

He lifts his gaze, eyes red. "Let me carry you. Close your eyes and let me carry you to the finish line because. I. Fucking. Love. You."

She laughs, blotting her eyes. "You say that, but I don't say it back. You have to *hate* that I don't say it back. I know *I* hate it. And I don't say it back because I know it would feel like a lie. If I love you, we don't stand here ... ten feet apart."

Jackson shrugs. "I'll wait."

Frankie grunts. "For how long?"

"Forever." Jackson doesn't hesitate. Not for a single second.

"I don't want you to wait! You've waited your whole life for the life that brought you to me. But I'm not the endgame. It's your daughter. Your sister. Your beautiful grandbabies. I am the goddamn pothole in your road. But I don't have to be. I'm giving you a pass to walk away."

He glances at his watch. "I appreciate your selflessness. But I'm waiting. And I need a shower. Don't burn the muffins. You forgot to set a timer." As soon as he gets to the bathroom, he calls Livy. "I need a huge favor."

CHAPTER FIFTY-THREE
FRANCESCA

JACK SPENDS the next two days doing his usual chores as if we didn't have a heated conversation. He smiles and winks. He tells me he loves me. But he keeps his distance.

This afternoon, he's a little off.

He constantly checks his phone, glances out the window, and paces the entry.

I'm on my third self-help book in a week. Seeing Dr. West requires me to leave the house. Sadly, I'm not there yet.

The doorbell rings, and I jump up from the sofa, high-tailing it to my bedroom.

"Frankie?" Jack calls.

I ignore him, locking myself in my room until whoever is at the door is gone and the door is locked again. According to my most recent book, locks have become a trigger for me since I was unlocking my car when that man attacked me.

It's not that I'm not making progress. I am. Today, I stay in the bedroom instead of going into the closet. That's progress.

I wait, but I hear chatter, more than one person. And it

366

sounds like they're in my house. Why would Jack let anyone else in the house? Footsteps get closer to the door. I jump and walk backward toward the closet.

Knock. Knock.

Holding entirely still, I wait for them to leave, for Jack to make them go. If it were him, he'd tell me.

"Frankie?" It's a woman's voice.

I don't speak, don't breathe.

"It's Livy."

My hand flies to my face. I want to cry. I want to scream. Why is she here? I can't meet his daughter when I'm entirely wigged out and mentally unstable. Why? Why did he do this to me? This isn't love. It's cruel and embarrassing.

"Can I come in?"

The lock clicks. I grapple with the closet handle, desperate to hide. But before I can, Jack opens the door.

"Frankie, meet my daughter Livy. She and Slade stopped by with Ryn and Wylder."

I try to convey my anger with an unblinking gaze even though I can't speak.

Stop by? He makes it sound like they were in the neighborhood. As quickly as he invades my space by unlocking the door, he saunters off. Livy smiles.

She's ... stunning. Long blond hair and the bluest eyes. She cautiously steps into my room and closes the door behind her.

Despite every inch of my body shaking, I manage the hint of a smile and a soft "hi."

"It's wonderful to meet you finally."

"You too," I murmur, hugging myself, nails digging into my arms.

She glances around my bedroom. "You have a beautiful

home. It's timeless and feminine. I finally have my own real house to decorate. You should help me. I'm not that great at decorating." When her gaze returns to me, she nods to the cream velvet bench at the foot of my bed. "May I sit?"

I nod.

"How can I help you?" she says, just like her father.

I'm too choked up to speak, so I pinch the bridge of my nose and shake my head.

"It wasn't his place to tell me, but Slade told me about Archer Sanford."

My gaze quickly averts to the side.

"In college, a man tried to rape me behind a convenience store. I was lucky because Slade saved me. Thankfully, my story was just a close call. My Aunt Jessica is ... well, she's my idol. The strongest person I know, times infinity. When she was young, she and a friend were kidnapped and tortured. Her friend died, but Jessica lived. And life was far from easy after that. She was raped during combat training. And years later, abducted again and tortured. She died. Uncle Luke had to bring her back to life. She is undoubtedly the greatest human I have ever known." Livy lowers her voice. "But don't tell my dad I said that."

I still can't look at her but manage a tiny smile.

"Not because she survived. That was the easy part. She's *lived*. She married the love of her life, and they have three children. Her glass is always half-full. Hell, I think it runs over every single day. She's not normal. She's not the average woman. I'm not even sure she's a mortal. But she represents hope and possibility. What's that Robert Frost quote? The only way to overcome suffering is to go through it? Or something like that. I guess I'm trying to say that I know you're suffering. And the only way past it is through it. But you don't have to go through it alone.

"There's a little boy in the other room who's love personified. And when he sees you, he'll assume you're his new best friend. He's going to want hugs and kisses. He'll grab your nose and try to hide it like my dad does to him. There's also a baby in the other room. She's peace personified. Holding her is like hugging a rainbow ... floating on a cloud. But if you're not ready for human touch or to be surrounded by people who care deeply, overstep boundaries, but fight fiercely for the ones they love, then we won't stay long. And you might want to stay in here until we leave." Livy stands. "There's no shame in whatever you decide. If it's not today ... we'll come back another day ... and another day ... but we'll never give up. We'll never abandon you." She smiles. "It's been a pleasure meeting the woman who has claimed my dad's heart."

With that, Livy leaves the bedroom, closing the door behind her.

CHAPTER FIFTY-FOUR
JACKSON

LIVY REAPPEARS with a tiny I-did-my-best shrug.

"Thank you," Jackson says. He's on the floor with Wylder, letting him walk on his back.

"It's heartbreaking. You can see it in her eyes; she desperately wants to shed her trauma skin and reengage in life." She sits on the sofa beside Slade and takes a fussy Ryn to feed her.

Heartbreaking indeed, Jackson thinks.

They chat and watch the wild child run around for the next hour; then, the bedroom door creaks open.

Jackson hooks his arms around Wylder when he tries to run past him. "Easy," he whispers in his ear, kissing the side of his head.

Frankie appears, fists nervously pumping at her sides and a shaky smile.

"Hi." Jackson smiles at her.

"Hi," she says softly.

"Frankie, this is Wylder, the wild child." He ruffles his hair, and Wylder shakes his head and giggles. "Wylder, this is Frankie."

"Frankie," he repeats her name.

"But Frankie's been feeling a little yucky, so you need to be gentle with her. Okay?" Jackson says, looking only at Frankie.

She draws in a slow breath and swallows hard.

Jackson lets go of Wylder, and he runs toward Frankie.

"Slade!" Livy cringes.

Jackson holds out his hand, signaling for Slade to let the wild child be.

When Wylder hugs her legs, Frankie stiffens like a cat thrown off a ten-story building. Her eyes remain wide and glued to Jackson, a silent plea for help.

He mouths, "I fucking love you."

Emotion fills her eyes, and she slowly squats so Wylder can throw his chubby arms around her neck and press his fishy lips to her cheek.

Frankie folds him in her arms and closes her eyes like he's giving her every breath she takes.

When Jackson glances at Livy, he smiles because she's wiping the corners of her eyes. In the next breath, Wylder wriggles free and runs to Slade.

Frankie stands, composing herself. "Can I get anyone something to drink or eat? Had I known you were coming—"

"You would have kicked me out," Jackson says.

She rolls her eyes. "I mean, probably."

Livy stands with Ryn. "I'm going to take wiggle pants to the potty. Frankie, would you like to hold Ryn for me?"

Frankie's not stupid. She's privy to the game. Still, it takes a little hesitation before she steps forward and holds out her arms. The swap can't occur without Livy touching Frankie, but Frankie's too mesmerized by Ryn to show any sort of aversion to her touch.

JEWEL E. ANN

Livy and Slade head upstairs to the guest bedroom with Wylder. And Jackson sits in the chair opposite Frankie on the sofa.

"This was quite the gamble," she says, cradling Ryn. "When they arrived, I wanted to die."

"I realized what you needed, but it wasn't me. If you couldn't handle Wylder and Ryn, I was going to change my mind."

Frankie glances up. "Change your mind?"

"I was going to say you were, in fact, broken."

She frowns. "Jack, this is a step, but I'm not cured."

"It's a step forward. You made it twenty-six miles. I said I'll carry you to the finish line." His lips twist. "I'd say you're at twenty-six-point-one-three-nine miles."

THE KIDS BREAK the tension and offer something to focus on that's not as heavy as Archer Sanford or Frankie's incident in the parking lot. She keeps her distance from Jackson and Slade, which shows that men are her trigger.

Jackson and Livy make dinner. Frankie remains quiet while they talk about Livy's job and give Slade a hard time about his new stay-at-home dad role. She occasionally glances up from her plate and smiles.

Just before the dishes are removed from the table, she clears her throat and asks, "Where are you staying?"

Livy and Slade share a look before aiming that same look at Jackson.

He finishes wiping Wylder's mouth. "They're staying here. You have two guest bedrooms."

"Only one of them has a bed. And I don't have a crib."

"Ryn sleeps with us. And if you have an extra blanket

and pillow, Wylder will happily sleep on the floor," Livy says.

Concern spreads across Frankie's face. "My floors are wood with a few thin rugs." She bites the inside of her cheek. "Maybe he can sleep with me." Frankie looks nervous as her gaze sweeps around the table, gauging everyone's reaction.

"He can be restless and wake up scared. I don't want to put that on you," Livy says, reassuring Frankie.

"I don't know what everyone's talking about. Wylder's sleeping with me." Jackson winks at Wylder.

"You're on the—" Frankie stops herself.

Jackson knows she's feeling guilty for him sleeping on the sofa, but nobody else feels guilty. Everyone understands what she's going through.

"He's a little guy with a big personality. There's room for both of us." Jackson collects the dirty dishes.

"Let me get all of this," Frankie says, standing. "You spend time with your family."

"We're taking an after-dinner walk," Livy announces. "Dad, you coming?"

"No. I'm going to help—"

"Go." Frankie plasters on a fake smile.

Jackson's brow furrows.

"Go," she repeats. "I'll be fine."

"I can stay and help clean up," Slade suggests.

"Maybe Frankie needs a little break from all of us. I'm sure this has been a lot. And while nobody wants to stick her with the dishes, perhaps a monotonous task and a little break from socializing is exactly what she needs." Livy amazes Jackson. She's so mature and astute, just like her mother.

Frankie gives Livy a silent look that screams 'thank you'.

But Jackson hasn't left Frankie alone since he arrived. And he's not sure she's ready.

Livy tugs on Jackson's hand. "Thirty minutes. She'll be fine," she murmurs.

"Go," Frankie says one last time.

Jackson returns a hesitant nod before following his family to the door. He hopes today wasn't too much. Thirty minutes is plenty of time for Frankie to regress. The slightest noise could send her running to her closet with a butcher knife in her hand.

CHAPTER FIFTY-FIVE
FRANCESCA

It's the small victories.

I manage to clean the kitchen without getting spooked. I still can't turn on the television or play music because those sounds might drown out the sound of someone breaking in or sneaking up on me. And I hate that.

Never in my life have I been worried about something like that in my own home.

The crew returns, and Jackson has a visible look of relief on his face when he sees me putting away the last few dishes. I smile, and it makes him smile. The good kind. The kind of smile he gives Wylder and Ryn.

"We're going to get ready for bed. It's been a long travel day," Livy says, nodding for Slade to head up the stairs with Ryn. "Slade will get Wylder ready for bed and bring him down when he's in his jammies and a clean diaper."

"Sounds good," Jackson says, his voice behind me as I drain the sink.

"Did uh …" Nerves hijack my voice. "Did you have a nice walk?" I turn. He's closer than ten feet—more like six.

"Yes." He slips his hands into the back pockets of his

jeans as if to let me know he has no intention of trying to touch me.

I hate that too.

I hate so much about my life right now because it doesn't feel like my life. I'm not myself. And I'm not sure I'll ever be the same again.

"Thank you for inviting them. And you're right, Wylder and Ryn were exactly what I needed."

Jackson's mask begins to slip. I know he's been trying so hard to be everything I need, never giving a glimpse of his needs until now. He looks lost and lonely—a palpable longing.

"Here you go," Slade says, carrying Wylder down the stairs and giving him a big smooch before setting him free to run to Jackson.

"Night," I say to Slade.

He gives me a tiny nod before disappearing back up the stairs.

"I set out an extra blanket and pillow," I say to Jackson while nodding to the sofa.

He lifts Wylder onto his shoulders. "It's probably not necessary. He'll sleep on my chest and act as a heated blanket. I'll be sweating by morning."

I nod. "Okay. Well, good night." I'm forced to get closer to Jackson to slide past him to my bedroom.

He could give me more space, but he doesn't. Instead, he eyes my every move. That longing gets more palpable until I feel his touch without actually touching him. And my pulse responds, sending nerves firing out of control. It feels like anxiety, but not the kind that makes me want to hide in my closet.

"Good night," he says while I bravely navigate our close proximity. "I love you."

The returned sentiment gets stuck in my throat, but it's screaming in my head. I love him too.

"Go get on the sofa. I have to brush my teeth," I hear Jackson talking to Wylder as I reach my bedroom door.

But Wylder's feet slap the wood floor behind me instead of getting on the sofa.

I turn. He runs past me and climbs onto my bed.

"Wylder," Jackson calls, yawning while sauntering toward my room.

"He's fine until you brush your teeth," I quickly say to stop Jackson from getting closer.

He abruptly stops, and I give him a sheepish grin.

"Okay. I'll be quick," he says.

I watch Wylder play on my bed. He hides beneath my sheet, and I can't help but grin. It feels good to smile like this. Steven used to love playing hide and seek. When he stayed with me, I'd build him massive forts under my piano. We'd pack the space with pillows, blankets, snacks, and flashlights.

Stepping into my closet, I change into my lounge pants and tank top. When I emerge, Jack's waiting, standing at my door, but he's not looking at Wylder jumping up and down. He's looking at me.

"Don't look at me like that," I say, feeling a little flushed.

He leans his shoulder against the door. "Like what?"

"Like ..." I drop my gaze. "Intimately."

"I don't know how else to look at you."

I nervously rub my arm. "I feel like you're silently asking for something I can't give you. I feel like you need intimacy."

"Frankie, I don't have to touch you to be intimate. Because I remember what it felt like to hold you in my arms, to kiss you ... to be *intimate* with you. So, *every* look is intimate. It's personal. It's me ... loving you from near or far."

I love this man with every part of what makes me a woman. Maybe I need him to take off his kid gloves, the way I needed Dr. West to drag the truth out of me. Jack won't touch me until I ask him to, but what if I can't bring myself to do that? What if I'm not that strong?

"Pa!" Wylder tosses a pillow off the bed and giggles.

"Come on, wild one, let's let Frankie get some sleep." Jack scoops him up and carries him down the hallway.

My heart makes a lunge, but it trips before reaching its destination. And I'm left with a whisper only to myself. "I'm the girl you kiss good night." I touch my lips for a second and close my eyes.

Archer raped me.

His daughter is responsible for Steven's death.

I survived gunfire.

I survived the loss of my twin.

Yet, a stranger shoved me against my car, covered my mouth, stole my purse, and tossed me aside. And *that* flipped my whole world on its head? It doesn't make sense. He didn't touch me like Archer did. He didn't say the things Archer said.

Did I experience the final straw phenomenon? Something so, in and of itself, minor, upending my entire existence.

I brush my teeth and head to my door to shut it as tiny feet race toward me again.

"Wylder!" Jack chases him. "It's bedtime." He gives me an apologetic frown, scooping him up again.

Wylder kicks and flails.

"When you shut your door, he'll settle down. He just sees your light on."

I nod, staring at Wylder and his discomfort from being held back. "How about a book?"

"I have books for him. But he doesn't want to have them read to him right now." Jack carries him to the living room again.

As I shut my door, I hear, "Wylder, you can't go in there. It's time to sleep, buddy."

My heart aches for him. It aches for me. It aches for so many reasons. I make my way to the living room. Jack is on the sofa, bear-hugging Wylder to keep him from me. Wylder sees me and stills for a second.

I smile and hold out my hand.

Jack eyes me for a breath before easing his hold on Wylder. The little boy slides to his feet and takes my hand. We make it two steps before he tugs in the opposite direction. When I glance back, Wylder holds his other hand to Jack.

"I'm sleeping here, buddy." He gives Wylder a shrug.

Wylder pulls on my hand more but doesn't let go as his other hand makes an impossible stretch toward his grandpa.

When Jack lifts his gaze to mine, I give him a little nod. He slowly stands from the sofa, keeping his attention on me while he accepts Wylder's chubby little hand. I lead the train to my bedroom.

Wylder finds his spot in the middle. Jack and I remain silent while we climb onto each side. I shut off the light, and that warm little body snuggles into my side. I could cry. If I didn't know better, I'd say Wylder is John reincarnated. He's here to show me that I'm not broken. I'm not alone. And I'm safe now.

As Wylder's body starts to melt and relax, and he slides into a slumber, I move my hand to rub his back. My fingers don't find his jammy-covered back; they find Jack's hand resting on it.

He quickly moves it, and I feel an instant pang of ... I'm not even sure. Regret? Sadness?

I lie still in the dark.

Silence.

A cocoon.

Maybe a breath. That's it. I take a real breath where my lungs fully expand, and I don't feel suffocated.

When I close my eyes, I don't see Archer.

I don't smell him.

I don't hear his voice.

I can't remember how I felt when that man put his hand over my mouth.

And I don't want to sleep because I'm scared this won't last. When the sun rises, it will bring all those memories back to life.

So, I focus on every inch of my body connected to Wylder.

Every long, deep breath.

And the beautiful, peaceful silence.

My hand falls from his back and stretches toward the center of the bed, lying idle, palm open.

Take my hand ...

The pads of Jack's fingers ghost across mine.

Tears flood my eyes, and I smile.

It's barely a whispered touch.

When it's gone, I bend my fingers to see if he's still there.

He is.

Our fingers lace together.

It fills me with such overwhelming emotion that I can't help but close my eyes. And when I close my eyes, I fall into a sleep unlike anything I've experienced.

———

I wake alone.

I stretch.

When I look at my alarm clock, it's ten thirty-five.

I grin.

Me! Yes, *this girl* ... she slept over twelve hours. Again, I stretch, then roll to the side and bury my face into the pillow before pulling the sheets to my face, inhaling deeply, desperate to catch a whiff of Wylder or Jack.

After a long shower, I dry my hair, dress, and go to the living room. Jack's on the sofa, reading a book from my bookshelf, *The Alchemist*.

"One of my favorite stories ever," I say on my way to the kitchen for coffee. "Where's everyone else?"

"They thought you were going to sleep for eternity, so they headed home."

I stop. "Are you serious?"

He keeps his eyes on the book and smirks.

I continue my quest for coffee.

"They went into the city."

"Why didn't you go?"

"Because I had some reading to do."

I roll my eyes, waiting not-so-patiently for my coffee. "Because you're scared to leave me alone."

"Scared for me. I don't know what I'd do without you."

I fucking love him.

I grab a sweatshirt and open the front door when my coffee's done.

"Um ..." Jack follows me. "What are you doing?"

I step outside for the first time in a week. "Thought I'd drink my coffee outside."

"Care for company?"

"That would be lovely."

We sit in my rocking chairs and watch a few neighbors take their dogs on a morning walk while the trees shed their leaves. The air is cool and crisp—my favorite time of year.

"I grew up on a farm. We had a huge pumpkin patch that my parents opened to the public every October. Corn maze. Apple cider. A hayride. John and I would dress up as scarecrows just to see if we could scare the little kids." I laugh. "But neither one of us could hold still that long. I love pumpkin spice, apple cider … pumpkin pie. All things fall."

Jack smiles, gently rocking beside me. "My mom used to sew costumes for Jess and me. I went through a heavy Star Wars phase. Luke, Han Solo, Yoda, Obi-Wan … and every year, my mom would say, 'Jude, I'll pay you money to choose something that's not Star Wars.' Jessica was the pleaser that time of year because she wore whatever Mom made her, no complaints."

I love that about him—the softer side to Jack.

"Did you ever imagine your life would go in this direction?" I ask.

"Never. I assumed I'd be more of a white-collar crime guy."

I giggle. "How so?"

"Well, I went to college and graduated with a degree in computer engineering with a minor in finance. A good Ponzi scheme seemed like a possible direction for me. But things never go as planned." He glances over at me, maybe because he feels the weight of my stare. "What?"

"You have a degree in computer engineering?"

"Yes. Did you think I was nothing more than a pretty

face with a bad habit of killing people?"

My lips twist as I shake my head. "I love that you never stop surprising me. Well, the good kind of surprises like yesterday's unexpected visitors. I know Livy and Slade plan to take Wylder home when they leave here, but I want to steal him. He's ... thousands of dollars of therapy all wrapped up in a pint-sized body with fishy kisses, the best hugs, and the most addictive giggle."

Jack returns his attention to the road. "Grief, trauma, depression ... they come in waves. I'm happy that you're feeling better today. I hope this is the beginning of great strides. But Wylder is leaving. And I'm not a therapist, but I think it might be a good idea for you to talk to someone or join a support group." He shrugs a shoulder. "Just to keep moving forward. There's work. Driving your car again. And I think you could use some better self-defense skills. I know a guy."

He's right on all accounts. And I know this because I have read enough self-help books to know that I might need help beyond those books for quite some time. But I'm turning a corner. I feel it. I know it. And I have Jack to thank.

"Can I say something aloud without you reacting? Without you speaking or responding in any way? Can I see if I *can* say these words outside my head without falling apart?"

Jack eyes me carefully for several seconds before nodding.

I don't look at him. I'm better, but I'm not *there* quite yet.

After a long inhale, I let the actual words see life beyond the dark recesses of my mind and the nauseous pit of my stomach. "Archer Sanford raped me on his piano. It didn't hurt because I let the important parts of me leave my body. At the time, I didn't feel him. I didn't feel anything until I met your gaze on me. And I felt embarrassed. I felt shameful. I felt ... at fault. And part of me felt like I, too, would have blood on my hands for the rest of my life. Days later, I thought about the events of that night, and I realized I never said the word 'no.' I never screamed. I didn't even fight him."

I'm on the verge of tears, but I'm so damn proud of myself for getting all that out without shedding a single one.

But when I turn my head, I realize my moment of great strength is Jack's final-straw moment. He doesn't move. His hands are gripping the arms of the chair, and his face is wet with tears.

The man I love is not heartless. He's not a killer. He's human.

He bleeds.

He feels pain.

And sometimes ... he cries.

I stand.

He doesn't move. Doesn't look at me. Doesn't blink.

I stand, stepping in front of him. Still, he doesn't acknowledge me. It's as if he's fighting everything to hold it together, but he can't hide the parts that leak to the surface. I can't imagine ever loving him more than I do right now.

Wedging between his spread legs, I curl up in a ball on his lap, face in his neck, hand flat against his heart. "If you carry me to the finish line, I'll carry you for the rest of our lives."

Ever so slowly, Jack's hands release the arms of the chair and embrace me. Head bowed. Lips pressed to my head.

He is my Baines. I am his Ada. And together, we will sail away to a future filled with unimaginable happiness.

EPILOGUE

Eight Months Later ...

JACKSON WAITS.

He worries.

What if she doesn't make it?

What if something happened along the 2500-mile journey?

How long would it be before someone told him?

If she has so much as a scratch on her, heads will roll.

He paces. Checks his watch. Then he heads to his basement to beat the shit out of his punching bag.

A quick shower, and he's back to his front window.

It's not that she's his whole world, but his world is better with her in it. His fingers itch to touch her, caress her soft curves, make her sing.

"She'll be here." Frankie laughs, sliding her arms around his waist and resting her cheek on his back.

Jackson blows out a long breath and turns in her arms. "She should have been here hours ago." He's visibly tense and jittery.

Again, Frankie chuckles. "Patience."

He frowns. "Is all of your stuff unpacked?"

"Yes. It's official. I'm jobless and shacking up with my boyfriend."

His nose still wrinkles when she uses the word *boyfriend*.

Frankie finished her year contract with the university and spent months in therapy. They racked up many airline miles with bi-weekly visits.

"And you've never been happier." He kisses her forehead.

"Not true. I'll be happier when you stop worrying. What if we steal a couple of grandbabies? They'll keep your mind off—"

"Can't. Slade took them to some indoor gym or play space. They won't be back until after lunch."

Frankie's lips twist. "So ... if I'm hearing you correctly, what you're saying is for the next three or so hours, there's a zero percent chance of little ones barging in on us?" Her fingers work the button of his jeans.

He stops her.

Frankie's jaw drops. "Seriously? Are you telling me no?"

"No. I'm telling you..." He turns them 180 degrees "...I need to face the window when we do this." He lifts her dress over her head. She's wearing nothing else. God ... he loves *all* the beautiful things about this woman. She gets him.

"I fear you love her more than you love me."

Jackson flits his gaze out the window for a quick check

before looking at her and smirking. "Jealous?" He lowers to his knees, holding her hips.

She laces her fingers through his hair and tugs it. "I've made her my bitch, while I'm pretty certain *you* are still her bitch. So no ... I'm not jealous."

He hums, and Frankie's hands press to the window behind her. They're hidden in a wooded lot, but her driver will get quite the view when she arrives. And Frankie should care, but Jackson knows she's missing the gene for modesty. Besides, he's great at multitasking. He can do this and keep an eye out for *her*.

"Jack ..." Frankie's head rests against the window while he spreads her legs wider, while his tongue and fingers work with great enthusiasm to pleasure her. "Don't ... fucking ... stop ..."

He doesn't stop but unbuttons his jeans, pulls down the zipper, and releases his dick, slowly stroking it.

Frankie tips her chin and bites her bottom lip for a second. "I love it when you do that."

He's flattered. Really. The day will never come when he doesn't want to please her in every way. However, this is less about her and more about him.

Does he want to have sex with her? Of course.

Is time of the essence? Unfortunately.

He's forced to move things along a little quicker so that nothing tragic happens, like ... he's on the verge of blowing his wad just as *she* arrives, and he's forced to choose between two of his favorite women. Today, it might not be Frankie, and he's only a little sorry about it.

"Not yet!" Frankie protests, on the verge of her orgasm, when Jackson stands, lifts her with her back pressed to the window, and drives into her.

"What the fuck ..." she's angry but still chasing that orgasm "...was that?"

He kisses her to shut her up and because he loves kissing her. He's close. So close to release.

Best day ever!

His hand squeezes her breast. She moans, and that's nearly all it takes. *Nearly* ... Then he hears screeching brakes and knows it's *her*.

"Don't you dare!" Frankie grips his shirt. He's never seen her this desperate. And it's so damn sexy, but ... *but* ... *she's* here!

He drops Frankie to her feet like a hot potato, tucks himself into his jeans, and flies out the door just as the truck backs into the driveway. Today marks the official day that his life is absolutely perfect. Finally, all of his women are home and safe.

"Easy," Jackson warns while the men unload Black Beauty in all her glory.

As he leads them to the house, he sees Frankie, and the day becomes a little bittersweet because three months from now, when she's still withholding sex from him, he'll be forced to look back upon this day and wonder if thirty more seconds with his mouth between her legs would have made all the difference in the world. But it's too late. He'll never know.

"I see my bitch made it," Frankie says between clenched teeth.

Jackson ignores her while showing the men where to put Beauty.

"Are we tuning it?" one of the men asks as they unwrap her and attach her legs.

"No. I'll tune her," Jackson says.

"Pfft ..." Frankie rolls her eyes. "Only one person in this room can properly tune this piano."

The two men nervously eye Jackson. He gives them a slight headshake, discouraging them from engaging with Frankie. Nothing good will come of it.

After the men leave, Jackson walks around Beauty, gently dragging his fingers along her smooth wood the way Frankie used to do. "I'll let you tune her," he says as a peace offering.

Frankie stands in the corner of the room, arms crossed, lips in a hard line.

"I'll let you play her first."

Frankie doesn't blink.

His shoulders drop into a hard surrender. "What's going to fix this?"

She rubs her lips together while snatching the tuning kit off the table. "You told Wylder you would teach him to play the piano."

"Yeah ..." Jackson replies with caution. He doesn't trust Frankie. She's too much like ... him.

"I've decided *I* will teach him."

"What if we alternate who—"

"I," she snaps, "will teach him." She sits at the piano and lays out the instruments like a surgeon.

He'd have to kill her if he didn't love her beyond reason. Wylder is his mini-me, despite Slade's ridiculous protests of the claim. It only makes sense that Jackson should teach Wylder to play the piano.

The problem is that Frankie has a look. A come-hither look. And she has perfect tits. An unforgettable ass. Don't even get him started on her pussy.

Jackson begrudgingly nods a silent acquiescence.

Maybe when Wylder's old enough to understand the magic of a woman's body, he can tell his grandson that he wanted to teach him, but ... tits and ass.

"Why are you—"

Frankie gives him an outstretched arm with a flat hand. "Shoosh."

The man without a submissive bone in his body sits in a chair and watches Frankie tune Beauty for the next hour. It's confusing. He's not sure where the greater jealousy lies. Beauty? Because Frankie's hands are all over her. Or Frankie? Because she's playing Beauty?

"Okay, maestro ... play something." Frankie steps away from the piano.

Jackson grins, standing and stretching his fingers in a dramatic display while strolling toward the piano.

"Take off your clothes before you play for me."

Jackson squints at her. "Is that your kink?"

"I'm too fucking *sophisticated* for kink. I simply know what I like."

Jackson tries to hide his amusement while he shrugs off his shirt.

Jeans.

Underwear ... depositing them on the floor by the piano bench. "And you like watching me play the piano naked?"

Frankie leans against the back of the sofa and crosses her arms. "We're about to find out."

Jackson smirks, taking a seat. "I fucking love you."

"Because I'm so smart and talented?" She pushes off the sofa.

"Nope." He starts to play a concerto in E minor.

"Because I challenge your stubborn ass?" She ambles closer.

"Nope."

Frankie runs her fingers along Beauty. Then she teases the nape of his neck while her lips settle beside his ear, and she whispers, "Because I'm the girl you kiss good night."

The End

ACKNOWLEDGMENTS

While I wrote this as a standalone, it came to life because my Jack & Jill fans showed this world and its many characters so much love. Therefore, the biggest thank-you goes to my readers of this series. It has been an honor and a dream to write this for you.

Jenn Beach (World's Best Assistant), thank you for being by my side and believing that I could make Jackson and his gray balls sexy again. We make the best team!

Emily Wittig, thank you for a beautiful cover. It's such a pleasure to work with you.

Thank you to my team with Valentine PR. I love being part of your awesome family.

Georgana/Nina/Joan Grinstead, my publicist, agent, and friend, thank you for always believing in me, even if you've never finished the Jack & Jill Series. Our friendship is so much more than you reading my all-time favorite series. I would never publicly call you out. We'll keep this between us. I'm going to do great things and make you proud for taking a chance on me (and most of my books.) Love you!

To my editing team, thank you for bending to my incredibly demanding and TIGHT publishing schedule for this book. Amy, Monique, Sarah, Leslie, and Kambra, I "adore" you.

To my Bookstagram team, ARC team, Jonesies, and all of the influencers who unrelentingly share my book releases, I'm always speechless and left feeling unworthy of that kind of love. You are the reason I'm living my dream. Thank you.

Thanks to my family for putting up with me obsessing over the Jack & Jill world. I'll stop talking about it and move on to my next obsession.

ALSO BY JEWEL E. ANN

Standalone Novels
Idle Bloom

Undeniably You

Naked Love

Only Trick

Perfectly Adequate

Look The Part

When Life Happened

A Place Without You

Jersey Six

Scarlet Stone

Not What I Expected

For Lucy

What Lovers Do

Before Us

If This Is Love

Right Guy, Wrong Word

The Fisherman Series
The Naked Fisherman

The Lost Fisherman

Jack & Jill Series

End of Day

Middle of Knight

Dawn of Forever

One (*standalone*)

Out of Love (*standalone*)

Because of Her (*standalone*)

Holding You Series

Holding You

Releasing Me

Transcend Series

Transcend

Epoch

Fortuity (*standalone*)

The Life Series

The Life That Mattered

The Life You Stole

Pieces of a Life

Memories of a Life

ABOUT THE AUTHOR

Jewel is a free-spirited romance junkie with a quirky sense of humor.

With 10 years of flossing lectures under her belt, she took early retirement from her dental hygiene career to stay home with her three awesome boys and manage the family business.

After her best friend of nearly 30 years suggested a few books from the Contemporary Romance genre, Jewel was hooked. Devouring two and three books a week but still craving more, she decided to practice sustainable reading, AKA writing.

When she's not donning her cape and saving the planet one tree at a time, she enjoys yoga with friends, good food with family, rock climbing with her kids, watching How I Met Your Mother reruns, and of course...heart-wrenching, tear-jerking, panty-scorching novels.

Receive a FREE book and stay informed of new releases, sales, and exclusive stories:
https://www.jeweleann.com/free-booksubscribe

Made in the USA
Monee, IL
25 October 2023

45142493R00223